BLACK, WHITE & "RUSTY"

BLACK, WHITE &
"RUSTY"

BY
DAVID J. PARKER

For Cathleen with best wishes, 6/00

Library of Congress Catalog Card Number 99-095512
ISBN 0-9674625-0-9

Published by
Buckaroo Press
P.O. Box 31834
Billings, Montana
dparker@wtp.net

To my wife Roberta—she is a miracle

Contents

Foreword

Black, White and Rusty, deals with the lusts, the loves and culture of the 1840s through 1860s, as it takes you on trails from the deep south, west to Texas, and north to Montana.

You will meet an array of characters. Malcolm Chandler, his family and a beautiful slave girl, Mary Annabelle will appeal to the intrigue of the story. You will smile at the goings on of two Indians, Right Nut and Left Nut. The treatment of the slaves will bring a tear, on one hand and on the other you will appreciate their culture. Overseers such as Mr. Hardnails will make you angry. The intimate details of love and lust affairs, will show you how life really was, for both the blacks and the whites.

During the Civil War, Rusty Montana Chandler, a handsome ex-slave travels west and gets a taste of the army, cattle business, and mining. Rusty's adventures hold your interest, with a new saga in each chapter.

Every character is fictional, the happenings could be very real to the time period.

BLACK, WHITE & "RUSTY"

CHAPTER 1

"Malcolm had purchased two fine field hands and
was more or less in the market to buy a young female."

The temperature must have been 100 degrees and the humidity hung like a wet blanket in the shed that housed the slave auction. Malcolm W. Chandler II stood near the back of the shed with sweat running down his back and into the crack of his ass.

Malcolm had purchased two fine field hands and was more or less in the market to buy a young female to help Bolo with some of the cooking and kitchen work. Bolo had been at the Cottontail Plantation for as long as he could remember. She was getting old. Several young females had sold, but they had sold pretty high and were not quite what he was looking to buy.

The auctioneer announced that she came from Cuba, which was interesting as all slave imports had ended in 1808, but there was still a bit of a black-market import from Barbados and Cuba. It was not usually announced at the auction if they had come from the West Indies.

Malcolm looked at the female form on the plat-form. She was draped in what looked like an old bur-lap sack, which did not hide the fact that she had a full figure. The sack-like dress was removed to reveal a most beautiful female body. Her hair was somewhat straight and unkempt. She had a bloody bandage on her left arm that would indicate a compound fracture if the arm were broken. The back of her burlap dress was stained with a reddish-brown blood that would indicate recent rape. Her ankle was bleeding from the chains that held her captive. Her skin looked dry and hard and was as black as the inside of a black cat. Her face did not have the wide, flat nose of most of the female slaves, nor did she have the large lips. Tears streamed down her face, and she glared at the potential buyers with a cat-like sneer. Her white teeth gleamed in a vice-like grip that would have cut the head off a ten-penny nail. She was young.

The auctioneer called, "What am I bid on this fine young wench?"

Malcolm's eyes met the eyes of the young slave. He bid. He could not believe he had bid on this wretched mess of a girl.

The auctioneer chanted, "I have a bid. Do I hear any more? No more bids. Sold to Malcolm Chandler of Cottontail Plantations."

Malcolm spent the night before at a political meeting with most of the power players of the South. He had reservations about slavery. He had heard talk, mostly by northerners, that you could raise cotton without slave labor and make it pay. Malcolm did not believe this for a second, but still slavery and handling slaves was a pain in the ass. His father had died the year before. He was very hard on the slaves, and Malcolm still had the same overseer that his father had employed. The overseer's name was Whip Smith. His reasoning for keeping the cruel overseer was the reali-zation that strict order must be enforced at all times.

Malcolm made his way through the crowd to his wagon. He had brought a trusted slave from Cotton-tail with him.

"Black Jim, I have bought three new additions for us. They are chained down in the slave quarters of the auction shed. Take some food, water, and blankets down to them and make them as comfortable as you can for the night. I have another meeting tonight. We will leave at first light in the morning." As an after-thought, Malcolm added, "I told the auction caretaker you would be coming. His instruction is not to un-chain them until I get there in the morning. I think it would be a good idea for you to stay right there with them until cockcrow."

Black Jim gathered together his bundle to take to the new slaves. It was always interesting for him to see the new slaves. In actuality, they were his new neighbors and working partners.

As he entered the auction shed, a large unkempt white man halted Black Jim.

"What you doin' here, Nigger?" the man de-manded.

"I 've got some food and blankets for Mr. Chandler's new people. He can't pick 'em up 'til mornin' and I'm to take care of 'em," Black Jim said.

"Chandler said nothing about you being black. I can't have you hanging around here all night. That could cause a bit of trouble," the man retorted.

"Well, could ya take this bundle to 'em?"

"Reckon I could," he grunted.

"It's two men and a girl," Black Jim added.

"I know who they are. That girl is a real bitch. I had to give her a good hard whip just before you came."

Black Jim left, wondering what would happen, especially to the girl. He had no cause to like the auction caretaker. Standing outside the closed door, he heard a woman cry out. By hanging around, he would only make more trouble for the new slaves and maybe even for himself.

Back at the wagon, he ate some salt pork and hard bread, wishing that Malcolm were there to take care of things. He fell asleep under the wagon. The sun had not begun to rise yet when he woke to a cool, humid morning. Malcolm had not returned from the room he had taken in town.

Black Jim readied the team with a fresh drink of water and a measure of grain. He wished Malcolm would hurry back. He was just fixin' to harness the team when Malcolm arrived.

With much surprise, Malcolm looked at Black Jim. "What are you doing here? I told you to stay with the new slaves."

"The white man at the slave shed sent me away," Black Jim explained. "Said he couldn't have no nig-gers hangin' 'round the auction shed."

"What did you do with the bundle of goods for the slaves," Malcolm asked.

"I gave it to the white man care taker, he said he'd give it to 'em. Said he had to whup the girl, and 'fore I left I heard a woman scream inside the shed."

"You get the team hitched up and meet me at the auction shed," Malcolm said.

Malcolm rapped on the door of the shed with good force. The caretaker finally opened up.

"You dirty-rotten, no good son-of-a-bitch! Why didn't you let my Jim take care of my people?" Malcolm angrily demanded.

The caretaker, caught off-guard, almost fell as Malcolm pushed him aside to get in the door.

The sight that greeted him was bad. Three humans lay in human offal. The girl was nude except for the burlap wrapped around her waist. The bandage on her left arm showed signs of fresh blood. She had a bad whip cut along her left shoulder. On closer inspection, he saw none of the blankets or bundle he had sent with Black Jim.

It was time for Malcolm to stand back and look at what he had bought. The first was a tall skinny lad of about seventeen. His arms were well muscled with large hands dangling from each. The face was flat with large, round eyes that showed a lot of white. He had on what were once white, baggy pants and a shirt in the same dirty white.

The other was short with a stocky, almost heavy build. He had broad shoulders and a wide ass, very curly, long hair, and a broad nose, with wide lips. His ankle was bleeding from the shackles that held him to the wall of the shed. His wide face and coarse features showed signs of defiance.

The girl was lying along the wall. Her lower half was covered with the rag burlap that she had on when she was sold. Despite her destitute state, she had a bright eye. Her breasts looked like two halved oranges with black raspberries pasted on them. Her lips were narrow with extremely white teeth showing behind them. Her hair was quite long and looked almost straight and very dirty. Her could-be-beautiful face was tear-stained. Well-formed arms and long legs brought Malcolm's manhood to attention, despite her filthy state.

Malcolm Chandler II was six feet tall with black hair and eyes the color of garnet. He had a sandy mustache that he wore in handlebar style.
First turning to the tall lad, Malcolm demanded, "What is your name?"

"My las' massah called me Tall Boy," he re-sponded.

"That is good enough for me, get on your feet," Malcolm said.

Now looking at the short, stocky slave, Malcolm said, "What are you called?"

"My mother called me Possum, but my las' mas-sah called me Joe," he answered.

"We have a Joe. We will call you Possum . On your feet." Malcolm ordered.

By this time the girl was on her feet, looking as though she was all cried and screamed-out, but she still held her head high and her back was as straight as a young willow.

"And what are you called?" Malcolm asked.

"My name is Bitch!" she yelled

Malcolm caught himself almost taking a step backwards. Black Jim just could not stand it and let out with a short laugh.

"Shut up, Black Jim, or I will take the nine tails to you," Malcolm warned. Then he turned to the young black woman and said, "I will tell you right now, little miss, we are not going to call you Bitch."

Malcolm scratched his head. "We must give her a pretty name," he thought. "From now on, you will be known as Mary Annabelle," he told her. The erect, female form before him repeated, "Mary Annabelle." She almost smiled as she spit on the floor.

"Black Jim, take these three out back and clean them up a bit. Leave about three feet of chain on the shackles, that way if they run they can't run fast. I am going to go buy them some clean clothes."

Black Jim came from a long line of slaves and was more-or-less proud of it. His mother had said that her dad was brought over from England very early and was one of the first slaves in the south. Black Jim had many tasks on the Cottontail Plantations. If there was fieldwork to be done, he was a willing hand. When the Chandler's entertained, he filled in as a server or a butler. When the Chandler stable had a race outside the plantation, he would accompany the regular trainer with the horses. Whip Smith was never allowed to lay a hand on Big Jim, a fact that had caused some com-petition between them sprinkled with a little bad blood. Black Jim was loved by all the whites and blacks on Cottontail Plantation. His wife was a large woman and worked in the fields. They had no chil-dren. Black Jim was a father and grandfather to all the children.

Black Jim took the three new slaves to the back of the shed where there was a well and an old rusty bucket. He filled the bucket with water. "Miss

Mary Annabelle you take this water, go behind that fence, and wash yourself up. Possum, you pump the water while Tall Boy washes up, and then Tall Boy you do it for Possum," Black Jim ordered.

Malcolm went to a haberdashery not too far from the auction shed. They had all kinds of clothes, and even some used ones that people brought in. Malcolm managed to find a mid-length, shift type dress in the used clothing. It had a blue background with a small flower print. For the men, he got two pairs of white, baggy pants and light blue work shirts. He also picked up a comb for Mary Annabelle.

Returning to the shed, Malcolm said, "Black Jim, here are the clothes for the boys. Get them on them and let's get out of here."

Malcolm walked over to the high-board fence and tossed Mary Annabelle's clothes over the fence.

"You threw them in the mud," she yelled.

The next thing Malcolm saw was a very black girl in a blue dress, with stringy wet hair that showed a lit-tle more curl than when it was dry. She did have a good lot of mud on her new dress. The bandage was off her arm and she seemed to be using it to run her fingers through her hair. There was a rather bad cut on her arm.

"Here, I forgot. I got you a comb," Malcolm said.
He tossed her the new comb, which she caught with her bad arm. Malcolm decided, then and there, that the arm was not broken. Just maybe he should have left her name "Bitch".

She almost smiled, then gave her dirty look, and spit on the ground. Malcolm had never hit one of his people in his life. He knew it was not his place to ask Black Jim to flog her. He reached in the wagon and got the horsewhip. He walked up so close to her he could smell the musk of her clean body. Sticking the whip right up in her face, he yelled, "Take a look at this!"

He saw tears start. Stepping back two steps, he cracked the whip like the sound of a rifle shot, and tossed it back in the wagon. Taking out his bone-handled knife, he cut a four-inch strip off the bottom of her new dress. He went back to the wagon and got a can of grease that he used on the wagon wheels, and sometimes for medicinal reasons. It was a combina-tion of bear grease and lard. He gently picked up her arm. The feel of her warm, soft arm went through him like a shot, and there it was again, the male urge. You could strike a match on it. He managed to get the bandage on her arm. "Let's load up and get out of here," Malcolm demanded. "Mary Annabelle, you ride up here in the seat with me."

Big Jim rode the bay plantation horse along side the wagon. He would sometimes spell off with Malcolm on their trip back to Cottontail.

CHAPTER 2

"Mary Annabelle says you killed a man in Cuba"

As the wagon bounced along the rutty, dirt road heading west, Malcolm took time to gather his thoughts. He had never been troubled with the purchase of slaves. Before, he and his father had left it up to Whip Smith. But, since he had to go to the city to attend the political meetings, he decided to get some new slaves and take Black Jim along to help. He wished now that he would not have taken on this mission.

His political meeting had been good and there was even some talk of running him for governor. He had enjoyed playing the piano for his political cronies after the meetings. He was an accomplished musician and loved to play. The Symphonic Association of the Southern States had offered to have him play at concerts.

"Mas Malcolm?"

"Yes. Mary Annabelle."

"We have to talk about the one you call Possum."

"Why must we talk about him?"

Mary Annabelle, in a low, husky voice whispered, "He killed a man and he practices Voodoo."

Malcolm sat up straight and reined in the team of mules. "Black Jim, put a rope on Possum, tie it good and lead him a few yards behind the wagon. He is probably getting stiff and needs some exercise. It is okay to remove the shackles, but watch him. Now, Mary Annabelle, what is it you have to say?" Malcolm asked.

"He's from the same plantation in Cuba that I came from," she explained. "The Massah heard noises in the blacksmith shop one day and found Possum standing over the body of the blacksmith with a hammer in his hand and the head of the blacksmith all pounded up like a dish of grits. The Massah was goin' to hang 'im. Then a trader came by and offered to buy 'im and send 'im out of Cuba. The Massah sold him and me to the trader."

"Why did he sell you?" Malcolm asked.

"He said I was always makin' trouble, and best to get rid of me. I was always teachin' the slave younguns to read. The Massah didn't like that."

"Can you read and write?"

"Only read, no write. I would borrow books from the big house on the plantation when no 'un was around, and teach the younguns, and myself. It is Spanish, no English," she answered.

Malcolm sat in silence as the wagon bounced along. Here he was, with several days to travel through near-wilderness country, with four slaves, one a murderer, and one a troublesome female. Tall Boy sat in the back of the wagon and seemed almost happy with his life. Malcolm wondered what his story could be.

"Black Jim, bring Possum back to the wagon and take Tall Boy for some exercise."

Malcolm checked his boot to see if his white bone-handle dagger was in its place. Malcolm's mother had lost her leg to a water moccasin bite. When old Doc Trueblood had to cut off his mother's leg, Malcolm asked him to save some of the bone. Malcolm then had the slave in the blacksmith shop make a dagger for him with a handle from the bone of his mother's leg. It was a fine piece of workmanship and both he and his mother were very proud of the dagger.

Malcolm looked at Mary Annabelle. He removed the keys from his pocket and took off her shackles. "You go back and walk with Tall Boy, and help Black Jim so that they don't run away. You don't want him to get away if you are going to teach him to read," Malcolm said.

Mary Annabelle jumped from the wagon, looking at her legs and her new freedom. She almost smiled and spit on the ground.

"Possum you get up here in the seat with me," Malcolm said. "Black Jim, take a rope and tie his hands behind his back."

As the caravan progressed up the trail, deeper into the wilderness, Malcolm looked back and saw that Mary Annabelle was walking with Tall Boy and Black Jim was riding on the big bay behind them.

"Now Possum, we are here where no one can hear us. Mary Annabelle says that you killed a man in Cuba. It is very obvious that we cannot have a murderer on Cottontail Plantation. What do you have to say for yourself?" "Mas Malcolm, I never killed the man. He was a bad man and always rapin' the young girls on the plantation. All the slaves knew about it, but were afraid to do anything as he was a good blacksmith and liked by the white massah. I heard a scream come from the back of the blacksmith shop. I ran to see what it was. Here was my wife with a hammer, poundin' the head of the blacksmith into the floor. My ten-year-old daughter lay on the floor naked. I grabbed the hammer and told my wife to grab the girl and run out the back. This she did. When the white massah got there, I was standin' over the body with the hammer in my hand. I just couldn' tell 'em what really happened cuz my girl needs her mama."

"You knew you would hang for what she had done?" Malcolm asked.

"Yessa, I sure did and I's not lookin' forward to it. My wife is a very good Nigger and I love my daughter. I hope they're in good order back in Cuba."

"Possum, what makes you think I would believe a story like that?" Malcolm asked.

Possum looked Malcolm right in the eye. He had tears rolling down his broad, black face. "Mas you just have to believe me. I'll be a good slave. Someday maybe you go to Cuba and buy my wife and daughter, they be good slaves too."

The first night, they had to camp out. Malcolm slept in the wagon and Mary Annabelle slept under. The men slept around the wagon. Nobody got much sleep but the night was uneventful.

The summer morning came on hot and humid as Black Jim cooked a breakfast of raccoon that Malcolm had killed the day before. That, along with coffee and hard tack, made everyone full and harmonious to start the day.

Midmorning, they came to a major river crossing. Being summer, the river was low, but the banks on each side were rocky and steep. All went well until the mules started up the steep bank to get out of the river. Halfway up, the doubletree on the wagon broke, sending the wagon crashing back into the river. Malcolm was on the bay. Black Jim, trying to hold the team, was pulled off the wagon headfirst. He crashed hard on his face into the rocky bank. Malcolm charged ahead on the bay to catch the mules. Mary Annabelle, Tall Boy, and Possum, being shackled to the wagon, crashed into the river as the wagon flipped over.

Malcolm caught the mules and tied them to a tree, rushing back to help the others. Black Jim lay still on the steep bank, his head twisted at an odd angle. Malcolm saw the other three struggling in the river as the current floated them down the river. The only luck of the day came when the wagon washed up against a log and the three were able to save themselves by keeping their heads above the muddy current. Malcolm crawled out on the log and was able to get the trio freed. Malcolm rushed back up the river to take care of Black Jim. He gently turned him over and saw that it was too late. Black Jim had broken his neck and was dead.

Possum and Tall Boy solemnly dug a grave on the riverbank while Mary Annabelle gathered a few wild flowers. In just the few days they had known him, all three liked and respected the big black slave. Malcolm made a crude cross of tree branches. It was going to be hard to tell Black Jim's wife and the rest of the plantation that they had lost him.

Their loss was almost total. All they had were the mules, the harness, and the bay plantation horse and saddle. All food and belongings went down the river with the wagon.

Malcolm had been over the road enough so that he knew it was only a day's ride to Left Nut and Right Nut's place. After getting the men on the mules and shackled to the harness, he mounted Mary Annabelle behind him on the bay. It was not long until she fell asleep with her head on his shoulder and her arms around him. He could feel her hard, firm breasts pushing into his back and her warm hand on his belly. Malcolm had a bad case of just plain lust. It was not uncommon for a master to bed the slave girls, but that was not Malcolm's style.

CHAPTER 3

"Right Nut and Left Nut were identical twins."

Left Nut and Right Nut were full blood Cherokee Indians. When the whites had moved the Cherokees west in the 1830s, the Nuts had been able to stay behind. This was partly due to the fact that Left Nut had married a white girl. She was a short, round, blue-eyed German girl who had been captured by the Cherokees. She was so white her name was Snowflake.

Left Nut and Right Nut were identical twins. The reason for their names was that they were born under a big black walnut tree, close to where they now lived. There were black walnuts all over the ground. The mother brushed away a spot and gave birth to a baby boy. She had no clue that she would have twins. She wrapped the boy in a blanket and went to the other side of the tree. She had a funny feeling. She brushed away the black walnuts and lay down. In a few minutes, out came another boy. Since they had been born on different sides of the nut tree she named them North Nut and South Nut. This in, Cherokee language, more or less translated into Left Nut and Right Nut.

Left Nut, Right Nut and Snowflake were known far and wide. They controlled a portion of the main road east and west. The cabin was located at the east end of a long narrow valley, with a clear stream running through it and a nice meadow for horse feed. Travelers would stop to rest in this very pleasant setting.

Right Nut was a very good hunter and provided deer, turkey, coon, possum and a variety of other meats for the pantry. Snowflake was a good cook and prepared excellent meals for travelers.

The Nuts lived in a rather large cabin, and had two smaller cabins they rented to travelers. Behind the cabins, there were cage-like quarters for slaves.

Malcolm and his exhausted party arrived at the Nuts' late on that hot summer evening. Snowflake was out getting a little wood and a pail of water in preparation for supper. She recognized Malcolm from previous visits. She called him Red Beard because of his red mustache, which gave emphasis to his black hair. She said it was his Indian name.

Malcolm stepped off his horse and helped Mary Annabelle to the ground. This sight was a big shock to Snowflake as she was used to seeing people from Cottontail Plantation traveling in much better style. These people were a mess, clothes in disorder, and dirty and very tired. Snowflake stepped forward and gave Malcolm a halfhearted welcome.

"Mr. Malcolm what happened to you?" she asked.

"Snowflake, we experienced a terrible event early this morning and we are in need of a meal and a place to rest." Malcolm then explained to her the past events.

"Red Beard you are always welcome at the Nuts," Snowflake said. "I will have Left Nut take the men to the creek and clean them up. I will take the girl right into my cabin."

Right Nut came out of the cabin in time to hear the conversation and volunteered to clean up the girl. This produced a strong cuff on the side of his head by his brother's wife along with a harsh retort to get some old clothes out of the loft and take the men to the creek.

"Red Beard, I will heat some water for you and you can have the first cabin," Snowflake offered.

It was a good hour later and pitch dark. Left Nut took plates of venison and hot bread down to the slaves caged by the creek. Mary Annabelle was chained to a post on the porch of the cabin and given some food and blankets. Snowflake would not have slaves sit at her table. In fact, it was a surprise that she would take the girl into her cabin to get clean. She even gave her an old dress and washed her blue flower print.

Right Nut had been out hunting and came in with a nice buck just as they were eating. He saw the girl on the porch, and it stirred his loins.

Right Nut's first comment was, "Who is that on the porch?"

Malcolm explained again how they happened to be there and all that had gone on. Right Nut was more or less the boss of the traveler's stop, so Malcolm asked if he could borrow a wagon to go on to Cottontail and return it in a few days, as Cottontail Plantation was only two days' travel away.

"Mr. Malcolm, I will trade you a first class wagon for that girl on the porch," Right Nut responded. "I will take her to the small cabin and try her out tonight. If she is any good we will trade."

Malcolm knew he was about to be had by the big Indian. If he did not trade, chances were he could not borrow the wagon. Then he would have to ride the mules and double on the horse all the way to Cottontail. This he did not relish, and the insides of Mary Annabelle's legs were rubbed so raw that even the black skin was quite incarnadined.

It was Snowflake who came to his rescue.

"Right Nut, what are you thinkin' of? We ain't havin' no slave around here. I don't believe in that slave system. If you were just a little darker, I would make a slave of you. And you ain't taking the likes of her to no cabin for the night. She belongs to Red Beard and it's going to stay that way."

Right Nut never had won an argument with Snowflake, but with the thought of having that young pretty black girl, he was not going to give up easily. He also knew that there was a streak of jealousy in Snowflake because it didn't make much difference who she slept with. The neighbors said that she could not tell Right from Left. Even though she was really married to Left Nut.

"Now Snowflake, you know I bought that good wagon from those travelers who were broke, and we have little use for it. If she don't work out, we can always sell her," Right Nut persisted.

"We are having no slaves, and that is the end of that. Go ahead and sell or loan the wagon to our friend, Red Beard. Eat your supper and shut up about this, or I will throw your supper to the dogs."

Right Nut sat sulking, his final statement before he started to the loft bed was, "Talk about wagon in the morning."

CHAPTER 4

"Massah Malcolm, can't we take off the ropes and let him set up"

"Possum, Possum! I got loose. We can make a run for it." These words were from Tall Boy. He had managed to get out of the cage and was running to Possum.

"You must be crazy man. They'd catch us before we got a mile. Didn' you see that hound the Nuts have up by the house? Not only that, I don' wanna run. Where'd we go?" Possum asked. "If I could get back to Cuba the hangman waits for me. If I go north, it's cold and maybe no job. It's almost daylight now. Go back and stay."

"This is the only chance I've ever had to be free in my whole life. I must take it," Tall Boy said.

"Unlock my cage," Possum ordered. "Now run if you must, but I'm stayin' here."

The eastern horizon was turning light gray as Tall Boy went past the cabin porch. The hound let out with a howl, just as Mary Annabelle woke and yelled in fright, not knowing who was walking by in the gray dawn. Tall Boy had broken a stay off his cage, and as the hound rushed at him he dealt a deathblow to the head of the hound. The hound let out with a low whine and dropped dead.

Malcolm ran out the cabin door just as Right Nut showed up at the door of his cabin. Malcolm had lost his gun in the wagon wreck, but Right Nut had a shot gun pointed at Tall Boy's head. Right Nut fired one barrel over the top of Tall Boy.

"Drop that club you black son-of-a-bitch or the next shot won't miss," Right Nut ordered.

Malcolm grabbed Tall Boy, spun him around, and pointed the bone-handled dagger right at his heart. The whites of Tall Boy's eyes were as big as horse turds as he dropped the club and fell to his knees.

"I was jus' comin' to wake you when the hound run at me and scared me so I hit 'im," Tall Boy explained.

Malcolm reached down, grabbed Tall Boy's ear, and cut it off.

"Get some rope and tie this black bastard hand and foot," Malcolm barked.

Tall Boy lay on the ground, bound head and foot.

13

"Now take him down and lay him in the creek until we are ready to go. That should keep him cool."

There was a shallow ford in the creek, about four inches deep, where the water ran over some sharp shale.

Snowflake looked at her dead hound, then, taking Malcolm's bone-handled knife, she cut open the dog. Removing the dog's guts, she rubbed them into Tall Boy's face.

"You killed my good dog. Maybe you like the smell and taste of him," she snarled. She rubbed in more and harder.

The two big Indians picked the bound man up and headed for the creek.

While Left and Right Nut did not practice slavery, they understood the white man's need for slaves and the discipline he must hand out to those who disobeyed.

They laid Tall Boy in the cold creek on his back. The blood from his severed ear made a red trail as the small creek rushed to the river.

Malcolm walked to the cages to let Possum out. Arriving at the cage, he noticed it open.

"How did you get the lock off, Possum?" Malcolm demanded.

"Tall Boy came and wanted me to run with 'im. I wouldn't go. I had Tall Boy open the cage so when you found me you'd have more trust for me."

Malcolm stood back and scratched his head. Possum got out of the cage and stood before Malcolm. Malcolm bent down and removed the shackles from Possum's legs. Possum looked at Malcolm, gave a big smile, then gave a half-hearted salute.

"Possum, you go get the mules and harness them. I will go try to bargain Right Nut out of a wagon," Malcolm said.

Arriving back where Snowflake and Mary Annabelle were standing, he gave a hard look at Mary Annabelle, then took off her shackles.

"Now, Mary Annabelle, you get a shovel and help Snowflake bury her dog."

Mary Annabelle looked with shock at Malcolm and her new found freedom. Snowflake went up on the porch and got a shovel. The two of them, dragging the dead dog off to a large tree behind the house, made for about the only pleasant thing that Malcolm had seen that morning.

Right Nut almost rushed up to Malcolm. "Come look at the wagon, it is almost new," he exclaimed.

The wagon was in good shape and much better than the one that he had lost in the river. He even noticed a can of the same bear grease and tallow under the seat.

Right Nut grabbed Malcolm's arm. "Now we must make a deal before Snowflake gets back. I will trade you the wagon for the slave girl. I will hide her until you are gone and then it will be too late for Snowflake to make a fuss."

" Right Nut, you are crazy. Snowflake would kill both of us. I don't want to be killed, nor do I want Snowflake as an enemy for the rest of my life. To top that off, I do not want to sell the girl," Malcolm retorted.

Right Nut looked disappointed as he reflected that he was loosing his best chance at a helper and a good piece of ass.

"Here is what I will do for you. I can see you and Left Nut need a good saddle horse. The big bay I have with me is a good horse. You drive the wagon to Cottontail and help me with the slaves. When we get to Cottontail you ride home on the bay, and he and the saddle are yours, and I'll keep the wagon. It will give you a chance to see all the Cottontail folks. You haven't been over for a long time," Malcolm said.

Right Nut mulled this offer over in his head. It would give him a couple of days close to the slave girl.

"Okay, lets get loaded before that slave we got in the creek floats away or freezes to death," Right Nut agreed.

They left Tall Boy bound and laid him in the wagon.

Malcolm observed that Mary Annabelle was studying Tall Boy, bound in the wagon, and tears were streaming down her face.

"Mary Annabelle, you ride in the back of the wagon and take care of Tall Boy. Don't let him die," Malcolm said.

"Massah Malcolm, can't we take the ropes off 'im and let 'im set up?" Mary Annabelle pleaded.

"We will let him bounce around, bound like that, for an hour or so. He will then know how good it feels to sit up," Malcolm replied.

They said their good byes to Snowflake, and Left Nut and were off to Wanderlust Lodge where they would spend the night before going on to Cottontail.

CHAPTER 5

"He handles a woman better than he hoes cotton"

They made pretty good time and arrived at Wanderlust Lodge at dusk. Wanderlust was owned by the Wanderlust Plantation and was located on the east side of their large holdings. The main lodge had a lounge and dining room with five sleeping rooms for white guests, and a slave's quarters in the back. Being an Indian, Right Nut was kind of in No-Man's Land. He could not stay in the main lodge, and of course he did not wish to stay in the slave's quarters. This was not going to give him much of a chance to get to the girl. Malcolm came to his rescue.

"I want Mary Annabelle to stay where she can care for Tall Boy during the night, as I plan on him being shackled and bound with rope. Right Nut, I wonder if you could stay with them in the stable tonight and keep an eye on them and the mules. Possum, you go to the slave's quarters and get a good nights' sleep. Have the team harnessed and ready to go at day break."

Right Nut had a smile from ear to ear.

The manager of Wanderlust Lodge was a woman in her mid-forties. She had been a madam in a New Orleans brothel. She was married to one of her customers, who had brought her north to Wanderlust Plantation where he worked as an overseer. He was a big drinker and a mean-spirited individual. On his way home one night he passed out, fell from his horse, hung up, and was dragged to death. He was not really missed much by anyone who knew him.

She was known far and wide as Madam Charlie. To help her run the lodge, she had three slaves—two females that doubled as cleaning maids and waitresses and a large black man that was bouncer and bartender.

Madam Charlie had overheard the instruction for the evening. She knew of Right Nut's lust for black girls. She jumped on Malcolm with both feet.

" Mr. Chandler, you will not be sending this Mary Annabelle off to no stable with the likes of Mr. Nut and that boy that looks most killed. That girl stays in the quarters with my girls. Their names are Pansy and Columbine. There are only two reasons for a girl to make love. Either she is in love or she gets paid. That Indian doesn't come under either heading.

Right Nut could have killed Madam Charlie!

16

The arrangements were then made for Possum to stay in the stable with Tall Boy and Right Nut. Possum spent the early part of the evening cleaning Tall Boy up and feeding him some supper sent down from the main lodge. After his ordeal, Tall Boy was feeling better and was ready to listen to the wise council of Possum.

"Tall Boy, you just can' be tryin' to run off. We all wants to be free and someday it'll happen. The only possible way now is with what I've heard called the Underground Railroad. It's where white people hide you and help you get to the north and freedom. I don' want any part of that as I still have hope that Mas Malcolm will go to Cuba and get my woman and lil' girl. If you thinks you want to run, you go underground. When you get settled in the slave's quarters at Cottontail Plantation, there'll be people who know how to help you. In the mean time, you work hard and do as the massahs tell you. I see you makin' eyes at that Mary Annabelle. You jus' stay away from her. She's big trouble. You'll be able to find yourself a good girl," Possum said.

Tall Boy looked at Possum with teary eyes. His head, where the ear was gone, hurt. His pride hurt. He was physically hurt. He said not a word to Possum about his wise counsel. He lay back on the hay and was soon asleep.

Madam Charlie had one other guest in her lodge. He was a drummer with a wagonload of supplies for slaves. He traveled from plantation to plantation with his wares. Malcolm had known him from past business dealings and they enjoyed a fine meal provided by their host. The conversation during the meal centered on slavery and cotton, as did most conversations of the period.

Mr. Silas Vender, the drummer, was also well known for bringing news and gossip from plantation to plantation. Mr. Vender told Malcolm that his brother-in-law, Bancroft Whitesides, had just returned from New Orleans with some new slaves. Bancroft owned the Hanging Magnolia Plantation. Malcolm had married Bancroft's sister, Glena Lee. Hanging Magnolia Plantation lay to the west and south of Cottontail for several miles. He would bring his slaves up the Mississippi and then overland, east to get to the Hanging Magnolia.

Malcolm was surprised to hear this news, as he and Bancroft were friends and worked together on projects that would benefit each other or their plantations. One of their common joint ventures was going together to get new slaves.

Mr. Vender also told of a slave uprising in the New Orleans area where one planter and an overseer were killed. The uprising was said to be caused mostly by voodoo and witchcraft, which was prevalent in the New Orleans area.

Malcolm took the opportunity to purchase some supplies from Mr. Vender. He got some slave clothing and some new shackles.

Mary Annabelle, finding herself alone in the quarters of Pansy and Columbine, took the opportunity to clean up and comb her hair. After the meal was served and cleaned up, the two slave girls returned to their quarters.

The girls had a lot to talk about, as girls do, and it always came back to men and boys. Columbine had a boyfriend who would sneak out of the field hands' cabin and visit her some nights, Pansy revealed.

"When that boy comes up here they make me take my blankets and go outside to sleep. One night, on 'is way home, he stopped by my blankets. I's happy to have 'im as Pansy had told me how good he was. Well she don' know what a man is. That boy ain't over three inches, and he don't know how to use it. Now that man of mine, Punch, he is a man! His business must be ten inches and when he makes love to you, you know it! He handles a woman better'n he hoes cotton," she boasted.

Pansy had to tell her side of this. "That Punch, he's so ugly I'd never let 'im in my blankets. I never did see 'is tool. That face is enough to make you sick—those big lips, flat nose and flat forehead. It'd hafta be mighty dark out 'fore I let 'im touch me."

After Mary Annabelle stopped laughing at her room mates, she asked, "Did either of you ever have a white man?"

Pansy told about her white man first. "I had the overseer's son push me down in the grass by the creek. I was 'fraid to fight so I just let 'im. It was no fun I tell you, but I got even. While he had me down I got hold of some saw grass and got it 'round 'is balls. Just as he started to get off, I starts to saw. I had no more trouble with 'im."

It was now Columbine's turn. "The overseer 'imself took me in the back of the gin shed and gave me some rum. It was pretty good and made me feel good. He wanted to make love to me. I's pretty drunk and kinda scairt, so I did. He seemed all tired-out, when we finished. He slapped me on the butt and told me to get outta there 'fore somebody came."

Mary Annabelle looked at the girls with disapproving eyes and told her story. "I got raped a lot on the old plantation in Cuba, both the blacks and the whites. It was even worse in the slave market where Massah Malcolm got me. I wants to find me a white man. I don' want nothin' to do with the black boys. I thought I might kinda like Tall Boy 'til he tried to run and lost 'is ear. I think he must have shit for brains. I got my eye set on Massah Malcolm."

Both Pansy and Columbine looked at Mary Annabelle like she was the one who had shit for brains. Columbine was the first to comment.

"Girl, you gotta be crazy! He's Malcolm Chandler the II. He owns one a' the biggest plantations. He 'as a wife and two little daughters. They stopped by Wanderlust once and I had to take care a' the girls. If'n you mess 'round with Mas Malcolm that Mrs. Chandler'll 'ave ever' inch a' hide you got stripped off'n you."

"I'm not goin' to stay on this Cottontail Plantation and work," Mary Annabelle replied. "Mas Malcolm will send me to a big city and keep me, buy me a nice yellow dress. He may get me a little dog to have on a leash. I seen Mulatto girls like that walkin' the streets of Havana. The people tell me they're kept by white men."

It was Pansy's turn to pass on some advice to Mary Annabelle.

"First thing girl, you ain't no Mulatto. You're black as they get. Lookit the palms of my hands. They're at least light color. Now lookit yours. They're black as night. White men don' like real black girls, and for sure, Mas Malcolm ain' goin' to make no mistress outta you. You'll be on your hands and knees scrubbin' floors at Cottontail, 'til you old as the moon. That's if you's lucky and he don' make a field hand outta ya."

"No Pansy, he already bought me a comb and nice blue dress," Mary Annabelle argued. "It got all messed up when the wagon fell in the river, but I 'ave it stowed away. I'll get it clean and look real nice. Not only that, I'm gonna be teacher at Cottontail and teach the black peoples' kids to read and write. When I get better at it I bet the white people'll send their kids to me to teach," Mary Annabelle said.

Pansy and Columbine looked at one another in astonishment. They almost felt sorry for her. She didn't think she was a slave. After a long silence, Columbine was the first to speak. "You know how to read an' write?" she asked.

"I know in Spanish and I can learn in English if I gets me some books," Mary Annabelle replied.

"An' where do ya plan on gettin' books?"

"Mas Malcolm will get 'em for me."

"He will not. White people don' wan' us slaves to learn books," Columbine said.

The three girls lay back on their pallets and fell asleep.

CHAPTER 6

"Right Nut had three things; a good horse, the saddle
and a love for black girls."

The morning came with a blast of humid heat. Possum had the mules
harnessed and the wagon loaded with the merchandise that Malcolm had
purchased from Silas Vender. The entire staff of Wanderlust Lodge was on
hand to see the Chandler party off for their final day on the road.

Tall Boy was looking much better and sitting up in the seat with
Possum, who was driving the team. Right Nut was on his new bay and on
his way back to Left Nut and Snowflake. He had a good horse and a good
saddle. He had not had his pleasure with any of the slave girls, and there they
were the three of them, Mary Annabelle, Columbine, and Pansy, looking so
pretty. Right Nut mounted the bay. He had three things: the good horse, the
saddle and love for black girls. Malcolm had decided it was time to let Right
Nut go home and not go on to Cottontail with them. He would just ride in
the back of the wagon with Mary Annabelle the rest of the way. When it got
right down to it, Right Nut was more trouble than he was help.

As they were pulling away, Malcolm reached into a bag of things he
had purchased from Silas Vender and took out a small, cheap Bible. He
handed it to Mary Annabelle. She took a look at it and waved it in the air
for Pansy and Columbine to see. Be damned if he had not given her a book!
As they were driving down the road, Mary Annabelle, in a low voice so the
men in front could not here, whispered, "That Possum, he damaged the
wagon part you call the doubletree, jus' so we'd wreck and kill Black Jim.
Then he thought he'd get to be the big Nigger on the Cottontail
Plantation."

Malcolm looked sternly at Mary Annabelle. "Mary Annabelle, you listen to me and listen good. When you get to Cottontail you say nothing, and
I mean nothing, about what you know, or think you know, about Possum. I
think you are making this stuff up, and for what reason I have no idea."

"You'll find he has a black heart," Mary Annabelle replied.

The wagon fell silent as it headed west toward its destination. Malcolm
took this time to reflect on his past week. No more was he taking a part in
handling the slaves. That would be left to Whip Smith and others. He
thought of the economics of the past few days. Lost were a good and valu-
able slave, and a good wagon. He had three unproven slaves that he had paid

quite a bit for. The abolitionists were always harping about how the slaves were treated. Only a few worried about the economics of the South and the slave system. Malcolm did not want to be branded an abolitionist, but he was going to take some time when he got home and put a pencil to the question of slavery. There had to be a better and more economical way to raise cotton.

Malcolm would have to console Black Jim's wife. As far as that goes, he would have to console the rest of the Cottontail population. Black Jim had been very well liked. He would turn Possum and Tall Boy over to Whip Smith. He still had Mary Annabelle to worry about. The old cook, Bolo, was set in her ways, and God knows that Mary Annabelle had a mind of her own. He saw no other way than to take a personal interest in her keep and training. It was also necessary to keep her with the household slaves and not give her a chance to spread rumors about Possum to the field hands - at least he hoped they were rumors.

The party arrived at Cottontail Plantation in late afternoon. The lane to the main plantation mansion was about a half-mile long. Horses from the Cottontail racing stables grazed along both sides. Bordering the paddocks that lined the way to the mansion were the vast, rolling cotton fields.

Evelyn Lucille, age eight, and Mandy Ann, five, were on the porch swing and saw their dad coming down the lane. They ran to notify their mother, who in turn notified the entire population of the plantation.

Mother Lady Chandler was first in the yard to greet them. Lady Chandler was from an aristocratic family in England and had arrived in the Southern United States at the age of eighteen. Even at that age, she was known as Lady. She married Malcolm's father and they had just one child. Together they had built the Cottontail Plantation. Mr. Chandler had passed away one year earlier, and she and Malcolm had carried on with the operation of the plantation.

Lady Chandler was an excellent judge of horseflesh, though she never rode. She was very active in the management of the racing stables and other horse and mule activities on the plantation. She had lost her leg when she was bitten by a water moccasin in the tall grass around the stable. It was from a bone in her leg that Malcolm had his dagger made. She wore long dresses of the period and had a crutch/cane combination that let her get around quite nicely.

Malcolm's wife, Glena Lee, was born on the same day as Malcolm on a large plantation not too far from Cottontail. They had played together as children, and it was always understood that they would be married. In spite of this, they loved each other very much and got along quite well. Glena Lee was tall with black hair, and deep blue eyes. She had a line of freckles across her nose, a constant source of disgust to her, but most people thought that it gave her beauty a certain charm. She was not involved in the operation of the cotton or the stables. Her time was spent with her girls and managing the big mansion.

She loved to entertain and was known for her lavish and well-planned balls and parties. The Cottontail Mansion had a large ballroom on the north side of the house with a large porch and a well kept lawn that gently sloped down to the passing stream. This was contrary to the home where she was raised, which had a ballroom with balconies on the second floor.

As the people gathered in the front of the mansion to greet the home-coming, Malcolm stepped down and immediately addressed Black Jim's wife. She knew something was wrong as he walked up to her.

"Black Jim is dead," he said.

The tears streamed down her face as Malcolm turned to the crowd and raised his hand for silence. Dead silence fell over the people of Cottontail.

"We lost our good friend Black Jim," Malcolm announced. He went on to relate, in a solemn voice, the details of the wreck and Black Jim's death. He told them of the grave along the bank of the river. Then he announced the plans to remember Black Jim.

"We will have a service, followed by a picnic, in honor of Black Jim this Sunday afternoon on the glade on the north side of the Cottontail Mansion. You will meet the new people as time goes on. Now go back to work."

Then Malcolm turned and said, "Whip, this is Tall Boy and this is Possum. Take them and get them settled in their quarters. Bolo, this is Mary Annabelle. Take her to the kitchen and get her settled."

Whip Smith walked up to the new slaves, looked them up and down, and gave them each a sharp slap with his riding quirt along the sides of their faces. It was lucky for Mary Annabelle as she was already going off with Bolo, or she may have gotten the same slap.

Whip said, "That was just a starter so you will know I am the boss. You will do as I say, when I say it. You will work from sun up to sun down. You will be severely lashed if you try to run away or show any sign of laziness. You work hard and do as I say and you will find good treatment."

When the trio got behind a slave cabin, out of sight of the others, Possum made a quick move, grabbed Whip's arm, and put a hammerlock on him. He wrapped the quirt around Whip's neck until he was unable to breathe. Possum, with his face just inches from Whip's and a death grip on the quirt around his neck said, "Mas Whip Smith, you ever touch me or my friend here, Tall Boy, and you are dead!"

Whip, his eyeballs out so far you could knock them off with a stick, and his face the color of a half-ripe blackberry, sank to the ground. Gasping, trying to get his breath, he returned an answer.

"You black bastard! You haven't got enough sense to pour piss out of a boot. I will flog every inch of skin off your black back!"

Possum took Whip by the hair and pulled him to a sitting position. He tightened the quirt around his neck. He did not choke him quite as bad this time as he did not want to kill him just yet. With his grip on a handful of hair, he shook his head from side to side.

"Guess you didn't understand me. If you ever lays a hand on me or my friend, I'll kill ya."

Possum released the stranglehold, but kept hold of Whip's hair, pushing his face again two inches from his own. He gave Whip the ultimatum.

"No one has seen you take this beatin'. I'll work hard and see to it that Tall Boy works hard. All you 'ave to do is treat us right," he sneered. He yanked Whip's hair just as he gave him a hard open handed slap across the face. Whip slumped back in a heap on the grass.

Whip had never dreamt of a slave giving him a beating and shouting demands. He thought he was going to die. He could feel his heart pounding in his rib cage. He looked up at the black man hovering over him and managed to gasp out, "Help."

Possum pulled him back and propped him up against a tree. "Tall Boy, get this man some water. I think we 'ave 'is attention."

Tall Boy came with the water. Possum tossed some in Whip's face and let him have a short drink. Possum backed off a little and looked at his victim.

Whip looked up at Possum and then at Tall Boy. "Did you loose that ear because you tried to run away?" he questioned.

Possum slapped him again, this time very hard.

Whip passed out, and Possum tossed more water in his face. Whip shook his head and studied Possum as he spoke.

"This ain' no time to change the subject," Possum sneered. "Just as soon as we make a deal, you can talk to Tall Boy all you wanna. Now, if'n you ever touches me or Tall Boy again, I'll kill ya."

Whip managed to gasp, "You have a deal."

"Tall Boy, help Mas Whip to his feet," Possum ordered.

As soon as Tall Boy had Whip standing, Possum gently washed off his face and gave him a good drink of water.

Speaking in his most friendly tone, Possum said to Whip, "Now let's he'p you walk a while, and 'ave some more water. We can' 'ave you goin' back lookin' like somethin' the cat drug in."

Possum managed a big smile for Whip.

CHAPTER 7

"He ran a slightly callused hand over her flat belly."

Malcolm found himself in the arms of Glena Lee with one daughter clinging to his leg and the other pulling on his coattail. He gave them all a kiss, picked up little Mandy Ann and walked to the mansion. They gathered in his mother's room, which was the old library when Mr. Chandler was alive. Lady Chandler had it changed over for her room as it was on the ground floor and she did not have to manage the stairs.

Malcolm told them of his adventures on the trip, how they had lost Black Jim, and how he had had to cut off Tall Boy's ear.

Then it was into the dining room for supper. Bolo had prepared a fine meal of fresh ham, summer squash, sliced tomatoes and hot bread. Malcolm was surprised to see Mary Annabelle helping the regular serving maid. She was dressed in the traditional uniform, black dress and white apron, of the Cottontail house slaves. She had a white scarf wrapped around her long hair. The other maid had very short, curly hair. Mary Annabelle looked quite pretty. She did her work with such amazing efficiency that you would have thought she had been serving forever. Malcolm could not help but ask, "Mary Annabelle, were you a serving maid on your old plantation in Cuba?"

"No Mas Malcolm. I was a teacher," she proudly replied.

The little girls looked at Mary Annabelle in amazement. They had never heard of, or seen, a slave teacher. Their teacher was an old maid that wore a black dress, high button shoes, and her hair in a bun on top of her head. They managed to look at each other and giggle.

Glena Lee looked to Malcolm for some type of explanation. All he could manage was to shrug his shoulders and keep on enjoying his meal.

It was a custom for Malcolm and Whip Smith to meet in the study and have cigars and brandy every evening and discuss plantation business. When Whip walked in, Malcolm was shocked. He was very pale, white as snowflakes on a polar bear's ass, and the side of his face was badly bruised.

In shock, Malcolm asked, "What on earth happened to you?"

"I stopped by the stable this afternoon and one of the horses jerked his head and hit me in the face," Whip explained. "It almost knocked me out. I usually don't go near the stable. I leave that to your mother and the groom, Shorty Rideout. I never did get on well with horses."

24

"You look terrible, have a cigar and pour yourself a brandy," Malcolm said.

Whip sat down. He looked exhausted.

"Well Whip, how have things been going? I can tell you, I am sure glad to be home. Our trip was not the best. The next time we need slaves, you are going to buy them and bring them home."

"Things have been going quite well," Whip answered. "That little slave girl, Liz, had her baby. I am not sure who the father is. Two of the boys are claiming the child. I decided it was best just to keep out of it and let them work it out.

"We have had two cotton buyers, and the price looks very good," Whip continued. "It's a good thing that you kept last year's crop. I told them they would have to see you when you got home."

"If they come back and I am not right here, sell them Warehouse Number Two. It is not the very best cotton, so when they look at it, you may not get the top price. We will keep Warehouse Number One for a while as it is top quality."

Whip, looking down at his feet, then asked, "What do you know about the two new boys you brought in?"

"The one called Possum is from Cuba. Says he knows nothing about cotton as he came from a sugar cane plantation. I kind of like him. and the last part of the trip he was as good of help as you could ask for. Now, that Tall Boy, he tried to run away and I had to cut off his ear and cool him in the creek for a while. I really learned very little about him. If you were wondering about where the big bay horse is, I had to trade him to Right Nut for the wagon after the wreck."

Whip Smith sat sipping brandy and smoking before he spoke.

"Malcolm, I am 48 years old. Both of our kids are away at school in Atlanta. I am wondering if it's not time for Mrs. Smith and I to get out of the overseeing, and move to Atlanta."

Malcolm was quick to reply. "Whip, you have been on Cottontail most of your life, and Mother and I could not bear to see you leave. If it is more money you want, I think we could work something out. You control slaves better than any overseer around. Please give this discussion some more consideration," he pleaded.

"I will talk it over with Mrs. Smith, but I wanted you to know what I was thinking." Whip Smith was afraid he had lost his touch, and he also had a fear of Possum.

Malcolm ascended the winding staircase to the master bedroom. Glena Lee was sitting at the dressing table in a bright red, silk dressing gown that Malcolm had given her for Christmas. He took her in his arms and she purred in his ear.

"Oh Malcolm, I am so glad you are back here with us. I missed you so very much."

She smelled of lavender powder. The touch of her buttermilk skin was as soft as a baby's skin. He gently laid her down on the bed as her robe fell aside and exposed her well-formed breasts, with nipples erect. Her nipples were longer than normal from nursing the little girls. The fact that her mother had long nipples also played a part.

Malcolm sat on the edge of the bed and removed his clothes, admiring his wife in her almost nude state. It was a rather hot summer night and they lay on top of the sheets, with no covers. He ran his lightly callused hand over her flat belly, gently fingering her belly button. She lay still, with her eyes closed, enjoying the feeling of his hands tingling her midriff nerves. The only sound in the room was her heavy breathing and now and then she would come forth with a low moan.

She let her soft hands rub his back, very gently massaging it. Her other hand found his flat stomach, and she massaged it with a slow motion, gently rubbing up and down. They were so happy to be alone, and they were starved for each other's affection.

Suddenly, the door to the bedroom opened, and a small voice whispered, "Mommy, I hear something downstairs."

Getting untangled and covering themselves with the sheets was not easy, as little Mandy Ann found her way to the bed.

"I hear something downstairs, and I am scared," the little girl repeated.

Malcolm could see his daughter's face reflected in the moon shining through the window. He would have liked to choke her.

"Here Little One, get in bed with your mother and I will go downstairs and check out the sounds you hear."

Malcolm put on a robe and went down the stairs. He could see a dim light coming from the kitchen area. By the dim candlelight and the moon's rays shining through the window, he could see Mary Annabelle. She was drying herself off with a rag towel as she stood next to a tub of water. From a small can on the counter, she began to rub tallow over her body, making it shine like a black diamond in the candlelight. She rubbed her breast, as the candlelight flickered on her flat belly. It was almost as if her belly button was winking at Malcolm. Her curly pubic hair ran in a fine line up each of her sides so that it appeared to be smiling at Malcolm.

She looked up and saw Malcolm standing a few feet from her. With one hand on her hip, she extended the other to Malcolm and said just one word, "Come."

Malcolm turned away, walked down the hall, and up the stairs. There, in the big double bed, lay his wife and little daughter, sound asleep. He walked to the day bed in front of the bay window, lay down and thought of what the night could have been.

Morning found him still on the day bed. Glena Lee had chased Mandy Ann back to her room and motioned for Malcolm to come to her bed. They made mad, tender love. He then dressed to start a normal day on a large southern plantation. It was going to be a hot one.

CHAPTER 8

"Mr. Archibald I want to buy a slave girl."

Right Nut had ridden for three hours when, Bang! Like a shot, it hit him. He had money. He could buy a slave girl.

The Nuts had always split the income from their traveler's rest. Right Nut had never spent a penny for anything. He saw Snowflake keep her money in a coffee can, so he just stuffed his in a sack behind the door.

There were times when Snowflake would ask him for money to buy capital improvements for the place. He always gave her the money out of the sack. They raised or hunted all their food. The only way to get anything, in Right Nut's mind, was to hunt it, raise it, trade or, on occasion, steal it. Just before he left with the Chandler party, he had stuffed a good supply of money in each pocket. Maybe if he had offered Malcolm money for the girl he would have gotten her.

He turned his horse and started back. He was going to buy that Mary Annabelle. Just as he turned the corner in the road, he saw Wanderlust Lodge and had another bright idea. He didn't have to go all the way to Cottontail. He could buy one of those girls from the Wanderlust Lodge. He hadn't gotten a real close look at them, but he was sure either one would do. He knew that Madam Charlie had no use for Indians, and she did not own the girls. He would have to find Mr. Archibald Wanderlust, the owner of the lodge and the plantation. He rode on past the lodge and turned down a lane that led to the main plantation house and the slave quarters.

As he rode up, two little boys saw him coming and ran to the house yelling, "Indians are coming, Indians are coming."

It had been quite some time since there had been any Indian trouble, but it was still on people's minds. Two men with rifles appeared on the porch and took dead aim on Right Nut. He threw his hands in the air and hollered at the top of his voice.

"I'm Right Nut. don't shoot."

The men lowered their guns and started to laugh. They had known Right Nut for many years and had stopped several times at his traveler's rest.

The larger and older of the two greeted Right Nut. "Welcome to Wanderlust. But what on earth are you doing here?"

Right Nut's answer was simple. "I came to buy a slave girl."

28

The younger man was Archibald's son. His name was Hamilton, but everybody called him Ham. Ham was known as the cock of the walk and a show off. He walked up to Right Nut's horse, took his horse by the bridle and looked him up and down. Then, in his own friendly greeting he said, "Well Indian, where did you get this horse, steal him? He's a fine looking animal for an Indian."

Right Nut sat up straight in the saddle, and did not return an answer to the cocky Ham. He figured him not worthy of an answer. He looked at Archibald, who was still on the porch, and said again, "Mr. Archibald, I want to buy a slave girl."

Young Ham let go of the horse and looked up at Right Nut. "Now where would an Indian get the money to buy a slave girl? I bet you stole that too."

Oh, how Right Nut would have liked to get down off the horse and beat the shit out of that Ham. But he knew that was not the right approach if he was to get himself a slave.

Right Nut, still ignoring Ham, reached in his pocket and handed money out to Archibald on the porch. Mr. Wanderlust counted the money. Then he turned to Right Nut and sternly demanded, "Maybe Ham is right. Where did you get all this money and that fine horse?"

Right Nut, in the best way he could, explained the deal of the wagon trade and the horse. Then he told of how, when Snowflake collected from travelers, she would give him money. He even had some more at home.

The Wanderlust's enjoyed the slave trade and did quite a bit of buying and selling. It was not uncommon for people to come to the plantation to buy or sell a slave. It was very uncommon for an Indian to show up to buy a slave.

Archibald Wanderlust asked Right Nut, "What kind of a girl did you have in mind?"

"I want one of those girls up at the Lodge," Right Nut explained. "I think their names are Columbine and Pansy. They are young and know how to cook and clean. Do I have enough money for one of them?"

Mr. Archibald Wanderlust looked at the big Indian. He knew it was important to get along with him. The Nuts controlled the eastern route to the ocean, and Wanderlust Plantation needed to get to the markets. Under most conditions, he would not have taken the offer for one of the well-trained girls. He addressed Right Nut in his best business voice.

"You and your brother are good neighbors, and friends. I would want more money from anybody else, but this is a fair offer, and you can have one of the girls. If it is alright with you, we will let Madam Charlie choose which girl she wants to part with."

Right Nut had a smile on his face from ear to ear as he answered. "Mr. Archibald, that is fine with me."

Right Nut dismounted, and the trio walked the short distance to the Lodge. Madam Charlie was quite surprised to see both the bosses with this not-so-clean Indian coming into her very well kept lodge.

Ham, thinking it was time to show his stuff, was first to speak.

"Mr. Nut here would like to purchase one of the slave girls here at the lodge. Which one would you like him to have?"

Madam Charlie started turning red at the neckline. By the time the color reached her forehead, she was steaming.

"I do not want to sell either girl. They work well together and are good workers. I suppose you would send me one of those crude girls out of the fields to train."

Mr. Archibald spoke up. "Madam Charlie, the deal has been made. Mr. Nut has paid good money for the girl."

He showed her the bills. "We thought it would be good for you to choose which girl he can have."

Madam Charlie knew when she was licked, but she was not ready to give up.

"Those girls work so well together, it would be a shame to break them up. I am sure Mr. Nut would be just as happy to choose one of the field hands."

An idea came to Right Nut. He reached in his other pocket and took out a handful of bills. "I guess if you don't want to break them up, I could take both of them."

Realizing what she had done, Madam Charlie's blood started to rise again. Ham, anxious to show his authority, took the money and looked at it. Then he turned to his father and said, "This is a very good offer. I think we should take Mr. Nut's offer and sell him both of the girls."

Archibald had been known to come up from the house at night and share Madam Charlie's blankets with her. Of late, she had been keeping her door locked and was getting kind of uppity. Archibald smiled to himself. What a good chance to get even and make the old girl go to work training two field girls to be house girls. He was quick to give his answer.

"That is a good idea Madam Charlie, to keep the girls together, and very thoughtful of you. Yes, that is what we shall do. Go get the girls."

Snowflake would be so mad she might melt.

CHAPTER 9

"Now an Indian was leading them away from every familiar thing."

Right Nut could not believe his good fortune. The money had meant nothing to him. But now, here before him, stood two slave girls. And they were all his. All he knew about handling slaves was how he had seen the white men do it. He borrowed two collars from the Wanderlusts', put them around the girls' necks and tied their hands behind them. He tied about thirty feet of rope to each girl. He got on his horse and started east, toward his valley.

The bay horse did not care for the rope and the girls behind him. He crow hopped a few times and the girls fell down. Right Nut had to let go of the ropes. Pansy skinned her knee, and Columbine got skinned up on her shoulder. Right Nut could see that this was not going to work. He dismounted and walked along, leading the horse and both girls.

As for the girls, they were scared to death. They had heard stories about Indians and what they did to their captives. Right Nut, with his shoulder length black hair and black eyes, looked very dangerous. Only a few minutes ago they were busy making beds. Now an Indian was leading them away from every familiar thing to the unknown

They were on the road for about an hour and not a word had been exchanged between the trio. It was Pansy who broke the silence.

"My feet hurt. Why can't I ride the horse?"

Right Nut walked on in silence for another mile. Pansy began to limp badly. She kept looking at Right Nut and he could see a tear in her eye. He stopped, untied her hands, and helped her on the horse.

Right Nut had to relieve himself very badly and was sure it must be the same for the girls. He finally stopped and took a pee in the road. The girls giggled. Columbine squatted down and peed. Pansy got off the horse. Here they were, all three of them peeing in the road, and they had barely said a word to each other. Pansy managed to whisper to Columbine, "Limp, act like you hurt. He'll let you ride."

After a while Columbine started to limp. Right Nut finally got brave enough to speak.

"Do you want to ride behind Pansy?" he asked Columbine.

" Yes, Massah Nut, my feet are very sore."

31

Right Nut stopped and helped Columbine up behind Pansy. This gave the girls a chance to talk. Pansy, who was the most forward of the pair, spoke first.

"I think Massah Nut has kind eyes. Let's be good to 'im and maybe he'll go easy on us. If you think 'bout it, it's our only choice."

" I'm scairt. I wanna run away and go back to Madam Charlie," Columbine answered.

"That we can't do. She'd send us back and we'd be whupped. We 'ave to make the best of it," Pansy scolded.

Just then a small buck deer stepped out in the road. Right Nut grabbed his gun and made a well-placed shot. The little buck dropped in the road. Right Nut was very surprised at what good help the girls were at dressing the buck. They turned the buck on his back and each took a leg while Right Nut dressed the deer.

The ever-alert Pansy said, "Massah Nut, cut out the back straps and I'll cook 'em for our supper."

It was in the shank of the day, and they were at a good camping spot with a small stream and a clearing. Columbine got right to work getting wood and cutting sapling sticks to roast the back straps. Right Nut cut out the back straps and sliced them in one-inch steaks. Pansy got the fire going. The evening meal was under way.

Sitting around the campfire after the good meal of venison, they all looked at one another. The girls went to the brush to relieve themselves. Pansy spoke in a low voice to Columbine.

"Massah Right Nut bought us so he could love us. He really doesn' need a slave. I say we let 'im do jus' that and he might give us a good home." Columbine, still scared half out of her wits, was ready to go along with any counsel that Pansy gave her. "I getta do it firs'. You're so wild with men, by the time you got done with 'im he'd be too tired to do me any good. I'll be easy on 'im so there's some left for you."

Pansy had to smile, as she knew that she was what the boys called a "very horny girl." She had always left her friend who came to her cabin, out of breath and in a big sweat. "When we go back to the fire, we'll get our blankets and spread 'em out. Then we'll spread Massah Nut's blanket 'tween ours. I'll get on my blanket and turn back to Massah Nut. You rub 'is belly. Now, don' wear him out. I kinda like 'im and wan' at least part a' 'im."

This arrangement was okay with Columbine. She was still scared of the Indian, and hoped that he had washed himself at least a little before he came to the blanket.

Things worked like clockwork. The girls got the bed all arranged. Right Nut had no choice but to get between them. This was just what he had been dreaming about, yet he was scared and a bit dumbfounded. He was not dumbfounded long, as Columbine's somewhat callused hand rubbed his belly, and was not long in finding him, which she stroked with great finesse. He loved it. Poor Pansy could not stand it, just laying there looking the other way. She turned over and took his family jewels in her hand. This kept them from bouncing on the hard ground and drove Right Nut out of his mind. He rolled off Columbine and Pansy gently took him in her arms. Things were soft as a cotton rope. She had been afraid of this. She kept up a gentle massage and placed his hand on her willing body. She was hot. It was not too long before she felt his blood begin to throb. She rolled over on top. There was never such a union. He felt like a peach seed in a ripe peach. She felt the warmth almost pushing at the tip of her pounding heart.

Right Nut woke in the night to the sound of croaking bullfrogs, ten thousand stars overhead, a good horse grazing close by, and a girl on each side. Was it just a nice warm southern night or was this pure heaven?

CHAPTER 10

"This is my daughter, Learnet Readwright"

Malcolm and Glena Lee were hand-in-hand, walking back to the stables. They had just finished choosing what horses Cottontail Plantation would enter in the big race.

It was the first week of October. The second week in October was the annual Harvest Ball and race meet at the Cottontail Plantation. This year they had seven other stables entered in the meet. This meant there would most likely be 200 or more people at the ball. Malcolm was going to use the occasion to announce that he would be a candidate for Governor. He had a large backing of planters, business people and educators. He would not give a long speech. He would write up his platform and thoughts and send it to the nominating committee next week.

While most all decisions about the horses were left to Shorty Rideout, the head groom, and Lady Chandler, Malcolm had wanted to make sure that his favorite horse, "Not-So-Fast", was entered in the race. Not-So-Fast lost his mother shortly after birth, and Malcolm and the little girls had raised him on the bottle. The name really fit the horse. Not only was he slow, he wasn't much to look at.

Evelyn Lucille had her heart set on riding in the race. Shorty and Lady Chandler had him entered right at the bottom of the list.

Malcolm and Glena Lee chatted and smiled as they thought how happy the little girls would be. Approaching the mansion, they noticed a rather shabby buggy with two occupants in it. A man, dressed in a black suit that was about four inches too short all the way around, stepped out and introduced himself as Amos Readwright.

"I am the younger brother of your children's governess and teacher," he announced. "This is my daughter, Learnet Readwright. It is with deep regrets that we must inform you that my sister, Miss Readwright, passed away this summer while home with her family."

This was a great shock to Malcolm and Glena Lee. They had never known her to be sick a day and their children truly loved her. Just in the last few days they had been wondering about her. She had planned on being back about a week earlier.

Amos wasted no time in getting right to the matters at hand.

34

"As you know, my sister truly loved your little girls. Her last request was that Learnet come to your plantation and take over her job as teacher and governess."

Now this was a shock.

Amos continued, "Learnet has completed her studies and is a very capable young lady."

Learnet stepped out of the buggy. She was maybe seventeen or eighteen, with a very fair complexion. She was tall and very skinny with rather coarse features. She wore a long, black dress with a dark blue bonnet. Beneath the bonnet you could see her auburn hair. She was not a beautiful girl, but one close to handsome, and her face reflected an air of authority.

Malcolm called to Tall Boy, who was tending the garden close by.

"Tall Boy, take the Readwrights' horse and buggy to the stable. See to it that the horse is fed and rubbed down." Then he turned to the travelers and said, "Please do come in and have some tea. You must be very tired. You have traveled a good distance."

The Readwrights' home was in a small town in southern Pennsylvania.

They took chairs into the library, which also served as a study, and Glena Lee rang for a servant. Mary Annabelle came and Glena Lee ordered tea and crackers for the guests.

Learnet had never seen such a pretty slave girl. Mary Annabelle had learned to carry herself with the grace of a young doe. The girls' eyes met as Mary Annabelle left the room to get the tea.

Glena Lee was still in a state of shock that this girl would come all that way and be so confident that she had a job. And that she could do the job. "Miss Readwright, I have several questions for you," Glena Lee began. "After living all of your life in the North, do you think you will like the South? How do you know you will like the children? What are your qualifications?"

Learnet rose to her feet, made direct eye contact with the Chandlers, and began to speak. "I read and I have studied much of the South: it's history, customs, and geography. My aunt has described your children in every detail, and I have never seen a child I did not love. I have finished my studies. I am very good with the English language, and I have a good knowledge of ciphers. You will find that I am a very dedicated and hard worker. It was one of my aunt's last wishes that I come to you, as she wanted your children in the best of care."

Learnet gave a slight bow in the direction of the Chandler's and took her seat.

Malcolm stood and took Glena Lee by the hand. "Will you please excuse Mrs. Chandler and me? We would like to talk this matter over in private."

They retired to the outer hall. "She certainly is confident for her age," Glena Lee said. "I say let's call the girls and let them talk to her. If they like her, I do not see how we could go wrong."

Malcolm agreed and they called the girls. "Miss Readwright's niece is in the library," he explained to his daughters. "It seems that Miss Readwright has passed away. Her niece, whose name is also Miss Readwright, would like to be your teacher. We would like you girls to come in and meet her."

"Do you mean our Miss Readwright is dead?" Evelyn Lucille asked. "I don't want any teacher except our Miss Readwright."

There were tears streaming down both girls' faces as the parents led them into the library. The girls had truly loved the old teacher.

Learnet stepped forward and knelt in front of the two little girls. Little Mandy Ann dried her eyes and said, "Can we call you Miss Readwright, just like we did Miss Readwright?"

"It looks like you have a job," Malcolm said. "Mary Annabelle, will you show Learnet to Miss Readwright's old room and help her unpack? Mandy Ann, you go along and help. Evelyn Lucille, you run to the stable and have Tall Boy bring the Readwrights' luggage up to the house. Amos, you had better stay with us a few days, get some rest and rest your horse."

Amos smiled.

"Mr. Chandler, I thank you. It was a long, hard trip and I am not as young as I used to be. I am a carpenter by trade. If you have any carpenter work to be done, I would like to do it. I do not like idle hands."

"As a matter of fact, I have," Malcolm responded. "We have wanted to build a stage in the main ballroom. We really have no slaves that are good finish carpenters. You may have Tall Boy to help you with the project. We have not owned him long, but he seems like a willing worker."

Amos did not believe in slavery or anything about it. The thought of having a slave to work with was most repulsive. He was a guest and he did not want to cause trouble for Learnet. He better keep his big mouth shut, build the stage and let the slave boy help him.

Learnet was shocked when she entered her new room. Family pictures adorned the walls, the closet was full of her aunt's clothing, and familiar books filled the shelves. Tall Boy was soon on hand with her modest belongings. Mary Annabelle took the bag, placed it on the bed, and opened it.

Learnet stopped Mary Annabelle saying, "I can do this."

She had never had anybody touch her personal belongings and she did not like it. On the other hand, the little girls stood, looking dumbfounded. They had never seen a white person unpack their own suitcase. Learnet looked at the people standing around her.

"You all go on downstairs. I will be down very shortly."

Evelyn Lucille went to her mother and told her that the new Miss Readwright was unpacking her own clothes. Glena Lee explained to the girls how things were different in the North and that people did not have slaves to do the work. Both of the little girls decided, right then and there, that they never wanted to live in the north. A household without slaves would not be a home.

Learnet combed her long, auburn hair and got out of her traveling clothes. It felt much better to be cleaned up after the long, hard trip. She went to the window to see the slaves coming in from the field. A man on a white horse rode with them. A girl that appeared to be pregnant stumbled and fell. The man on the horse struck her with his whip. She placed her hand over her mouth to keep from screaming.

Conversation at dinner was a discussion of the new stage to be built, and that the girls would start their lessons in the morning.

Glena Lee was glad to get the girls out from under foot as she had much work to do for the Harvest Ball.

The house was quiet with sleeping people, when Learnet heard a very light rap at her door. She had been sleeping and had just rolled over. Awakened, she lay quietly when she heard another rap, rap. She was half scared, but got out of bed and went to the door. "Who is it?" she whispered.

"Me, Mary Annabelle," came the whispered reply.

Learnet opened the door a crack. "What do you want?"

"I want to talk to you."

Learnet slowly opened the door. There stood Mary Annabelle, dressed in black panties and a black shawl. She put a finger to her lip to indicate quiet and gently pushed the door open. She looked scared.

"Miss Learnet, will you teach me to read English? I can read Spanish, but I must learn to read English so I can teach the slave children."

Learnet looked her up and down.

"I would be happy to help you learn to read," she offered.

"No one must know. The Massahs don' want the slaves to learn or be schooled. Maybe Massah Malcolm wouldn' care. He gave me a Bible. I thought I could learn from it, but I don' understand the words. The words don' sound like the words we speak. I heard Lady Chandler and Mrs. Glena Lee talkin'. They were sayin' it's not a good idea for slaves to even talk much to each other. Mr. Whip Smith caught me down at the slave quarters showin' a slave boy my Bible and he whupped me good."

Learnet looked shock.

"Mary Annabelle, you go back to bed. I will talk to Master Chandler tomorrow, and ask if it will be okay to give you schooling."

Mary Annabelle, in an almost too loud voice, said, "No, no. He will have to say no. It makes no difference how he feels. The whole South doesn' want slaves to learn and he'd just hafta see it didn' happen. Please don' say nuthin'. Jus' teach me in secret," she pleaded.

"Please Mary Annabelle, leave my room. I will talk to you in a few days after I am more settled."

CHAPTER 11

"He grabbed the knife and cut off Hoke's right ear."

The moon was full and sending an eerie light through the trees where twenty male slaves sat in a circle around a large oak tree. Deep in the forest, between Hanging Magnolia Plantation and Cottontail Plantation, the dominant male slaves from both plantations had gathered.

They sat with their knees folded, beating imaginary drums with their hands and chanting in low voices. Real drums would send out a very negative alarm to the slave owners. Dressed only in breach cloths, they raised from the sitting position and the cheeks of their buttocks were painted white. They danced around the tree, bending and flashing their white asses to the full moon. These voodoo rituals had been going on since Possum had come to Cottontail. He was the doctor of the voodoo, the guru. The dance around the tree continued with their white asses making a salute to the moon.

The dancing stopped. The group formed a circle around Tall Boy and Possum. From a gunnysack, Possum removed a red rooster. The rooster did not seem happy with where he was, and for good reason. Possum held the rooster while Tall Boy removed his head. While the rooster was jumping around like a chicken with his head cut off, (which he was), the slaves began the dance again, showing their white asses to the moon. When the rooster was dead, he was passed around the circle. Each man took one feather from the bird's breast. The rooster was then buried in a pre-dug hole at the foot of the oak tree.

Each man would take the feather with him. When he wished to put a hex or voodoo on his enemy, all he had to do was to place the red rooster feather in his enemy's bed or shoe, anyplace where the person would come in direct contact with it. Then the voodoo gods would destroy his enemy.

Each man, in turn, pointed his white ass at the moon and sat down. Possum stood by the tree and spoke to the men.

"Since our las' meetin' I've learnt many things. You mustn't tell a soul what I'm about to tell you. I can't even tell you who passed this learnin' on to me. The white men in Washington have a paper. This paper has the rules for all men. The paper says all men are equal. The paper says all men can keep guns. The person who tells me these things says that the people in the North believe in this paper and will help us. The people in the North think it's against the rules of this paper to whup us, sell off our children, and rape our women."

A short, stocky slave jumped to his feet. He stood before the others and announced, "Have some news. Most of you know of the Underground Railroad that the northern people have to help us escape. You also know there's never been a good connection in our part of the South. That has changed. There's a roadside stop east of here that is owned by two Indians and a white woman," he explained. "Two months ago, one of the Indians bought two slave girls. This lady, whose name is Snowflake, was very mad. She didn't believe in slaves. She made the Indian who bought the girls marry one of 'em if he wanted to keep 'er. He had to free the other girl. He did like the girl and she liked him so he married her. The other girl was freed, but she likes this lady, Snowflake, and stayed and is working for her wages. This lady, Snowflake, will hide runaways 'til they make contact with the people in the Underground Railroad."

Possum took charge of the meeting again. "You all have enough to eat. If you behave, you seldom get whupped. In many ways we have less worries than the whites. Give it much good thought before you run away."

The twenty black men then disbanded and disappeared into the woods, each going his own way. Tall Boy had not gone 100 yards when two men grabbed him. Without a word, they cut off his other ear. His assailants then silently vanished into the dark.

Possum was just emerging from the dark woods when two men grabbed him. Possum was quick and strong. He had heard Tall Boy's muffled scream, so he was on the look out. Possum gave a twist, breaking loose and grabbing the men by the back of their necks. With a hard slam, he banged their heads together with great force. He knocked them both colder than a cucumber. He studied the faces in the moonlight. It was Whip Smith and his son, Hoke Smith, home from school on a visit.

Possum saw a knife in Whip's belt. He grabbed the knife and cut off Hoke's right ear. Then he cut a swallow fork in Whip's left ear. A swallow fork is a v-shape cut used to ear mark cattle.

Just then, Tall Boy appeared, with blood rushing out the side of his head. He looked at the overseer and his son lying on the forest floor. "It's time to run. From now on, we're run away slaves."

Possum had a million thoughts in his head. He'd never see his wife and daughter again. Malcolm would never find them now. If he went back he could be hanged, or at the least, badly beaten. He'd almost liked being a slave on Cottontail Plantation. He liked Malcolm and knew he was a decent person that he could work with. Now, in a fit of temper, he had lost it all. He looked at Tall Boy and asked only one question, "Which way is north?"

Chapter 12

"Lets go to Cuba for a vacation and holiday."

What a beautiful day it was, as Malcolm rolled out of bed and look to the east, as the sun rose over the cotton fields. He had slept in, well really not slept, as Glenna Lee was still in bed. Glenna Lee sat on the edge of the bed, brushed here hair and said to Malcolm. "Let's go to Cuba for a vacation and holiday. We can take Mary Annabelle as she speaks Spanish. She can act as governess for the girls, interpreter and handmaid. I know you mentioned once that you would like to bring Possum's wife and girl back to him. He is such a good man and has become a real leader of the Slaves. It seems to me that Whip Smith does not like him. For the life of me I fail to see why. He is such a good worker and everybody else loves him. The race and Harvest Ball are only three days away. I would like to go right after that."

Malcolm was about half dressed as he spoke.

"That sounds like a great idea. We sold the No.2 Warehouse of cotton to an English buyer yesterday. It brought the best price we ever had, so this would be a good time to go. The only thing that could hold us up is that Whip Smith has mentioned that he would like to retire and move to Atlanta to be with his children. After breakfast I will go to the slave quarters and talk to Whip, you talk to Mary Annabelle."

As Malcolm approached the slave quarters he could see something was not right. The field hands that should have been in the fields were not, they were just kind of milling around and talking. The slaves who were assigned to the house and to the stables to ready for the weekend were just starting to the Mansion and the Stable. Malcolm went to Olaf, a slave that they had bought from a Norwegian Sea captain.

"Olaf, where is Whip Smith?

"Mas Malcolm he is not here this morning."

Up on closer observation Malcolm saw that Possum and Tall Boy were also missing. Malcolm did not like this unrest. In his loudest voice he shouted to the slave.

"The field hands will get to field right now!! Olaf is in charge. Olaf you do a good job and keep them working. You who are assigned to the stable get up there right now and report to Shorty. The rest of you go to the main house and report to Lady Chandler."

The worst nightmare of the plantation owners was a slave uprising, and this morning had all the earmarks of one. The slaves divided into the three groups and started to work. There was some grumbling, but for the most part the unrest was somewhat subdued.

Olaf seemed delighted with his newfound authority, and the slaves seemed to pay attention as they marched to the fields.

Malcolm walked the short distance to the Smith's modest home and knocked on the door. Mrs. Smith slowly opened it.

She had a bandage in her hand, and seeing Malcolm, she turned a gray shade of white, saying in a shaky voice, "Mr. Chandler this is not a good time. Could you come back later?"

A voice from the back of the house came.

"It is OK Clemintine, we have to talk sometime."

Clemintine was a small dark woman who pretty much stayed to herself. It was rumored she was of colored blood, a subject that never came up. Clemintine opened the door. Malcolm saw Whip and his son sitting at a rather messy breakfast table with bandages on their heads. The fresh blood was showing through. Malcolm was in shock. He took a chair at the table, which had been recently occupied by Clemintine. He did not wait for and invitation to sit down.

Whip did not wait for questions.

"Malcolm I have worked for you and your Father on Cottontail for a long time. I feel I have done a good job and almost feel a member of you family. I should have quit when I spoke of it several weeks ago. I have let you down. It was a chain of events that I am responsible for in some ways, and had nothing to do with in other ways. As you can see I have lost control of the slaves! Before you ask any questions I will start from the first and try to explain the events of the past two months to you."

Malcolm was thankful that he had been told not to ask questions as he certainty did not know what to ask. Whip Smith continued.

"It all started the day that Possum arrived. You will remember that I struck him and the Tall Boy just before I took them to their new quarter. When we were out of sight, Possum grabbed me, took my quirt and choked me down. He forced me to promise that I would never whip him or the boy. He said in return that he would work hard and keep the boy working. I thought he was going to kill me. You remember that day when I came to see you all bruised up. We both kept our bargains and things went quite well until last night. One night I happened to be out on my porch and I saw a girl come out of Possum's cabin. I kind of smiled and thought, well old Possum got a little ass tonight. Then I noticed she started to the Mansion, I tell you she moved so quiet and sly in the night, just like a female bobcat. I saw it was Mary Annabelle. I stepped back in the shadows and waited until she got close and I called to here in a soft voice. She stopped but did not run and did not seem to be afraid. I ask her where she was going.

She looked straight at me and said.

"The man slaves are having a voodoo meeting in the forest down by Magnolia Plantation, on the night of the full moon."

"Then she ran. I have never seen anyone run faster."

Clemintine had served Malcolm a cup of coffee. He took a drink and said nothing, waiting for Whip to continue the story.

Whip went on.

" I had heard of these meetings before, but I did not know where they were held. To tell the truth I could see little harm in them. Voodoo is an African religion, and probably has as much credence as Christianity or Buddha or what not. If I had thought there was talk of helping runaways or of the Underground Rail I would have investigated further. I talked to some of the slaves, and there seemed to be none of this. As near as I could tell they seldom met. Yesterday morning Hoke got home for a school vacation. I ask him if he would go with me to see just what was going on. We had no trouble finding the place. They had made a small clearing around a big oak tree. We hid ourselves and waited.

Just as the moon was coming up here they came 20 of them all males. Some of ours, and some from Hanging Magnolia. They all had on only breach clothes and their asses were painted white. They beat imaginary drums and mooned the moon with their white asses. Then they killed a rooster passed it around and buried it under the tree. There was no doubt that Possum was the leader and Tall Boy was his helper. As they held their short meeting it was very hard for us to hear. We did make out the words, *White man's paper, Snowflake and Underground Railroad.* Hoke and I decided this was enough for some action. Since they had all left single, we would catch Tall Boy and cut off his other ear. Then we'd catch Possum and castrate him. Hoke is a very strong young man, and I am not bad. We had no trouble with Tall Boy, and his other ear is gone. Possum is the strongest man I have seen, we attacked him from behind. I don't know just what happened. When we came to, Hoke had lost an ear, and he had earmarked me. We both have terrible knots on our head, he must have slammed us together with such force it knocked us out".

Whip removed the bandage from his head showing the damaged ear to Malcolm. Whip went on with the story.

"I am sure by this time Tall Boy and Possum have informed every slave on the plantation. I can never show my face here again. Possum will have to be punished, but by someone else. As soon as it is dark my family and me will be on the road to Atlanta. Malcolm, I feel very bad about everything and having to leave you like this, but I am sure you can see it is for the best. It was a funny thing when Hoke and I came to, we each had a red feather inside our shirts.

Malcolm was a man of even temper, but he was mad. How could this pair be so dumb to think that harming the Tall Boy and Possum in the way that they had planned help keep control of the slave.

Malcolm let on like nothing had happend.

"Before you go, I need your help. I am going to write a note to Bancroft Whitesides. On your way to Atlanta, will you stop by Hanging Magnolia and give him the note?"

Malcolm wrote.

> DearBancroft;
> Some of your slaves have been holding voodoo meetings with mine in the forest between our Plantations. Keep a close watch and don't let any of your slaves attend these meeting.
> I heard you say you had a young overseer in training to take over for Luke Loggerhead. I can not recall the young man's name. Could I please borrow him for a few days. Whip Smith will explain in detail. Please send the young man immediately as I am leaving at once to catch 2 run away slaves.
> Malcolm Chandler.

Whip Smith read the note, and seemed surprised to find that two slaves had run. He asked Malcolm. "Which slaves have run?"

"Possum and Tall Boy. I must be off. I want to catch them. I still think Possum is a good man."

Malcolm arrived at the stable just as Shorty Rideout was leading Not-So-Fast out for a work out. Malcolm took the young strong horse and headed east at full speed.

CHAPTER 13

"You're push'in my heart up in my neck"

Possum and Tall Boy had run and walked fast most of the night. They were just east of Wanderlust Lodge when the sky was turning gray in the east. They crawled under a cut bank not too far off the main road. It was well concealed, and they felt pretty safe.

Tall Boy had lost a lot of blood by running and not taking care of the wound where his ear had been removed. He was quite weak. Possum washed his ear off with creek water and got the bleeding stopped.

It was well past noon when the pair awakened. They were both quite young and tough and felt much better after the sleep. Possum, who woke first, watched Tall Boy sleeping. "What am I doing here?" he asked himself.

Tall Boy then woke, and Possum said, "I'm goin' back. I don' wanna be a runaway slave. Bein' a slave is bad, but bein' a runaway slave is worse. You can come back with me or you can run. If you decide to run, I'll tell you all I know, much of which I didn't pass on at last night's meetin'."

Tall Boy did not take long to answer. "I'm goin' to run. I've had both my ears cut off. Mary Annabelle is the only girl I ever liked and she won't have nothin' to do with me. I wanna go find out 'bout the white man's paper that'll let me have a gun, and be equal. I have nothin' to lose the way I see it."

Possum reported to Tall Boy all the information he had. "You saw the new girl that came to Cottontail to teach the little white girls. She's teachin' Mary Annabelle to read and some other things. This has to be a secret 'cuz the Massahs don' want the slaves to learn. Mary Annabelle came to my cabin the other night. She told me about the white man's paper. She called it a Bill of Rights and there's another paper called the Constitution. She says it gives ever'body freedom, 'cuz it don' say nothin' 'bout the fact that you're a slave and you don' count. She wanted me to fix it so she could come to the slave quarters at night and teach the slaves how to read and all 'bout those papers. I told her I'd see what I could do. Now, Tall Boy you pay attention. This's what the white teacher told her about Snowflake.

"You 'member when we stayed at the Nut's place and you lost your first ear?" Possum continued. "Well, this Right Nut, he went to Wanderlust and bought those two maid girls. Did you see 'em when we stayed at Wanderlust?"

44

Tall Boy thought, and then answered Possum. "Yeah, one of 'em was Pansy. She was short. The bigger one was Columbine. I din't think I'd ever see her again, but I did take a shine to that Columbine."

Possum went on. "The white teacher stayed at the Nut's place on 'er way to Cottontail. She got to know Snowflake pretty well and 'ere's what's goin' on. Snowflake was so mad at her brother-in-law for buyin' slaves, she said if he din't set 'em free, she'd kill 'im. Left Nut, her husband, backed her up. So Right Nut freed the big girl and married Pansy. Snowflake was so mad at the way white people treat the slaves she joined the Underground Railroad. You hurry on to the Nut's place. Snowflake'll hide ya and get to the right people so you can go north. I'll tell Massah Malcolm that you bled to death and died. Maybe he won' come lookin' for ya."

They shook hands. Tall Boy started for the Nut Place, keeping off the road and out of sight. Possum got right in the middle of the road and started back to Cottontail. He had not gone far when he heard a horse coming. He stepped off the road into the brush. Then he saw that it was Malcolm on Not-So-Fast, coming at a good clip. Possum stepped out of the brush in front of the horse and raised both hands. Not-So-Fast shied, and Malcolm almost lost his balance. He recovered and, needless to say, he was dumbfounded to see Possum.

Possum spoke first. "Mas Malcolm, I wanna go home."

"Where is Tall Boy?" Malcolm demanded.

"He's dead. The Smiths cut him real bad, skinned off the whole side of his head and cut way down his neck. There was nothin' I could do. He bled to death."

"Where is he now?"

"Buried him best I could deep in the woods. He din't die real fast. He say he din't wanna be buried on white man's land. He liked the forest and wanted me to bury 'im right where he died."

Malcolm had some second thoughts about this story, but he had the slave he really wanted and they could spend hours looking for Tall Boy's grave. And he was not sure he really wanted to find it.

Malcolm tossed Possum a rope.

"Tie this around your waist. We are going home."

They were off. Possum followed along behind Not-So-Fast back to Cottontail.

It was dark when Tall Boy arrived at the Nut Place. He had no idea what to do. Hiding in the tall reeds along the creek behind the outhouse, he could see the light from two cabins. His vantage point was not far from the outhouse. It made sense that somebody would have to go to the outhouse sometime. He made his way behind the outhouse and removed a very small board from the back. He did not have to wait long until the door opened and the moonlight shown through the door, displaying the outline of a woman. When the door was closed he could not see a thing. He had to take a chance. In a low voice he called out, "Columbine!"

It was a good thing she was on the pot or she would have messed her pants. After she gained some composure she said, "Who is it?'

"I'm Tall Boy, the slave you seen at Wanderlust who's a runaway and had 'is ear cut off. I've run away again. I's told that Snowflake could hide me and get to people of the Underground Railroad."

Columbine looked behind her and saw one large, white eye looking through the crack in the outhouse. She did remember the tall slave with one ear cut off. He was rather handsome even with one ear off and being tied hand and foot.

"You come 'round front where I can see you," she said.

She opened the door and could not believe what stood before her. A tall, not bad looking boy, with both ears off and blood caked on the side of his head. Her only question was a logical one. "What happened to you?"

He gave her a short version of the past night.

"You come in this outhouse. I'll go to Snowflake and find out about hidin' you and get you some food."

In a few minutes, she was back with a plate of biscuits and a shank of venison. The outhouse was a two-holer. He devoured the meal. He was very hungry and the food was some of the very best he had ever tasted. Columbine had brought a jar of warm water and some bandages. She gently washed his head and bandaged his ear. He never thought it possible to go to heaven in an outhouse.

When he had finished the meal and was all bandaged up, Columbine outlined the plans. "Left Nut and Snowflake are goin' to a village east of here in the mornin' for supplies. When the moon goes down you go to the wagon in front of the cabin. It has high sides and a false floor. Take out the two loose planks in the floor and lay 'tween the floors. There are some deer hides to lay on. It takes about four hours to get to the village. When you arrive there, Snowflake'll tell you what to do."

Then a strange thing happened. Like magic, they fell into each other's arms. The outhouse was not too large and they both stood up, still locked in an embrace. Tall Boy's hands found a way under her dress and he could feel her soft warmth. She let forth with a low moan and said, "Tall Boy, you is tall all over. You are pushin' my heart up in my neck."

She slid to the narrow floor with him on top of her. Her legs were spread as far as she could, and his were up pushing on the side of the outhouse to get more penetration. Pumping, pushing and pulling they reached a climax as high as one could. Just as they reached this climax, she ran a large sliver in her butt off the wood floor. The smells of the two hot bodies and the smell of the outhouse blended to make a strange and strong odor. The door sprung open, and in a tangle of arms and legs they rolled out into the October moonlight.

They lay together until the moon went down, and made their way to the wagon in front of the cabin. She helped him get between the floor and went to bed. She was so excited she could not find sleep. She had never felt this way before. She sat up in bed. The sliver in her ass hurt bad. She got up, walked to the window and looked at the wagon, knowing he lay beneath the floor. Then it hit her. "Tall Boy, I'm in love with you," she said to herself in a low voice.

No way could she let him be taken away and never see him again. Columbine went back to bed to devise a new plan.

CHAPTER 14

"The crowd would hang Right Nut."

Malcolm and Possum reached Wanderlust Lodge just before dark. Malcolm took Possum to the slave cages and went to the dining room for supper. The dining room was filled with guests that were headed to Cottontail for the races and the Harvest Ball. Malcolm used the opportunity to talk politics and try to determine what the people wanted in a Governor. Slavery was the main issue, and how best to keep slaves from revolt. He began to put together his thoughts for his platform for the coming election. He had over a year until the election.

The next morning he went to get Possum. Possum went to the creek and washed up. Malcolm gave him some breakfast. Then he explained his plan to Possum.

"I am going to borrow a horse so you can ride on to Cottontail. When we get there, we will tell everybody that you chased Tall Boy to try to bring him back. When you found him, he was bleeding to death and there was nothing you could do. It was then you realized that you were lost and wandered in the woods until you found the road and I found you."

Possum lifted his hands in the air, bowed his head and said, "Massah. Massah Malcolm, you are a fine man."

It was not hard to borrow a horse for Possum. Most of the guests going to Cottontail had extra horses that they intended to put in the races. Malcolm still had much to say to Possum so they rode close together on the road and talked.

"Possum, what about this Voodoo? You are said to be a Guru and leader of this so-called religion. We can not have this going on with the slaves at Cottontail. I want no more of this or any more meetings of any kind. If you do not obey me, you will be dealt with severely."

"I believe in voodoo. It is my religion," Possum responded. "But, I belong to you and if you say I can't practice my religion, then I can't. Voodoo has strong powers."

Due to the strong horses, they got into Cottontail by mid-afternoon. The place bustled with activity as many of the guests had arrived, and still more were coming in. Most of them were camping, however Malcolm and Glena Lee had two special guests staying at the mansion. One of the special

48

guests was Glena Lee's parents, Mr. & Mrs. Whitesides, from the Hanging Magnolia Plantation. The other was the Lieutenant Governor.

The rumor had spread like wildfire that Snowflake Nut was a part of the Underground Railroad. It was thought that Right and Left Nut were also involved. Malcolm was in conversation with the Lieutenant Governor and his brother-in-law when Bancroft Whitesides made the suggestion that the best thing to do was to burn the Nuts' place to the ground.

The Lieutenant Governor suggested that if the place were burned that the state would brand it accidental. However, he suggested the best thing might be to send a mob to hang Snowflake. That would probably stop the Underground Railroading. And it would not inconvenience anyone as the community used the Nut Place. At any rate, something had to be done, and with most of the community gathered here at Cottontail, it would be best to do the job tonight.

Malcolm was horrified. The Nuts had done wrong. Yet it seemed to Malcolm that it was very wrong to take the action recommended by the Lieutenant Governor and Bancroft.

Malcolm was actually sick to his stomach. He walked out on the porch and looked down the lane just in time to see Right Nut approaching. He was riding a mule and leading the bay that he had traded from Malcolm.

Now he *was* sick. The crowd would hang Right Nut on sight. He walked to the front gate and then ran as fast as a thirty-something man could run to reach Right Nut. Out of breath, he took the mule by the bridle and turned him around.

"Get back to your place," Malcolm warned Right Nut. "They have found out that Snowflake is trafficking in slaves and if you are seen here they will hang you."

"But, I came to run the bay in the races," Right Nut argued. "I am a slave owner now and want to race. The bay is a very fast horse. These people all stay with us and are our friends. They won't hang me. You are just mad because Snowflake helped your boy with no ears to escape to the North. He took our Columbine with him."

Malcolm looked shocked. "Did you say that Snowflake helped Tall Boy run north?"

Now it was Right Nut's turn to look shocked. "I thought you knew about that or I wouldn't have said anything. It was probably somebody else."

Malcolm was as mad as he could get. "You Indian sonuvabitch, I should kill you right now! I don't have time or I would. You turn the mule loose, get on the bay, and don't stop until you get home. Pack up your brother and Snowflake and get out of the country. I was going to try and save you, but this has gone too far. As soon as the races and Harvest Ball are over, I will lead a mob to hang all of you and burn you out."

Right Nut had the saddle off the mule and on the horse. He looked back at Malcolm once over his shoulder as he rode east.

Malcolm walked back to the mansion with the idea of stalling the war party on the Nuts for the weekend. He soon found it was not necessary as the subjects had changed and everybody was partying. The good news was, nobody had missed him or seen him talking to the traitor of an Indian.

The plans were laid for the next day's races. There were to be five races with five horses in each race. The winners of each race would be raced against each other in the evening. Following the last race, the Harvest Ball would be held. Drawings were made to decide which horses would be in the races. Not-So-Fast was in the second race. Southern Splendor, a horse that belonged to the Wanderlust Plantation, was in the fifth race. Southern Splendor was the grand prize winner from last year, and the heavy favorite to take it all again this year.

Evelyn Lucille wanted to ride Not-So-Fast. Her father set his foot down and said no. She was an excellent rider and judge of horses for her age. Lady Chandler would have let her ride, but father knows best. The jockey for Cottontail Plantation was a small slave boy named Half-Pint.

The races had all been arranged and everybody was drinking rum and wine until the wee hours. The little Chandler girls and two little slave girls got hold of some wine. They hid under the porch of the mansion and drank two bottles. The first adult to notice was Glena Lee as she witnessed poor little Mandy Ann leaning over the porch rail as sick as she could be. Evelyn Lucille was giggling and staggering around the lawn. Nobody saw that the little slave girls were passed out under the porch. Malcolm and Glena Lee got the girls to bed. Glena Lee, who had a little too much herself, decided it was her bedtime and went to bed.

Malcolm went back downstairs to mingle with the guests. He was surprised to see that the entire party had departed. Mary Annabelle was cleaning up the bar, and Learnet was helping her. They were talking and laughing like a couple of mourning doves. Malcolm thought it strange that the white teacher would be helping the slave girl. He could see nothing wrong, so he slipped out the double door and walked down the glade to the creek. He sat down to do some thinking.

Things were happening fast. He hated to admit it to himself, but there were a few things that he did not have a good handle on. He had yet to see the borrowed overseer his brother-in-law had sent over. He wondered if Right Nut had got the message and left the country. In a way he was a little sorry for being so hard on him. On the other hand, he had to get his family out or they were as good as dead. He had not talked to his mother about the final arrangements for the races, but assumed they were all going well.

Suddenly the silence was broken by a small voice whispering, "Would you like a Mint Julep?"

Malcolm looked up to see Mary Annabelle standing over him. As she leaned down, she let the neck of her blouse sag, exposing those firm breasts. He took the drink. There it was again—male hormones reacting. Never in his life had any female aroused him so quickly and completely.

"Mary Annabelle, I have some questions for you," he said.

She sat down, uninvited, and so close they almost touched.

"Is Miss Readwright teaching you to read?" he began.

Without a moment's hesitation she answered. "Ho no. She's already done that. She has some fine books, very easy to learn from. Now I'm teachin' her to read and speak Spanish."

So much for the first question. So Malcolm posed his second question, "Are you teaching the slave children to read?"

"No," she quickly responded.

She thought about giving him more of an explanation, as she had been trying very hard to do just that, but couldn't get the cooperation of any of the slave children. She did have two older slaves she was teaching to read, but that was not the question.

Malcolm could feel the affects of the Mint Julep added to his other drinks. He could also feel the heat from her body. She reached out to take the glass from his hand and their hands touched. He let the glass drop to the grass and took her hand. She squeezed his hand and let her head drop in his lap. He could feel her warm breath on his member. He ran his hand down the back of her blouse as she opened his pants and took him. She was gentle with him as his hand found her soft breast. The feeling for both of them was utter ecstasy. She took his hand, holding him tightly, as throbbing blood rushed through him.

His hand found her legs as she gently rolled on her back. The next thing he knew, she moaned with pure pleasure. The climax they reached, if it could have been put to music, would have been a masterpiece. He rolled off into the soft grass. She got up, straightened herself, and disappeared into the dark night. From this union would come a child.

CHAPTER 15

"Evelyn Lucille lead Not-So-Fast to the starting gate."

Morning came to Cottontail with a light fog over the infield of the racetrack. Horses, people, kids and slaves all mingled and made ready for the first race. It was a festive and happy occasion. The weather had cooled off, which would make it better for the horses.

Shorty Rideout found Malcolm rubbing down his horse for the first race. It was a small gray filly named Tinker Bell. This was the young horse's first race, and would serve more or less as a training program. Shorty had told Half-Pint not to push the young filly. Shorty approached Malcolm and asked if they could talk in private. They moved off to the side.

"Mr. Chandler, you know how Not-So-Fast was always very tender over the hips when we rubbed him down? When you took him and gave him that hard ride the other day, it seems to have helped him. I had Half-Pint work him out yesterday afternoon, and he is very fast. Tom Wanderlust is taking all bets on Southern Splendor to win everything. I bet all I could with him that Not-So-Fast would take it all. I did not have much money. I think you should teach the braggart a lesson, and make a big bet with him that Not-So-Fast wins it all. But wait until after Not-So-Fast wins his first race. I told Half-Pint to try and win by not more than a head so the horse wouldn't look too good."

"How can you be so sure the horse is that fast?" Malcolm queried.

Shorty smiled. "I have been training horses all my life and I have never seen a horse run like him. I would be willing to bet that there is not a horse in all of the South that could beat him."

Malcolm looked across the paddock and saw Not-So-Fast trying to eat the straw bonnet off Evelyn Lucille's head as she led him around.

"Shorty, I now know why you have such brown eyes. It is because you are so full of shit. I think the best advice you gave me was to wait until he wins."

Shorty, laughing and shaking his head, walked off.

The first race went off without a hitch. A big black that the owner had brought all the way from New Orleans was the winner by a length and a half. The horse's name was Black King, and it looked to Malcolm to be the horse to watch.

Evelyn Lucille led Not-So-Fast to the starting gate. She wore what was left of the straw bonnet. The horse had his head down and pushed her along. Once in the starting gate, he still kept his head down, and no matter how hard Half-Pint tried, he could not get him to pay attention.

Then they were off. Not-So-Fast got off to a slow start and was a length behind the pack at the first turn. Evelyn Lucille stood by the finish line with her head bowed and her eyes closed. Malcolm, standing beside her, heard her saying over and over, "God make him run, God make him run."

On the backstretch, he was in the middle of the pack and running hard. As they started for home he was third and Half-Pint was not whipping. He even looked to be holding him back. About fifty yards from the finish, Half-Pint gave him his head and one whack with the whip. Not-So-Fast shot out like a bean fart and won by a head.

Evelyn Lucille looked up and cried, "Thanks!" She jumped up and down and shouted with pure joy. The bad news came as Half-Pint was riding him back to the winner's circle. He had come up lame and was favoring his right front leg. After getting the ribbon and the check as winner of the second race, Evelyn Lucille led him over to Shorty. Shorty picked up his foot and, at first, could see nothing, but on closer observation he saw a small gravel that had worked into his foot. Shorty removed the gravel. He sat Evelyn Lucille up on the horse and said, "You ride him around slowly for about ten minutes to cool him down. Then rub him down good. It doesn't look too bad. I think he may be able to run in the last race."

Cottontail and Half-Pint had one more winner in the fourth race. It was a little bay mare that, like Tinker Bell, was not expected to win. Her name was Eve as she was the first filly that had been born to the Cottontail Stable in about two years. This left Cottontail in the finals with two horses and only one experienced jockey.

Evelyn Lucille was quick to pick up on this and begged to ride Not-So-Fast. It was not lady-like for a female to straddle a horse, and a girl jockey was unheard of. Malcolm was dead set not to let her ride. Lady Chandler thought it a grand idea. Shorty kept out of it the best he could, but knew in his heart that the girl would do a good job. Lady Chandler finally won and was Evelyn Lucille ever a happy girl. Lady Chandler took her to the stable and dressed her in boy-jockey's clothing. They were not trying to hide the fact that she was a girl, but the more she looked like a boy, the better.

The horses were in the starting gate—Southern Splendor, Not-So-Fast, Black King, Eve, and a horse from Atlanta name Muddy Eye, named for his one glass eye. Eve did not want to load in the gate and gave Half-Pint quite a hard time. All were ready and they were off. Black King took a length lead, and Muddy Eye was second at the first turn. Southern Splendor was dead last. In the backstretch, Not-So-Fast had pulled into a strong second when all hell broke loose.

There was a dense, wooded area along the track in the backstretch. It was at that moment that a flock of wild turkeys decided to cross the track. The flock numbered about thirty as they crossed, some running and others flying low, they flew and ran right into the tightly bunched field of race-horses. Eve tossed Half-Pint ten feet in the air. Black King fell over a running turkey and got up with a broken front leg. Southern Splendor turned and ran the wrong way. Muddy Eye tossed his rider and ran into the infield. Not-So-Fast almost lost Evelyn Lucille, but she managed to get him turned into the infield where he just put his head down and munched the good green grass.

When things were sorted out, Half-Pint was knocked cold and they laid him on the grass. Black King was led off the track and shot. Malcolm got Doc Trueblood to look at Half-Pint. His shoulder looked to be out of place. Doc, who was hell to drink, had been in his cups. He took a look at Half-Pint and announced that they would have to cut off his leg. Malcolm could see there was nothing wrong with the boy's legs. Malcolm took the old doctor by the arm and led him out of the area. Doc Trueblood loved to cut off legs. Possum showed up with a pail of water and splashed it on Half-Pint. He came to and got up on a pair of usable legs, his shoulder was out of place. Possum took him by the shoulder, gave it a jerk, and it went back into place. Half-Pint puked.

The racing committee declared the race a non-race, and the wagered money was returned.

Everybody was so busy with the races they had not noticed two wagons on the main road heading west. The wagons were driven by Indians, one accompanied by a white woman, the other a black girl. Their cargo was household goods.

The races were over, the horses stabled and everyone readied themselves for the Harvest Ball.

CHAPTER 16

"Oh, how he wished he had not succumbed to his male lust."

The Harvest Ball was not a formal affair, as was the Christmas Formal, which was held during the holidays. It was not a country Ho-Down either, but a mixture of the two.

Malcolm mingled among the guests, trying to keep his mind off what had happened between he and Mary Annabelle. He hoped that she would be discreet about it. He could see that she and Learnet were becoming good friends. He thought of sending Learnet and her father back north, but the little girls loved Learnet, and she was a very good teacher. And, if Mary Annabelle had already revealed their affair, this plan was of no value.

He could sell Mary Annabelle. This would create problems also. She waited on Glena Lee hand and foot. How would he explain his action to his wife? That was a good question no matter what happened. He felt that all eyes were on him and that the guests were whispering, "Did you know that Malcolm fucked that pretty slave girl last night?" Oh, how he wished that he had not succumbed to his male lust.

Malcolm saw Bancroft and the Lieutenant Governor off to one side talking in hushed tones. There was a very short man in the conversation with them. Not only was he short, he was also very slight of build. Malcolm thought it must be one of the jockeys, but he did not remember seeing him before.

Bancroft spoke first. "We were just discussing what to do about the Nuts and that slave runner of a Snowflake. Mr. Hardnails, here, has volunteered to lead a group to burn them out and hang that white woman."

Malcolm looked at Mr. Hardnails.

"I have not had the pleasure of meeting Mr. Hardnails," Malcolm said.

Bancroft looked surprised. "I am very sorry. I just thought you two had met. Mr. Malcolm Chandler, this is Mr. Hardnails. Hardnails is the overseer that I sent over when Whip Smith was called to Atlanta."

The two men shook hands. Hardnails had the small hands of a child and a grip to match. Malcolm could not imagine how this man could oversee slaves. He could not even see over a fence.

Bancroft continued, "Hardnails is an excellent man with the whip. He can hit a horse fly at twenty paces. He also has a special whip that has a small metal blade on its end. I have seen him cut a chunk out of an unruly slave's ass the size of a plum. He has been in charge of several hangings over in Arkansas. Our plans are to send Hardnails and about ten good men. They are to leave for the Nuts immediately and should be back in three days."

Hardnails spoke up. "Mr. Chandler, your slave Possum has asked to come with us on this little party to get rid of the Nuts. He is one of the smartest and best working slaves I have ever seen. It has been a real pleasure to work with him."

Malcolm's only thought was that this whole adventure could come to no good. What was it with Possum wanting to go hang Snowflake? He must stop it until cooler heads could prevail.

Mary Annabelle then approached the men and said, "There is a man at the front gate who says it is very important that he sees Mas Tom Wanderlust, and I can not find him."

"I will find him for you. Thank you Mary Annabelle," Malcolm responded.

Malcolm had seen Tom Wanderlust earlier, arm in arm with the Lieutenant Governor's wife, headed to the guest cabin where Wanderlust was a guest. The Lieutenant Governor's wife was known to be a bit horny. Before Malcolm went to find Tom, he first went to see whom it was that wanted him. He found Silas Vender with his wagon at the front gate.

"You have a message for Tom Wanderlust?" Malcolm inquired.

"Yes. It is from his father," Vender answered.

"Tom is indisposed at the moment. If you would trust the message with me, I could deliver it later. I am glad to see you, as we need some clothing for the slaves. Do you have any with you?"

Silas Vender's face lit up like a white bean in a black ass.

"Yes, I sure do. I purchased half a boatload of slave clothing at the seaport. It is imported from England and of the highest quality. In fact, I have two more wagons out on the main road. This message is about the Nuts pulling out. I came by their place and it was abandoned. Then I went on to Wanderlust Lodge, and Old Man Wanderlust tells me that when the Nuts came by on their way to Indian Territory, and he bought the place from them."

"Silas, why don't you bring in your wagons and park them in the infield of the race track," Malcolm said. "There are many planters here and you could do a lively business before they go home in the morning. When you are all set up, come in to the dance. There are many southern belles here to dance with."

Silas extended his warmest thanks for Malcolm's hospitality and started off for the road.

Malcolm shouted after him, "What about the message for Tom Wanderlust?"

Silas turned on his heel and handed Malcolm a sealed envelope. Malcolm made his way to the guest cabin and knocked gently. There was no answer, so he rapped a bit harder. The voice of Tom Wanderlust came from the inside.

"Who is it, and what do you want?"

"It's me, Malcolm. I have a message from your father."

Tom opened the door a crack and reached out for the note. He was wrapped in a towel and was out of breath.

Malcolm addressed Tom with the voice of authority. "Mr. Vender delivered this note and told me some of what was in it. Could you please read it and give it back to me? I want to take it back to the ball to stop a mob from going to the Nut's place. You can trust that I will not disclose your activities or your where-abouts."

This was a deal that Tom was most happy to make. He was not a bit interested in the rest of the guests knowing that he was with the Lieutenant Governor's wife. He went back into the cabin and read the note.

> Tom,
>
> Please come home as soon as possible. The Nuts stopped by. I took Snowflake as prisoner for slave trafficking. Left Nut said that if I would let her go I could have their property. I took his deed to the property. Somehow in the night, Snowflake escaped. I think they are headed for Indian Territory.
>
> I have sent Madam Charlie and two slaves to take over and hold the Nut property. This leaves us very short handed, could you please come home?
> FATHER

Tom went back outside and handed the note to Malcolm to read. After reading the note, Malcolm commented, "You better destroy this note. It almost incriminates your father in helping Snowflake escape. The crowd up at the ball is after blood, when it comes to Snowflake. You get some clothes on, and we will go back together and explain that the Nuts have left, and that the Wanderlusts are the new owners of the Nut property. This will keep them from going and burning the property. If they desire, they can check with Silas Vender for more details. Get the Lieutenant Governor's wife dressed. She can walk in with the two of us and people will think we were just getting some air."

The three of them found their way back to the ball just as Whitesides, Hardnails, and three others were leaving for the stable. Malcolm shouted for them to stop. In an authoritative and slightly disgusted tone, he said, "You all go back to the ball and dance with our pretty southern women. Mr. Vender has arrived and tells us that Tom and his father have bought the Nut Place. The Nuts have fled. I don't think that the Wanderlust family would take too kindly to your burning down their property."

There were many disappointed faces, especially the face of the little Mr. Hardnails.

"You better go tell Possum we are not going," Bancroft told Hardnails. "He is at the stable and has the horses ready."

Malcolm went back inside to find Glena Lee. They danced in each other arms. Malcolm told Glena Lee that he did not think it was a good night for him to announce his plans to run for Governor. She told him that everybody was waiting for him to play the piano.

After the dance he sat down and played his heart out for about an hour.

CHAPTER 17

"It is so wonderfully romantic about you and Mary Annabelle"

The morning following the ball, Malcolm woke early. Looking at his beautiful wife, asleep, with her black hair flowing over the white pillow, he wondered how he could have ever been untrue to her.

Malcolm arrived in the kitchen for one of Bolo's good breakfasts. He saw Mary Annabelle and another slave girl washing a mountain of dirty dishes. She smiled shyly at him. Even with a white turban on her head and soapsuds up to her elbows, she looked beautiful.

Learnet was eating biscuits and gravy at a small table in the corner of the kitchen. Malcolm got a plate of biscuits, a thick cut of ham and two fried eggs, and joined Learnet.

"Learnet, you look very chipper this morning. Did you have a good time at the dance? I noticed that you hardly missed a dance."

"Oh, Mr. Chandler! You cannot imagine the fun I had. You southern folks sure know how to make a person feel at home."

"Did you find the one and only Prince Charming," Malcolm chided.

"No, I do a lot of dreaming about my Prince Charming, and I know what he will be like. The time for him is not yet. I want to teach a few years," she replied.

"You are a smart girl."

As Malcolm finished his breakfast and started to leave Learnet said, "Mr. Chandler, when you have time I would like a talk with you."

"That would be fine. I will drop by your room after the girls' lessons this afternoon. I must go now and see our guests off."

By noon the guests were gone, along with their horses. Silas Vender had done a land office business. He gave Malcolm a beautiful pair of black riding boots for the use of the infield. He asked if he might stay until morning as he hated getting such a late start. Malcolm assured him it was all right to stay as long as he wished.

Malcolm knocked on Learnet's door and was greeted with a cheerful "come in". The girls were still at their desks. Learnet had Malcolm sit down and each of the girls read aloud and demonstrated their skill in ciphers with the teacher showing them flash cards.

After the recital, Malcolm gave a polite applause. It was obvious that the girls were doing very well in their studies. The girls got up from their desk, gave their father a polite curtsy, and left the room. Malcolm asked the girls to leave the door open. Learnet gave Malcolm a smile, like a cat with a bowl of milk, and thanked him for stopping by.

"I think it is so wonderfully romantic about you and Mary Annabelle," she purred.

Malcolm turned as white as a polar bear in a snowstorm.

"Mary Annabelle is so in love with you," Learnet continued. "And your encounter on the glade the other night was the very high point of her life. She says she knows you love your wife, but it is really nice that you love her too. We have become really good friends, and I was so pleased when she shared every detail with me. It was just the most romantic! She swore me to never tell a soul, as she wants to share your love, it would ruin the entire affair if everyone knew. She did ask me to have this talk with you, because she says whenever she is alone with you she just gets tongue-tied.

"This is even when her tongue is not as busy as it was on the glade. She says your style is very good, and is as smooth as a fine piece of polished jade. She said she never had such a wonderful feeling."

Malcolm could stand no more.

"Shut up, just shut up. I am not in love with Mary Annabelle. It was pure male lust, along with too much to drink. It will never happen again," Malcolm shouted.

"Mr. Malcolm don't be mad. You can trust me to never tell a soul," Learnet chided. Then she added, "Unless, of course, you send me or my father away."

Malcolm turned red with rage as she continued.

"You know, I am sure that my father is sleeping with your mother. I think, next to you and Mary Annabelle, that is just the most romantic. It almost makes us brother and sister."

Malcolm rose and made his way out of the room. Learnet had furnished him with about all the information he could handle for one day. As he passed his mother's room he saw her sitting, working on her cross-stitch. He entered the room and closed the door.

"What is this I hear about you and Mr. Readwright?" Malcolm demanded.

"Oh Malcolm, do come in. I will have Mary Annabelle bring us some tea. I have wanted to talk to you, but we have both been so busy. I think the Harvest Ball went very well. It was too bad about the turkeys and that last race. I just bet that Evelyn Lucille and Not-So-Fast would have won."

"Mother! I did not come here to discuss the turkeys or horses or Harvest Balls. What is this about Mr. Readwright?"

"Well I am not sure what you have heard, but Amos and I are seeing each other on a rather intimate basis. He is not the strong character of your father, but he is a fine man. He is kind, and a hard worker. He has done so much around the plantation since he has been here. He seems to just have a way with the slaves. I have never seen a man get more work out of a slave than he does, and he does it so easy that the slaves just seem to love him.

"I have talked to Glena Lee and she says you want to take Mary Annabelle and the girls and go to Cuba on a holiday. It will be the only chance for the girls to learn Spanish. I think that is a wonderful idea. I would like to have Amos stay at least until you get back. With Possum and Amos we can run the plantation in good shape. Please get rid of that Mr. Hardnails. He is a very cruel man. I heard that, on one plantation where he worked, he would line the children up next to a wall and pop one eye out of each child with that whip of his. I can not imagine what Bancroft sees in him."

Mary Annabelle entered the room with the tea, and as she sat his on the serving table, her knee brushed his. There it was again. Male lust.

He had to keep the teacup over it to prevent his mother from noticing. Just as his loins were settling down, Mary Annabelle came back, leaning over to place a plate of cookies on the table. He spied those youthful, lush mounds of black breast. OH! Not again.

Lady Chandler saw Amos coming down the hall and invited him in for tea. Malcolm studied this six-foot man that didn't weight over 155 pounds. His pants were always between his ankles and knees and his shirt sleeves about two inches above his wrists. His neck resembled the neck of a giraffe and his Adam's Apple stuck out an inch and a half. Malcolm hoped, for his mother's sake, that he was good in bed.

Malcolm addressed Amos in a formal voice.

"I understand you are staying with us a little longer than planned."

Amos gave a big, sheepish smile and said, "If it is all right with you, Mr. Chandler. Your mother has asked me to stay a while longer."

Malcolm smiled at Amos. "Mr. Readwright, Mother is still the big boss here. If she wants you to stay, you have my most earnest blessing."

It was decided that while Malcolm and family were in Cuba and Learnet had no pupils, she could take a class of slave children and teach them. This was to be an experiment to see if the slave children could learn. They were to be taught nothing except modest reading. Malcolm hoped the other planters did not find out about this, as they were dead set against teaching the slaves anything. If they did find out, it would be damaging to his political career. Malcolm figured that these black children would always be slaves and it would be much better for them and the white population if they had some education.

After three days of preparation, the family was loaded into the large buggy. Olaf was chosen to drive as he was a good teamster and got on well with the little girls. Olaf had a great time teasing and playing with them. They would take Mr. Hardnails as far as Hanging Magnolia Plantation. There, they would pick up Bancroft Whitesides, Glena Lee's brother, and he would go along to bring Olaf and the buggy back. He had shipping business on the river, and this arrangement would work out very nicely. When they had said their good byes, Olaf turned to the girls and asked, "Conds snaka norski dag?"

They laughed and asked him what it meant.

"It means, can you talk Norwegian today," Olaf said.

He said, before he came to Cottontail, when he was on the Norwegian freighter, he could speak Norwegian. He thought that if the girls were learning Spanish, they might just as well learn Norwegian also.

CHAPTER 18

"Good Lord, she had a miscarriage."

Somewhere west of Fort Smith, Arkansas the Nuts were making camp for the night. There was a hard north wind, and it looked like it could snow. The Nuts had never seen snow, nor had they ever been so cold. The wind blew up Snowflake's dress, and it was cold enough to freeze the balls off a brass monkey. Pansy lay under a crude lean-to that sheltered her from the wind. It was the best that Right Nut could do for her.

Her baby was not due for several months, but the way she felt, she could have it any minute. They were about out of money, and Right Nut had rented Pansy to a man going west to hunt buffalo. He had passed a dose of the clap to Pansy, and she had passed it to Right Nut. Pansy was pretty sick, running a fever, and had a bad case of diarrhea.

Snowflake was trying to get a fire started. Left Nut was taking care of the teams. The teams were thin and weak. As Snowflake got a small rabbit stew boiling, she spoke to the others gathered around the fire.

"I don't know why I tried to help these slaves escape. They really had it pretty good. Look at all of us, about to freeze, and very little to eat. I would give anything to be back in our valley."

The beleaguered party looked up to see a troop of bluecoat soldiers approaching from the west. A young lieutenant stepped off a well-fed horse and asked, "Where are you folks headed? Is there anything we can do for you?"

Snowflake was wrapped up in a blanket, Indian style. Right Nut and Left Nut were also wrapped in blankets by the fire. Poor Pansy lay close by, not even knowing what was going on. This rainbow collection of people, without adequate warm clothes or blankets, found a soft spot in Lieutenant Marshall's heart. He was stationed in Fort Smith with orders to patrol Indian Territory. The territory was huge and, the truth be known, their patrols seldom got very far from the Fort.

Snowflake rose from her seat by the fire. She knew that she would have to do the talking as Left and Right were scared to death of soldiers. With what the Cherokee tribe had been through, it was good for an Indian to be leery of soldiers.

"Mr. Lieutenant, my sister-in-law is very ill. Do you have a surgeon in your troop?"

63

"No Madam, we do not. Corporal Potts is our medic. I will have him take a look at her. Corporal Potts, forward and have a look at this nigger girl," the lieutenant commanded.

After feeling Pansy's head and taking her pulse, the corporal announced, "She is a very sick girl. About the only thing I can do is give her laudanum."

As he turned to get the medicine from his saddlebag, Pansy doubled with pain and screamed. She lay quiet as the corporal raised the blood-soaked blanket to find an embryo of a child.

"Good Lord, she just had a miscarriage. If I can get this bleeding stopped, I think she may be alright now."

Snowflake had a new dog she had picked up on the trail. The dog got up from his place by the fire, picked up the small embryo and took it to a sandy bank just outside camp and buried it.

Right Nut remembered his mother telling a story of an Indian girl who was bleeding to death, and they stuffed moss in her to stop the bleeding. The corporal, who was wondering just what to do, was surprised when Right Nut handed him some moss and gave instructions. Having no better idea, the corporal did as he was instructed. In a matter of minutes, Pansy had stopped bleeding and opened her eyes.

The soldiers gave Pansy an extra blanket. Right Nut thanked the corporal and gave him a twist of tobacco. The corporal did not use tobacco, but knew it was a great gift for an Indian to give. He accepted it to avoid offending Right Nut. Lieutenant Marshall mounted the troops and rode on toward Fort Smith.

The next morning Pansy was strong enough to travel. The party had not gone two miles when they arrived at a modest sized creek. They made camp again, even though it was still very early. They washed Pansy. There was also some very good feed for the teams. Right Nut took his rifle and soon returned with a nice deer. Snowflake went for a walk and returned, saying that there were good logs about a hundred yards up the creek, suitable to build a cabin. It was decided that they would build a cabin and start a trading post.

Work on the cabin went well. The weather was cold but not unbearable. They were up to the fifth log when two men rode into their camp.

"We heard there was a runaway slave girl with you people," a big, unshaven brute grunted. He rode a small buckskin mare. As he spoke the words, he pulled his gun and pointed it right at Left Nut's head. Pansy and Snowflake were washing some clothes about twenty feet away from the cabin. Right Nut was out hunting. Pansy, seeing that Left Nut would be killed if she ran, walked right up to the big man's horse.

"I am a free slave and I have a husband who is out hunting," she stated.

The big man looked down at her and said, "You are a scrawny little thing, but I guess somebody would pay a price for you. Hank Knife, get down off that horse and tie this little girl up. We don't put no stock in this free slave stuff. You are a nigger, and you will sell. You do anything foolish and this buck here will be on his way to the happy hunting grounds."

Hank Knife tied Pansy's hands and ordered her to get behind him on the horse. This whole process took less than two minutes. The big man fired a shot so close to Left Nut's head that he could feel the wind from the bullet. They wheeled their horses and were off. Left Nut scrambled for his gun, but was too late. Pansy was gone.

It was about an hour before Right Nut got back. He was riding the bay he got from Malcolm and had bagged a coon and two rabbits. Upon learning about Pansy, he started out on the trail of the kidnappers. The tracks were very visible and he moved at a good pace. Then the tracks vanished. They must have heard him coming and left the road to hide in the woods. They would be coming from behind him. He got off the bay and slapped the horse on the ass. The bay ran down the road around a bend and stopped to graze. Right Nut checked the loads in both his pistol and rifle. He hid in the brush, making sure to stay as close to the road as possible. He had only waited about ten minutes when the riders appeared.

The big man with the beard must have gotten suspicious, as he stopped his horse and held up a hand to stop the others behind him. Right Nut took the opportunity and shot him right between the eyes. He fell off the right side of the horse. Right Nut could not shoot again for fear of hitting Pansy. He grabbed Hank Knife's horse by the bridle and, with the other hand, grabbed Hank Knife's left leg. With a lift/shove combination, he dropped him off on the right side of his horse. Right Nut held his gun about an inch from Hank Knife's face. Hank Knife made no attempt for his gun. He just raised both hands and shouted, "Don't shoot, don't shoot. I am a brother Indian."

Right Nut, on a closer look, saw that Hank Knife was an Indian. He grabbed the gun from Hank Knife's belt and tossed it away.

In the meantime, Hank Knife's horse had turned and ran back toward Nut's camp at full speed with Pansy behind the saddle screaming bloody murder.

Right Nut saw that Hank Knife was indeed an Indian.
"I was just riding with Old Bill. I meant no harm. Don't shoot me," he pleaded.

Right Nut now observed that Hank Knife was really only a boy of sixteen or seventeen. Right Nut holstered his gun. "What kind of an Indian are you?" he asked the boy.

"I am a Pawnee. The tribe ran me out, because I had a young mother and I would go to the blankets with her. My father was much older and he ran me off. I rode east, and took up with Old Bill. Don't shoot me. I will work hard for you. I am a good hunter and good with a horse."

"You may be a hard worker, but you are still a Mother Lover," Right Nut exclaimed.

Right Nut took out his pistol and shot Hank Knife right behind the ear. Right Nut could not put up with a Mother Lover. He rolled his body in the brush, jumped on the buckskin horse that had belonged to Old Bill, and went back and picked up his horse and headed home.

That evening, Right Nut and Left Nut went back and buried the bodies of the old outlaw and the young Indian.

A few days later, when the Nuts were working on getting a roof on the cabin, Captain Marshall and his patrol stopped by. Marshall had been promoted since his last visit. Snowflake was quick to notice the new bars on his shoulder and congratulated him. He was very pleased.

The captain got right to the point and asked the Nuts if they had seen an older man and a young Indian.

The Nuts looked at one another in silence. Right Nut was the first to speak.

"They came by here a few days ago and I killed them both."

Snowflake almost fainted. She knew that the soldiers would hang him.

The captain looked at Right Nut through military eyes.

"Mr. Nut, you can not go around killing people."

Right Nut jumped down off the roof where he had been working.

"Mr. Captain, these were very bad men. They tried to take my wife. They said she was a runaway and would take her back for a reward or sell her."

The captain stepped off his horse and looked Right Nut straight in the eye. "It makes no difference if they were bad men. You can not take the law into your own hands and be judge, jury and executor. However, in this case you are lucky. Those two men ambushed one of our patrols north of here and killed a soldier. If we had caught them, we would have hanged them. You saved us the trouble. I should give you a medal, but next time you be very careful about taking the law into your own hands."

The troop headed west, and the Nuts went back to work on the Nut house.

CHAPTER 19

Malcolm and Glenna Lee were in the cabin suite making love."

The boat trip down the Mississippi to New Orleans was a real pleasure for the entire Chandler family. Mary Annabelle worked with the children to learn their Spanish. They were ready learners and had a fair command of the language by the time they arrived at New Orleans.

Malcolm took the opportunity to do a little gambling. Malcolm was good with cards, and by the time they arrived, he had accumulated considerable winnings. This left Glena Lee free to wander the decks and visit with other passengers. It also gave her time to sew on her quilt blocks. A few years earlier, she had made a quilt for Evelyn Lucille, and was now making one for Mandy Ann.

Mary Annabelle had a small cabin next to the Chandlers' stateroom. When she was not with the children, she waited on the family hand and foot. Glena Lee mentioned many times that she had never seen such a willing worker. When she was not teaching or working, she stayed in her cabin. She tried to work mostly in the afternoon, as she was sick in the morning. She never had a mother or anyone to tell her the reason for her morning illness. It worried her a great deal, but she did not mention it to anyone. It was good news for her the day before they reached New Orleans, she was feeling much better. Her breasts were still very tender to the touch. She would lay awake at night thinking of ways she could get Malcolm into her cabin for the night, or even a little while.

The day before they landed, Malcolm and Glena Lee were in the cabin suite making love. Mary Annabelle had the girls in her cabin at Spanish class. It was only these occasions that the Chandlers had a chance to make love. Today, they had enjoyed each other in a form of lovemaking they especially enjoyed. She would take her long, soft black hair and encircle his erect manhood with the hair. She would put a soft hand around the hard organ enclosed in the hair and gently rub him to orgasm. He would apply his soft and active tongue to her most sensitive and private parts. They would climax in a world of psychedelic color and true love. But after this lovemaking, she always had to wash her hair.

After their lovemaking session, Glena Lee asked Malcolm if he had talked to Possum to find out where they might find his wife and little girl.

Malcolm informed her that he had not mentioned to Possum that they were even making the trip to Cuba. He was afraid that Possum would get false hopes, as it was going to be no easy job to find her, let alone get her bought. He planned to talk to Mary Annabelle about it, as he knew they both came from the same plantation and that it was a sugar plantation.

They had checked into a suite of rooms in downtown Havana. The little girls were playing in the courtyard. Malcolm and Glena Lee were in the drawing room. They had asked Mary Annabelle to serve them some tea. Then they asked her to sit down and join them for tea.

"Mary Annabelle, would you like to go with Glena Lee and me to your old plantation and see if we can find Possum's wife and little girl?" Malcolm asked.

If it had been possible, Mary Annabelle would have turned white.

"No! No!" she exclaimed.

With this emphatic response, Malcolm decided to drop that line of questions.

"Then could you tell us where the plantation is and a little about it?"

"It is two days' ride in a wagon from Havana. I think it would be east. The name of the main sugar plantation is Sula Grande. The other part of the plantation is a cattle ranch. I have never been to it and don't know where it is. I heard the massahs call it Rancho Grande."

"Do you know the name of the masters who own the rancho and the plantation?"

"No, they live in Spain."

"Would you go with me to interpret so I could ask questions around Havana as to where we might find the rancho and the plantation?"

"When in Cuba, I must stay in the hotel at all times to take care of the girls and Mrs. Chandler," Mary Annabelle answered.

"That will be all for now Mary Annabelle. Please go get the girls and ready them for dinner. We are due in the dining room in forty five minutes."

As Mary Annabelle left the room, Glena Lee, with a downcast look said, "Mary Annabelle said she would interpret for us when we came to Cuba. Now she refuses to leave the room. The girl is so good, but sometimes I fail to understand her at all."

Malcolm responded, "I agree with you. I do not understand where she is coming from. Maybe she is wanted for murder in Cuba, same as Possum. I am going to find out what she is up to. We will instruct her to take the children to the beach in the morning. We will tell her it is kind of a field trip for their Spanish lesson. She will be instructed that we will rent a rig and come by the beach and pick them up about noon and have lunch at a waterfront café. If she refuses to do this, I will take appropriate action. If it is all right with you, I will not go to the beach and lunch. I want to snoop around the

Havana business community and see what I can find out about the Sula Grande Plantation."

When Mary Annabelle was called in and told of taking the girls to the beach, she seemed excited and not the least bit afraid to go out in Havana. At the last minute, Glena Lee decided to go with the girls and Mary Annabelle, and not wait until later. She had had diarrhea all morning and did not feel well. It would do her good to get out.

The afternoon at the beach was wonderful. The girls loved the warm, clear Cuban water. Going home time came much too soon. Just as they were getting out of the coach, a large well-dressed man approached.

"I see you ladies have been to the beach. This black girl here belongs to me. She ran away about six months ago."

He took Mary Annabelle by the arm with a firm grip and pulled her away. The little girls screamed. Glena Lee had her parasol in hand and hit the man with all her force along the side of his head. He loosened his grip on Mary Annabelle and she pulled away and ran behind Glena Lee, who had her arm and parasol cocked for another strike.

Crowds of onlookers began to gather. The big man rubbed the side of his head but made no attempt to regain his prey. Policemen came and asked the big man what was going on.

"That black girl belongs to me. I bought her several months ago. Then she came up missing. I was glad to find her, and I want her back," he explained.

The policeman looked at Mary Annabelle and asked her if that was true.

She answered in a shaky voice with tears running down her cheek. "No, he stole me. I was on Sula Grande Plantation, and he stole me to put in his brothel. I could not stand it there, so I ran."

"My husband bought her at an East Coast slave auction in the United States," Glena Lee explained. "We have the papers. This man has no claim on her."

The policeman looked at Mary Annabelle and could see that she was in mortal fear of the brothel owner. The little girls were clinging to her sides.

"We are going to let the girl stay with this family," he said.

The police had had some trouble with the brothel owner before and could see no reason to do him any favors. "You just be on your way and never bother this girl again."

As he turned to walk away, the big man said, "She is too black anyway. Those black girls don't sell very good. Now you take those yellow girls they are the good ones."

Glena Lee thanked the policeman and rushed the girls and Mary Annabelle off to the room. She was not good at trying experiences like they had just been through. She lay down on the bed and the girls went to play in the courtyard. She was awakened by a cool sea breeze coming through the window when Malcolm opened the door. She told Malcolm about the policeman and the man that tried to take Mary Annabelle away to become a whore.

Malcolm reported that he could find no plantation named Sula Grande Plantation. Everyone he asked said there were many big plantations. He did learn of a large sugar plantation and cattle ranch owned by a Spanish family. It was about sixty miles to the east. It was decided that they would rent a rig and go east. The map showed several villages that looked big enough to have accommodations. It was also decided to take Mary Annabelle, as they deemed it unsafe to leave her alone at the hotel.

The morning brought a cool breeze and a warm Cuban sun. Malcolm could not help but wish that he could move Cottontail Plantation to a climate like this.

Glena Lee was not feeling well when she awoke. She still had diarrhea and a slight fever. She really did not feel like going, but on the other hand it was probably just the change of food and water. Several of the tourists in the hotel were complaining of the same troubles.

The coach they ordered for the trip east to try to find Possum's family was a large carriage with a driver and one outrider. The outrider was for protection, as they would pass through much remote country where outlaws were common. The driver who owned the horses and coach was a man of Spanish descent and spoke English, French and Spanish. His name was Castro Valdez. The outrider was a black man named Tomtom. Castro said they would not travel great distances each day, as he did not want to tire the horses or his passengers.

The first night out, they stayed at a small resort on the beach. It was a great place to swim in the warm Cuban waters. They all went for a swim. They had their own cottage, and there were two other cottages with American tourists. One was a couple on their honeymoon, and the other was an elderly couple.

The older couple had been at the resort for a week. Malcolm learned from the old man that there was an overseer from a large plantation staying in the main lodge. Immediately, Malcolm went to the lodge and found the man, whose name was Jose Fleet. It turned out that he was not an overseer. He owned a large plantation, the Azucar Plantation, right next to the Sula Grande Plantation. He said that the Sula Grande Plantation was not a very good neighbor. They kept to themselves and had guards posted at all gates.

Malcolm stayed and visited with Mr. Fleet about running a plantation in the southern U.S., and how it was done in Cuba. Mr. Fleet invited the Chandler party to be his guests at his plantation. It was only a few miles from Sula Grande Plantation. They drank dark rum and smoked Cuban cigars until after midnight.

On his way back to the cottage, Malcolm encountered Mary Annabelle and Tomtom coming up the road, hand in hand, on their way back to the cottage. He felt a pang of jealousy.

Mary Annabelle dropped Tomtom's hand and stepped alongside Malcolm. She bid Tomtom good-night. He turned and went back to the stables where he was sleeping. Mary Annabelle was very emphatic about telling Malcolm that they had just been for a walk on the beach. When they arrived at the cottage, they found Glena Lee and the girls asleep. This was just as well because Malcolm would have found it a little awkward coming in at that hour with Mary Annabelle, no matter how innocent. On her way to her room, Mary Annabelle reached down and gently rubbed Malcolm's ever-so-hard manhood. That was all it took for him to go off in his pants, as she slinked off in her feline manner to her quarters.

CHAPTER 20

"Did you see what I saw"

The full moon was shining through the trees as Possum and Olaf sat under the big tree in the forest where they had held the Voodoo rituals. The slaves of Cottontail and Hanging Magnolia Plantations had asked Olaf and Possum to get rid of Mr. Hardnails. Mr. Hardnails had taken his whip and popped the left eye out of an eight-year-old slave boy.

"I don't believe in all this Voodoo business," Olaf said.

Possum looked at Olaf and said, "You just told me when they took you out of Africa, you were a religious man. Voodoo was an African religion. How can you turn it down now? The white men have taught you Christianity. Why do you believe in a man that was hung on a cross for a bad man when it makes just as much sense to place a hex on a person that you want to get rid of?"

"Your Voodoo gives me nothing to look forward to," Olaf responded. "In my Christianity, I will go to heaven when I die, if I'm good. I can go to church with the other slaves and even the white man. I can sing and pray and it makes me feel good. God will forgive me for killing a bad man. When I was taken out of the jungles of Africa and placed on the slave ship, things were very bad. Many died, and many were very sick. Then one day a Norwegian freighter pulled alongside. I was shackled to a mast. The captain of the Norwegian freighter called over to the slaver captain, 'Do you have one good man I could buy for my personal servant?' The slaver captain calls back, 'How 'bout this boy shackled to the mast?'

"I was on the Norwegian ship for five years, the captain was very good to me. The ship went all over the world but never did get back to Norway. Then the orders came for the captain to go home. We pulled into a seaport on the East Coast of the U.S. The captain couldn't take me to Norway, so he sold me at the auction. In the five years I was on the ship, I learned Christianity, and it's good."

Possum spoke up after a long silence. "You 'member when we wanted to get rid of Whip Smith and his mean boy? I put the feathers under their shirts and the next day they were gone. That was my Voodoo at work. You can't do that with your Christianity."

The two slaves argued for about half an hour about the best way to get rid of Mr. Hardnails. Kill him outright, or place a feather under his mattress.

Possum finally won out. They would try to place a red feather in his bed or on his person. The plan was for Olaf to lure Hardnails out of his cabin by making animal sounds outside his cabin. Possum was to sneak into the cabin and place the feather.

It was a dark night, no moon, as the two crawled silently up behind the cabin. The cabin was small with only one small window in the back. There was a light coming through the window. Olaf was first to peer in the small window. He took so long that Possum finally had to pull him down so he could get a look. Possum raised his head and peeked into the candle lit cabin. Possum took a quick look and slumped down beside Olaf. Possum was the first to speak.

"Did you see what I saw?"

"Yea, I couldn't believe my eyes. Let's crawl back in the brush and rethink our plan."

After much discussion, it was decided that they would do nothing. They would go back to Cottontail and tell Lady Chandler about their amazing discovery. Lady Chandler would tell Bancroft Whitesides, and he could do what he wanted with Mr. Hardnails. There was no doubt in the two slaves' minds that, when Bancroft found out the truth, that Mr. Hardnails would be gone. How they wished Malcolm was home.

The next morning, Olaf and Possum were at the mansion at daybreak. Bolo fed them breakfast while they waited for Lady Chandler. Bolo was getting old, but she was still the best cook around.

Lady Chandler arrived in her robe for breakfast and was surprised to see Olaf and Possum in the kitchen. Olaf spoke immediately.

"Lady Chandler, could we see you in private?"

This was a very strange request for two field hand slaves. "Yes, let me get a cup of coffee, and we can go to the study."

Olaf started the story.

"Mr. Hardnails popped a boy at Hangin' Magnolia with 'is whip and popped 'is eye out. We think that's very bad treatment for the slaves. The boy's mother said he was doing no harm. Last night, Possum and I went to see Mr. Hardnails. We peeked in his cabin and he was taking a bath in a wash tub. Well, this is hard to believe, but Mr. Hardnails is a girl."

Lady Chandler's mouth opened, and her chin dropped to about three inches above her belly button.

"You have to be mistaken. I have talked with Mr. Hardnails on several occasions. It is impossible. Oh, I wish for Malcolm. He is so good at these crises, and I am so poor. Olaf, go to the stable. Tell Shorty you need a rig and a team. You and I will go to Hanging Magnolia. Possum, you go to the stable and get Not-So-Fast and ride into town and get the sheriff. We will all meet at Hanging Magnolia. We may need to use that old magnolia tree one more time."

It was unheard of to call the law in to settle a dispute between slaves and their master. Double unheard of when the suspected perpetrator was a white man. Lady Chandler's reference to the magnolia tree was from the olden days and the way that the plantation had gotten its name. There was a large magnolia tree on the hill overlooking the plantation. The tree was used to hang slaves that tried to run away. It was always said that the lower branches were used to hang the children.

Lady Chandler had never seen a hanging from the tree. In fact, she suspected that there never was a hanging, just a story to keep slaves in line. If this was true, that this Mr., Miss, or whatever it was, had popped an eye out of a child, and passed him or her off as a man, she would ask Sheriff Laws to hang the person. The old tree would get some use.

Lady Chandler and Olaf arrived at the Hanging Magnolia well before Possum could get there with the sheriff. Bancroft was out in the front yard and greeted the Lady with all southern respect.

"Lady Chandler do come in. What a pleasant and unexpected surprise."

"Bancroft, I am afraid this is not a social call. May I bring Olaf in with me? This involves him and your apprentice overseer."

"Yes, yes. Olaf is always welcome at Hanging Magnolia," Bancroft assured them.

They were escorted to the study, and a servant was summoned to bring refreshments.

"The reason we are here," Lady Chandler began, "is your so-called Mr. Hardnails almost caused a riot among the slaves on both of our plantations. He whipped a young boy and popped his eye out. Possum and Olaf went to his cabin last night. I must admit, their plans were to rough him up for causing all this pain and suffering to the young slave. What do you think they found when they arrived at Mr. Hardnails' cabin? I will tell you what they found. Mr. Hardnails was bathing and Possum and Olaf discovered that HE is a female. I have the sheriff on the way to take him, or her, into custody."

Bancroft Whitsides rose and walked behind his chair. He placed his hands on the back of the chair. His face was a deep scarlet and his hands, clutching the back of chair, exposed snow-white knuckles.

"Mrs. Chandler, I must tell you at the onset, your behavior in this matter is completely out of line. Your slaves had no business on the Hanging Magnolia! Their intent to harm Julie is inexcusable! If you do not order it, I will have Malcolm flog them until they have no skin as soon as he gets home. I shall meet Sheriff Laws at the gate and tell him we have no business for him at Hanging Magnolia. Now that Julie's identity is known, I will tell you the entire story," he continued.

"As you know, Mr. Hardnails, Julie, came to Hanging Magnolia about eighteen months ago as an apprentice overseer. She knew she could never be an overseer if anyone knew her true identity. She was only here a week when I accidentally discovered she was a young lady. I confronted her and told her she would have to leave. One thing led to another and, as we discussed the matter, we fell in love. In fact, I must have just left her cabin last night when your slaves came to do her harm. If they would have harmed one hair on her head, I swear I would have killed them!"

He reached for a nearby stove iron, and was about to hit Olaf when he thought better of it. Then Bancroft continued, "You might just as well know it all. Julie was going to leave Hanging Magnolia and go to Atlanta in just a few days. This would be the end of 'Mr. Hardnails'. She would change back to a young lady, which she is very much a lady. Then, just before the Christmas Ball, I would go to Atlanta, find this beautiful young lady, bring her to the Ball, and announce our engagement. No one would ever know it was Mr. Hardnails. Now you have gone and ruined the whole plan."

Lady Chandler had had enough. She got up to go and fainted.

Chapter 21

"I don't feel well I think I will stay home with the girls."

Glenna Lee was happy to find out that they had been invited to stay at Mr. Fleet's Plantation as guests. She was tired and not herself. They had a guest cottage that had a large front window looking to the beach and the bay. She could sit in the window and watch the girls and Mary Annabelle play on the beach and in the water.

Malcolm borrowed the horse that Tomtom was riding as guard and outrider. He rode to the front gate of Azucar Plantation and was greeted by a large black guard who asked his business at the Plantation. He said he was a sugar buyer from the United States and was interested in buying 2 or three boatloads of refined sugar. He was instructed to go to an office building that looked about a mile up the road. While riding up to the office he noticed a Blacksmith shop and service building off to the left. He knew that it was a blacksmith that had been killed by Possum's wife. He took a detour to the shops. A slave was shoeing a fine looking horse. Malcolm noticed what a fine job the young slave was doing shoeing the horse. He thought, I should try to buy this young man. The young man saw Malcolm and let down the horse's foot and looked up at him. His black body was glistening with sweat.

After some idle greetings, and short discussion of the weather, Malcolm asked, "Do you know any thing about the Blacksmith that was killed here buy a slave named Joe?"

The young man pickes up the horse's foot and went back to work. Malcolm rode on to the office building. On entering the building there was an old man behind a desk piled with paper work. So far he had lied, and was turned down in conservation. It was time to get to the heart of the matter.

In his most commanding voice, yet as friendly as possible, he greeted the old man.

"Good day, I am Malcolm Chandler the II, I'm a cotton planter from the United States. I am at Azucar Plantation to try to find the wife and daughter of one of your ex-slaves."

The old man lay down his quill pen and looked over the rims of his glasses. He looked at the tall figure before him with the red mustache and the jet-black hair. With a look of authority, and before the old man could say a word, Malcolm said, "I am looking for the wife and daughter of a slave called "Joe", who is said to have killed the plantation blacksmith. Do you know where I might find them?"

"They were sold along with several other slaves."

"Do you know where they may be now?"

"They were sold to the plantation just to the west, a Mr. Fleet I believe. Now good day to you."

Malcolm got on his horse and rode down the road and out the gate with-out looking to either side.

Malcolm and Glenna Lee had been invited to dine with the Fleets that evening.

Malcolm arrived home just before dusk. He found Mr. Fleet visiting with Glenna Lee in the living room of the guesthouse. Glenna Lee greeted him with a hug and kiss.

"Mr. Fleet, was wondering if he could borrow Mary Annabelle to serve at the dinner tonight. His main serving girl had a baby this afternoon. I told him that would be fine, as the girls are old enough to stay alone in this safe cottage."

Mr. Fleet spoke. " I most appreciate this generosity."

Malcolm spoke up. "Before you leave, could I talk with you for just a minute?"

Mr. Fleet stopped as he was headed to the door.

Malcolm went on with his question.

"Did you buy some slaves from Azucar Plantation?"

"Yes, I believe our overseer did just that, and not too long ago."

"Was there a woman about 30 with a little girl in the deal?"

Mr. Fleet scratched his head and said. " I am not sure, but our overseer will be at the party tonight. He took care of the transaction. We can ask him."

He turned and left the guest cottage. Where Mary Annabelle was waiting in the carriage with his driver to go to the main Hasendia.

Glenna Lee put on her light green full-length dress. There were many White Margarita Daisies growing around the guest cottage. She had picked a few and arranged them in her black hair. Just as she was about to leave the dressing room she became very ill and vomited.

When she entered the living room she was very white and gaunt. Here hands were wet and cold as she took Malcolm by the hand.

"I do not feel well, I think I will stay home with the girls. You hurry on and go or you will be late."

Malcolm looked at his wife and could see that she was very ill.

"My dear I will stay home with you, you do not look well at all."

"No, no, you go on, the Fleets are expecting you."

They had not called for a carriage, as they had planned to walk to the Hacienda in the warm Cuba air. It was not a long distance.

Malcolm walked along the beach to the Fleet's Hacienda. It was a beautiful evening and a full moon was breaking the horizon. It was not a big dinner party. The only people present were Mr. & Mrs. John Fleet, their daughter and her husband, Mr. & Mrs. Roland Round, the Fleet's teen-age son, John Fleet Jr., and the overseer, Mr. Gonzales and his wife. Mrs. Round was about 8 months with child. Malcolm was very proud of Mary Annabelle, the way she did the serving and was so pleasant to everyone.

After the meal, Roland, John Sr., Pedro and Malcolm retired to the study for Cuban Cigars and Brandy. A very good dark Cuban Rum was also available. Malcolm had the chance to ask if there was a Mother and Daughter in the new slaves that had been purchased from the Azucar Plantation. Pedro said there was such a pair and he would ask in the morning if her husband's name had been Joe. There was much good conversation about sugar cane, cotton, and good horses. The subject of Glenna Lee's illness had come up, and John Sr. had volunteered to send for a doctor in the morning. Malcolm said it was best to wait until morning, as he was sure it was stress of the trip and change of food and water. Time flew by, and it was time for Malcolm to go home. Mary Annabelle had finished helping the other slave girls clean the dishes. It was decided that she and Malcolm would walk home together.

The moon was shining on Mary Annabelle's jet-black hair that hung to her shoulders. Her short black serving skirt showed ample young and well-rounded legs. The loose white blouse exposed her firm, round breasts. She took Malcolm's hand. He did not pull away. Off to the left there stood a small grove of palms. There seemed to be an unseen force that turned their path in the direction of the palms. As they entered the grove, the shadows of the trees gave a romantic look to soft green moss that grew under them. Malcolm just could not help himself and took her in his arms. He could feel her small heart pounding at his chest, the firm breasts pressing against him. She ran her arms around him under his shirt, and the touch of her hand aroused him to the male limits. She stepped back and let the skirt and blouse fall to the moss, as she untied his belt and took him in her soft warm hands. They lay down on the cool moss with her head cradled in his arms. She rolled on her back, as his lips found the firm erect nipples. Malcolm could not ever remember the feeling of any thing so grand as her long black legs entwined around him, as he entered her willing body.

Malcolm watched her dress in the warm Cuba moonlight. He did not notice the small bulge in her normally flat stomach. There had not been a word between them. Then Malcolm asked, "Please do not mention this encounter to your friend Learnet when we get home." She answered with a word that Malcolm had never heard a slave use before. She simply said, "OK."

Just before daylight, Glenna Lee began to shake and call out in cries that were not one bit normal. Malcolm gently shook her, but her ridged body did not respond. She felt cool but was very sweaty. He ran to the back of the house where Mary Annabelle slept on a pallet.

"Run to the Fleet's Hacienda and fetch Mr. Fleet. Tell him to send someone for a Doctor—Glenna Lee is very ill."

Mary Annabelle was up and out of the house and off to the Fleets as fast as her young strong legs would carry her. Malcolm went back to Glenna Lee. Her breathing was shallow, and he could barley feel her pulse. He placed a wet cool cloth, on her head then got dressed and went to the girls' room. They were just getting up, and he told them that their mother was very ill, and for them to play in their room until he called them. Malcolm went back to look in on Glenna Lee. She was dead.

Malcolm was in the living room with his head in his hands and large tears dropping on the floor when John Fleet and Mary Annabelle came in. John and Mary Annabelle went to Glenna Lee. She had vomited just before death, and she looked terrible. Mary Annabelle took John by the arm and led him back to the living room.

"I will go clean her and the room up. Please keep the girls and Mas. Malcolm out until I am ready."

John gave a nod and went to the side bar and poured a brandy for Malcolm.

"I have sent young John Jr. to the village for Dr Lopez. It should take about an hour for their return"

Malcolm nodded, and both men sat in silence.

Mary Annabelle went to the kitchen and got a pail of water. This was no easy task for a young girl. She washed Glenna Lee, changed the bed, and arranged her black hair flowing over the white pillow. She did a very good job, and Glenna Lee looked beautiful. Then she very carefully removed a red rooster feather from the hem of Glenna Lee's nightgown. She placed the feather in the palm of her hand, went to the open window and blew the feather out into the morning air.

CHAPTER 22

"The only families at the services were Chandlers, Fleets, and Gonzales."

There was a Catholic Cemetery and a Black Cemetery, but there wasn't a cemetery for Protestants for miles. Mr. Fleet spoke of a grove of palms with a moss-covered floor between the Fleet's hacienda and the guest cottage. He said it would be a fine resting-place and someone would always be around to care for the grave. Malcolm thanked him for allowing them to bury Glena Lee in such a beautiful spot.

Mandy Ann and Evelyn Lucille were devastated by the loss of their mother. It had been so sudden. When they had gone to bed she was only a little sick. When they got up she was gone. Mary Annabelle did everything she could for the girls, but it was not like having their mother.

Mr. Roland Round was a Catholic and had some religious training and did a very fine job of giving a sermon for Glena Lee. The only families at the service were the Chandlers, Fleets, and Gonzales'. Mary Annabelle and a few other slaves stood in the background. Mandy Ann sobbed uncontrollably throughout the service. Malcolm had tried his best to comfort her, but with little success. After the service, all of the white folks went to the hacienda for refreshments and a light lunch. Malcolm had never had such a loss, and nobody could feel it more. He was one thousand miles from family and, while the Fleets could not have been kinder, they were still not old friends. The poor little girls just could not understand and every chance they had they clung to Malcolm or Mary Annabelle.

After the services and refreshments, Pedro Gonzales approached Malcolm.

"I have the slave woman and her daughter, the ones that you were interested in, waiting outside."

Malcolm, in his grief, had forgotten the main purpose of his mission to Cuba. Malcolm went outside with Pedro and found a rather large, almost white, woman and a little girl who was white, except for her black eyes, and very short, curly black hair. It was hard for Malcolm to believe that Possum had ever had anything to do with this pair. They spoke no English. Pedro interpreted for the woman.

Malcolm asked her when her husband had been sold. She answered that it had been about four years ago. She said her husband was not the girl's father. The father was a white man.

Malcolm turned to Pedro and said, "This is not the woman I was looking for."

Pedro and Malcolm walked back to the hacienda, and Pedro asked Malcolm, "Would you take the little girl as a gift? You have the two girls. She would be a good playmate and grow into a good servant for them. She is a very smart little girl. Mary Annabelle is good with children, and she would not mind having one more to care for."

"Why do you want to be rid of the little girl?" Malcolm asked.

"She is what I call a Too Girl, and Too Girls don't make good slaves. Not only that, I could get more work out of the mother if the girl was gone," Pedro answered.

"What is a Too Girl?"

"A Too Girl is one that is too white and too smart," Pedro explained.

"So, you want to get rid of this Too Girl, by giving her to me?"

"I think it would be much better for her to grow up with white children, and growing up in the United States would be better for her as well."

Malcolm thought that perhaps the father was Spanish and wanted to get his daughter out of Cuba. It was a distinct possibility that her last name should have been Gonzales.

"What would the mother have to say if I was to take her?" Malcolm asked.

Pedro eyed Malcolm with a look of suspicion, thinking Malcolm should be smarter than that. "She belongs to the plantation and Mr. Fleet," he tersely answered. "The mother has no say in the matter."

"I will get back to you on this matter tomorrow," Malcolm said.

Malcolm got the girls back to the guesthouse and put them to bed. It was very hard to think that Glena Lee would not be coming in to kiss them good night. As he left the room he could hear soft sobs. He got a glass of brandy and went out on the veranda. He took a seat and sipped his brandy and lit up a cigar. It was time to gather his thoughts and make some decisions. First, he must leave Cuba and get back to Cottontail in the next day or two.

As to finding Possum's wife and child, he knew that Pedro Gonzales knew more than he was telling. He wished he had time to look around the plantation. He would bet good money that there was another woman with a little girl. To think that he would even take the little white girl was crazy. He would have so much to do, raising his own two girls, now that Glena Lee was gone. On the other hand, if she were left here, the little white slave would end up as a whore in a Havana brothel. It was just such girls that the Cuban men liked.

The little girl was already pretty. It would be a shame for that to happen to the child. Mr. Pedro Gonzales knew this also. One decision that Malcolm did make, sitting on the veranda at the Fleet's plantation, was that he would not run for Governor. The other decision was that he would have no more contact with Mary Annabelle! He didn't dare get rid of her now that Glena Lee was gone, because she was so good and kind to the children. He needed her very much, but not laying on her back under a palm. Malcolm finished his brandy and went to bed.

The next morning, there was a small rap at the door. Malcolm was close to the door so he opened it. Looking out, he saw nothing, then looking down he saw the little white slave girl. She said something in Spanish that he could not understand. He called for Mary Annabelle.

"She say's her name is Loupe and she wants to play with the girls," Mary Annabelle explained.

Loupe had on a sack-like dress that looked to be homespun. Her curly hair clung to her head in ringlets. She was barefoot and not too clean.

Malcolm looked down at the little girl, who managed a big smile, and ordered, "Clean her up and let them play. Give her one of Mandy Ann's dresses."

Loupe had found a new home.

Malcolm got Tomtom to help him pack and prepare to leave. He gathered all of Glena Lee's things, except her jewelry, and had Tomtom take them to Mrs. Fleet to do with as she saw fit. Mary Annabelle was busy with the children, so most of the preparation for the journey home was left to Malcolm. As darkness fell on the island, they were all packed.

Malcolm walked to the main hacienda to bid the Fleets good-bye, as he wanted to leave very early in the morning. He stopped by the palm grove and sank to his knees to pray for Glena Lee. He then visited with the Fleets until midnight. He thanked them for all they had done for him and invited them to visit Cottontail. He left money to put up a nice headstone for Glena Lee. The subject of little Loupe never came up. Sometimes, to leave a situation in a state of mystery, is the best policy. This time as he passed the grave, he did not stop, but in a strong and friendly voice he said, "Good-bye Glena Lee, until we meet again."

The party arrived in Havana, and managed to rent the same suite of rooms as they had before. It would be two days before a passenger ship to New Orleans was to leave. Mary Annabelle would not let the girls go out of the hotel and they could only play in the courtyard. It was amazing how fast little Loupe learned English, and how the other girls were quickly able to converse in Spanish. Malcolm used his time to buy some souvenirs for the folks back at Cottontail.

The trip back to New Orleans was uneventful. Malcolm had good luck at the tables. Nobody, except little Loupe, got seasick. Mary Annabelle had the other girls play nurse so they had fun taking care of poor Loupe.

CHAPTER 23

"I would hate to see him go to prison, as you know he is family"

Sheriff Laws helped Possum and Olaf return Lady Chandler to her home. The two slaves went to work in the fields. Lady Chandler was feeling much better when she got home, and she and the sheriff had refreshments in the study.

Lady Chandler addressed the sheriff. "You must do something about Bancroft's outrageous behavior. He allows that whatever-it-is to pop eyes out of children. He is harboring a girl that poses as a man. He even has the gall to say that he loves her. I hate to see him go to prison, as you know he is family. Our dear, dear Glena Lee is his sister. Something must be done."

"Lady Chandler! Bancroft Whitesides has broken no laws," the sheriff injected. "I will speak to him about the terrible treatment of the child, however there is nothing that I can legally do about it. The child does belong to him. You must understand that I agree with you. This kind of treatment of slaves must not be tolerated. But there is no law that says a girl can't dress like a man. And about him loving her, we can only hope he changes his mind. Please try and understand. Just let things rest a few weeks. We will see what Malcolm and Glena Lee have to say when they get home. Sometimes time is a very good cure."

Lady Chandler took her fan and, with rapid fanning, tried to cool down.

"Sheriff Laws, I know you are right, but this is so terrible. What will Bancroft's parents do when they find out? They are such nice people. They are quite old and it will be so hard on them."

The sheriff started to let himself out, then turned and said, "We must let the people of Hanging Magnolia work out their problems. I will, however, notify some of the other planters about the cruel treatment of the slaves. Sometimes a little peer pressure is also a good cure." Then he added, "while Malcolm has been in Cuba, I have been working on his campaign for Governor, and he is developing tremendous support."

Bancroft had gone directly to Julie's cabin after the altercation with Lady Chandler. Julie was just mounting her horse to go to the fields to see that the slaves were still working. She had one whip in her hand and another tied on her saddle.

"Julie, stop, we have to talk," Bancroft called out. "Your secret has been discovered."

She tied her horse to the rail outside her cabin, and they went inside. Inside, Bancroft explained how the slaves had seen her bathing last night and that Lady Chandler had come over and raised holy hell—not only about her disguise, but the fact that she had taken an eye out of a child.

Julie uncoiled her whip and popped a fly off the stove across the room. It sounded like a rifle shot in the close quarters of the cabin. She then sat down on the bed and looked at Bancroft through the eyes of a wounded bobcat.

"What should I do?" she asked.

"You better get out of here and go to Atlanta. Those two slaves last night came to do you harm or maybe kill you. The fact that they found out you are a girl will not change their thinking. Our slaves are also very upset. It is a good thing that I got to you before you rode out to the fields. It is not likely that we will be able to control them as long as you are here."

"I guess what you are telling me is to get out. I love you very much. I guess this ends my career as an overseer, but nothing will stop me from enjoying whipping those slaves."

"I love you too, but there will be nothing to love if the slaves get to you. Your horse is saddled. Get on him and go out the back way. Take the old road and ride fast. I will come to Atlanta in about a week, as we planned, and work out our future."

Bancroft watched her horse disappear in the distance. He sat down and gathered his thoughts. No way was he going to Atlanta and renew a relationship with the little bitch. His family and Hanging Magnolia Plantations were too important to him. It was a good piece, but it was time for other things. He would go to Cottontail in the morning and apologize to Lady Chandler. Then he would go to the slave child and do what he could for the child. He would also see to it that an apology was rendered to the entire slave populations on both plantations. How could he have thought he was in love with a person who displayed such despicable behavior? It is only about six inches to the end of a erection, but sometimes hard to see beyond it.

Early the next morning, Bancroft was at Cottontail Plantation. He explained how he had sent Julie on her way, that he was not going to follow her, and that he was on his way to talk to the slaves. He had called a doctor to look at the child who had lost an eye. Lady Chandler accepted his apologies and felt very good that he had come to his senses.

Bancroft found the slave child in one of the slave cabins. He was a boy of about six. He had a crude bandage on his head. The doctor removed the bandage. It almost made Bancroft sick. A large gaping hole nearly exposed the child's brains. The doctor cleaned the wound and dressed it in a clean bandage. The little boy sat up and ate some soup brought to him by his mother.

The doctor informed the boy that, of course he would only have one eye, but he would be able to see pretty well. Bancroft told the mother that as soon as the boy was feeling better he could go Cottontail to Learnet's school. This was a great concession for Bancroft, as he had always been very adamant that slaves should not be educated.

After the doctor had gone, Bancroft called the slaves together and apologized for the terrible thing that had happened to the boy. He also said that Mr. Hardnails had been sent packing. A murmur of approval went through the crowd. They all went happily back to work. Bancroft felt that he had held off a possible uprising.

Two weeks passed and Bancroft personally delivered the little one-eyed slave to Learnet's school. Learnet was glad to accept the new pupil. She explained to Bancroft how important it was to give the slaves an education, as someday they would all be free. If they were educated, they would be less of a burden on the south and the entire nation. Bancroft explained to Learnet that they would never be free. To even think or say such things was treason to the south and to the southern lifestyle. They had very different views, but their remarks were friendly. Bancroft did notice a nice ankle under Learnet's long dress.

The time was drawing near to go to the river to pick up Malcolm and his family. Bancroft was the one to do this chore. He prepared the big buggy and chose one of his slaves, a young man that had been very loyal to Hanging Magnolia, and was a good worker. In fact, he was the father to the little boy who had lost the eye. His name was Conway.

Conway was a fair hand with a team of horses. Bancroft let him drive the buggy, and Bancroft acted as the outrider. Lady Chandler insisted that they take Not-So-Fast so that Evelyn Lucille could ride him at least part of the way home. Bancroft rode a big roan with a glass eye, and they tied Not-So-Fast behind the buggy. Lady Chandler also sent a list of supplies that they were to bring home for the Christmas Ball. She told them to deliver it to Glena Lee, and she would know what to do.

When they arrived at the river, the boat was a few days late. Bancroft got a room at a hotel with slave quarters in the back. Conway slipped off and got drunk. Somehow, he got out on the balcony of a building overlooking the street. He took a piss over the side and happened to piss on the local sheriff as he was walking by. Needless to say, the sheriff was a little pissed off. After a few good lashes with the whip, he threw Conway in jail.

Bancroft spent the next day looking for Conway and, when he finally found him, he bailed him out. Bancroft also gave him a few lashes. Conway was about to decide that getting drunk just was not worth it.

Bancroft spent some of his layover time gambling in the bar at the hotel. He had bad luck and lost a bundle. He told himself that cotton was high and he could afford it, which, in part, was the truth.

He did manage to get one of the bargirls to his room for the night. She was a little blond with ample breasts. She wore a velvet red outfit that exposed most of her sales points. He noticed, when she took off her clothes, that she was not as clean as he would like but what the hell.

The next morning he found that she must have had ninety percent of the crabs and lice in the South. She left fifty percent of them on him. He bathed and picked, jumped in the river, and bathed and picked again. By the time the boat carrying Malcolm and his party got in, he had about rid himself of the pests.

The boat whistle blew, and it pulled into the dock. Malcolm had everybody dressed in black for the departure off the boat. He spotted Bancroft standing on the dock. Mandy Ann and Evelyn Lucille ran to Uncle Bancroft with tears in their eyes. He did not have to ask what had happened, he only wanted to know how.

CHAPTER 24

"Lets sneak down to the stable and steal No-So-Fast."

Malcolm related the story of Glena Lee's death to Bancroft. Bancroft and his sister had not been really close, but it was still a devastating loss. He was very concerned about how it would affect his elderly parents. Glena Lee had always been the apple of their eyes.

Bancroft, recovering from the shock of losing his sister, asked, "Who is the little girl?"

"She is a slave girl whom I received as a gift from a man that I suspect was her father. My plans are to raise her to be a servant for the girls. But, I fear my plan is not going to work. She is too white and they treat her just like a sister. Mary Annabelle treats her with the same respect that she gives my girls. I am going to have to raise her as an adopted daughter.

I would appreciate it if you would keep it under your hat that she is of colored blood. Mary Annabelle and the girls know nothing of her background. From this day forward she will be known as Loupe Rose Chandler. She is a smart girl and seems to fit well in any situation."

Evelyn Lucille was thrilled that they had brought Not-So-Fast. She mounted him. Conway was on the big roan, and Malcolm, Bancroft and the girls were in the buggy. They were off to Cottontail Plantation.

Bancroft told Malcolm that he was acquiring tremendous statewide support as a gubernatorial candidate. Supporters had already set up headquarters for him in Atlanta. Malcolm was tired, he had lost his wife, and he had a large plantation and stable to care for. The last thing on his mind was to be Governor. His decision not to run was going to stick, but he did not come right out and reveal this to Bancroft.

In late afternoon, they stopped at the Old Log Inn. It was a rustic Inn, displaying no elegance of the South. Evelyn Lucille had ridden Not-So-Fast all day, and it was such fun for her. This was not so fun for Mandy Ann and Loupe Rose. It caused some quibbling and rivalry and especially put Mandy Ann's nose out of joint. Adding a little fuel to the fire, Malcolm said Evelyn Lucille could sleep in his room, as it had two beds. Mandy Ann and Loupe Rose shared a bed in the next room. They all enjoyed a nice dinner of passenger pigeon. The Rustic Inn kept a hired hunter to supply the Inn with pigeons. It was a house specialty.

Conway was to sleep at the stable so he could watch the horses. He managed to find some whisky in one of the saddlebags hanging in the stable. He had a great little one-man party. Mary Annabelle had a room at the back of the Inn.

The little girls' room echoed with conversation.

"Loupe Rose, are you asleep?"

"No."

Mandy Ann was silent for a minute and then said, "Let's sneak down to the stable and steal Not-So-Fast. We can hide him in the woods in the morning so that Little Miss Uppity will not have her horse to show off. She acts like such a smarty."

The little girls got up and dressed, not putting on shoes. Their feet were tough from all the barefoot playing they had done in Cuba. They tiptoed out of the Inn, managing to suppress their giggles. Once outside, they ran to the stable. The door squeaked with an eerie sound as they opened it. It was very dark in the stable. They could hear Conway snoring on his pallet not too far from the squeaky door. After his one-man party, he was out of it. They found Not-So-Fast in a back stall. They led him out behind the stable and deep into the woods. After tying him securely to a tree, they started back. They had not gone far when Loupe Rose asked, "Are you sure we are going the right direction? We have been out here a long time, and I don't like the creepy noises in this forest."

Mandy Ann, who was a few months older and a natural leader, answered. "Don't be a fraidy cat. It is only a little farther, and we will be right at the door of the Inn."

They walked on for a time, and Loupe Rose began to cry.

"Mandy Ann! You don't know where we are anymore than I do. I am cold and my feet are sore. I am going to stop."

Mandy Ann's bravery diminished as she turned to Loupe Rose and started to cry.

The girls huddled together under a big tree and cried some and slept some. Despite the fact that they had sense enough to wear their coats, they were very cold.

It was just turning daylight when they heard something like the noise a horse makes when he blows his nose. It awakened both girls and they were terrified. As it got a bit lighter they could see that they were only a few yards from where they had tied Not-So-Fast.

"Turn the horse loose," Mandy Ann told Loupe Rose. "He will go home and all we have to do is follow him. Horses always know the way home. Maybe we can get home before anybody wakes up."

Loupe Rose untied Not-So-Fast, and he nosed the heads of both girls as if to kiss them good-bye and took off on a high lope. In the thick timber, there was no way the girls could keep up. They hugged each other, and both started to cry.

Conway had just awakened with a sick stomach and a headache. The stable door was open, and he was sure he had closed it. Just at that second, Not-So-Fast came trotting up to the stable. Conway caught him and put him back in the stall. Conway scratched his head and asked the horse, "Just how did you get untied and out of the stable?"

He looked around and saw that no harm was done. He could see no reason to tell his master that the horse had gotten out.

At the lodge, breakfast was being served and Mandy Ann and Loupe Rose did not come down for breakfast. Mary Annabelle went back up the stairs to the get the little girls. She found the room empty and screamed that the girls were gone.

Malcolm was the first to reach the empty room.

"What on earth could have happened to the little girls?" Bancroft stated.

"They probably got up early and went to the stable. I'll go look for them," Evelyn Lucille suggested. She reported back that they were not at the stable, and Conway had not seen them.

Everybody spread out in all directions of the lodge calling the girls' names. It was Bancroft who found them huddled under a tree. They were cold, their legs were scratched and their feet were bleeding. Bancroft alerted the others that he had found them, and by the time he got them to the Inn, everyone had assembled.

There was much speculation about what had happened. It was hard for the girls to explain just what they did or what there intentions were. They tried to tell the truth but it always came out the wrong way. Conway did not help their story by saying there was no way that they could have stolen the horse when he was right there.

Finally Malcolm said, "We will just forget all this. You are safe and that's what counts." He put them in the back of the rig with a big blanket. They covered their heads and it was not long before you could here their giggles coming from under the blanket. Evelyn Lucille gave them turns riding behind her as they progressed along the road.

It was about noon when they saw a wagon stalled in the road. Upon arriving at the scene, they observed that it was a slave trader with an old wagon and five slaves chained on the rough board seats. One of the slaves was a very thin boy who appeared to be about eleven. The rest of the slaves were quite old, or had something wrong with them. The slaves were in very poor condition, and showed signs of abuse.

The wagon had lost a wheel. Malcolm and Bancroft helped the trader fix his wagon. While they were fixing the wagon, Mary Annabelle asked if she could give the slaves something to eat, as they looked very hungry. With permission from Malcolm, she fed the five slaves. They ate like it had been a long time between meals. When the wagon was fixed Malcolm took charge.

He told the trader to sit down, and that he wanted to talk to him. The trader leaned up against the wagon, and Malcolm started his tongue lashing on the trader.

" It is obvious that you are going from plantation to plantation buying slaves that are of little value to the owner. I can see that these men and this little boy have been badly mistreated, and you do not feed them. It is your kind that gives the northerners all the ammunition to argue that there is widespread slave abuse. We have extra food, and I am going to give you some for these slaves. I am going to send word out to the rest of the planters not to trade with you anymore. For the benefit of our beloved South, I want you and all of your kind out of business."

When the trader was getting in his wagon, Bancroft reached up and grabbed him, pulling him to the ground and pulling his collar so tight that he almost choked. "Give me the key to these chains. I am taking this little boy with us," Bancroft ordered.

The trader protested, all the while digging in his pocket for the key. "You can't do this. He is my slave. I will sell him to you for a good price."

"I am not buying, I am taking."

The trader handed Bancroft the key. He took the boy and put him in the buggy with the little girls. The girls pulled away from him, holding their noses, as he did not smell the best.

Due to the late morning start and time spent with the trader, they could not make it to the next Inn by nightfall. They would have to camp out. They had plenty of food and warm clothes. It was getting late in the fall, but the weather was warm, and it was going to be a nice night.

Mary Annabelle took the new little boy to the creek and washed him and his clothes. He refused to speak a word. While his clothes were drying over the campfire, Mary Annabelle put one of the girls' dresses on him. Everybody got a good laugh, and if you had watched close, you would have seen a slight smile on the boy's face.

While camp was being made, Bancroft dug a hand line out of his duffel. He gave it to Conway with instructions to go to the river and see if he could catch a catfish for supper.

Conway beamed with pleasure, as he loved to fish. The section of the small river they camped on had a backwater that was famous for large catfish. Conway found a large flat rock out in the river and tossed out the line. He had no results, so he tied the line to his big toe. His toe was big and flat at the end. He gave the line a couple half hitches and a slipknot around the big toe and laid back on the rock and fell asleep.

He was awakened with a slight tug on the line attached to his toe. He stood up and reached down to get the line, when the very large catfish decided to head for the middle of the backwater. It pulled Conway off balance and into the river. There wasn't much current, but it was impossible for him to swim with the big fish pulling so hard on his toe. He struggled to reach shore, as the fish made another run. It felt like he was going to pull the toe off. His toe hurting and the fish pulling, he tried to swim, this time going completely under. It looked like the end of poor Conway. Then, from out of nowhere, he felt someone grab him by the shoulder and pull him to shore. Conway, gasping and spitting river water, finally got the stranger to see his bleeding toe. It was a great relief to Conway when the man quit trying to pull him up the bank while the fish was trying to pull him back into the river. The stranger grabbed the line and pulled in what must have been a forty-pound catfish. The line was pulled deep into the flesh of his toe, so they had to cut the line to release him from the fish.

Conway looked at the big stranger and asked, "Man, who are you? And thank you. I think you saved my life."

The big man gave Conway a long look before he answered.   " M y name is Bally. I'm a runaway slave. When I heard you coming, I hid in the brush and watched you fish."

Conway told him the white men were camped not far away, and that he better be on his way before someone came.

"I'll tell 'em I had trouble with the big fish, but I made it to shore by myself. Thanks again."

Bally moved off into the brush, and Conway bandaged his foot with his shirt and started back for camp.

Back at camp, Malcolm took his bone-handled knife and cut the line out of Conway's toe. He looked up at Bancroft, who was watching the operation, and smiled.

"Last summer when I was bringing the slaves back to Cottontail from the market, I said that I would never let myself get into a position like this again. Here I am again. By the way, Bancroft, why did you rescue that slave boy today? You've never been known as one who treats his slaves very well."

Bancroft shrugged his shoulders. "I guess you have finally made me see the light," he replied.

Chapter 25

"What a terrible time for male lust."

The camp for the night was pretty cozy. The girls had a makeshift tent made by hanging blankets on the buggy with their beds placed under it. Mary Annabelle placed her blankets just outside the girls' tent. Malcolm and Bancroft were under the limbs of a large oak tree, and Conway fixed a place for him and the new boy not far from the campfire.

Mary Annabelle cooked up a big batch of the fresh catfish. The entire party enjoyed it very much, and the new boy ate enough for three little boys.

While they were sitting around the fire after supper, Bancroft noticed the new boy staring into the fire, not looking from side to side or even acting like he heard the conversations. Bancroft went to the fire and took two lids off of the cooking pots. He went behind the little boy and slammed them together with all his strength. Everybody, except the little boy, just about jumped out of their skin. The boy did not move and continued to stare into the fire.

Everyone looked at Bancroft as if he had lost his mind.

"This new boy is deaf and dumb. It is no wonder he will not talk with us. We had better give him a name."

Evelyn Lucille spoke up. "He eats so much catfish, let's call him "Catfish."

There was a murmur of laughter around the fire. The name "Catfish" would stick.

Malcolm lay in his blankets, staring at the moon, and his thoughts went to the Governor's race. If as much support existed as Bancroft had said, maybe he should run. In his mind, it was going to take someone like himself to save slavery and the southern lifestyle. He knew that whatever he accomplished towards retaining slavery would only remain for perhaps one more generation. The end of slavery was on its way, one way or the other. For the most part, the rest of the world had abandoned slavery.

When he got back to Cottontail he was going to try a new system with one of his slave families. He had a back forty-acre field that was difficult to farm. He was going to let a slave family build a cabin on it and farm it. He and the slave family would share the crop, in fact that is what he would call them, was "sharecroppers."

Malcolm heard a noise and raised up. He saw Mary Annabelle getting ready for bed over by the buggy. With the glow of the dying fire, she was silhouetted against the night sky. As she turned, he could see her flat tummy was not so flat. His heart sank. With no doubt in his mind, he realized that Mary Annabelle was going to have his baby. He could say it was one of the slave boys. He could sell her now before anyone knew. He wondered how it would play out if he ran for governor.

He could let things take their course and let the chips fall where they may. Somewhere, deep inside, he wondered how it would be to share a child with Mary Annabelle. Malcolm fell into a restless sleep.

Sometime after midnight the entire camp was awakened by a blood-curdling scream. Malcolm jumped up and grabbed his pistol. He saw a fat raccoon making its way across camp. One shot, and the coon rolled over. Mary Annabelle was sitting on the ground holding her foot. The raccoon must have been attracted to camp by the smell of food. Finding none, he had taken a big bite out of Mary Annabelle's toe. She was scared to death. Malcolm went to her and she put her warm arms around him. What a terrible time for male lust. The entire camp was up, wondering what had happened, except Catfish, who slept right through the commotion. They got a bandage on Mary Annabelle's toe. Malcolm took a good look at the raccoon and it looked healthy. He was quite sure that it did not have rabies. It would take a few days to tell for sure.

Breaking camp in the morning went smoothly. With the two slaves hobbling around with their sore toes, the girls decided to name the camp the "Bad Toe Camp."

Travel went well, and Bancroft took the opportunity to tell Malcolm of his affair with Julie, alias Mr. Hardnails. Malcolm could hardly believe that Mr. Hardnails was a girl. He had to laugh that he and everybody else had been misled.

"She is out of your life for good?" Malcolm asked.

"I hope so. For sure, I am not going to Atlanta and look her up. You never let your sex drive get in the way of your good judgment. I wish I could be more like you. I guess I should find someone and get married."

Malcolm made no comment, but thought, "if he only knew."

Malcolm and Bancroft made plans for a memorial service for Glena Lee. It would be held at Cottontail a few days after they arrived home.

The party pulled into Hanging Magnolia early in the afternoon. Malcolm and Bancroft went immediately to the main house and found the Senior Whitesides. Grandpa was in the swing on the porch. When they told him of the death of his only daughter, he placed his head in his hands and wept.

After what seemed like a long time, he raised his head, and with tear filled eyes, he said, "We had better go tell her mother."

Mrs. Whitesides was wrapped in a blue and white afghan that she had knitted a few years before. Her rocking chair came to a stand still when the men entered her room. She greeted Bancroft, but seemed to have no knowledge of who Malcolm was.

"Mother, this is Malcolm. You remember, Glena Lee's husband," Bancroft explained. "We have come to bring you bad news."

Mrs. Whitesides had only been able to walk from her rocking chair to bed for quite some time, and she looked very frail. She still did not seem to recognize Malcolm. Malcolm kneeled down and took the thin and aged spotted hand in his.

"Mother Whitesides, Glena Lee and I were in Cuba on a vacation, and Glena Lee became ill and died."

The old lady raised up from her chair. She walked to the window at a brisk pace. She opened the window and shouted in a large voice, very uncommon to her.

"Glena Lee is dead! Glena Lee is dead! I wish to join her! I wish to join her!"

With that, she walked to her bed, lay down, and closed her eyes. Bancroft went to her side, picked up her hand and felt for a pulse. Looking at his father and Malcolm, with tears in his eyes, he announced, "She has no pulse."

They spread a sheet over her and helped the old man back to his porch swing.

Malcolm and Bancroft were very busy the next few days. It was decided to hold funeral services for Mrs. Whitesides and a memorial for Glena Lee at the same time. They would be held on the glade between the creek and the mansion at Cottontail Plantation. Mrs. Whitesides was laid to rest in the family plot about one hundred fifty steps west of the Magnolia Tree that gave the plantation its name. The services were well attended by slaves and whites alike.

The strangest things sometimes happen at funerals. When the preacher was giving the sermon for Mrs. Whitesides, a stray dog trotted up to the coffin and raised his leg on it. Then when they were taking the coffin up the hill for burial, a wheel fell off the wagon, spilling the coffin and its contents out on the road.

A few days passed, and things became normal on the Cottontail Plantation. Learnet canceled her classes for the slaves until the first of the year. This enabled her to get the three Chandler girls brought up to date. Now they could all speak Spanish, and occasionally she conducted the class in Spanish.

Amos and Lady Chandler seemed to get on very well, and there was talk of marriage. He would slip out of her room every morning, then go down and visit with Possum and Olaf, never telling them what to do, but just giving them guidance. With this strange management team of Possum, Olaf and Amos, the work was getting done on Cottontail better than ever. Amos would spend the rest of the day doing carpenter work around the plantation. He had seen Catfish over at Hanging Magnolia, and the boy seemed to have no guidance. He took a liking to the lad and asked Bancroft if he could buy him.

Amos, the old hard northerner, buying a slave! If his old friends up in Pennsylvania ever found out, he would be very embarrassed. Bancroft liked the boy, but found him to be a great deal of trouble, and he was more than glad to give him to Amos. Amos built him a modest, clean shack out behind the mansion. They learned to communicate with each other by using a series of hand signals. Catfish became very loyal to Amos. He would follow him everywhere, help with his carpenter work and run errands.

He seemed to have no interest in normal childhood activities. Together, Amos and Catfish made Lady Chandler a wooden leg. She could get around much better and was very appreciative to both of them.

Mary Annabelle and Learnet were still best of friends. However, no matter how hard she tried, Learnet could get no information about her affair with Malcolm. Mary Annabelle had given her word to Malcolm not to talk, and there was no way that she was going to. Learnet was beginning to suspect that maybe it was over. With Glena Lee out of the picture, maybe, just maybe, she should make a try for Malcolm. He was older, but he was very rich and handsome. Mary Annabelle was still managing to hide her pregnancy, but she would not be able to much longer.

It was a very dark, rainy night as Learnet lay in bed thinking. Malcolm had to be lonesome. He had to want a woman. God knows she wanted a man. She got all worked up just thinking about it. About two in the morning, she could stand it no longer. Slipping out of bed, taking off her pajamas and slipping on a light robe, she gently padded down the hall toward Malcolm's room. The closer she got to his door, the more worked up she got. She had to stop and lean against the hall wall to catch her breath. She could just feel his arms around her and imagine him gently pressed to her waiting body.

Just as she reached the door, she heard it opening and slipped back into the shadows. Mary Annabelle quietly closed the door behind her and made her way down the hall in her cat-like stride. Mary Annabelle walked so close to Learnet in the shadows that Learnet could smell the musk of recent sex.

Learnet made her way back to her room. That Black Bitch, that dirty rotten Black Bitch.

CHAPTER 26

"I have given it considerable thought and decided to run for Governor."

It was a very warm Sunday for so late in the fall. Malcolm came down to breakfast, and the two little girls jumped all over him. They wanted to go riding. They were too young to go alone, and Evelyn Lucille was not quite old enough to send as their chaperone. Malcolm said he would take them for a long ride, since it was such a nice day.

Evelyn Lucille opted to stay at home, as she had schoolwork and was reading a good book. The entire family happened to get to breakfast at the same time. Malcolm looked around and decided that now would be a good time to make his announcement.

"I have given this considerable thought, and I have decided to run for Governor! It will be a very tough fight, as I am running on a very liberal program. It may be that some of the southern people will call me a traitor. It is my belief that in order to save slavery and our southern life style, we must make changes. We do not have to make these changes overnight. My platform will be to start educating the slave children and teach them to read and learn arithmetic, usingthe whip only when absolutely necessary. I will also recommend that it will be illegal to free a slave."

All the adults at the table thought that it was a wonderful idea.

"I will make a trip to Atlanta next week to kick off my campaign," Malcolm continued. "I will take one slave with me as my servant, but I have not yet decided who that will be. I plan to speak with Possum and Olaf to see whom they could spare and who they wish to recommend."

Bolo, who had heard all this, decided that she could speak her mind and not get whipped.

"Massah Malcolm and Lady Chandler, I need more he'p, I'm gettin' old. You gots me, Mary Annabelle, and she's a willin' worker, but you'all keep her busy with other things. Liz comes up and he'ps some. With the Massah runnin' for Govnuh they'll be more dinners and parties. I need more he'p."

Malcolm and Lady Chandler looked at each other, and they smiled an understanding smile. It was very unusual for a slave to speak up in this manner.

97

"Bolo, this is Sunday, and the slaves are not working. I can hear the slaves singing around the slave quarters right now," Lady Chandler said. "You go down and talk to them. Find a young girl who wants to be a cook and house slave and bring her up. Amos will be happy to build her a shack out by Catfish's. I shall be very strict that no one gives her orders except you. You will be in charge. I know we always get you help and then have them doing other things. So, right now, I am giving an order. Anyone who asks Bolo's new girl to do anything will get thirty lashes."

Everyone laughed and Bolo swelled up to twice her already ample size. She disappeared and returned a short time later dressed in her best dress. Giving a clumsy curtsy she said, "I's off to get me a slave."

Malcolm looked at Mandy Ann and Loupe Rose. "You girls get your riding clothes on, and we will start a campaign for governor by calling on some of our good neighbors."

Amos and Lady Chandler got ready and went to church.

When Amos and Lady Chandler got home from church it was such a nice warm day they went for a walk down along the creek. They came to the old swimming hole and decided to go skinny-dipping. When they got their clothes off they looked like two half-melted snowmen. They put their clothes behind some rocks and had a great time splashing in the creek. When they went back to get dressed, they found that a beaver had eaten almost all of Lady Chandler's wooden leg.

While Lady Chandler and Amos were swimming, there was an interesting drama playing out up at the mansion. With everybody out of the house, Evelyn Lucille had a good idea. She went out back and got Catfish. She was afraid to take him up to her room, so she led him deep in the woods. She had heard the older people talk of sex and she thought it was time to give it a try. Catfish was perfect, because he could not tell. She got him to take off his clothes, and she took off hers. He stood looking at her, with his little thing dangling between his legs. She knew this was not right. She thought about giving him a kiss. That's what the big people did, but she just could not bring herself to kiss him. How did older people do this sex thing? Catfish just stood there in the warm afternoon with his little thing hanging between his legs. In utter frustration, she had him dress and they went back to the mansion.

When Malcolm brought the little girls home, about suppertime, they were worn out. They opted for a cold chicken leg and a bowl of porridge, then headed off to bed.

Bolo took the opportunity to introduce her new helper during supper. She was a girl of about sixteen with dark, curly hair that clung to her scalp. She stood about five feet tall and was rather plump. Her broad nose and large lips showed her African heritage. She had a big smile that flashed even, white teeth and her black eyes sparkled. Her name was Alzora.

That evening, Malcolm called in Possum and Shorty Rideout to talk about the upcoming trip to Atlanta. He needed Shorty to decide which good, strong horses were available, and he needed Possum to help pick a servant to take along. Shorty suggested that one horse should be Not-So-Fast as he was gentle, strong and fast. The other was a big dapple-gray. He was a five-year-old and a very strong animal. His name was Big Blue. Malcolm didn't know much about him. Shorty assured him he was a good horse.

After much discussion about which slave to take, it was decided that Possum would go. This was very much to the satisfaction of Possum. Malcolm liked Possum and he was a very good worker and a leader. Still, Malcolm wondered about Possum. One thing that bothered him was that when he told him he could not find his wife and daughter in Cuba, Possum dismissed it. "Ho well she pro'bly wouldn't like it here anyway," Possum had said.

Malcolm later discovered that Possum had taken in one of the slave girls, she was only about seventeen. Malcolm knew that Mary Annabelle had been seen on several occasions coming out of Possum's cabin late at night. It was rumored that she was teaching him to read, and he was teaching her Voodoo. Mary Annabelle had told Malcolm that she had never had sex with anyone but him since coming to Cottontail.

A couple of uneventful days passed, and Malcolm and Possum rode out for Atlanta. There were good-byes and well-wishes. Evelyn Lucille hated to have Not-So-Fast gone for so long.

Malcolm was barely out of sight when Mary Annabelle went to her quarters and put on some tight-fitting clothes and went about her work. She said nothing. With Malcolm gone, she thought it would be a good time to make her condition known. By sunset, rumors were flying over about half the county, among both blacks and whites. Learnet had not had much to do with Mary Annabelle since the night in the hall. Now things had changed. That night, when Mary Annabelle had the girls tucked in, she went to see Learnet.

Learnet had her speech memorized.

"Mary Annabelle! I suppose that is Malcolm's baby?"

Mary Annabelle tried not to smile as she hung her head and said, "Yes."

"What is Malcolm going to do when he finds out?"

"He already knows."

"He will have to sell you. He can't have a nigger baby when he's running for governor. There are other things he could do, but they are too terrible to talk about. Are you going to tell who's baby it is?"

"No."

"Well! I am going to tell everyone I see."

Mary Annabelle had to hang her head again so Learnet could not see her smile. This was just what she wanted Learnet to do.

Mary Annabelle raised her head and looked straight at Learnet, her black eyes flashing and penetrating.

"You don't be calling this baby a nigger baby. It is Mary Annabelle and Master Malcolm's baby. It ain't no nigger baby." She spun on her heels and left the room.

When she was sure she was gone, Learnet went straight to Lady Chandler's room. A knock on the door produced Amos, who said that Lady Chandler was in the kitchen.

"May I come in and wait? I have a private matter to take up with Lady Chandler," Learnet said.

She entered, and Amos showed her to a chair and departed to get Lady Chandler. It was not long before Lady Chandler returned.

Learnet got right to the point.

"That baby that Mary Annabelle is carrying is Mr. Malcolm Chandler's."

Lady Chandler sank into a chair.

"No! Learnet you are mistaken. Who on earth told you that?"

"Mary Annabelle herself and not ten minutes ago."

"You know Malcolm well enough to know that he would not have sex with a slave girl. Why, Malcolm is a fine southern gentlemen and very true to Glena Lee. It is obvious that this baby was conceived before the death of Glena Lee."

"They had sex the night of the Harvest Ball, and they have been having it ever since. Just the other night, I saw her coming out of his room," Learnet persisted.

Lady Chandler got out of the chair and opened the door. "You leave this room at once and never, never repeat what you have told me to anybody."

When Amos came back, Lady Chandler hugged him and said, "We must ask Learnet to leave Cottontail."

Amos held her out at arm's length. "What on earth do you mean?"

"She is spreading the ugly rumor that the baby Mary Annabelle is carrying is Malcolm's child."

"How can you be so sure that it is not his child?" Amos asked.

"Not my son Malcolm. There never was more of a gentleman. He would not think of such a thing."

"Lady, please sit down. We will discuss this like adults. First, we should do nothing until Malcolm gets back. Learnet is doing fine with the children.

I love you and love it here at Cottontail. The smart thing to do is to do nothing for a while and see how things play out. The plantation is doing very well. Let's not upset the apple cart."

"Oh Amos, do you really love me? You have never said that before."

"Yes, I really do and I think that we get on with each other very well for older people."

They were locked in each other's arms when a knock came at the door. It was Learnet.

Learnet entered the room and asked to speak with them.

She said that she had a letter from an academy in Philadelphia offering her a teaching job. She had applied before she had come south and had never heard back from them. They now said they had an opening. "When I came south, I planned on freeing and educating all the slaves," Learnet continued. "To that end, I have made some progress. Now, in my own mind, I am wondering if it is such a good idea to free the slaves after all. Things are not nearly as bad as I was led to believe by the people of the north, but it is a system that I would just as soon be away from. Father, I know you like it here and I think you are in love. Father, it is very hard for me to do, but I am leaving you and Cottontail. The stage to the railroad comes by the main road in the morning and I am going to go home and take the new job."

Amos took her in his arms. "My dear, dear daughter. This is strange, as I have been thinking that you should get out and try your wings without me. You go do your packing. I hate to see you go. Please promise that you will come for a visit next summer."

Learnet took Lady Chandler's hand and smiled.

"You all have been very good to me. I see a true light shine when you look at father. I wish you all the happiness in the world."

As Lady Chandler stood looking at Learnet her thoughts were, "you bitch, I am really glad to be rid of you." But instead, she said, "Learnet, it has been such a pleasure to have you at Cottontail. You did very well with the girls. Have Mary Annabelle help you pack."

"No, I will pack," Learnet quickly replied.

The next morning, Learnet was on the stage. She had not gone far when she opened her purse. There was a red feather in it. She thought, "I wonder how that got there?" She placed it in the palm of her hand and blew it out the stage window.

CHAPTER 27

"You probably remember me as Mr. Hardnails."

When Malcolm and Possum arrived in Atlanta, they were very tired, and so were the horses. They found a good livery stable and checked the horses in. The manager of the livery said they had an empty stall where Possum could stay.

Malcolm gave Possum some money for food. Malcolm hired a hack and went to a fine Atlanta hotel. He cleaned up and went to the bar before he went to supper.

He was surprised to find Golden Finch. She was the daughter of the owner of one of the largest shipping empires in the entire world. It was headquartered out of New Orleans. They also had a large plantation. Ladies were not allowed in the bar alone, so her valet accompanied her. Malcolm had met Miss Finch several years ago when she was much younger. He had heard that she married a French Count and had moved to France.

She was dressed in a floor length yellow dress of lace and taffeta. Her shoulder length, auburn hair framed a beautiful face with a peaches and cream complexion. She asked Malcolm to join her. They had a couple of drinks and three got to be a crowd, so she dismissed the valet. Golden explained to Malcolm that she had been divorced and back in America for about a year. She was living on her father's plantation east of Atlanta. She was in Atlanta doing some Christmas shopping. She said she and the French Count were just not made for each other, but he had given her a large settlement.

They had a few drinks and dinner. Malcolm could just see, "I want to go to bed," written all over her face, but he was too damn tired. He made a date with her for the following evening. In the conversation that evening, Golden had mentioned that she had seen the campaign headquarters that Malcolm's supporters had set up not too far from the hotel. Malcolm wondered, even more than ever, who was setting it up and who was running it.

The next morning he had no trouble finding his headquarters. They were about a block west of the hotel. There were nice posters on the windows, and the place looked pretty official.

He entered the office, and a small young girl jumped up from behind the desk.

"Mr. Chandler, I am so glad you have come. I do hope you don't mind me taking the liberty of organizing your campaign headquarters. I tried to contact you, but learned you were in Cuba."

Malcolm looked at this rather pretty girl and he had no idea who she was.

"My name is Julie Penn," she continued. "You probably remember me as Mr. Hardnails."

She reach behind her desk, took out a whip, popped down one of the posters hanging in the window, and said, "I had little to do while I was waiting for Bancroft to come and get me. We are getting married. I knew you were going to run for governor, so I took it upon myself to get things going. I had hoped that Bancroft would be here before this.

Oh, I am sorry, please sit down. I will get you some coffee. You have a tremendous amount of backing. It will be no trouble getting you elected. I have talked to the present governor and he is not going to run. He said he would give you his backing. I have written to Washington for the backing of the President, but I have not heard back yet. Now that you are in town, I will start scheduling appearances and speeches. I think we should start with a rally in the City Park tomorrow. Outdoor appearances give a homey feeling that will help to attract the poor whites. You know we don't want them, but we have to take them. They do vote."

Malcolm raised his hand and almost shouted, "Stop!"

"First off, who is paying you?" he demanded.

"Nobody yet, but I know you will. I have already collected a great deal of money for you. I know you will spend some of your own money, so we have no financial worries. You just go take care of whatever business you have in Atlanta. You probably want to do some Christmas shopping. Be in the City Park tomorrow for your first speech. I will have it ready for you later this afternoon. You may want to practice your presentation this evening. Stop by this office again about four o'clock. I am so glad you are here. Now we can really get to work. There is just one thing I want understood. I will want a good state job when the election is over."

"Please, Miss Penn just slow down."

"Slow down? NO! We must work very hard. Elections are not won by slowing down. You run along so I can write the speech. And be back at four."

In order to collect his thoughts, Malcolm left and returned to his hotel room. Women, of course, could not vote. What on earth would the male voters think of this very aggressive woman running the show? What would the voters think when they found out that she posed as a man and popped eyes out of children? Could she really get a crowd at the City Park tomorrow?

He decided he had better go over and see if he could get in to see the Governor and find out what he really did tell Miss Penn. And he had better do it before four o'clock. Malcolm had met the Governor, but did not know him well. He was not sure the Governor would even remember him.

Arriving at the Capitol Building, Malcolm asked to see the Governor. The Governor's assistant said, "Oh yes, Mr. Chandler. The Governor is expecting you. I will tell him you are here."

The assistant was back in a few minutes and told Malcolm to go right in.

"Mr. Chandler. Our next Governor," the Governor said. "Miss Penn sent a messenger by just a few minutes ago to say that you would be stopping by. It is good to see you again."

"Governor, what do you know about this Miss Penn?" Malcolm asked.

"All I know is that she is one very good campaign manager. The women here in the office don't care for her. She is a bit aggressive, especially for a woman, but the women don't vote. Where on earth did you find her?"

"I didn't. She found me. She worked for Bancroft Whitesides on Hanging Magnolia Plantation for a while."

"Oh yes, I know Bancroft. Fine man, fine man. I guess she did mention that she knew Bancroft."

"Did she mention that she disguised herself as a man, so she could act as an overseer?" Malcolm asked.

"Well, that little devil. That is why I say she is quite a girl."

Malcolm decided to drop the subject. He and the Governor spent a half-hour discussing politics and the state of the south. As Malcolm was leaving, the Governor's parting words were, "Miss Penn has asked me to appear on the speaker's platform with you at the park tomorrow. I will see you there."

From the Capitol, Malcolm went back to his room to find that a package had been delivered. The package contained a new suit and a note from Miss Penn.

> Dear Mr. Chandler:
> Please find this new suit. Please wear it for your speech tomorrow.
>   You are a very handsome man, but you dress a little too much like a rich planter.
>   The crowd we have tomorrow will want a more common man.
>   Thank you: Julie Penn

Malcolm tried on the suit. He felt that it made him look like he just stepped off of a hay wagon. It was nearing four o'clock and time for him to pick up his speech. He planned to pick up the speech, then give the speech that he wanted to give. When he got to his campaign headquarters, Miss Penn was out. A young man was manning the desk.

"You must be Mr. Chandler. Allow me to introduce myself. I am Peter Penn. Julie is my younger sister. I help out here at the office from time to time. She had to go to the park to ready things for tomorrow. Here is the speech she has prepared for you."

He handed Malcolm what must have been ten written pages. Malcolm put it in his pocket. He looked at the young man and asked, "What do you do when you are not here, manning the office?"

"I run the family lumber business," he replied. "We have mills and also some retail outlets. Julie was connected with the business. Then she went to work for Hanging Magnolia Plantation. She is very good at handling slaves, and we sorely missed her at the mills. Now that she is engaged to that Mr. Whitesides, who owns that big plantation, she has resigned from the family business. Says it's just too much for her to do."

"Has your sister always been this aggressive?"

"Oh no! When she was helping me in the lumber business, she was much more aggressive. She says it's nice to be able to relax a little."

"Did you know that she disguised herself as a man when she was at Hanging Magnolia?"

"Yes, yes. Wasn't that smart of her? She really proved herself in that job."

Malcolm went out the door hoping that there were no more of the Penn family anywhere on the face of the earth. In the solitude of his room he read the speech.

My fellow Southern American's, I welcome you here to City Park to announce my candidacy for Governor of our great state.

We will never bow to the pressures of our northern neighbors to free our labor force.

In order to meet the challenge, we must lay the whip down, and pick it up only when absolutely necessary. We must educate the children of our labor force. Not in our history, not with facts and figures. Rather, we must teach them modest reading, and the foremost lesson is to teach them discipline, to be loyal to their masters and to be loyal, hard workers.

We must pass a mandatory death penalty for anyone assisting any of our labor force to escape.

There are those of you who want war with the North. I am not as optimistic as some in thinking that our boys could win a war. With the industrial might of the north, it would be a hard battle and much bloodshed. If you elect me Governor, we will have no war, and we will maintain our black labor force.

Malcolm read through the entire ten pages. He made some changes and cut out about half of it, as it was repetitious. By and large, it was his thoughts as if she had crawled into his head and taken them. Nobody, except his mother, seemed to give a damn if she misrepresented herself as a man. The shit might hit the fan when she found out that Bancroft was not coming to marry her.

For now, he would give the speech and let things play out for a few days. He called for some hot water and prepared for his date with Golden Finch.

CHAPTER 28

"When you look you see only one direction when you listen you see all directions."

A cold November wind blew across the plains of central Indian Territory. Right Nut and Pansy were huddled in a small tent, just about to freeze. They had left the trading post and gone west. It was rumored that there were lots of buffalo to hunt in central Indian Territory. Right Nut had always dreamed of hunting buffalo, but so far they had seen no buffalo and it was very cold. Right Nut had managed to kill two big wolves. In fact, they were using the skin as a blanket this very night. The soft, warm fur was very welcome.

They had just drifted off to sleep when they heard one of their horses squeal. Right Nut grabbed his rifle and rushed out of the tent. In the moonlight, he could see a wolf attacking Pansy's good pinto pony. Right Nut fired a shot, and the wolf ran off into the darkness, and the pony went down. Right Nut was a good shot, but somehow he had missed the wolf and killed the pony. Right Nut went back to bed.

In the morning he got up and skinned the pony. He knew of a small band of Cheyennes camped to the southwest, and they had a lot of horses. He took the two wolf hides and the pony hide and rode toward the camp. He left Pansy in camp and said he would be back in about a day and half. He was sure he could trade the three hides for a new pony.

Right Nut's camp was hidden in a grove of trees along a creek surrounded by rimrocks, and he felt sure that Pansy would be safe. Pansy had come a long ways towards becoming a frontier woman from the time when she was a slave. She had learned to use a gun and was able to handle it pretty well.

When Right Nut was gone, Pansy stayed in the tent and kept her gun handy. When it was time to relieve herself, she went out to a patch of willows behind the tent. A young fox was not far off and caught her scent. He sneaked up behind her and ran his cold nose-you know where. She jumped and screamed. Looking over her shoulder, the fox looked as big as a wolf. Pansy's pants were still around her ankles and she fell on her face, skinning her knee. She tried to run again without pulling up her pants and fell down again, skinning the other knee. The little fox was just as scared as she was, so when she got to the tent and her gun, he was long gone. This was the last time she left the tent without her gun. Right Nut had told her to stay in the tent and listen for any strange noises. He had said, "When you look, you only see one direction, but you listen in all directions."

Pansy missed her baby whom she had left with Snowflake and Left Nut. Snowflake, having no children of her own, loved the little boy with all her heart and took very good care of him.

Evening brought with it a cold wind. Pansy was huddled in her tent when she heard a sound outside. Opening the tent fly for a peek, she saw two men. They were on mules and had a small pack donkey. They wore long, black robes, and they had iron crosses hanging from their necks. Pansy had never seen a priest, but she had heard of them and knew that they were good people. She stepped outside and welcomed the strangers.

A tall thin man introduced himself as Father Clinton and his friend as Father O' Nixon. He then asked if they might camp with her. They explained that they had been sent by the church and God to go west to bring Christianity to the Indians. The good fathers pitched their tent and picketed their livestock. It was a cold windy night, but Pansy made the best of it and made them a good venison stew, which they partook of with relish.

Pansy went to her blanket and listened as the fathers made ready for bed. She heard Father O'Nixon say, "Father Clinton, I am sure the little lady next door would appreciate it if we paid her a visit tonight. She is probably quite cold and lonesome. I am sure that our vows of celibacy do not count in a situation of this kind. I think it would be best if you visited first."

Now, Pansy had been raped before. She knew better than to fight. Right Nut had brought along some beaver traps, and they were lying off to the side of the tent. She set one and placed it close to her blanket. The good Father Clinton opened her tent and stood over her with a kind smile.

"Miss Pansy, I have brought you a kind offering." He raised his robe and displayed his flesh.

Pansy took a look and gasped. She forgot about the trap and reached out to the kind priest. She tossed back her blankets and accepted this giant with relish, every inch she could. They both moaned and groaned. Poor Father O'Nixon was hearing all this in the next tent and getting all worked up, waiting his turn.

On his way out of the tent Father Clinton said, "My dear, I will send you Father O'Nixon."

Pansy lay in waiting and thinking, she felt a little bad about cheating on Right Nut, but that big man was really worth it.

Father O'Nixon entered the tent and raised his robes. He was a short, heavy man and, under the rolls of his potbelly, Pansy could see about two inches. As he lowered himself, she could smell his sour breath. She reached for the trap and let it snap on his balls. He was out the door yelling like a man that had a steel trap on his balls. She listened to the two priests trying to free poor Father O'Nixon. The next morning, the priests were nowhere in sight. The trap, with bloody jaws, lay in the tall grass. Pansy decided that it was best if Right Nut did not hear about her company. It was a good secret to keep to herself.

Despite the cold wind, Right Nut made good time going to the Cheyenne camp. The camp was much larger than when he and Pansy had visited it a few weeks earlier. Most of the Southern Cheyenne had arrived for their winter camp, and there were thousands of horses outside the camp.

Cheyenne Chief Passing Water welcomed Right Nut. Right Nut was a Cherokee brother. He explained how they had lost a pony and wanted to trade for a new one. The chief invited him to smoke and have supper. They would do their trading in the morning. The Cheyenne women prepared a fine meal of dried buffalo. Right Nut was told to sleep in a lodge of a young warrior named Falling Water, son of Chief Passing Water.

Falling Water had only recently left his father's lodge and was in the process of courting a prospective wife. He was not too happy with his guest, as it meant there would be no maidens creeping into his tent.

The next morning Right Nut found a young Cheyenne girl in a soft, white doeskin dress outside his lodge. She was holding two pinto ponies.

Using sign language and broken English, Chief Passing Water explained, "A moon ago, when you passed our way, you had a black wife. A black wife could be bad medicine for a warrior. You say your village is small, just you and your brother. Your brother has a white wife. Bad medicine. You take this Cheyenne maiden for your second wife, and she will bring you good medicine. From now until you die, she will be yours. Call her "Cheyenne Star" in honor of our great tribe, and the maker in the sky. The great Chief Passing Water will sleep good tonight, and for many moons, knowing he has given a Cherokee brother a fine wife."

Cheyenne Star gave a soft smile to Right Nut and came forward.

The great Chief Passing Water talked on. "Take these two ponies. Now both your wives shall ride."

Right Nut was not sure how Pansy would react to this second wife. It looked good to him. She was pretty. They left the Cheyenne camp and headed for Right Nut's camp. Right Nut wished that he had camped with them so they could camp one night before getting back to Pansy. It was only a half-day's ride and no reason to stop before he reached his own camp.

It had snowed a little during the night, but the sun had come out, and most of it was gone by the time Right Nut and Cheyenne Star left the camp. Right Nut was very proud he had a second wife, two ponies, and still kept his wolf and pony hides. Pansy would have been proud of him if he had kept the hides and got the ponies, but this second wife?

The Indian girl was a very willing worker and helped Pansy with the evening meal, carrying wood, and hauling water. Pansy began to think that this second wife might be a good idea.

That night, as Right Nut and Cheyenne Star panted, groaned, and made passionate love next to her in the tent, she was not so sure it was a good idea.

CHAPTER 29

"I hear you are sniffing around Golden Finch"

Malcolm had a fine evening of dancing and dining with Golden Finch. She was a true southern lady. She had been married to a French Count for seven years. They had a son who was six, but her ex-husband received custody of the boy since he was a French citizen. She wanted to bring him to the United States and told Malcom that she missed the boy very much. Her husband had left her a large cash settlement plus a large vineyard and winery in southern France.

She said she could not go to the City Park to hear him speak, as she had plans to leave for home early in the morning. He walked her to her room, and she gave him a peck on the cheek. She said she could not invite him in, as it was the wrong time of the month for her. She did promise to be his date and special guest at the Winter Ball at Cottontail.

When Malcolm arrived at City Park he could not believe his eyes. Thousands of people all cheered as he stepped down from the rented carriage that had brought him. True to her word, Julie Penn had the speaker's platform loaded with dignitaries. Julie was not on the platform, but standing down at the stairs that led to it, giving last minute instruction to everyone near the platform.

She informed Malcolm that he would be the second speaker, and after him, the Governor would speak. The Mayor would introduce him, as the Mayor was a much better speaker than the Governor was.

The Mayor introduced himself, then addressed the audience. "We have with us today our next Governor. He is the most forward thinking man in the entire south. He is owner of one of the south's most successful plantations. And his forward thinking is the reason for its success. With his forward labor policies he is able to extract the most efficient and productive output from his black labor force. He has recently experienced the tragedy of losing his beloved wife. However, this tragedy did not stop him from coming to the aid of our beloved south. He is a devoted family man with two little girls, and on a recent trip to Cuba, he adopted an additional little girl."

(At this point in the speech, Miss Penn handed the Mayor a note).

"The little lady has just handed me a note," the Mayor said. Then he read to the audience. "As President of the United States of America I take

great pleasure in endorsing Malcolm Chandler II for Governor of your great
State."

There was only a modest cheer as the President was a northerner.

"What more can be said?" the Mayor continued. "It is with great pleasure, as Mayor of this great City, that I give you our next Governor of this
great State, Malcolm Chandler II."

There was a great burst of cheers as Malcolm took the platform. He
gave his speech, following very close to the way Miss Penn had written. He
was a forceful and eloquent speaker, and the speech was extremely well
accepted.

When he had taken his seat, a heckler shouted. "He is no southerner,
he is a northerner, and he won't fight for us. We educate these niggers and
they will revolt and they won't work."

Miss Penn, who had made her way to the platform, took a whip from
under her long dress and popped a hole about the size of a quarter in the
shoulder of the heckler's shirt. You could see a little blood.

The crowd got a great charge out of this and gave Miss Penn a cheer.
The Governor gave a short speech which, like all the speeches, had been
written by Miss Penn. The very enthusiastic crowd broke up. Malcolm made
his way back to the hotel.

At the hotel he ordered a hot bath, then sent a message over to Possum
at the stable to have the horses ready to go by noon the next day. After the
bath and dinner, he retired to the bar and discussed politics with some of the
gentlemen in the bar. From the information he gleaned from them, he was
sure that he had a good base vote for Election Day. There were some that
believed that strict discipline was imperative in order to keep the slave system in line.

Up early in the morning, Malcolm made his way to the campaign
office. He wanted to give Miss Penn some last minute instructions, or receive
some, which would most likely be the case. He also wanted to take this
opportunity to discuss Bancroft and tell Miss Penn that his chances of showing up in Atlanta were very slim.

He found her in the office, dressed in a long green velvet dress, white
elbow-length gloves, a black hat with lace brim, and a parasol. She greeted
Malcolm and told him of her plans to make a campaign tour of the state.
Her brother had lent her a buggy and a driver from the Penn Lumber
Company. She would close the office, since there wouldn't be much happening before the late summer months. She invited Malcolm to come along
on the statewide tour. He declined, saying he had too many obligations at
Cottontail Plantation. He offered her some money, but she declined, saying
they had plenty of contributions to cover the trip. The trip would also serve
to raise campaign funds. Then the subject of Bancroft came up.

"Mr. Chandler, will you please level with me about Bancroft? He should have been here weeks ago."

"It seems that Bancroft has had second thoughts about you. Your behavior, with the deception of being a man and the fact that you cut an eye out of a young child, was more than poor Bancroft could take."

"Would you please deliver this message to him for me?"

She handed Malcolm a sealed envelope, imprinted with flowers and laced with the smell of lavender.

Just then her carriage, a black Brougham drawn by a white team and driven by a handsome slave, arrived. Malcolm assisted her into the carriage. She leaned out the window and remarked to Malcolm,   "I hear you are sniffing around Golden Finch."

"I guess that is a rather crude way of saying that we did enjoy each other's company one evening."

"She would be a good catch. Her daddy is owner of a bank as well as that big plantation. It is rumored that the Frenchman left her a bundle. You stay right on top of that, if you know what I mean. She would be a good catch and make a great First Lady for the State."

The carriage pulled away.

Malcolm hired a hack and made his way through the streets of Atlanta to the stable. He found no one around, so he dismissed the driver and went to the back of the stable.

There, in a back stall, he found Possum. Possum had a nanny goat jammed up in the corner of the stall and was making love to her with every inch he had. Possum jerked away and the goat made a jump for freedom. Despite the cool day, the sweat was pouring off Possum.

As he tried to catch his breath, Possum said, "Just tryin' to teach that dumb goat a lesson, she got in and ate most our horses' feed las' night."

Malcolm decided that it was best to just let this subject drop.

"Get the horses, and lets get started to Cottontail."

They had ridden in silence for an hour or so when Possum said, "I was at City Park yesterday when you talked. Mary Annabelle tells me there's a paper in Washington City that says all people are equal and that ever'body can have a gun. How come you don' tell the people 'bout that?"

"That paper is called the Constitution and it only applies to white people, not slaves. How did you get to the City Park?"

"I jus' walked. There weren't much goin' on at the stable. A slave can travel 'round pretty good in Atlanta if he behaves hisself. How can it be if the paper says we're equal that it don't apply to slaves? We're people."

"That is just the way it is, and it will never change. Don't you go worrying your head about it."

They rode on. It was not too far to the village where they would spend the night. Malcolm could use the rest and a drink.

CHAPTER 30

"Mother, the baby is my child"

Malcolm and Possum arrived at Cottontail Plantations in good time. The ride home had been cool, but without incident.

Malcolm dismounted at the mansion and sent Possum on to the stables with the horses. Amos met Malcolm on the porch.

"Your mother is in the study. You better go talk to her before you talk to anyone else."

His first thought was that his mother had become ill. She was far from ill, as he opened the study door. Her greeting was cold and sharp.

"Come in and close the door. That little hussy of a Mary Annabelle is pregnant. And, if that is not bad enough, she is telling everybody it is your baby. I, of course, know that is out of the question. You must get rid of her. She has managed to run off Learnet. Now we have no teacher. Mr. Finch, of Finch Plantations, was by the other day and offered a good price for her.

"I should have sold her, but I wanted to get the air cleared about this baby, so I waited until you came home. The Finches are very good to their slaves. I know the baby is not yours, but just the rumor is enough to hurt your campaign and be very hard on the family."

"Mother! The baby is my child."

Lady Chandler fainted dead away. Malcolm called for help and Mary Annabelle rushed to the rescue. Seeing what happened, she ran for the smelling salts and gave Lady Chandler a good whiff. Mary Annabelle had kneeled down to administer the salts, and Malcolm took her by the arm to help her up. Just the feel of her soft warm arm and there it was again. Instant hard-on.

Lady Chandler slowly regained consciousness. With her big belly and flowing black hair, Mary Annabelle seemed to radiate the entire room. Lady Chandler dismissed Mary Annabelle with a sharp order.

"You get out of this room at once!"

Malcolm sat and looked at his mother. Her face was flushed, and tears appeared in her eyes. He addressed her in a commanding tone. "Mother, please try to understand. The deed is done. There is no going back. I have worried and given this much thought. I have thought of selling her. I have thought of denying that the baby is mine, saying it belongs to one of the slave boys. None of this solves any problems. If she claims the baby is mine

114

and I say it is not, chances are the baby will resemble me enough to make me out a liar. We will let her raise the child here at Cottontail. We will not give it the Chandler name. We will see to it that it gets an education. I must ask for your cooperation in this matter. Please do not make a fuss over it, just let things go on as normal. You know that Mary Annabelle is one of the best slaves we have ever had. I see no reason for that to change.

As for the politics of this matter, we will just let it play out. Thomas Jefferson was said to have black children. Please think about this. I must leave now, as I have an important message to deliver to Bancroft."

As soon as Malcolm had left the house, Lady Chandler called Mary Annabelle to her room. She addressed her in a stern, but friendly, manner.

"Malcolm has said that the baby you carry is his. I can see that I must accept this. Please, for the sake of the girls, don't say any more than is absolutely necessary about this.

I ask you to take good care of the child, but do not bring it into the mansion. I want as little family contact with this child as possible. You abide by these simple rules, and I will accept this terrible situation, and things can go on as normal as possible."

Mary Annabelle bowed her head and answered a barely audible, "Yes." Then she went directly to Lady Chandler's room. Checking to see that nobody was looking, she entered and removed a red feather from under Lady Chandler's mattress. She knew that this was the best she was going to get for her and the child.

Malcolm arrived at Hanging Magnolia Plantation and asked for Bancroft. Ojean, the head house servant, answered the door.

"Massah Malcolm, what brings you to Hangin' Magnolia? It's very good to see you again. Do come in."

"I would like to see Bancroft, if he is not busy."

"Oh, he be busy awright. He's in the study doin' book work, but he always gots time to see you."

Malcolm was shown to the study. Bancroft sat at a desk, with his foot bandaged and propped up on a chair. He did not get up to greet Malcolm.

"Come in and help yourself to some brandy and a cigar. I have the damn gout, and it is killing me."

Malcolm did just that. He helped himself to a glass of brandy and a cigar. Then he took a high-backed chair so he could look out the window.

"I have a message for you from Julie Penn."

Bancroft stiffened, but said nothing, as he took the note and began to read.

My dearest, beloved Bancroft,

I have missed you so much. I am sure it was the pressures of the Plantation that kept you from me. Please do not come to Atlanta now as I am on a statewide tour on behalf of Mr. Chandler. You undoubtedly know that I am working in his behalf as manager of his campaign for Governor.

Shortly after I arrived in Atlanta, I had a miscarriage. The baby was a boy and it showed that it was of colored blood, this of course had to come from your family, as I was not bedding any niggers. The doctor said that I probably could not have any more children, this is okay, as I really did not want any. With you being of colored blood, I really think it best for us not to have any. I will come to Cottontail Winter Ball. I have a new dress that you will just love.

I will arrive a few days early and we can plan our wedding, as I want to get married right after the Winter Ball. I will be very busy with Malcolm's campaign later on in the year.

Please make arrangements for our wedding at the little chapel in the Village.

I love you.

Julie

Bancroft handed the note to Malcolm, who read it and had to smile.

"You are on your own on this one, she is very much a take charge girl."

"I am not going to marry her. It is most likely she has the colored blood."

"You have to let her come to the Winter Ball, as she is very important to my campaign, and I asked her to come."

"You take her to the Ball, even marry her if you wish, I want nothing to do with her."

" I can't take her to the Ball. I have already asked Golden Finch to be my date and special guest."

Bancroft looked at Malcolm and asked, "Did you ask every woman in Atlanta to come to the Ball?"

"Yes, I did ask several and a good many men. It will be good for my campaign."

Bancroft shook his head and said, "This is going to be a very interesting Winter Ball. Do you plan on announcing that you are the father of Mary Annabelle's baby at the Ball?"

"No! I have discussed this with Mother. We decided to keep Mary Annabelle and let her have the baby and raise it. I ask you, please do not discuss or gossip about this baby."

That ended the conversation, and Malcolm headed home. He was not sure just how Bancroft felt about him. He hoped, beyond hope, that he could still be a good friend with him.

On his way back to Cottontail Mansion, he found Amos working in the blacksmith shop. There was an old man in the village with only one leg, and Amos had volunteered to make him a wooden leg. Malcolm stopped to talk with Amos.

"You better make that leg out of a wood that beavers don't like."

Amos laughed and assured him that he had learned his lesson about beavers and wooden legs.

"Where is Catfish? He is usually just like your shadow."

"He is missing. We can not find him anywhere. He has been gone for several days. I gave up our search this morning. I guess he ran away."

"That is impossible, he loved you. He would never run away."

At that moment, a shadow fell over the door of the blacksmith shop. Both men looked out and saw an elephant standing in front of the shop. Perched atop the elephant was little Catfish. He had a smile on his face from ear to ear. Amos went out and helped the boy down. The elephant started to walk away and, with a stick, Catfish stopped the elephant and brought it back to the shop. He rubbed the elephant's trunk and the huge beast wrapped his trunk around the small body and set him back up on his back. Catfish beamed with smiles of delight. As hard as Amos tried, he could not get any information out of Catfish about where the elephant had come from, or where Catfish had been. The animal walked as though his feet were sore. Amos and Malcolm decided that the pair must have traveled quite a distance.

Amos scratched his head. "You know the other day Catfish and I went to the Village. I remember him looking at a circus poster on the wall of the general store. I can't remember where the circus was, but there was a picture of an elephant on it. Do you suppose that Catfish ran away to see the circus?"

Malcolm tried to make signs to Catfish to ask about the circus. He jumped around like a monkey and swung from a rope in a tree, then he marched like he was beating a big drum. Catfish smiled and nodded that he understood.

"He sure acts like he has seen a circus. You don't suppose that he stole that elephant?" Malcolm asked Amos.

The two men began to laugh, and then it dawned on them, what were they going to do with an elephant, let alone one that was most likely stolen?

They motioned for Catfish and his elephant to follow, and they walked toward the mansion.

On the way, they had to pass the plantation's vegetable garden. The elephant decided it was time for supper. He relished pulling carrots, and ate pumpkins, vine and all. Catfish sat on his back and seemed very happy to see his pet getting something to eat. Malcolm and Amos tried to save the garden. It is not easy to save a garden from a hungry elephant. When they arrived at the mansion, Catfish ran back to his little shack and returned with the circus poster. He proudly showed it to Malcolm and Amos. It showed that the circus was playing in Savannah, a good long way from the plantation.

By this time, quite a crowd had gathered. Catfish sat on his elephant, smiling and acting like a king. Malcolm's three girls came to see the elephant. Catfish slid down, took his stick and poked the elephant, and the elephant very carefully lifted each little girl, one at a time, up on his back. Catfish walked around the yard, and the elephant followed like a dog. The girls squealed with delight. After a while of giving people rides, the elephant went under a big tree and lay down. Catfish ran to his shack, got his blanket, and curled up by the elephant's huge head. In a matter of minutes they were both asleep.

Malcolm woke to a strange sound. He went out on the porch and saw the elephant in the creek spraying himself with water and pulling the long grass along the creek bank. Catfish sat on the bank, and once in a while the elephant would spray him with water. His only thoughts were how to get rid of this elephant.

Catfish saw Malcolm on the porch and came to him, pointing at the elephant and smiling. Malcolm sat Catfish down and tried to sign to him that the elephant must go. The elephant tried to follow Catfish up on the porch. He placed his huge front foot on the step and it crumbled. He did not stop until every step and the floor of the porch was crushed. The porch finally gave completely away, and came crashing down on top of Malcolm and Catfish.

No one was hurt. Malcolm finally got Catfish to understand that he had to take the elephant to the paddock with the horses. Upon entering the paddock, a colt about three days old ran up to the elephant. The elephant took one sniff of the colt and decided it didn't like colts. He picked up the colt and slammed it to the ground, killing it instantly. Catfish managed to get the elephant back on the lawn. As the plantation's population got out of bed, they came to see the elephant. Catfish was having the time of his life giving rides on his pet. This was at least keeping the elephant out of trouble.

Malcolm saw two men riding up the lane, he was most happy when he saw that one was the sheriff. They reined up and stepped off their horses.

The sheriff introduced the man with him as Mr. Threering. The sheriff explained that several days ago Catfish had shown up at the circus. He had shown an interest in the elephant and seemed to have no owner or family so Mr. Threering let him help the elephant trainer take care of "Huge", that was the elephant's name. Then one morning Catfish and the elephant were missing. He explained that it was hard to follow the animal, as the boy and animal only traveled at night and hid in the forest during the day.

Malcolm was only too happy to have Mr. Threering take the animal. He was a kind, jovial sort and promised not to press charges against Catfish. He had an attachment that went around the elephant's neck to lead him behind the horse. He explained that the elephant was very well trained and would follow the horse. As they started down the lane Catfish began to cry and ran after the elephant. The elephant turned and lifted the boy onto its back. Amos went and got the boy off the elephant and explained to him that the elephant had to go home.

Mr. Threering started off again and the same thing happened. Amos again retrieved the boy. This time Mr. Threering asked if he might buy the boy, as he was good with the elephant. Now Amos, being a northerner, did not believe in selling human flesh. On the other hand, he could sure use the money. To clear his conscience, Amos drew a line in the dusty road between him and the elephant, signing to Catfish that he could go with the elephant or stay with him. Catfish put one foot on each side of the line and would not give an inch. Finally, after much signing and a few tears, Catfish stepped over the line on the elephant's side. As they went down the road Amos stood on his side of the line with tears in his eyes and cash in his hand.

CHAPTER 31

"Daddy what is he doing, did he hurt my mare?"

It was only five days until the Winter Ball. Julie Penn had not shown up or even been heard from. This pleased Bancroft very much, but was a worry to Malcolm.

Silas Vender had been by with his Christmas merchandise and delivered a note from Golden Finch saying she would arrive the day before the ball. Lady Chandler, with the help of the house girls, had made ready for the ball. She was surprised at what good taste Mary Annabelle had in decorating the ballroom. In fact she really liked the girl, but every time she looked at her big belly and knew that it was Malcolm's child she almost got sick.

Silas Vender had told Malcolm of a horse trader who had come down from Canada with a large string of horses and mules. He was going to sell them at auction in a town not too far from Cottontail. Malcolm decided to take Shorty Rideout and Evelyn Lucille to the sale with him. What he really needed was a new jack. He kept a good jack to breed mares and raise mules for the cotton fields, and his old jack had died.

When they arrived at the auction place, they spent a day viewing the man's sale offering. He had one big sorrel jack that Malcolm really liked. He knew that it would be very popular and very expensive. He also had a pair of matched ponies, both pintos, that Malcolm wanted to buy for the little girls for Christmas. His racing stock did not look that great, however there was a pen of two-year-olds that showed some promise.

He told Evelyn Lucille that she could buy one. He thought it would be a good way for her to learn this aspect of the business world. She was the happiest girl in the world. She spent the rest of the afternoon in the pen with the young horses. That night she could not sleep, thinking which one she should buy.

She was in love with two of them, a dun and a steel gray. She woke her dad up at four a.m. and wanted help with her decision. Her dad told her that was an easy decision.

"Buy the best one," he said.

It so happened that the little dun was the very first horse to sell. She had decided on him. She had never been to an auction and got all mixed up, raising her own bid. The auctioneer was very nice to her and explained that

120

she had raised her own bid. Then she got nervous and missed the bid, and the horse sold to someone else. She looked at her dad with tears in her eyes.

"I thought you told me the steel gray was the best horse," Malcolm teased her.

The big jack came into the ring, and he really looked good. The owner had cleaned and trimmed him up. His handler showed how gentle he was by jumping on his back and picking up his feet. Malcolm was right, he did cost a lot, but Malcolm had one of the best jacks in the entire South.

The ponies sold together, and Malcolm got them without paying an arm and a leg. Near the end of the sale, the steel gray came in. Evelyn Lucille had caught on by this time, and she got her at what Shorty and Malcolm thought was a very good price.

Getting ready to take their new purchases home, they first tied one pony to the buggy and then tied the other pony to his tail. Shorty had ridden a saddle horse and he led the new jack. The gray mare was tied to the other side of the buggy.

What they did not know was the little mare was in heat. When the new jack saw, her he went wild. The breeding of a jack to a mare is a very dramatic sight for one whom has not witnessed it. A jack has a very large male organ for the size of the animal. The braying of a jack is loud and a different sound. The jack bit the mare on the neck, brayed very loud, and mounted her. When the jack removes his organ from a mare, the head of it is about the diameter of a dinner plate. It comes out with a sound very much like plunging a toilet.

Evelyn Lucille watched this whole process with horror.

"Daddy what is he doing? Did he hurt my mare?"

"No honey, he is just mating with your mare. He is planting a seed in her, and in eleven months you will have a little baby mule."

After some thought, Evelyn Lucille commented. "It would be a lot easier with a rake and a hoe."

The party started on their way back to Cottontail. The gray mare pulled back some at first, but soon learned and led right along.

They had not gone far when Evelyn Lucille asked, "Daddy, did somebody do that to Mary Annabelle to make her belly so big?"

Malcolm felt the sweat starting as he answered. "Yes." He was very happy when the conversation did not go farther.

Evelyn Lucille was thinking as she rode along. "I think that must be what big people call sex. I don't know what I would have done if Catfish had done that to me," she thought silently.

When they passed through the little village, Malcolm saw that Julie Penn's team was tied to the hitching post in front of the chapel. Malcolm did not try to look her up, as he did not have time to talk with her. When they arrived at Hanging Magnolia, he passed the information on to Bancroft about what he had seen. They left the little ponies at Hanging Magnolia, as it was a good place to hide them from the little girls until Christmas.

Back in the village at the little chapel, Julie was talking to the minister. She was surprised to discover that no arrangements had been made for her wedding. She explained to him that there would be a wedding. She gave him the date and time and informed him that about fifty people would attend. Then she went across the street to the café and made arrangements for a reception. She said there would be about two hundred people, and she wanted it catered on the glade at Cottontail Plantation. She said to send the entire bill to Penn Lumber Company in Atlanta.

Then she was off to Hanging Magnolia. She got off at the main house and sent her driver to the stable with the team. When he answered the door, Ojean, the house servant, did not recognize her as Mr. Hardnails. She asked to see Bancroft. She was dressed in a long dress and had quite long, blond curls hanging out from under a straw bonnet. She looked quite nice. She was shown to the study where Bancroft was still laid up with gout. She took his hand and gave him a kiss on the cheek. With a big smile, she lifted her skirt and said, "Look, no underwear."

This was too much for Bancroft. He stood, took her by the hand, and led her to his bedroom. They spent the entire afternoon locked in each other's arms, legs, mouths and what have you. About midway into this afternoon of mad passion, she announced her plans for the wedding. There was no way that Bancroft could say no, and he was not real sure he wanted to.

He did manage to get a promise out of her that she would never reveal that she was once Mr. Hardnails. As far as he knew, Malcolm was the only one who knew, and he could swear him to their secret.

The Winter Ball was a huge success. People from all over the state arrived, dressed in their best finery. Golden Finch chose a black and brown velvet gown that was not as full as most worn during the period. Her long, auburn hair flowed over bare shoulders. She danced and conversed with the guests in the form of a true southern lady. Golden was an excellent dancer and dripped with grace and southern charm. She won the heart of every man and the admiration of every lady.

Julie Penn looked very nice in her green dress. She could not keep her hands off Bancroft and seemed to enjoy dancing with anyone. Due to the gout, Bancroft did very little dancing, and it was hard for him. Despite her best efforts, it was apparent that the women at the ball did not really like her. Before the night was over, she had asked every man at the ball to be sure to vote for Malcolm.

Mary Annabelle's job for the night was to check the guests' coats. Malcolm had Amos build a half-door to the cloakroom that would conceal Mary Annabelle's condition.

Malcolm gave a short speech that was laced with a little politics. It was very well received. Malcolm played the piano during intermission, and this too was very well received.

Julie announced her wedding engagement to Bancroft during the intermission. The wedding date was set for New Year's Day, and everybody was invited to the reception on the glade at Cottontail. This was news to Malcolm. Then, as the dance progressed, she distributed her fifty invitations to those she believed to be the fifty richest people at the Ball. This behavior did not set well with many of the guests.

The ball ended about three a.m. Malcolm had had a bit of bourbon and so had Golden Finch. Malcolm walked her to the door of her guestroom. She looked up and down the hall and almost pushed him into the room. She sat down on the bed and removed her shoes.

"Malcolm, I guess I am a bit drunk, but I have thought about the opportunity that we missed that night in Atlanta and we are not going to miss another chance. We are not kids. Please come here."

He walked over to where she sat on the bed. She unbuckled his belt, and his pants dropped to the floor. She massaged him with a soft and pleasant vigor. She stood, turned around, and he unlaced her dress. It fell to the floor.

They fell back on the bed, and she opened a jar of some light green ointment that was on the nightstand. It had the soft smell of mint. She applied a generous portion to him and did the same to herself. It gave him a gentle, warm feeling as she pulled him on top of her. She teased him until he was almost insane with desire. With the tingling of the ointment and the action of the lubricant, when she did open to him he almost wished he had a plank nailed across his ass to keep from falling in. They were both tired, and the session of lovemaking was short but wonderful. They fell asleep in each other arms.

Malcolm tried to leave her room without being seen and bumped into Mary Annabelle in the hall.

CHAPTER 32

"Pansy took Cheyenne Star to the outhouse and showed her how to us it."

Snowflake was busy serving supper to a family of immigrants on their way west when she saw Right Nut riding in with Pansy and the Indian girl. Left Nut was in the trading post with some customers. Pansy did not want to cause a scene in front of her paying guests. After the trio had put their horses away, Snowflake fed them in the kitchen. Cheyenne Star had learned only a little English so Snowflake could speak freely.

"Who is this girl?" Snowflake demanded.

Right Nut knew that he had better start his defense early.

"She is Cheyenne Star. She is a very good worker. A Big Chief of the Cheyenne gave her to me. He said no Indian should have only a black wife."

Snowflake was so mad.

"Who will feed her, where will she sleep? She can't speak English. She will be homesick without her people."

Right Nut had expected the questions and had had a couple of days to think of the answers.

"She can eat with us, she will sleep with Pansy and me. Pansy has already taught her to speak a few words of English."

Pointing at Pansy, Cheyenne Star said, "Pansy." Pointing to her husband, she said, "Right Nut."

Then she got up and started to work, clearing the dishes. Snowflake knew that they had to have more help for the growing business. If they all wanted to sleep together and if she would work, what the hell? She'd give it a try.

Right Nut explained that there were no buffalo, but he had some nice wolf skins that would bring a good price in their Trading Post.

Pansy took Cheyenne Star to the outhouse and showed her how to use it. She thought this was very strange, but learned quickly.

Things at the Nut Road House and Trading Post went very well for the next few weeks. Right Nut had lost a lot of weight, but in the process he had both Pansy and Cheyenne Star with child. Snowflake was getting a middle age spread, and Left Nut began jealously eyeing Right Nut and his two pretty young wives.

It was in the dead of winter and colder than a well digger's ass. Business was slow, so Left Nut decided to go west. He had heard some of the guests at dinner talking about vacations, and he decided he needed one. He didn't dare tell Snowflake, or she would not let him go. Especially if she knew that he was planning to bring home another wife. He told Right Nut about his plans and swore him to secrecy.

One morning when Snowflake was busy with guests, he slipped out to the barn and left. When Snowflake found him missing, she was very worried and wanted Right Nut to go find him. Then she found most of the cash out of the jar was gone, and two of the best horses were also missing. Right Nut finally had to give in and tell Snowflake about Left Nut's planned vacation. He did not mention the fact that he also planned to bring home another wife.

Left Nut had ridden for several days. His camps had been cold and lonely, yet it felt good to be out alone. He finally found the Cheyenne winter camp. Chief Passing Water mistook him for his friend, Right Nut, whom he had given the wife. In a mixture of Cherokee, Cheyenne and English, communication attempts went down hill quickly. Left Nut could not understand why the Chief was insulted when he requested a wife. The chief called a council meeting and the elders decided to take Left Nut prisoner. It made no sense for a man to come back for another wife and bring no ponies to trade.

He was turned over to the women, they stripped off his clothes and gave him a breechcloth. They took his horses, saddle and packs. They drove wood splinters under his fingernails and made him scrape buffalo hides. The only good news for poor Left Nut was that he did have a small, warm lodge to sleep in.

The women beat him, worked him, and made fun of him. Left Nut was a willing worker and behaved himself. In about a month he had gained the respect of most of the Cheyenne women, and he had also learned some of their language.

He thought for sure that Right Nut would come for him, but the weather was cold and Right Nut never showed up. One day, he asked the head squaw if he might speak to the chief. He was able to explain to the Chief that he was Right Nut's twin brother. The Chief had never heard of such a thing and sent him back to the women. The Chief told the council that the prisoner was a liar, as no two men looked exactly alike.

There was one middle-aged squaw that only had one arm and was very ugly. None of the braves would take her for a wife. She also had a problem with her nose constantly running. In fact, her name was Running Nose. On the night after the council meeting, when the Chief sent him back, Running Nose slipped into Left Nut's lodge. It was dark in the lodge and

Left Nut was very lonesome so he welcomed her to his blankets. She was so delighted to finally have a man that the next morning, she went to the chief and asked that Left Nut be made her husband and accepted into the tribe. The Chief thought this a good idea. Even though he thought Right Nut was a liar, he had been a good worker and caused no trouble.

After a short ceremony, which Left Nut did not understand, Running Nose led him back to his lodge. She just looked awful in the daylight. She expanded his lodge and made him a fine meal. A little later a young brave brought back one of his horses and a saddle. The weather had turned very bad and Left Nut knew that he could not travel back to Snowflake even if he could get away from Running Nose.

Left Nut slept very little that night. He must make a break for it as soon as possible. His life with Running Nose was unbearable.

The next morning it was raining and below freezing, coating the entire camp with a sheet of ice. One could hardly stand up. Running Nose was fixing breakfast in their lodge. It got pretty smoky so Left Nut went outside to get some air. He noticed a squaw bundled in a blanket beside one of the lodges. With great care to keep from falling, he made his way to the poor creature. Much to his surprise, when he pulled back the blanket, he found Cheyenne Star.

She was very close to death. He called for Running Nose. Together they managed to get Cheyenne Star into their lodge. Slowly they gave her water and let the breakfast fire warm her. She finally opened her eyes. The first thing she saw was Left Nut, whom she mistook for Right Nut. Cheyenne Star covered her head and began to sob. Running Nose gently removed the blanket from her head, this time she saw Running Nose. She grabbed her in a giant hug and sobbed how happy she was to be home.

The storm broke the next day to a bright winter sun. The Cheyenne winter camp was about out of food and wood. The bright day was spent gathering wood, and a hunting party was sent out.

Cheyenne Star had run away from Right Nut and Snowflake in the dead of winter. Her journey to the Cheyenne winter camp had been dangerous and very cold. When she was only about a mile from the village her pony fell on the ice and dumped her. Before she could recover, the pony ran off. She walked to the village, but was about dead and very disoriented. She slumped down beside the lodge, and that was where Left Nut had found her. She had hated it with Snowflake and Left Nut. The thing she hated the most was the outhouse. It smelled badly. She did not mind the work, but sorely missed her friends in the village. Pansy would seldom let her share Right Nut. She was so happy to be home.

Left Nut asked Cheyenne Star to go to Chief Passing Water and tell him that he was not Right Nut and that he no longer wanted a wife. He just wanted his two horses and packs and be allowed to go home.

Cheyenne Star made a good case for Left Nut, and the Chief said it was all right to go. There was a break in the weather, and Left Nut was very happy to ride out of the village. He got a late start and made it about ten miles east of the village when he decided to camp. He made a small shelter and built a nice fire. He was about the happiest Indian on the southern plains. Along about midnight he felt something crawling into his blankets. It was Running Nose. He did not need this.

CHAPTER 33

"I am about 5 legs behind."

Things at Cottontail had settled back to their regular routine. The Winter Ball guests had all gone home and Christmas had been a success. The little girls loved the new ponies and learned to ride with great success.

It was the day before New Year's Eve and New Year's Day was the wedding day for Bancroft and Julie. Bancroft had many thoughts about this marriage. He did not think he really loved her, then again he got on well with her. Maybe he did not know what love was. She was excellent in bed, and he felt sure that she loved him.

She had gone to Atlanta to get some of her things and had arrived back that afternoon. Bancroft had given her a slave girl as a maid. In fact it was the older sister of the young fellow she had popped the eye out of. She was a very faithful fourteen-year-old girl named Alicia.

Julie had asked Golden Finch to be her matron of honor. Malcolm was to be the best man. Malcolm was happy to have Golden back at Cottontail for a visit. Even with Julie's pushy manner, she and Golden seemed to be good friends.

Julie's bridal gown was white lace with a bright red sash. She had a long, white veil that draped down to her belly button. For something borrowed and something blue, she borrowed a pair of blue underpants from Golden. For something old, she wore a diamond necklace that had been her grandmother's.

Golden's dress was white cotton with a red belt. She wore red shoes. She did not plan to stay long, so she had loaned her only underpants to Julie.

The organ played, "Here Comes the Bride." Julie's brother was to give her away, as he was her only family. When they reached the altar, there was no minister. They waited and waited some more. Finally, a young slave boy ran in the back of the chapel and handed Bancroft a note. It read:

> Very sorry. I have become very ill and can not make the wedding.
>
> Get someone to perform the ceremony and I will sign the certificate.
> Signed,
> The Right Reverend Royal Flush

Bancroft turned to the congregation and read the note.

"Is there anyone here who has had any religious training?" he asked.

Amos rose from the pew. "I have been raised a Quaker in Pennsylvania and would be happy to perform the ceremony."

In truth this went over, literally, like a fart in church. With this southern congregation, it was a poor place for a Yankee Quaker to perform the ceremony, everybody thought. But no one objected, and Amos took his place behind the altar and read the marriage vows for the couple.

The two little girls, Mandy Ann and Loupe Rose, had been placed in charge of getting the rice and distributing it to the guests to toss on the new bride and groom. They got into the kitchen and took some black pepper and laced each bag they handed out with pepper.

Just outside the chapel, everyone was lined up to toss the rice, and when they did, the bride and groom went to sneezing and coughing. The scene was utter chaos. Nobody knew what was wrong, so they just kept tossing the rice and pepper on the poor couple. The little girls were nowhere to be found. If only they would have looked up in the large Georgia pine in the churchyard, they would have seen the girls, with hands over their mouths to restrain their giggles.

The wedding party made their way to Cottontail for the reception. Julie took Alicia to the room assigned to her and was having Alicia help her out of her gown. Just as Alicia was unlacing the corset, Julie let a big fart. Poor Alicia could not help but giggle. Julie turned and slapped her with all her force, knocking the poor slave girl to the other side of the room.

"You black people can not do anything right. If Bancroft had not made me give up the whip, I would teach you a lesson you would not soon forget."

Alicia gathered herself and, with tears streaming down her black cheeks, went back to helping her mistress dress.

The reception on the glade went very well, with everyone enjoying themselves. The only disturbance was when Mandy Ann and Loupe Rose, dressed as Indians, came riding through the party at top speed and shouting blood curdling war cries. It was a good way to show off the Christmas ponies.

That evening, with the entire guest population gone, and Julie and Bancroft off on their honeymoon, things were quiet at the Cottontail Plantation. Mary Annabelle helped Malcolm get the girls to bed early.

Malcolm, Golden, Lady Chandler and Amos had a tranquil dinner, served by Mary Annabelle, out on the veranda. This could not help but make Lady Chandler a bit nervous, wondering if Malcolm had mentioned to Golden the reason for Mary Annabelle's condition. Lady Chandler had loved Glena Lee very much. It was hard to see Malcolm with this new lady.

With her long, auburn hair and her buttermilk skin, with so much southern charm, she would be perfect for her son.

Amos dropped his fork, and as Mary Annabelle bent over to pick it up, she managed to expose the hard black bosom with the ripe blackberry nipple to Malcolm. There it was again. Instant hard-on.

After a nice meal of rabbit stew garnished with mustard greens and okra, the ladies retired to the study. There was chill in the night air. Malcolm and Amos remained on the veranda and smoked and sipped brandy.

"I suddenly have found myself in the wooden leg business," Amos said. "I made some for friends and people heard about it, and they have been sending in orders. I am about five legs behind. I was wondering, with things slow now in the winter, if I might get a couple of slaves to help me until spring planting starts? I am getting a very good price for the legs and would be happy to pay for the use of the slaves."

"Amos, you have been a great asset to this plantation. Your visits to the slave quarters each morning and meetings with Possum and Olaf seem to make things run very smooth, and the slaves seem very happy. You use all the slaves you want. The one named Black Butch appears to be very handy around the shop. You may want to try him."

"When I talk to Possum and Olaf in the mornings, I pass along some of my Quaker training to them. They seem to respond very favorably to a peaceful approach."

The next morning there were good-byes to Golden, who was off to France to see her son and take care of some of her business affairs. She had made arrangements with an importer in Savannah to buy her entire production of wine. This made things so much simpler than trying to market it all over Europe.

Malcolm met with some of the leaders of the community to persuade them to build a school in the village. That way they would not have to replace Learnet, and he thought it would be better for the girls to mix with some of the other white children from surrounding plantations, and some of the white village children.

CHAPTER 34

"May I ask why you are turning against Mr. Chandler?"

Bancroft and Julie took her brougham and the white team as far as the railroad and then took the train to Savannah. Alicia was with them. This was her first time away from the plantation, and she was scared to death.

By the time they had ridden the train to Savannah, Alicia had begun to relax a little. She tried very hard to please Julie. The poor child had to endure several hard slaps and many tongue-lashings. Bancroft tried to persuade Julie to be patient because the child would learn and she was doing her best.

They had a fine room in Savannah and spent many hours on the waterfront and in the best cafés. This was a hand in hand honeymoon and both parties enjoyed it very much. Bancroft was always surprised at what a lady his wife could be when the situation demanded it. An example of this was when Golden Finch invited them to the finest restaurant to dine with her and her new wine broker. It was the day before her ship was to sail to France. They had a fine dinner at a cabaret that served some of Golden's finest wine. Bancroft and Julie, both modestly full of fine wine, enjoyed their bed until about ten the next morning.

After getting dressed, Julie announced that she was going to go visit Malcolm's competition in the race for governor. She told Bancroft that she needed to analyze the competition. He was a lawyer that no one seemed to know very much about.

When she entered his office she saw a small, but very rotund, man behind the desk. He was bald and sported a pencil-line mustache. What hair he had was black. He had a stub cigar in the corner of his mouth and brown tobacco juice running down his chin. Julie introduced herself.

"Mr. Filmore MacScumber, I am Mrs. Julie Penn Whitesides. I am Campaign Manager for Mr. Malcolm Chandler."

"The hell you say. What do you want with me?"

"I was wondering if you would like to be the next governor?"

"Well, of course I would. Why else would I be running."

"I am in a position to guarantee you the governor-ship if you will do exactly as I say. But, you must guarantee me a good state job when you win."

131

Through his fat pudgy eyelids, Mr. MacScumber studied her with barely visible eyes. "Mrs. Whitesides, let me get this straight. You are the campaign manager for Mr. Chandler, yet you come in here and tell me you can promise me this election?"

"Mr. MacScumber, you are not a very attractive candidate, but you do seem to hear well."

They both sat in absolute silence. Mr. MacScumber broke the silence. "You had better come to my private office."

He took Julie into a small room where a spinster looking middle-aged woman was working on some books. The room was unkempt and littered with law books.

"Miss Passion, would you please excuse us?" Mr. MacScumber ordered. Miss Passion took her books and retired to another office. When the door was shut, Julie took over.

"I have written a handbill which we will distribute all over the state three days before the election. It contains enough damaging information about Malcolm Chandler that you will receive well over fifty percent of the vote. Of course it is most important that no one knows that I am behind this. There will be no lies in this handbill. I will go on working very hard for Mr. Chandler. I will do a good job,"

"Just what will this magical handbill say?" he asked.

"Oh, no. You do not get that information until three days before the election. You must not make any public appearances or give any speeches during the campaign. I understand that your good friend and poker playing buddy, Mr. Ike, has a printing press in his basement."

"Yes, Ike does have a press. He has done work for me from time to time."

"I want you to arrange for me to use that press in private. I will print the handbills and put them in a safe at the Southern Bank and Trust. You will hire ten riders on fast horses and three days before the election, I will instruct the bank to release 500 handbills to each of the ten riders. There will be instructions packed with the handbills for each rider. If you want to be governor you will do exactly as I say."

"How do I know I can trust you?"

"My good man, because I have you by the balls. If you want to be governor, do as I say. It is your only chance. I can get Chandler elected in a heartbeat."

"May I ask why you are turning against Mr. Chandler?"

"He changed some wording in a speech I wrote for him, and he expressed some ideas about handling slaves that I do not agree with. That should give you some idea as to why it is always best to do as I say, and only *what* I say."

"I will give this some thought," MacScumber said. "You drop by tomorrow."

"Your thinking time stopped as soon as I entered your office. You tell Mr. Ike that I will be at his place tomorrow night to do the printing. I will see you after the election. You have someone clean you up for your Inaugural Ball. I will be waiting for you in the governor's office when you get there. Good day Mr. MacScumber."

Julie gave Bancroft the excuse that she had to meet with some political people about Malcolm's campaign and left the hotel in the early evening.

She arrived at Mr. Ike's house and was taken to the basement, where she found a rather modern printing press. She had the paper delivered early. It was well after midnight when she finished packaging her ten bundles of handbills enclosed with instructions to each of the riders. She placed them in a trunk, and as soon as the bank opened the following morning, she deposited them in the safe.

The morning found the party packing to catch the train for their return home. Poor little Alicia dropped one of Julie's dresses. Julie went into a rage and slapped the girl very hard, then took her hand and broke her little finger. Bancroft was appalled at his wife's behavior and helped Alicia put a splint on her wounded hand.

While waiting to board the train, Julie caught her heel in the board platform and twisted and sprained her ankle. A young black porter and Alicia helped her to her feet and did all they could to make her comfortable. When Alicia was taking Julie's shoe off, she had a chance to give the ankle a good twist, much to Julie's protest.

As the train made its way through the gray winter day, with soot drifting in the windows, from time to time Bancroft tried to comfort Julie. He did not pay a lot of attention to Alicia's aching hand.

Julie took Bancroft's hand, looked into his eyes and said, "I think we should leave the plantation and move to Atlanta."

CHAPTER 35

"His name will be Rusty Montana."

Spring had come to Cottontail Plantation. The planting season was in full swing. The daffodils and dogwoods were in bloom, and there was new growth on the trees. The new schoolhouse was finished, and a search for a new teacher was under way. One of the applicants was Learnet Readwright. The girls' schooling had been interrupted through the winter, so it was decided to operate the school during the summer months.

Mr. Whitesides had passed away, and Bancroft had been very busy with the operations of Hanging Magnolia. Julie was spending most of her time in Atlanta working on Malcolm's campaign. They had not been able to move to Atlanta, as Julie wanted to do. Bancroft was very cool about the plan.

Golden Finch was due back from France in a few weeks.

Malcolm had gone to Atlanta to work on his campaign with Julie. Amos and Lady Chandler, with the good counsel and help of Possum and Olaf, were managing the Cottontail Plantation.

One beautiful spring morning, Mary Annabelle entered the kitchen. Her belly was flat, and she had a bundle in her arms. She fixed a spot in the corner of the kitchen, lay down the bundle, and prepared for work. Bolo and Alzora stood looking at each other with open mouths. Bolo walked over and opened the bundle.

Looking up at her through garnet eyes and a shock of red hair, was a baby boy. There was no need to open the blanket to see the sex. He looked all boy. He was not black, but a dark shade of brown. Bolo lifted the child into her arms as Alzora came to look at the child. The baby looked back and gave forth with a happy coo.

Bolo turned to Mary Annabelle and said, "Child, it's obvious you had a baby las' night. You sit right down. You can't work for a while. You must be very weak. Havin' these babies has killed many a women, and here you are as if nothin's happened."

"Havin' a baby don' amount to much. I woke in the night and had a bad belly ache. It got worse and worse. The next thing I know, there's this baby 'tween my legs howlin' his lungs out. I got up, cleaned things up, and let him suck a little while. That really feels good, lettin' him suck. I love him so much."

134

Bolo unwrapped the baby. "Child, we must clean him up a little better. Alzora, you get a tub of warm water."

Bolo lowered the boy in the pan, took a kitchen knife and cut the cord and tied it off. When the baby was all clean, Mary Annabelle took him and let him nurse for a short time. They made Mary Annabelle sit while they finished cooking breakfast.

Lady Chandler, as usual, was the first down for breakfast. Mary Annabelle jumped to her feet and helped serve breakfast. Lady Chandler did not notice the change in Mary Annabelle, until she heard a baby crying in the corner of the kitchen.

The ever-helpful Bolo picked up the baby and brought it to Lady Chandler. She knew better than to hand the baby to its grandmother. She slowly opened the blankets. When Lady Chandler saw those garnet eyes and red hair, she fainted dead away. After the smelling salts had been administered, Lady Chandler sat and ate her breakfast in silence.

There was some to-do over the baby, as the household had their breakfasts. Mandy Ann commented that he was not very pretty. Loupe Rose wanted to hold him, and Evelyn Lucille hoped he didn't grow much, so he would be a good jockey. Mandy Ann suggested that he should be named "Rusty", as he was the color of rust.

Mary Annabelle took both of Mandy Ann's hands in hers and looked the child in the eyes. "Mandy Ann, that is a very good name. We will call him 'Rusty Montana'. Montana means mountain in Spanish, he will be the brown mountain.

Malcolm arrived home from Atlanta, tired and out of sorts. Julie had run him ragged with speeches and talking to the press. It was late when he arrived, and he went directly to bed. It was about two in the morning when the familiar rap-rap came to his bedroom door. He had not heard it for months. It did arouse his loins, yet he knew better. Mary Annabelle was still very pregnant.

He opened the door and was greeted by Mary Annabelle with Rusty Montana in her arms. She took a seat on the bed.

Malcolm lit the lamp and shined it on the baby. Even in the poor light, he could see the red hair, and noted a definite resemblance to himself in this very small bundle. Mary Annabelle handed the baby to his father. Malcolm took him with a feeling of reserve. That feeling soon left as the child gave him a smile and coo.

"I wanted you to meet your son in private," Mary Annabelle said. "He is a handsome boy and will grow to be a great man, just like his father. I will not bother you with him, and I will try to be a good mother. I love him very much and I truly hope that you can learn to love him too. His name is Rusty Montana. In a few days, I will come and warm your bed."

She took the baby and slipped out of the room and down the dark hall.

Malcolm sat down on the bed where Mary Annabelle had been. The spot felt warm, and there it was again. Heated loins.

He put his head in his hands to slow his swirling thoughts. "I am now the father of a black son. A slave."

He wondered if Lady Chandler had seen the baby. He wondered if he could keep the arrival of Rusty Montana confined to Cottontail Plantation, at least until after the election. He felt good about Mary Annabelle. He knew she would be a good mother for the child. He had always wanted a son, now he had one. Would he ever be able to take him hunting, play ball and go on trips?

Should he give him his last name? Would it be possible to show any love to the boy? Was he sorry he had fathered the boy? No. He could not help but feel warmth towards Mary Annabelle, another emotion that society would never let him show. There were probably thousands of black children across the South that were fathered by planter's overseers and other white fathers. He wondered if they all felt, in some ways, the way he did.

If elected governor, he wondered if he could solve any of the growing social problems of the South, to say nothing of the economic problems. He knew it would take several generations. He wondered if the girls knew that the rust colored baby was their half-brother? Should he tell them now or later? Malcolm fell into a restless sleep.

Malcolm arrived at his mother's room the following morning before she could get to breakfast. He was admitted with a noticeable lack of a smile or her usual friendly greeting.

"I suppose you have seen your son?" she asked tersely.

"Yes, and I think he is a very handsome boy."

"Malcolm, what has come over you? He is a red headed nigger."

"His name is Rusty Montana, because he is the color of rust, and will be strong as a mountain.

"If you polish something that is rusty, it will shine. You cannot polish that baby."

"Mother, don't be too sure about that. He may polish up just fine. You do not have to accept the child, which I know is a lot to ask, but could you please be pleasant about this matter?"

He knew that many of the same questions that had bothered him had to be bothering his mother. He took her by the hand, and they went to the kitchen for some of Bolo's flapjacks and salt pork.

As the baby got a few days older, the three girls just took him over. They played with him just like he was a doll, dressed him, and would get him back to Mary Annabelle's breast in time for meals.   Bolo worried that the girls would kill him for sure, the way they handled him. She found them down by the creek one day and the girls were trying to teach the baby to swim. She scolded Mary Annabelle and told her she must pay closer attention to what the girls did with the little boy.

One day they were playing down by the stable and forgot they had the baby and came back to the mansion without him. When Mary Annabelle asked about him, the girls looked at one another and ran off to the stable to rescue him. He was mad and dirty, but no worse for the wear. Evelyn Lucille fixed a makeshift cradle to strap on the dog, so that he could learn to ride. Her thoughts were that a jockey had to train early. It was rather strange. Nobody seemed to think that he even had a father. It was just Mary Annabelle's baby and everybody on the plantation, black and white, loved little Rusty Montana.

CHAPTER 36

"He took Running Nose and went to the post."

Spring had finally come to Indian Territory. Left Nut had come home about two months earlier. After receiving the cold shoulder from Snowflake for a few weeks, she had at length, taken him back to her blanket.

When he found Running Nose in his camp last winter, Left Nut did not know what to do with her. He didn't dare bring her home. He was scared to escort her back to the Cheyenne winter camp for fear they would make him prisoner again. He couldn't find it in his heart to turn her out in the cold.

There was a small military post not too far from his camp. He took Running Nose and went to the post. He could not make the military understand that he wanted them to take her back to her people. Part of the reason they didn't understand was because nobody wanted to escort the squaw to the camp in the dead of winter. He finally devised a plan. He told Running Nose that she could have anything in the store that she wanted.

"All you have to do is go in, put what you want under your blanket, and walk out."

This sounded like a great deal to Running Nose. Then Left Nut went to the guards and squealed that she would be stealing. She went to the store and put some ribbons and a pound of sugar under her blanket. When she got outside the door, a guard stopped her and asked to see under the blanket. When he found the stolen goods, he took her into custody and locked her in the guardhouse. It was nice and warm and she would be fed. Left Nut saddled up and headed east as fast as his horse could go.

Now Left Nut was home. Spring was in the air. A meadowlark would cut loose now and then with his familiar warble of the spring, while Left Nut sat in his chair on the south side of the cabin soaking up the sun.

The sky was shedding a gentle rain one afternoon when a U.S. Marshal showed up at the Nuts' trading post. He told them of a real bad desperado who was on the loose and thought to be in the territory. He asked if he could put up a wanted poster. The poster showed a tough looking hombre and read, "$500.00 Reward. Dead or Alive." The man on the poster wore a large hat and a beard.

Not long after the poster was placed, a clean-shaven man wearing a derby hat arrived. Right Nut had spent his life hunting and keeping his eyes

138

open and alert. He suddenly realized that this was the same man on the poster. He got Left Nut off to the side and revealed his discovery. After a close look, Left Nut decided that this was the man. Right Nut was pretty disappointed that Pansy was with child, otherwise he could rent her to the stranger and when they were in bed, he and Left Nut could overpower him and earn the reward. It was Left Nut who came up with the plan.

"Let's rent Snowflake and then we can catch him."

Right Nut was skeptical about this.

"Snowflake is your wife. You have never rented her. She may not go for the deal."

"You're right. She is my wife. I know her pretty well and, for $500.00, she would go to bed with the devil.

Snowflake resisted at first, then with the thought of the large reward, she gave in. They fixed snares up on the bed so that Snowflake could slip it over his leg or arm and give the signal to them, and they could pull the snare and have him.

The Nut brothers hid in the next room, with pistols drawn, ready to pull the snare at the signal. Somehow in the confusion, Snowflake got the snare on her own leg instead of the desperado's. She thought they were all ready and gave the signal. Left Nut pulled the snare, jerking Snowflake out of bed onto the floor. Right Nut charged in with his pistol.

"You got me! Shoot the son-of-a-bitch," Snowflake hollered.

It was dark and Right Nut shot in the general direction of the sound and shot Snowflake in the shoulder. The desperado ran out of the cabin without his clothes.

When things settled down and they got the lamp lit, they found the wounded Snowflake, and the desperado gone. It was too dark to go hunting for him, so they doctored Snowflake's shoulder and waited until daylight. The wound was pretty bad, and Snowflake would be out of commission most of the summer. She was one mad German.

At the first gray light, Right Nut and Left Nut went on their manhunt. They had not hunted long when they saw him, wrapped in a blanket he had found, trying to catch a horse in the horse pasture. The horses wanted nothing to do with him with the blanket flapping over him in the half dark, and they kept running off.

"The poster said dead or alive," Right Nut told Left Nut.

He took careful aim and shot him. He hit him in the upper neck, and the man toppled over, dead. Now, due to lack of planning, the Nuts had a problem. The marshal was not around, and they did not know how to collect the reward. The days were getting warmer, and their man would not keep long. In fact, as the sun came up and the morning warmed, there were already big blue blowflies in the wound.

Their first thought was to get the body to Fort Smith where there was a marshal's office. This plan had its problems. It was a three-day trip, and with Snowflake laid up and Pansy ready to give birth, it would leave the trading post short-handed. Not only that, but by the time they got to Fort Smith, the face on the body would be too decomposed to be recognized by the officials.

The other plan was to take the fastest horse and make a dash to Fort Smith to get the marshal. This idea had some of the same problems as taking the body.

Then Right Nut had an idea. There was a bank along the creek that consisted of very good clay. They could make a cast of the desperado's face. When the marshal came back they could show him the cast. They would bury the body, and if necessary, they could dig him up for proof of identity. Thus they could collect the reward.

They got the cast made, and it turned out pretty good except it was backwards. This would have to suffice for now until it was completely dry. Then they decided that the head and face would last longer if they took it to the Ice Cave, which was only a day's ride. They cut off the head, covered it with the good clay, and let it dry a day in the sun. Right Nut took the head and buried it as deep in the cool Ice Cave as he could. Now all they had to do was wait for the marshal.

While waiting for the marshal, they chipped the clay mask from the cast of the face. It looked pretty good but nothing like the picture on the poster. Something had to be done. They took some black horsehair and gave the head a scruffy beard, and put one of Right Nut's old hats on the cast. That did the trick. It was an excellent resemblance to the poster.

In about a month the marshal showed up. They presented him with the cast of the likeness of the desperado and told their story. The marshal was impressed, but said that he could not pay because they did not have a body. Off they went to retrieve the body. When the marshal saw that it had no head he said it would not do for identification. Right Nut rushed to the Ice Cave to get the head, but he found that he had not buried it deep enough, and the varmints had dug it up. The head was gone. He gathered a few pieces of the clay they had on the face and took it back to the marshal.

"I know you people and I believe you," the marshal sympathized. "But my superiors will never believe this story. They must have real solid evidence to prove the identity of the body. They will say you could have killed anybody, removed the head and made this statue from looking at the poster."

The marshal mounted his horse, tipped his hat, and rode away. The head sat in the corner of the trading post for years.

CHAPTER 37

"It is easier to apologize than ask permission."

The campaign was in full swing by the time of the Harvest Ball at Cottontail. Lady Chandler and Mary Annabelle had done their usual good job of decorating the ballroom.

Evelyn Lucille was developing into a pretty good artist. She painted a mural on the wall behind the stage. It was of a racehorse just crossing the finish line, and the jockey was a red headed colored boy. The horse resembled Not-So-Fast. Everybody gave her good marks for the painting. Lady Chandler insisted that she change the hair color of the jockey, which she did. Then, on the night before the ball, she sneaked down and changed it back to red.

She was very proud of the red-headed baby. She had figured out that he must be her half-brother. She said not a word to anybody what she was sure of. If she was going to have a brother, he was going to be a famous jockey. She wanted to show him off the night of the ball. She asked her dad if they, meaning her and the little girls, could dress him up and show him off the night of the ball.

"Daddy, Mary Annabelle has to work the night of the ball. We girls are always taking care of Rusty anyway. Can we just bring him early for a little while? Everyone will want to see him."

"No, not this year. He is too little. Maybe next year you could bring him."

As soon as she got the "no," she knew she had made a mistake. She should have just brought him and said nothing. It was easier to apologize than to ask permission. Now if she brought him, it would be against her father's will. This, she did not think would be wise.

Golden Finch arrived a few days before the ball. She saw baby Rusty in the kitchen. "Oh, what a cute baby. Who's is it?" she asked.

Mary Annabelle stepped up proudly to claim the child. Golden was holding the child.

"I didn't know you were married. I would like to meet your husband."

She took a closer look at the baby and gasped. "I do believe I have met the father. These plantation owners just can't stay away from you pretty slave girls."

It was poor timing, but at that moment Malcolm entered the kitchen. Golden looked at Malcolm and in a very friendly voice said, "Congratulations on this fine son."

Malcolm turned the color of the yet-to-be-invented stoplight. Everyone in the kitchen seemed to work a little harder and bowed their heads a little lower. Mary Annabelle faced the wall and smiled. This was the first step towards her child's acceptance into southern society.

That night, when Golden went to Malcolm's room, she wore a special gown and her best perfume. She slipped into bed and cooed into Malcolm's ear.

"Please give me one of those handsome babies. We could be married right after the ball."

Up to this point, Malcolm had a first class erection. With Golden's request, it melted like a July icicle. She lay by him a few minutes and tried to get his manhood interested, but to no avail. He could hear the sound of her weeping as she slammed the bedroom door.

The next morning when Malcolm came to breakfast, there was Golden holding Rusty and feeding him grits. She gave Malcolm a big smile and handed the baby to Mary Annabelle to finish the job.

"Could we please talk in private?" she asked.

Golden and Malcolm went out in the hall.

"I am very sorry about last night. I just got a little carried away. I do think it is time we at least talked about marriage. We seem to be fitted to each other. I have no problem with your slave child. In fact I have never seen a child that so many people seem to have a genuine love for. It would be my hope that you could refrain from taking Mary Annabelle to your bed."

Malcolm took her in his arms.

"I am the one who should apologize for last night. I guess it was just the mention of a baby. I am not proud of the way Rusty came to be, however, in spite of myself, I am proud of Rusty Montana. Let's end this conversation now. We will pick it up, with serious consideration, after the election."

"I understand and agree," Golden responded.

They kissed and went back to the kitchen.

Bancroft arrived at Cottontail leading a big, good looking, long-legged buckskin behind his brougham. He said he had bought him from a horse trader out of Virginia. He was going to put him in the Harvest Race. Evelyn Lucille looked him over and ran right to Shorty Rideout, who managed the races.

"Put that big buckskin in the same race as Not-So-Fast. He won't see anything but Not-So-Fast's tail if he doesn't have too much dust in his eyes."

Shorty had a lot of confidence in Evelyn Lucille and Not-So-Fast, but the big buckskin looked awesome. Evelyn Lucille had been really working with the Cottontail racing stable. She had made up her mind that Cottontail horses were going to win every race, and Not-So-Fast would win the last race, making him champion.

Every evening before the races, if anyone would have been watching, they would have seen a short, small figure dressed in black, enter Not-So-Fast's stable. The figure carefully lifted his front left foot and placed a nail at the base of the frog of his foot. The nail was not so far in that it would hurt him until he ran and drove it in deeper.

Then the figure patted Not-So-Fast on the nose and said, "Now you can run fast until about the end of the back stretch. When they find the nail and remove it, you will be okay."

The first race went well, and Half-Pint won by three lengths on one of Cottontail Plantation's horses. The second race was the race with Not-So-Fast and the big buckskin. Evelyn Lucille and Not-So-Fast took an early lead, with the buckskin a length behind. This formation held until the end of the backstretch and Not-So-Fast pulled up lame. The big buckskin went on to win the race.

Evelyn Lucille took the lame horse to Possum. She was crying and devastated. Possum picked up the foot and found the nail. He pulled it out and looked at it very closely.

"Honey, somebody's put this nail in 'is foot. We've never had any nails like this. Look at it, it's a nail with a large head like they use on some kinds of roofin'. We've never used 'em here at Cottontail."

"I know just who it was," Evelyn Lucille stated. "It is that awful Julie. I know she is a bad person. I have had that feeling every since Bancroft brought her here. You wait till I get my hands on her."

Evelyn Lucille began to sob in earnest. Possum managed to quiet her and then asked, "Can you keep a secret?"

"Yes."

"You come by my cabin tonight. Don't let anyone see you and you must never, never tell anyone of our meeting."

"Okay."

That night, by the dark of the moon, Evelyn Lucille had never been so scared in her life, as she made her way to the slave quarters. Every dry leaf she stepped on sounded to her like a rifle shot. She imagined dark forms behind each tree. She finally arrived at Possum's cabin. There was a dim light in the window. She rapped on the door and the door opened, but there was nobody in the cabin. She just about ran away when she heard a small female voice say, "Don't be afraid. Come to the window."

Then she saw a rope tied to the door. It ran to the small window in the back of the cabin. Whoever opened the door was outside the window. She froze with a fear that she had never known. "Come to the window," a male voice said.

She slowly made her way to the window. The two voices, in unison, began a low, scary chant. The voices as one, but there was really two or more, gave her instructions. "We have a small gift for you."

A stick came through the window. Tied to the stick with a small thread, was a red feather.

"Take this red feather," the voices continued. "You must never say you have it. You must never say a bad word about Julie Bancroft. You must never accuse her of laming your horse. Put the red feather in the very toe of her shoe. Ask no questions. Now go back."

The voices melted back to the low chant, as Evelyn Lucille slowly backed out of the cabin with the red feather clutched in her hand. When she got to the mansion, she sat down on the porch swing and looked at the feather. Her heart was going a mile a minute. She looked up and saw a figure almost floating as it came from the direction of Possum's cabin headed to Mary Annabelle's cabin.

One thing that Evelyn Lucille had learned from her Dad was to think things out. The cool fall breeze flowed through her hair as she sat swinging on the porch. The best way to handle this was to go right to Julie and confront her. Then she would deny the act, and she had no proof. It would just make her look foolish. She did not understand this red feather business, but in some way it must be to punish Julie. What a joke! How could a feather in her shoe do her any harm? She had to smile at the two slaves trying to hide under the window. Anybody would know that it was Possum and Mary Annabelle.

The next morning, Evelyn Lucille got Mary Annabelle off to the side and asked, "Just what is this business about this red feather?"

"I know nothing about a red feather."

"Oh yes, you do. And if you don't tell me, I am going to father and tell the whole story about last night."

If it had been possible for Mary Annabelle to look pale, she would have looked pale.

"I think this red feather business has something to do with you slaves and Voodoo. You know you are not to practice Voodoo at Cottontail. I will make you a deal. If you will take this red feather back and get rid of it, or whatever, I will say nothing of this to anybody. It will leave me free to deal with that little snip of a Julie in my own way. There is one more thing. When Rusty is older, you are not to teach him any of this Voodoo stuff. He is to grow up to be a Christian as well as a great jockey."

Mary Annabelle took the feather. She would keep it in case she needed it. She would never, but never, get involved with practicing any Voodoo with a white person. They were not smart enough to understand.

CHAPTER 38

"Every chance she got, she preformed a sex act on Malcolm"

The Harvest Ball was a huge success. Amos had built Lady Chandler a new, improved leg and she was able to dance again. His leg business had grown so much that he had to buy two slaves of his own. It was very compromising to his Quaker upbringing.

Malcolm was able to keep Rusty Montana more or less hidden from the guests. Lady Chandler almost had one of her fainting spells when she saw the little redhead in Evelyn Lucille's mural. She scolded Evelyn Lucille, but that was all that came of it.

Evelyn Lucille was still very, very upset about the races. She devised a well thought out plan, and she was ready to confront Julie. She waited until just before Julie was ready to leave for Atlanta.

She took a nail and placed it, just the way it had been placed in Not-So-Fast, in the foot of one of the horses in Julie's white team. She knew this would do little harm to Julie or the horse, but it should deliver the message. Then, the next time she saw Julie, she would casually ask if one of her team had gone lame on the way to Atlanta. What she did not know, was that Mary Annabelle had taken the feather she had given back to her, and managed to place it in the toe of Julie's shoe.

Malcolm and Golden had secretly made plans to hold their wedding in the rotunda of the state capitol building after his inauguration.

After Golden had left, in the middle of the night, the familiar rap-rap came to Malcolm's door. It had been so long that he just could not turn her away. He had never made love to anyone who gave him more pleasure than Mary Annabelle. He was very worried about another baby, but she assured him that she had talked to some of the slave women and they had a method. This, at least, set his mind free to enjoy the pleasures that this black girl could give him. If only she was white, he could love her. Did he love her? A question he did not like to ask himself. He would lay awake at night waiting for the rap-rap and wishing she were white.

The three girls could not be seen without Rusty. Usually they had him propped on a hip, carrying him. One day they had him tied on behind Loupe Rose on her pony. He came loose and bounced along on the hard road for a spell. It skinned him up a little. He hardly let out a whimper. They took him to the creek and washed the gravel out of the shoulder that had taken the hit. It was bleeding some, so they took him back to his mother. The next day the girls fixed a better method to tie him behind the saddle, and they were off again. When they took him on long rides, they would get Mary Annabelle to milk herself into a bottle so they would have lunch for Rusty.

Malcolm was president of the new school board. They had not picked a teacher yet, but had ruled out Learnet Readwright. They voted unanimously that they should have a teacher from the South. This was a disappointment to Amos, as he would have liked to have his daughter closer. A girl from just outside Atlanta won the board's vote as the best candidate.

Malcolm was going to Atlanta, as the election was only two weeks away. It was agreed that Malcolm would interview her, and if he liked her, he was instructed to hire her. That would be his first order of business on arrival. He decided rather than taking a rig, he would just ride Not-So-Fast. He would have loved to take Mary Annabelle, but thought better of it. He would rent a small house and hire, or buy, a housekeeper.

On the way, Malcolm ran into the slave trader that sold Catfish to Bancroft. Despite Malcolm's warning, he was still in business, dealing in worn-out or handicapped slaves. He had a young girl with him who had been born with one short leg. She looked to be in her late teens. She seemed to have a good spirit, despite her deformity. She showed every symptom of bad treatment. Malcolm bought her.

He took the measurements of the girl and wrote instructions to Amos to fit her for a new leg. Then he hired a messenger and sent him back to Cottontail with a rush order for Amos. The messenger was to deliver the new leg to Malcolm in Atlanta. It was not far to Atlanta, so he just let the new girl ride behind him on Not-So-Fast.

They had not ridden far when he felt his manhood on the rise. It seemed to him, if he got close to any young black girl, this happened. She was holding onto him to keep from falling off. Her hand dropped and she felt his stiff manhood. She let out a little giggle and undid his pants. Her hand enclosed on him. Reins went slack and Not-So-Fast took this as an invitation to graze on the tall grass in the barrowpit. There he was, sitting on a horse in the middle of the road, with a black girl giving him pleasure. This was no behavior for the future Governor. He was most happy nobody came along. He gathered up the reins and, at a fast clip, headed to Atlanta.

Upon arriving in Atlanta, they went directly to Bancroft and Julie's house, located behind the larger Penn family home occupied by Julie's brother. Julie was in the yard practicing with her whip. Malcolm was not happy with this behavior, but she assured him it was all right, as she had done this since childhood, and the neighbors just took it for granted.

"Besides I need the practice," she added. "You may want to appoint me warden of the state penitentiary when you become governor."

Bancroft and Julie could not understand why Malcolm had purchased this crippled girl. Malcolm said nothing but thought, if they only knew, he had gotten his money out of her already. The new slave's name was Pegie, and Julie took her to the Penn family slave quarters, giving her a good pop with the whip when they were out of sight of Malcolm and Bancroft.

Julie had already rented a house for Malcolm, and, as luck would have it, had a small cabin for Pegie. Pegie's new leg arrived, and she was delighted with it. It took her a while to get used to it. She was a very good housekeeper, but kind of a nymphomaniac. Malcolm noticed the next door neighbor sneaking to her quarters at night. Then the next night, the other neighbor would come over. Every chance she got, she managed to perform a sex act on Malcolm.

On the fourth day before the election, Julie and Bancroft had Malcolm over for a nice dinner. They had a large ham with squash and some of Golden's French wine. The atmosphere was electric with the excitement of the election. There was no way that they could lose. Nobody even knew the name of the other candidate.

Plans were made for the Inaugural Ball, and there was much discussion of political changes in the state. They were going to be able to save the south. The new policies would strip the northerners of all the ammunition that they were using against the South.

The next morning, Malcolm was so sick he could not get out of bed. He called for Pegie. She did her best to comfort him and brought him hot milk for breakfast. He had cramps and diarrhea. Midmorning, Julie showed up. She said she heard he was sick, and Malcolm silently questioned how that could be. Pegie and he had never left the house. He was too sick to worry about it, so he let it drop.

Julie overlooked telling him about the poster that was all over town, and she knew it was all over the state.

VOTE FOR
MAX MACSCUMBER

HERE IS WHAT MALCOLM CHANDLER II STANDS FOR:

- ✔ He wants to educate the labor force. He has a private teacher for his slaves.
- ✔ He has said: "We must not punish our slaves!"
- ✔ He believes that the North would win if it every came to war.
- ✔ He has stated that someday all slaves will be free.
- ✔ **This man is a northern sympathizer and a traitor to our beloved South.**
- ✔ If this is not enough, he claims to be an honest family man, while he cheated on his poor, ill wife and fathered a child from a slave girl.
- ✔ He smuggled a little slave girl out of Cuba into the U.S.

VOTE MAX MACSCUMBER

CHAPTER 39

"Pegie showed up hand in hand with Catfish."

During Malcolm's short illness, a strange thing came over Pegie. She made no sexual advances towards Malcolm. The neighborhood men were not sneaking in and out of her cabin. He had noticed this change a few days before he became ill. The answer came that evening. Pegie showed up, hand in hand with Catfish.

"Mas Malcolm, I'd want you to meet Mr. Catfish. He don' talk but 'is owner tells me 'is name is Catfish and we're in love. He works with elephants at the circus. Would you please buy 'im so we can be together?"

Catfish smiled and stepped forward and shook Malcolm's hand. You could see in the lad's face that he was glad to see Malcolm again.

"Pegie, how did you come to meet Catfish"

"Well now, Mas Malcolm, you got me this good leg. I can walk pretty good now. The other night when you went to dinner with Miss Julie and Mr. Bancroft, I went to the circus. I met Mr. Catfish, and we just fell head over heels in love."

"Pegie, could this wait a few days? Tomorrow is election, and I have a thousand things on my mind."

"I sure hope you decide to buy 'im. You see, I'm goin' to 'ave a baby. Well, you know how I am, it's hard tellin' who the daddy might be. I got Mr. Catfish to understand this, and he don' care if I 'ave a baby. He just loves me so much. I think he's tryin' to tell me he likes babies."

Malcolm slapped his hand to his forehead.

"Yes, yes, I will try to buy him."

The thought of another red headed slave without a father was just more than he could handle right now.

Pegie planted a big kiss on her Mr. Catfish and, arm in arm, they walked away.

Malcolm went to his campaign office, and it was closed and boarded up. He could not find Julie. He went to her brother's home and was informed that they had not seen her since the day she visited him when he was sick.

He wondered how much damage this poster would do. He felt sure that it would not be enough to defeat him. When he walked on the streets of Atlanta, he was not greeted as friendly as he had been prior to the arrival

149

of the poster. Another thing that worried him was he was uncertain if the poster had been distributed statewide or just in Atlanta.

That evening, the eve of the election, he was having dinner at an Atlanta hotel by himself. Golden was in France and would be home in about a week, after the election. He missed her. He was lonesome and needed to talk with someone. There were a few of his political cronies around the hotel, but those that were there seemed to avoid him.

He was both surprised and happy to see Julie and Bancroft come in. They said they had just returned from a swing around the state to exam the damage done by the poster. He invited them to have dinner with him.

"Just what do you know about this poster that is all over town?" Malcolm asked Julie.

Julie hung her head and did not answer. Bancroft was the first to speak.

"It has been distributed all over the state, and I hate to report that it seems to be doing some damage."

"I have been able to see that here in Atlanta, but I was just not wanting to admit it. Do you think this means that this Max MacScumber, whoever he is, will win?"

Julie raised her head, and tears were running down her cheeks.

"Oh, Malcolm, I feel so bad. I feel that this is my fault. I never dreamed Max would do this. Frankly, when I visited him on our honeymoon, I never thought he had enough sense to pour piss out of a boot. I guess I was wrong."

Malcolm took her hand and said, "It is in no way your fault. The best-laid plans sometimes go astray. Besides, we are not beat yet. There is a good chance that it has not done a lot of harm."

Julie pulled away from his hand. Her eyes brimful of tears, she began her story.

"Malcolm I have to confess to you and everybody around you and Bancroft. I hardly know where to start. I have done some terrible things and now the doctors tell me I am going to die. First things first. When I came to Hanging Magnolia Plantations as Mr. Hardnails, I was very happy. I enjoyed the power, a power never known to a woman of the South. When that fell apart, I decided I had to have power. I had to show myself and set an example for other women of the South who sit around in lace and fan themselves. I knew there should be a better road for us. Setting up your campaign seemed the way to go, and it went well.

"Then, when you came to Atlanta and showed your strength by changing the speech I wrote you, and in other ways, I felt my power slipping, and I was very mad. It was then that I decided that I could not control you. So I went to Max MacScumber and explained to him that I could hand him the election. All he had to do was do as I said. I wrote and printed the bulletin.

I had riders distribute it all over the state. At the Winter Ball, the women were rude to me and thought me terrible. They were the very ones I was trying to help.

"I now feel as low as a snake's belly. The harm is done. I cannot go back. I cannot fix it so that poor Evelyn Lucille can win the big race. I can not give the little boy back his eye. I am very afraid that I have fixed it so you will not win the election. The last few days, Bancroft and I have been at the doctor, not out in the state as we said. I have been having terrible headaches, and I have this growth in my head. The doctor says it is a fast growing tumor, and I will not live long. I guess it is God's punishment. I know sorry is not enough, but I am sorry."

By the end of the week, the vote was in enough to show that Malcolm had lost the election, and Julie Penn Whitesides was dead. No one ever found the red feather in the toe of her shoe.

BOOK II

CHAPTER 40

"The Union's General Sherman is only a few miles north and coming our way."

The sound of cannon fire echoed off to the north. The population of Cottontail had gathered in the ballroom. Some of the familiar faces were missing. Lady Chandler had passed away in her sleep about five years earlier. After her death, Amos had moved his leg factory back to Pennsylvania. Loupe Rose had moved to New Orleans and was reported to be the mistress of a Spanish trader.

When the first word of the war came to Cottontail, Possum came up missing. It was rumored that he had joined a black unit of the Union Army. Many of the younger slaves had defected. Malcolm had never married Golden. She came to Cottontail for long stays, and they were good friends. There was no cotton crop in the ground, and the doom of the war was upon them.

The gathering consisted of Mary Annabelle and her tall, handsome son Rusty Montana; Olaf, who was very gray and bent; Evelyn Lucille and her husband Colon.

Colon Webster was the son of Foster Webster, who had bought Hanging Magnolia from Bancroft Whitesides a few years before. Mandy Ann, who had become a teacher, was teaching in the local school. There were several other loyal slaves in the gathering.

Malcolm, with hair turned to silver-black and his mustache a silver red, took his place on the platform.

"My dear family and loyal servants. The Union's General Sherman is only a few miles to the north and coming our way. He is burning everything as he heads south. Those of you who wish to get away must leave now. Rusty has managed to have horses ready for any of you who wish to leave. As for myself, I am going to stay and try to defend the plantation as best I can."

Olaf and several of the older slaves chose to stay with Malcolm to the end. Evelyn Lucille and Colon chose to stay. The room grew silent as Mandy Ann took the platform.

"I, too, will stay, but not with the idea of fighting to the death to save what is gone even before it is burned. Our beloved plantation is, in all reality, no more. As bad as I hate the coming blue coats, it is not the end. They will pass. We must rebuild our land, our homes and our school. I ask that all of you who stay will help me to rebuild. This includes you, father. I know you feel old and very down, but let us not make this the end."

Rusty rose to his feet.

"In my heart I cannot see myself fighting with the Union. Slavery is bad, and our people have suffered much, but I am worried that the suffering has just begun. With Master Malcolm's permission, I would like to take the remaining horses from the stable, and along with my mother, head west for a new beginning."

Mary Annabelle rose with tears streaming down her black face.

"My good son Rusty, I love you. You are my life. It is time to say goodbye. I wish to stay with Master Malcolm."

With much hugging and many tears, the meeting broke up. Malcolm called Rusty and Mary Annabelle into the study.

"Rusty Montana, while you are my son, I have never been a father to you. It is too late to make it all up at this late date. While I have not shown it, I have from a distance and in my own way, loved you like a son. I want you to take the Chandler name. From this day forward, you are Rusty Montana Chandler.

"I have some Confederate money, but it would be worthless to you as it will not be honored out west. I have managed to collect some gold during my lifetime. Gold is always good. It is not a lot, but please take it. By my count, there are forty horses and twenty mules in the stable. The Union soldiers would give anything to get their hands on them. Leave today and drive them west as fast as you can. I guess the Emancipation Passion Proclamation gave you your freedom. In any case, here are papers from me giving you your freedom, and a bill of sale for the horses. Here is the knife made from your grandmother's leg. She never accepted you, but I know she would be proud for you to have it. You can not trail all the horses by yourself. You and Sigrid, Olaf's son, have been good friends since childhood. Take him with you to help you. Now hurry! I have already told Sigrid he was to go with you, and he has the stock ready to go."

Rusty gave Mary Annabelle a hug. Then, holding her at arm's length, he looked into her black tear-filled eyes and said, "You have been the best mother anyone could ever have. I will miss you so much. You take care of

Master Malcolm. After all this terrible killing and plundering is finished, I will return to get you."

Rusty kissed his mother and shook Malcolm's hand. He was out the door and off to the stables.

The two young men, almost boys, rode and drove hard the first day. They passed some Confederate infantry troops who tried to commandeer their horses. A horse was one of the most sought after items in the entire nation. The war was literally being waged with horsepower. The Confederate commander could not understand how one black boy and one brown boy had so many good horses. Rusty kept the commander busy talking while Sigrid moved the herd as fast as he could. When Rusty figured Sigrid had the horses a good distance, he wheeled his horse and took off, leaving the commander to wonder what had happened.

When he caught up with Sigrid, the horses had scattered from hell to breakfast. They had run through a farmer's cornfield and created much damage. They found fifteen grazing in a graveyard. The farmer, whose corn they had damaged, was very upset. Rusty gave him a horse to shut him up. After he was given the horse he softened a little and let the boys use his old corral to hold the horses as they gathered them.

There was a small town not far from the farm and they found ten head of their horses tied behind the jail. The sheriff eyed the boys suspiciously when they asked for their horses back.

"Now how could a pair of black boys like you come on to these fine horses? I bet you stole them."

Rusty tried to show that he had a bill of sale for the horses from Malcolm. The sheriff locked them up as horse thieves. After much argument, the boys resolved to give the ten horses to the sheriff so they could go. He released them with the warning never to show their faces in town again. By the time they got out of jail it was well after dark. It was after midnight when they got back to the farmer's corral. They slept on the ground until daylight.

Rusty knew just about all there was to know about horses. He knew that, even if they found the rest of the horses, it would not be long before the same thing happened again. With small towns, farms and plantations along the way west it was going to be very hard to get this bunch of horses that were not broke to trail, to the west. Things did not look good. After the encounters with the Confederates and the sheriff, it was obvious that everyone was going to try to commandeer the horses.

Rusty approached the farmer to try and sell him six of the horses in the corral. The farmer said with the war and all, he had no money. Rusty had learned horse trading from Shorty Rideout before he died. Rusty offered a deal.

"You give me enough rope to tie the nine horses I have left together. I saw an old saddle and an old set of harness in your barn. Give me an IOU for the balance. I will give you a bill of sale for the six horses. After the war I will come back and collect on the IOU. If I fail to show up, the horses are yours."

The farmer scratched his head.

"Where did a black or brown, or whatever you are, learn to deal like that?"

"That's none of your business. Do we have a deal or not?"

"I will make the deal, but I get to pick the horses."

"You pick one and I'll pick one," Rusty said.

The farmer could not help but laugh.

"Boy, you are some kind of a trader. I'll get some foul scrap, and I will write this up."

"I will write it up," Rusty said, "and Sigrid here can make his mark as a witness."

It was almost noon before they had the horses all in a string. The two wearing the harness looked a little out of place. This made no difference to Rusty. The farmer had come to respect, and like, Rusty Montana, and he told him of a trail to the north that stayed away from most towns, farms and other gatherings. In fact, it ran mostly through forest country, but it would get them west.

CHAPTER 41

"I am Rusty Montana, and I would like to have a look
at your guns"

Rusty Montana pushed Sigrid hard to get as many miles each day as they possibly could. They had gotten some food from the farmer, but it was running short. The further west they got, the more they realized that they needed guns. They had seen turkey, deer and rabbits, but had no way to harvest this bounty. They tried to stay away from any populated areas as much as possible. Rusty had heard of a trading post not too far ahead of where they were camped. He detailed Sigrid to guard the camp and the horses while he went to the post to buy a gun.

Rusty was dirty, unshaven and certainly did not look his best as he entered the post. There was a very pale white woman in her mid-fifties behind a well-stocked counter.

"Good day Ma'am, I am Rusty Montana Chandler and I would like to look at you guns."

This was the first time he had ever used his last name and it made him feel very proud. The white woman looked him up and down.

"You got any money?"

"Oh, yes Ma'am."

Rusty displayed a small portion of the gold Malcolm had given him.

She led him to a rack of rifles and a display of pistols. Rusty was wishing that he knew as much about guns as he did horses.

"Ma'am, I must be honest with you, I know little about guns. My friend and I are headed out west and we need two rifles and two pistols. I will have to trust you to show me which is best for our needs."

She kind of liked the young brown man, and he had a familiar air about him.

"Please don't call me Ma'am. My name is Snowflake. Guns are very hard to come by with the war going on. I don't have as big of selection as I should have. She took down two Springfield's and two Colts. These are my very best in stock. I see you're riding a pretty good horse. The army came by and took all of our horses the other day. I would trade you this rifle for that horse, and you can pay the balance with your gold. It's going to take more gold than you showed me."

Snowflake kept staring at Rusty. He felt as though her eyes were going right inside of him.

"I will trade you this horse and another good one for all four guns."

"You don't appear to be a horse thief, but where did a brown boy like you ever come by good horses."

Rusty dug Malcolm's bill of sale out of his pocket. Snowflake read it, and the bottom line was signed by Malcolm Chandler II. Snowflake looked at Rusty. Except for the color, he was the spitting image. She walked around the counter and flung her arms around the surprised boy and wept. To a very surprised Rusty, it seemed like an hour when he finally pushed her back at arms length and look at her. She took a deep breath and dried her eyes.

"I knew you father very well, and by the looks of you your mother must have been that pretty slave girl, for the life of me I can't think of her name right now. Your father saved me and my family at one time."

She told the story of how Malcolm had warned her that a lynch party was on the way to their place to hang them, when Malcolm warned them. He told of how he managed to be where he was, and that his mother was indeed Mary Annabelle.

"You go back to your camp and get the horses and your friend. We have plenty of pasture for them, after losing our horses, we know how to hide them. Now hurry, and we will do our trading in the morning."

When Rusty and Sigrid arrived back at the Nut's Trading Post, Snowflake had gathered all of her family. Right Nut and Pansy had a daughter that was sixteen. She had the black complexion of her mother, but the high cheek bone and the long straight black hair of her dad. The loins on both Rusty and Sigrid tightened a bit when they were introduced to this beauty. The young girl's name was Hazel. Right Nut said he did not want her to have an Indian name. She took Rusty and his horses to a secluded pasture not visible from the trading post or the road. On the way back to the house they held hands and kissed and rubbed each other some, but they knew they had to be back to supper soon. Poor Rusty had inherited from his dad the trait that a black girl gave him an instant hard on. He asks Hazel to meet him in the barn after dark. She gave a shy nod of her head yes. Snowflake and Pansy fixed a wonderful supper of pork, venison, potatoes and okra.

When the supper was finished, Right Nut broke out a bottle, and they all told what they knew about each other and the old days before Rusty's birth. Snowflake was so glad to be reminded of the old days. They were the best part of her life. Times had changed and were changing very fast.

That night Rusty and Sigrid were to sleep in the barn. Rusty was as busy as a cat trying to cover shit with cotton in a windstorm, trying to figure a way to get Sigrid out of the barn. He had heard Malcolm and others talk about snipe hunting. When they got to the barn he suggested that it was a bit early to go to bed and maybe they should go hunt some snipes. He took Sigrid out in the Nut's garden and gave him a sack to hold open while he went to drive the snipes to him and into the sack. He told Sigrid that it might take a while. He had only been in the barn a few minutes when Hazel Nut arrived. They were like all teenagers and thought that they were the first to discover sex. They kissed and rolled around on the blankets. Rusty Montana got so excited. Their sex was completed with some satisfaction. It hurt her a little, and she bled on the blanket. She got dressed and went back to the house, thinking all the time that sex was not all that much fun.

This whole sexual experience had only taken about twenty minutes. Rusty went out to the garden and had Sigrid come in to bed. He said he could not find any snipes to drive into the sack. He did not tell Sigrid it was a joke, because he thought he might want to use it again.

The next morning at breakfast Snowflake asked the boys if they would like to stay a few days. They could do some work that was needed, for their keep. The horses needed a rest, and the boys loved the food. The thought of getting Hazel Nut on the blanket again did pass through Rusty's mind.

About midday, Captain Marshall and a troop of black soldiers arrived at the Nut's trading post.

He was almost ready to retire from service when the war broke out. He had been assigned the job of escorting new recruits to the cavalry based in Texas. This unit would later become the 10th cavalry. This was a unit of black soldiers to help keep the Southwest Indians under control. The Nut's had known Captain Marshall for years and considered him their friend. It was a shock to see him with a troop of blacks. Rusty and Sigrid were splitting wood, they were very leery of the bluecoats. Rusty could overhear the conversation of the Captain and Snowflake. The Captain was asking if the troops could lay over a day or two. They needed a rest and to find some one to shoe their horse, as their farrier had taken ill and was sent back to the fort.

Rusty stepped forward. He gave the white officer a half-hearted salute.

"Sir—My name is Rusty Montana Chandler, and I am a very good farrier."

The Captain looked Rusty up and down. He liked the looks of the young brown man.

"Would you like to join our unit?"

"No sir—I would like you to hire me to shoe your horses."

"I had planned on hiring a white man to shoe the horses. If a black man does it, he would have to be a member of the unit."

"That is very hard for me to understand why the color of a man who you hire to shoe the horses makes a difference."

"That is just the way the Army works."

Rusty went back to chopping wood.

Rusty and Sigrid joined the colored troops for supper that night and sang with them around their campfires. That night when the boys retired to the barn, Sigrid announced that he would like to join the troops.

"It is about my only chance at a job, and it will give me a way to get to the west where we want to go. Rusty—Why don't you join and be the farrier?"

"I do not want to be a soldier. I will try again in the morning to get hired on as a civilian farrier. Then I could go west with you and the rest of the troops."

Rusty got up at four a.m. and found the Captain's horse. He had noticed the day before that it was one of the horses that needed new shoes. He had an extra set of shoes in his duffel. He did the very best he could do shoeing the big black horse, and it was an excellent job. Captain Marshall came out later to check on the horse. He noticed the new shoes, picked up a foot on the horse, and gave it a good look. Rusty took this opportunity to walk up to the Captain.

"Captain—I wanted to show you that a black civilian could do a good job shoeing a horse. My friend Sigrid is going to join your outfit. I want a job with the army shoeing horses. I can also doctor sick horses, I can train horses. I have almost lived in a stable all my life and I had a very good teacher that taught me all he knew about horses. You pay me a dollar a day and I will keep the horses shod for you. I will ride with the troops until you get to Texas then you can fire me.

"Why don't you want to be a soldier?"

"I have other plans. There is one other part of the deal. I have nine horses of my own. I will be taking them with me to Texas. The Army can use them on the way for pack animals and extra horse, but I want it understood that they are my horses when we get to Texas."

Captain Marshall liked the red-head. Looking at him he must have had a white father. He was offering two things that were most needed—nine extra horses and to do the shoeing.

"Was your father a white man?"

"Yes-Sir!!

"I guess regulation say nothing that I can not hire a half white man. You have a deal"

"Good I will write a contract as to what we discussed and you can sign it."

Late that afternoon, the supply wagons for the troop came in. They had been running a day behind.

Sigrid was sworn in and issued a uniform—Pvt. Sigrid—he was so proud.

The Captain announced that they would leave the next day.
Rusty gave the contract to the Captain, and he signed.

> Contract between the US Army and Rusty Montana
> Chandler.
> Rusty agrees to act as farrier and help care for the troops
> horses. The Army agrees to pay Rusty a dollar a day. The
> Army can have the use of Rusty's eight horses until they
> arrive at Calvary headquarter in Texas at which time this
> contract becomes null and void.
> Captain Horace Marshall . . . . .June 16th 1862
> Rusty Montana Chandler . . . . .June 16th 1862

The Captain signed.

Rusty did not need as many guns as he had first bargained with
Snowflake for. They finally settled that he would get a rifle, a pistol, ammunition, and a buckskin shirt for one horse. Snowflake picked out a small gray
mare that Lucile Evelyn had once bought at an auction. The mare was pretty old but very gentle. Rusty was happy with the deal, as he was not sure the
mare could make it all the way to Texas. Rusty also had to give Snowflake
the old saddle and the harness. Snowflake was so happy just to see the
Chandler boy that she tossed in the deal a pair of buckskin pants.

The next day a well-organized troop, with a new trooper, a farrier and
eight head of extra horses headed southwest.

As Rusty rode along his thoughts were---

How could you beat a deal like this, new buckskins, a little love'n, and
an escort to Texas.

CHAPTER 42

"You got a smart mouth for nigger kid."

The troop was one day from the Red River. When they crossed, they would be in Texas. The Captain called Rusty off to the side.

"For the rest of the trip we are going to need a scout to go ahead and look for camp sights and check for hostiles. It is unlikely that there are any Confederate troops in this area. It is very possible there are rebel bands that are sympathetic to the South. I would like you to take on the position of scout along with your other duties."

"I would be happy to do the job. Two men's work, then two men's pay."

The Captain had to laugh. He thought, "This kid will go places."

"I would have to check with the President himself to give you a raise like that. How does fifty cents a day more sound to you?"

Early the next morning, Rusty rode ahead and was about a mile from the Red River when he rounded a bend and ran smack dab into a camp of very rough looking men. The next thing he knew, he was looking into the barrel of a large caliber rifle.

"State your business kid."

"I am a free black man, and I am going west for a new start."

"We hear there is a troop of Yankee Blue Coats somewhere in the area. You got anything to do with them?"

"I don't know nothin' about the Yankee's. I try to keep out of the way of all soldiers. Now put that gun down before you hurt somebody."

The man raised the gun a little higher and leveled it at Rusty's head.

"You got a smart mouth for a nigger kid. Get down off that horse. We are going to let you go, but we are going to cut your nuts out first. We got all the niggers in Texas we need."

Inside, Rusty was scared, but he could not let this bastard see his fear.

"Sir, if you plan on harvesting my balls, you will have to shoot me first."

A woman dressed in buckskin rose off a log and pushed the man's gun down. Up until this point, Rusty thought she was one of the men.

"This here boy has some real guts. How would you like to join our out-fit? We hunt Yankees and rob banks."

161

The big man with the gun looked at the woman and said, "We ain't takin' no niggers in our outfit."

"Shut up Jake. How 'bout it kid? You want to join up?"

"That sounds real interesting. What's my cut?"

"We split everything equal."

At this point, the one called Jake piped up. "Jackie, have you lost your ever-lovin' mind? We are takin' no niggers. And for sure we ain't givin' a cut."

"Shut up Jake. How 'bout it kid, is it a deal?"

"I would really like to join an outfit like this, but I have a better deal for you," Rusty answered. "I have a friend a few miles back in camp. He's the best shot in the territory and really hates Yankees and banks. I will go get him, and we will both work for the price of one."

"Is this guy another nigger?" Jake demanded.

"Oh, no. He's only half black. His mother was an Indian. He told me what tribe, but I can't remember."

Jackie came over and shook hands with Rusty. "What's your name kid?"

"My name is 'Pint of Poison Piss', but most people just call me 'Piss'," he answered.

"That's a good name, Piss. We're the Jake and Jackie Gang."

"I'm going to ride back with this kid to make sure there ain't no funny stuff," Jake said.

Rusty's heart sank to the bottom of his stomach. He busied himself devising a plan. When they had ridden about a mile from the outlaw's camp, Rusty dropped behind. He pulled the knife, made from his grandmother's leg, and ran his horse up along side of Jake's. He slipped the knife blade up under Jake's rib cage and into his heart. With eyes wide, Jake turned and looked at Rusty, then slipped off the horse to the ground. Rusty put his spurs to his horse and headed for the troop.

Rusty reported to the Captain what had gone on with the Jake and Jackie Gang.

"How many in the gang?" the Captain queried.

"There are six men and Jackie left in the camp. I sure hated to kill a man. I hope I did the right thing."

The Captain assured him that he had done right. The Captain ordered his men forward.

"What are you going to do?" Rusty asked.

"We are going to ride in and take them."

"Captain, they are well armed and dangerous. Why don't you let me take Sigrid. We can pick up Jake's body and ride into their camp with it across his horse. We will take our time, and you send the rest of the men to surround the camp. When they are looking at the body and asking what happened, you can take them without a shot. I would hate to lose any of our men, which we very easily could if we go charging in on the camp. I told them I was coming back to get a friend, so they will not be suspicious of us."

Captain Marshall was glad no one else had heard Rusty's plan. It would not be good if the men knew Rusty was calling the shots, but he had to admit that it made a lot of sense. He halted the troop and outlined the plan to them. Rusty and Sigrid took off down the road for the body.

Rusty and Sigrid got Jake's body tied on his horse and rode into the outlaw camp. Jackie rushed to Jake, grabbed him by the hair, and lifted his head.

"Jake's dead. What happened to him?"

This was when the troop was supposed to move in for the arrest, but no troop showed up. Rusty looked around and said, "He got stabbed."

Jackie looked up at Rusty and asked, "Who stabbed him?"

"I did. He got to insulting me and calling me a Nigger."

"Piss, you should not have stabbed him, but what the hell. Let's get him in the ground and be on our way."

The male members of the gang dug a shallow grave and very unceremoniously dumped Jake in. Still no troop showed up. Sigrid had taken off his uniform and was in old clothes. He had kept his government issued side arm. When Jackie noticed the gun, she asked, "Where did you get the side arm?"

Rusty could see that Sigrid was scared to death. "He shot a Yankee soldier right between the eyes and took it," Rusty offered.

It was getting dark and still no troop. Jackie handed out a cold supper of jerky and hard tack. At bedtime, Jackie took Rusty by the hand and led him off in the woods.

"Since you killed Jake, I guess you will just have to take his place."

Back in the dark woods, under a big oak tree, were some not-so-clean blankets. Jackie stripped off her clothes and crawled into the blankets.

"Get in here boy and old Jackie will show you a real good time."

Rusty stripped and crawled in. The odor was not the best, but when Jackie reached and began to stroke him he got pretty excited.

"My God boy, you are hung like a Shetland pony."

Rusty closed his eyes and did as he was told. They rolled, bounced, and rubbed most of the night. Come morning, Rusty was so worn out he could hardly get up from the blankets. Jackie looked even worse in the morning. He just couldn't stand it. He threw up. As bad as she was, she had taught him a lot about sex and he wished he had had this experience before he met Hazel Nut.

One of the gang had some side pork fired up when Jackie and Rusty came into camp. Sigrid was on one side of the group and Rusty on the other. Rusty motioned to Sigrid and they pulled their guns.

"Nobody move and put your hands in the air. You are under arrest by the U.S. Army."

The element of surprise was in the boys' favor. Jackie went for her gun.

"You dirty no good sons-of-bitches."

She barely had the words out when Sigrid shot her in the heart. She managed to get a shot off that went wild before she hit the ground. Rusty and Sigrid tied up the rest of the gang. Sigrid stayed to guard them while Rusty went to find the wayward troop.

Rusty had not gone too far when he saw the troop arriving. They were coming in the opposite direction from where they were supposed to be.

"Where in the hell have you been? We heard some shooting," Captain Marshall demanded.

Rusty was more than a little disgusted with the Captain. He knew he had been lost, but he held his temper.

"We have the gang in custody. We had to kill the ring leader."

In order to save face, the Captain said no more, and ordered the troop to get the prisoners.

They took them to a small village on the bank of the Red River, to turn them over to the local sheriff. When they arrived, they discovered there was no local sheriff, and they had to turn them loose. This made one of the outlaws very happy, as he had a Mexican wife and child in the village.

The troop crossed the Red River and headed southwest.

CHAPTER 43

"The woman was tied, spread eagle, on the ground."

The troop made their way southwest with little trouble. The late June weather was hot. They saw a few wild longhorn cattle each day. One day, while on scout, Rusty killed a nice yearling steer. In the troop there was an ex-slave that had been a butcher. He helped Rusty skin and dress the animal. The troop enjoyed a good meal of fresh beef. Rusty repeated this process about once a week.

As they moved west, they saw more Indian sign, but no Indians. Then one evening, on a ridge off to the left, appeared a band of Comanches.

The Captain gave the order to halt. "Rusty, you go up and find out what they are up to."

"I don't know a thing about Indians."

"You are the only scout we have. Now get a move on."

Rusty rode toward the band of Indians, having no idea what to do. He got within about fifty yards and stopped. The Indians just looked at him. "Well fuck it," he thought. He spurred his horse and rode right into the group, extended his hand and shook hands with anyone who would shake with him. The Indians were just as surprised, as Rusty and the leader said a few words in his Indian language and made signs with his hands. Rusty had heard of sign language. He made some signs that he thought might mean friend. The Indians all looked at one another and laughed. What he had signed was "take me prisoner." The Indians surrounded him and motioned for him to come. He rode off with them.

Captain Marshall was watching all this through his telescope. When he saw Rusty ride off with the Indians, he had no clue what was going on. It was almost dark, and there was no use following or making any other moves. He ordered the troop to make camp. He would send someone to investigate in the morning.

While Rusty was riding with the Indians, he noticed one of their horses limping. He stopped and got off, picked up the horse's foot and removed a gravel out of the horse's foot. He got back on his horse and they rode on. The Indian horse was no longer lame.

"The Brown Man is big medicine," the Indian leader said to his comrades.

There were six Indians riding with Rusty, and when they arrived at the Indian camp, there were two more in camp. The two remaining in camp were guarding two white children and a woman.

The woman was tied, spread eagle, on the ground. One of the children was a boy, about twelve, who was tied to a post. His hands were purple from the ties. The other was a girl, about three, and she was not tied. She sat by a make shift lean-to with a tear stained dirty face.

When they arrived, one of the braves dismounted, pulled aside his breach cloth, and violated the poor woman. Rusty stood in shocked anger.

The Indian rolled off the woman, and another took his place. This was all Rusty could stand. He grabbed the brave by his long, black hair and pulled him off the woman. He slammed his knee into the Indian's groin with all his force. The Indian doubled over with pain. Rusty walked over to the boy and cut him loose with the white, bone-handled knife made from his grandmother's leg.

The Indians stared at Rusty, who stood there with the knife in his hand. It seemed like an hour before anyone moved. Seeing the Indians frozen in their tracks, Rusty went to the woman and cut her loose. The woman ran to her children, put her arms around them, and huddled next to the lean-to.

Rusty asked the woman if she could speak to the Indians.

"No."

Just at that moment, one of the Indians got brave enough to make a lunge at Rusty. Rusty still had his knife in hand and carved an eight-inch gash in the Indian's upper right arm. The Indian stepped back and gasped for air. Rusty trimmed a piece of hide from the lean-to and bandaged the Indian's arm to stop the bleeding.

Then he turned to the woman and said, "Feed the children and then get two of those Indian ponies. Put the boy on one and you and the girl get on the other."

The woman said, "No English. German."

The little boy spoke up, in broken English. "I speak English."

Then he translated the order to his mother in German. She went to a pot of stew on the small fire and fed the little girl. The boy got the ponies, then he and his mother ate from the pot.

The Indian who seemed to be the leader dropped to his knees and began to chant.

"Brown Man, Brown Man. His medicine is bigger than the Comanche Nation. We are the bravest warriors in the tribe, yet he comes to our camp and makes us look like fools. Our raid on the farmer was successful. We got a strong woman and two children, one horse and a mule. We sent the farmer to the happy hunting grounds. Now he wounds two of our good warriors, he takes our captives, and he eats our food. He helps our lame horse, he helps the wounded warrior. The Brown Man. His medicine is strong."

Rusty could not understand a word, but he sensed that he had the upper hand. He walked behind the kneeling chief and kicked him in the ass, sending him sprawling in the dust. He then dumped the balance of the stew on the ground and kicked the ashes across the Indians' camp.

The lean-to and the robes hanging inside started to smolder and smoke. He motioned for the Indians to mount the remaining horses, which they did. One of them, in his haste, left his rifle on the ground. Rusty picked it up and handed it to him. He pointed to the west, slapped the chief's horse on the rump, and he bolted out of camp with the others following.

The poor woman, who was sitting on an Indian pony, was still in the nude and looked very bedraggled from her recent experience. Rusty picked up one of the Indian robes that had not burned and wrapped it around the woman.

A full moon washed the Texas landscape in a bath of soft light, as Rusty and his party made their way toward the encampment.

The boy, whose name was Wolfgang, told Rusty of the Comanche raid on their farm. He said they saw the Indians coming, and his mother hid her six-month-old baby boy under the floor of the cabin. The savages had not burned the cabin and he had to take his mother back to see if they could find the baby. He knew that his father was dead, because he had seen the Indians cut his body into small pieces.

Rusty and his party arrived at the camp at about three the following morning. He woke the Captain and gave him a brief account of his ordeal with the Indians. He asked for permission to leave as soon as he and the family had a little rest. He wanted to make an attempt at rescuing the baby.

After a short sleep, Rusty met with Captain Marshall.

"Rusty, we are still a week out of headquarters. We need you to scout for us and shoe our horses. I will send Sergeant Frisbee and let him pick a good private to assist him in returning the family home."

There were three white men in the outfit, the Captain, Lieutenant MacWell, and Master Sergeant Frisbee. Lieutenant MacWell was a very quiet officer, but very capable and hard working. Sergeant Frisbee was an airhead, and would be unable to pour piss out of a boot without directions written on the heel. At least that was Rusty's opinion.

"Captain, please send Sigrid and me," Rusty requested. "Private Arnold has been helping me with the shoeing, and he can make out until you get to headquarters. Lieutenant MacWell has been over the trail every time you have brought recruits. He knows the way. Sigrid and I can ride hard. We won't be gone more than four days. Two days back to the family's farm, and at that point, two days to catch up with you."

Captain Marshall was silent, but he was thinking.

Here was a basic black boy who would not join the Army. If the truth were known, he had taken over the command. What the hell? He had taken recruits from the east coast to Texas several times. Why was he worried about a few days? He had had a command for almost twenty years.

"Take Sigrid and some of the best horses. Do your best to catch up in four days."

"Thank you sir."

Rusty and his party were soon ready to head east. The mother was still quite bewildered and kept asking questions that made no sense, such as, "when does the boat leave for Germany?" Wolfgang was a very courageous child, and did his best to help his mother and sister through this difficult time.

The two units parted. Captain Marshall and his troop headed west, and Rusty and his party headed back east. Rusty Montana was not out of ear shot when he heard the Captain order Sergeant Frisbee forward to act as scout. A shiver went down Rusty's spine. With Frisbee as scout, they would be going in circles.

The sun was high in the sky, and the temperature was near 100 when Sergeant Frisbee galloped back to the command. His horse was lathered and winded.

"Captain, Captain, large war party just ahead."

Frisbee was right. He had led a large, well-armed war party of Comanche's right into the troops. The battle only lasted a matter of moments. Not one of the Tenth Cavalry recruits was alive. Captain Marshall, with an arrow through the calf of his leg, managed to hide under a burned out oak tree.

CHAPTER 44

"Slim let Otto up and rode off."

Rusty Montana and Sigrid rode east with the German farm family. The woman and the little girl rode on one horse, and Wolfgang and Sigrid on another. Rusty Montana rode out in front a mile or so to scout.

The first night, they camped on a small stream under a canopy of trees. A June thunderstorm rolled over in the night and soaked both people and gear. The woman, whose name was Irmagaard, woke at all hours shouting in German. Wolfgang said she made no sense.

In the morning they got up and spread their blankets out to dry while Sigrid made a breakfast. Rusty killed a couple of prairie chickens the day before. Those, along with some hot biscuits, made a tasty breakfast. Wolfgang and his little sister, Hilda, especially enjoyed it. The morning was hot and humid, a typical east Texas June morning, when they set out on the trail.

The sun was low in the west when Wolfgang asked to stop. "Our farm is just around the next bend."

The party rode on with caution. As they got closer, they could see that the Indians had burned both the house and the barn. They spooked two wolves into the woods as they approached.

Wolfgang said he had not seen a fire when the Indians took them away, but it was very possible that one of the Indians had stayed behind and burned the buildings.

The faint sound of a crying child came to the party as they approached the burned out cabin. The cabin had a dirt floor and the hiding place for the baby was in a small cellar-like structure under the floor. This had saved the baby.

Wolfgang jumped off his horse and ran into the ruins. He picked up his baby brother. The wolves had dug the child out from under the floorboards and chewed off his left foot. Rusty analyzed the situation and was not sure if they had arrived just in time to scare off the wolves, or if the wolves just did not like the taste of the kid.

The bleeding had pretty much stopped. It was easy to see that the poor child was very dehydrated. The fact was, the child was so dehydrated that the cheeks of his ass looked like two white raisins. The Indians had killed the family milk cow, and she lay a hundred yards out in the field. Rusty sent

169

Sigrid to see if, by chance, the milk would still be good. Sigrid came back holding his nose and a small amount of blue liquid in a cup. He reported that one of the cow's teats fell off in his hand when he tried to get the milk. Rusty's mind went to work, the wild longhorn cows!

"You stay here with your family," he instructed Wolfgang. "Take care of them. Sigrid and I will see if we can find a cow, kill her and get some milk. Sigrid, you go up the creek and I will go down. Shoot any wet cow you see."

Rusty had not gone far when a whitetail doe stepped out of the brush, she had twin fawns at her side. He took careful aim and shot her down. Deer have very little milk, but it is very rich. Rusty managed to get enough milk to cover the bottom of the cup. He rushed back to the family. They added some water to the doe milk and literally poured the milk down the baby. Within a few minutes, the baby was improved.

Wolfgang handed the baby to his mother. She looked down at the baby, and she snapped.

"Oh my dear little Hans, and you Wolfgang, you are here. Where is Hilda?"

Hilda came running to her mother.

"Those awful Indians killed your father."

Looking around she then announced, "They destroyed our farm."

Wolfgang looked at Rusty with a big smile. "Mommy is back. She knows me. She knows little Hans and Hilda."

The children huddled around their mother and she tried to hug them all at once.

Rusty salvaged what he could of the family's personal belongings. He pumped water from the well so the mother could clean up Hans and Hilda. She seemed happy, considering the circumstances. She asked Rusty to bury the remains of her husband. This was a nasty job. His remains had been scattered by wolves and other varmints. The fact that they had been under the hot Texas sun for several days did not help.

The sun was going down, which gave some relief from the heat. He found what he thought were most of the farmer's remains, and decided it was too late to dig a grave. It would have to wait until morning.

Rusty had just gotten the fire going, and Irmagaard was cooking some of the fresh doe meat, when Sigrid came riding in. He had a pail half full of good longhorn milk. He also reported that there were quite a bunch of wild longhorns about three miles away from the farm. Irmagaard fed the baby, and put a fresh bandage on the little stump.

When all was settled and most were asleep, Rusty had many thoughts. He wanted, in the worst way, to get back to the troop. How could he leave this family?

They had nothing. He wondered how near a neighbor might be. Things had been so hectic that he had forgotten to ask Wolfgang.

The warm morning found the family sleeping while Rusty and Sigrid dug a grave and shoveled in the remains. They mounded it up, and the family found a pretty nice grave when they awoke. Irmagaard gathered the family around, and with heads bowed, she spoke a few words in German.

Wolfgang pulled at Rusty's leg and said, "I don't think God in Texas understands German. Would you please pray for my father in English?"

Mary Annabelle had raised Rusty as a Christian and had made him do some Bible study. He remembered the twenty third psalm and managed to say it for the boy. "The lord is my shepherd; he maketh me lay in green pastures. He leadeth me beside still waters..."

The boy looked up at Rusty. "Boy, oh Boy, Mr. Rusty! That was good! I bet the Texas God understands that."

Rusty discovered that there was another German family about four miles to the south. It was decided that Wolfgang and Rusty would go to the neighbors, and Sigrid would stay with the family. This way Wolfgang could act as interpreter.

On the way to the neighbors, Rusty and Wolfgang came on to some cowboys working cattle. They hid in the brush and watched. The cowboys would rope the cattle, tie them down, and brand them with a hot iron. Rusty had never seen this before and Wolfgang explained that this way they could tell whose cattle were whose. He said that his dad had branded some cattle, and their brand was W̱.

Wolfgang also told him that the tall cowboy had been at their farm talking to his dad. Rusty decided to ride in and talk with the cowboys. Rusty noticed that there were several cattle with the W Bar brand.

Rusty introduced himself to the tall cowboy, who in turn said his name was Texas Slim, and then he introduced the rest of the cowboys. The cowboys stopped their work as Rusty told his story of the Comanche raid and the rescue of the woman and children from the Indians. This story was enough to gain the respect of the cowboys.

"Do you know anything about who shot the cow?" Texas Slim asked. "It looked like it had just been shot yesterday."

Rusty explained that Sigrid had shot the cow for the milk. The cowboy laughed.

"If you boys had a dairy you would soon be out of business," Texas Slim joked. "We found the dead cow and thought there were rustlers or Indians. Just couldn't figure why anyone would just shoot a cow and let it lay. The cow you shot was a W Bar cow, so I guess we can't hang you for rustling."

The cowboys had another good round of laughs as Texas Slim mounted his horse and lay a loop on the head of a cow with a full bag of milk. One of the other cowboys grabbed the cow's head and held her while another cowboy milked a pail full of milk.

Texas Slim handed the milk to Rusty and said, "That's the way to do it, and you always have the cow. While we are working here, don't worry about milk for that baby. We'll get you all you want."

Rusty hung the pail of milk on a tree limb and he and Wolfgang went on to the neighbors. Their farm was located on a small creek. The cowboys were working on a plateau and the farm was down a very steep hill. Their name was Gunderslung. The family consisted of the farmer, Otto; the wife, Clara; and two daughters, Phyllis, seven, and Alga, seventeen. The family was very happy to see Wolfgang, but they acted very suspicious of Rusty. Wolfgang talked with Otto at lengths about what had happened. Alga, who was very tall for her age, wore a cotton dress that hung on her slim body, showing every curve. Her long, blond hair was in two long braids. She could speak English well.

While Wolfgang and Otto discussed a plan for the orphaned family, Alga sidled up to Rusty and asked if he would like a drink of water. He accepted, and she brought a bucket of cool water from the creek and handed him a dipper full. Then she and Rusty were talking about nothing in particular, when Otto turned and saw his blond daughter talking with the black man. He lost it. He picked up a neck yoke, and made a dash at Rusty. Rusty Montana was caught completely off guard. Otto hit him in the head with the neck yoke. Rusty's knees buckled and he went down like a falling star, blood running from his head. Alga ran to the house crying.

Wolfgang ran to Rusty and washed the wound with some of the water from the bucket. Clara came from the house with a towel and helped Wolfgang doctor Rusty. Wolfgang demanded to know why Otto had clubbed his friend for no reason.

"I don't want no niggers talking to my Alga."

Otto went to the barn and soon returned with a team. He hitched them to a wagon. He told Wolfgang that he would go to the burned out homestead and get the rest of his family. Rusty, still too dizzy to ride his horse, rode in the wagon. They made their way up the hill. The party stopped at the tree and picked up the milk. The cowboys had moved on to a new location.

That evening, the two families were more or less settled at the Gunderslungs' farm. Otto and Clara would do all they could to help them rebuild. Wolfgang assured his mother that he could do the work of a man and could protect the family once they had rebuilt.

Otto treated Rusty and Sigrid as though they were not even there. In fact, he told Wolfgang to tell them to ride out. He did not want the likes of them hanging around. Poor Wolfgang was at a total loss. In his almost thirteen year old mind, he did not know what the hell to do. He needed Otto's friendship, yet he and Rusty had become good friends. After all, Rusty Montana had saved his family.

Rusty saw the dilemma and offered a solution. "It is time for Sigrid and me to be headed west. Sigrid is a soldier, and I work for the Army. The captain will be wondering what has happened to us. We don't mind riding in the night."

Irmagaard and little Hilda came forward to hug Rusty Montana and thank him. Rusty told her that he would send word north to a man that made wooden legs to fix a leg for her baby so he could learn to walk. Otto pushed them back.

"Irmagaard, if you are going to be a nigger lover you can't stay here." Rusty and Sigrid reined their horses west and rode out.

Early the next morning, Texas Slim and his cowboys rode into the Gunderslung's farm. One of the cowboys was a black man. Slim dismounted and asked Wolfgang if there was anything they could do except bring milk for the baby.

Otto puffed out his chest, and informed Wolfgang to tell the cowboy that he wanted that black cowboy off his place. Poor Wolfgang was really in a pickle now. If he did as he was told, he would sure make Slim mad. Finally Otto pointed to the black cowboy and indicated he wanted him gone. Slim stepped up to the German, gave him an opened-handed slap that rattled his teeth, and pushed him in the dirt. Otto was managing to get up, when he found a cowboy boot on his chest, with considerable pressure. Otto lay squirming under the pressure of the boot while Slim smiled at Irmagaard and informed Wolfgang to tell his mother that they would brand some cattle with the W Bar to help them get a start.

Slim let Otto up, mounted his horse and rode off to work.

CHAPTER 45

"What were you doing to the German girl when her dad got so hot?"

When Rusty and Sigrid reached the trail where they were to meet up with their unit, they saw no indication that a military unit had passed. They started to back track up the trail.

Soon darkness engulfed them. This was their third day out since leaving the German families. The Captain would be beside himself with anger. They made camp and sat around the fire bull-shitting.

"What were you doing to that white German girl that got her dad so hot?" Sigrid asked Rusty.

"I was just talking with her. I am not really into white girls. Now you take black girls or Indian girls, and that's a different story. They say there are a lot of Mexican girls around the fort. I think I will like Mexican girls. You remember that Hazel Nut? Now I liked her. It was her first time with sex, and I don't think she liked it too good."

"I never have been with a girl in that sex way, stuff. I sure would like to. That white German girl would have been just fine for me," Sigrid offered.

"You be careful around those white girls. The white men don't like us blacks fooling around with them. You will get yourself killed."

The boys sat and watched the fire. Sigrid broke the silence. "The German, Gunderslung, sure didn't treat us very good. But that's one good thing about being an ex-slave, you don't have to learn what it is to be badly treated."

The boys were camped back in the trees where their fire could not be seen from the trail. They heard a noise coming from the direction of the trail. It was a scuffling sound and then kind of a moan. Rusty crept to the edge of the brush where he could make out the trail in the dim moonlight. He saw a man dragging himself and moaning with every step. As the man got closer, he could make out the uniform. He stepped out in front of the man and saw at once that it was Captain Marshall. Rusty helped the wounded Captain to the camp. By the firelight he could see that the Captain's left leg was in bad shape.

"I tried to get the arrow out and I broke it off. Part of it is still in my leg."

The leg was swollen and blue. Rusty, with his ever faithful bone-handled knife made from his grandmother's leg, made a quick-as-a-wink cut in
the Captain's leg. The Captain let out with a long, wailing cry and blood and
arrow parts gushed out on the ground. Rusty made the Captain go lay down
in the creek so the cool water could wash the wound and lower his fever.

Just as the Captain got into the creek, the boys heard a hell of a roar
from up the creek. They looked up in time to see an eight foot wall of water
headed right for them. They scrambled to get the Captain out of the creek
to safety, but to no avail. They could only save themselves on the slick
muddy bank. The last they saw of the Captain was his head bobbing in the
turbulent water as he rushed toward the Gulf of Mexico. They had commented earlier in the day about the huge black clouds off to the north. It was
the first flash flood either of them had seen.

They finally arrived at headquarters. Sigrid reported to the commander and informed him of the loss of the recruits. The commander immediately sent out a detail to bury the bodies and investigate. Rusty presented his
contract to the commander and received his back pay. The commander said
there was nothing the Army could do about his horses, they were Rusty's
loss. He had lost every horse that he had left the plantation with, but he still
had some gold and the pay the Army had given him.

Sigrid was assigned to a barracks. Rusty made his way to the small
town that was supported by the army camp. It consisted mostly of small
shacks and cribs that housed prostitutes. At the far end of the sprawling
town was a new building with a freshly painted sign that read *Saloon and
Rooms*. Rusty tied his horse to the hitching rack in front and went in. The
place looked new, and was decorated in red velvet with crystal lights and
black leather furnishings. The back bar was ornately carved dark wood. The
bartender was washing some glasses. Behind the desk was a very pretty
Mexican girl. Rusty Montana spoke to her in Spanish, which made her
bright smile even brighter.

"I would like a room and some hot bath water."

"Maybe a nice girl to go with the room?" the girl asked.

"Would that nice girl happen to be you?"

"Si`, Senior."

"I have been on the trail a long time. I just want to clean up, eat a good
steak, and rest for tonight. You are a very pretty girl. Maybe tomorrow
night."

The brown-eyed beauty tossed her long black hair and frowned.
"Tomorrow is a long time."

Rusty thought, "She is such a pretty girl. What the hell is the matter
with me? I should take her right now." The idea of buying a girl was a turn
off.

She gave him a smile and the key. Just as he turned to go to the room, he heard a female voice from the back room.

"Marie, who's out there?"

Rusty would know that voice anywhere. It could not be anyone else. He pushed poor Marie out of the way and went to the back, into the living quarters. There, at a kitchen table, sat Loupe Rose. Her first reaction was fright, and then she saw that it was Rusty Montana. She ran to him and they embraced.

"Marie, get us a bottle of good whisky and two glasses."

Rusty sat down at the kitchen table in absolute amazement that he had found his sister, Loupe Rose. She told her story of how she ended up in west Texas.

"When I left Cottontail, as you know, I went to New Orleans. I fell in with a Spanish merchant. He had two big houses, one where he and his wife lived, and another that he let me live in. He visited about twice a week.

"As time went on, I asked a girl to stay with me as I had many unused rooms in the house. It turned out she was a prostitute. She would have gentlemen in and give me a cut of her pay. Then I got another girl. Before long, I had eight girls, and I was making money hand over fist. I would hide the girls as best I could when the Spanish trader came to visit. He had to have known what was going on, but he said nothing.

"He did not show up for almost two months," Loupe Rose continued. "Then, much to my surprise, I read in the paper where he had died. The next thing, a banker came and said that the house had sold, and I would have to move. I had some money, and the war was causing a lot of trouble. I heard that the place to go was Texas. I guess that is about it. I just finished building this place. In fact you are one of the first guests. Rusty Montana, it is so good to see you. Do you remember when we used to tie you to our ponies and take you everywhere with us?"

"Loupe Rose, I guess I was too small to remember that, but I sure remember that you were always the one on the Plantations who would help me. You always treated me like a brother. Not like a half slave/half brother, half white, and half black. I am so glad I found you."

"What are you going to do now that you are in Texas?"

"I really haven't made up my mind yet. The commander says he will give me some horse shoeing jobs. I see these cowboys branding these wild cattle. I don't know much about being a cowboy, but it looks like if you want to work you could build a herd pretty fast."

"Well, until you make up your mind, you stay right here with us. If you want, you can do some work around here for your keep. If you don't, I love you and will keep you anyway."

"Thank you very much Loupe Rose. I will be happy to do the work you need."

"I see that Marie has got eyes for you already. She is a nice girl."

"I just don't buy girls. I am not ready to fall in love and settle down. If she wants to sleep with me just for the sport of it, I would be glad to oblige her."

Loupe Rose laughed. "You are a tough one Rusty Montana. I will leave that up to you and Marie."

They sat at the table and talked and drank. Marie brought them a huge steak and some fresh baked bread. Rusty could hear the crowd beginning to gather in the bar.

"It sounds like you have a booming business already."

"Yes. I need more girls. I don't suppose you would go south of the border and bring me back six or seven new girls?"

"Loupe Rose, I must admit that sounds better than branding cattle or shoeing horses. Let me sleep on that."

Rusty and Loupe Rose made their way to the lobby and up to the bar. Loupe Rose introduced Rusty to a middle-aged, rather heavy cowboy.

"Rusty, this is Bull Short. He has a lot of cattle and he brands more every day. Bull this is Rusty Chandler, my kid brother."

Bull looked a bit shocked until Loupe Rose explained the relationship.

"Rusty may want to talk to you about going to work as a cowboy. But first he is going to Mexico and bring me back some pretty girls for this establishment. Maybe he can find a filly that satisfies you. Bull here doesn't like any of our girls except Marie, and she seems to prefer the younger men."

Loupe Rose was polite enough not to mention his big belly or his bad breath. The trio sat and drank and talked.

Finally, Rusty Montana said, "Mr. Short, I will make you a deal. I will bring you back the prettiest girl in all of Mexico for your very own, if while I am gone, you will put my brand on every fifth critter you brand."

Bull Short pondered only a moment before he responded. "With these conditions—if I do not like what you bring me, you have to endorse your brand over to me so all the cattle are mine."

Rusty realized he was not dealing with a fool. "How does this sound? I will give you two brands: the R-Bar and the C -Bar. When I get back, if you don't like the girl, I will sign over all the R-Bars. I will keep all the C-Bar cattle. You keep a good tally. I will be back in about a month. If you like the girl, I keep both brands."

Bull Short scratched his head. "You have a deal," he answered. Then they shook hands.

Rusty spent the next two days getting his gear ready for the trip to the border and helping Loupe Rose hang the new sign on the hotel. *Loupe Rose's-Rooms-Meals-Drinks.*

That night Sigrid came to the hotel, and Marie would not let him in. She explained that only officers were admitted, no enlisted men. This made Rusty Montana hopping mad. He realized that if he had not been kin to Loupe Rose, he would most likely not be welcome. He talked to Loupe Rose about the rule. She explained that if they let in enlisted men and men of color, the officers and white cowboys would not frequent her establishment. Besides, she explained that there were a lot of places the soldiers could go. There was another saloon in town and plenty of girls in the shacks and cribs. Rusty realized these were the rules, and there wasn't much he could do about it.

He went outside and told Sigrid that he was going to Mexico to get six or seven more girls for Loupe Rose. As for Sigrid, he was happy he was in the army. He had had about all the adventures with Rusty he could handle for the time being. He liked the warm cot and the thirteen dollar monthly salary.

Sigrid and Rusty went over to the other bar and had a drink. It was not long before a small, fat Mexican girl attached herself to Sigrid. As Rusty went back to the hotel he thought, "Sigrid will find out what sex is all about before morning."

CHAPTER 46

"Bull Short, if that is the kind of woman you want, that is what you will get."

It was a hot July morning when Rusty was readying to head for the border to hire the whores for Loupe Rose. He promised Loupe Rose that he would not hire any of the girls without trying them first.

He slung a large water bag over his saddle. In the saddle pockets he carried about two day's worth of food in the form of jerky and hard tack. Loupe Rose gave him expenses and enough money to buy a buckboard and a team to bring his quarry back to her hotel.

The cow camp where Bull Short was working cattle was not out of his way, so he decided to stop and cowboy a few days before he made his way south. He learned to rope, brand, and other general cowboy stuff. Bull was true to his word and branded the cattle agreed upon with Rusty's brand.

"Rusty, now you listen good!" Bull Short said. "I will tell you just what kind of a woman I want. She must be tall, with long black hair. She must be a hard worker, willing to cook and clean. No Indian blood, Spanish blood only. Young, I don't want anything to do with a woman over seventeen. She must be a virgin, or at the very least, never been married."

"Bull, if that's the kind of woman you want, that is the kind you will get."

After a few days of hot and uneventful riding, Rusty hit the Rio Grande. There was a Mexican farmer working the river bottom raising corn and peppers. Rusty stopped and asked about the town and what the accommodations might be. The farmer was very kind to him and said that he was welcome to stay in his modest hacienda and he could keep his horse in his corral. That evening, he and the farmer drank tequila and talked. Rusty learned a great deal about the community.

The next morning Rusty felt like he had drank too much tequila, but in general he was pretty happy. He would ride into town, buy a buckboard, and get to work finding the girls for Loupe Rose.

He started to dress and could not find his boots. Looking around, he saw that his saddlebags and guns were gone. Looking out to the corral, he could not see his horse. That bastard farmer had taken everything he had.

He had gone barefoot as a child, but as soon as he stepped out into the gravelly yard, he could see that his feet were too tender to get far. He could find no shoes in the house. He went to the door, and saw a man leading a burro toward the farmhouse. The burro was hooked to a cart that carried a woman with two small children.

The man explained that they owned the farm, and that his wife's father, who lived in another village, had died. The family had to leave the farm to go to his father-in-law's funeral. They had left the farm in charge of a man called Roberto. It was Roberto who had robbed Rusty. The family had never owned a pair of shoes, so there was not a pair of shoes for Rusty to borrow. The farmer told Rusty that a neighbor had recommended Roberto, and there was a possibility that he might know where Roberto had gone.

Rusty borrowed the family's burro and started out in the direction the farmer had told him. The little burro was a dun color and had a black stripe down his back. Folklore says that burros with this coloring are direct descendents of the burro that carried the Virgin Mary to Bethlehem. A burro is a very friendly, loyal animal. They have a tendency to be very cautious, which sometimes interprets into being very slow. After an hour's ride in the Rio Grande valley heat, Rusty found the farm described by the farmer.

Rusty knocked on the door, and a pretty Mexican lady answered. "Is Roberto here?"

"Oh si`. He just got home. He is out back showing the children how to shoot his new guns. Roberto has been working and his boss gave him guns, a fine horse, and many nice things. We can live much better now."

Rusty could hear the shots coming from the back of the house. He went around the side, picking up a stick on the way. He peeked around the corner and saw Roberto firing at a tin can. Two small children were watching. With all the lung force he could muster, he jumped around the corner of the house, pointed the stick at Roberto, and hollered, "Drop that gun or I will kill you and both kids."

Rusty rushed and picked up the gun. The children were laughing, thinking it was all a game, since Rusty only had a stick pointed at their father. Rusty did not point the weapon at Roberto, but laughed with the children, and messed the hair of the little boy.

"We had too much tequila last night and your father brought my horse and other things over to your house for safe keeping. That was very nice of your father."

Rusty went to his saddlebags and took out two coins and some paper money. He gave each of the children a coin. Then he handed Roberto a few bills and thanked him for keeping his stuff overnight.

"Roberto, if you don't mind, I would like to have my boots back."

Roberto sat down and took Rusty's boots off and handed them to him. Rusty got his horse, took the burro by the lead rope, and rode away from the happy family. The children were laughing, and Roberto was standing in bare feet watching Rusty go down the lane.

Rusty delivered the burro back to the farmer and rode into town. He figured the best place to find whores was at the whorehouses. It was still a little early for the girls to be up, so he just rode around town looking at the sights. He rode down a small street and saw a short and not too thin girl doing laundry. She had a baby about eighteen months old that was playing in the mud under the wash stand. He watched her for a spell and could see that she was working hard.

"Seniorita, my name is Rusty. Would you like a new job cooking for cowboys in Texas?"

The girl looked up from her work. Rusty could see she was mostly Indian. There was just something about her that made him know she was a good woman.

"Si`, I am a good cook. I can cook rice and beans. I make good tortillas, I can cook beef, and cowboys like all those things. My husband was a cowboy, but a bull gored him, and it is just me and little Fellipe. My name is Silva."

"You be at the town square Friday morning. I will have a wagon to take you and Fellipe north to your new job. We will have other girls going, so please travel light."

Rusty knew this was the kind of wife that Bull Short needed. She was exactly the opposite of what he had ordered. He wondered how he was going to convince Bull that this little fat Indian was the wife for him. Oh, what the hell. He had several days to worry about that.

By late afternoon he had cased the town pretty well and found what looked to be the best brothel in town. He went in and was greeted by a middle-aged woman in a green dress that displayed most of her ample female parts.

"We don't serve colored men here," she stated.

Rusty, as always, got mad at these racial rebuffs, but he managed to hold his temper.

"My name is Rusty Montana Chandler. I am not looking for the services of your girls. I am hiring girls to work in a very respectable house in Texas. I was wondering if you might have an excess of girls?"

The Madam looked the handsome brown man up and down. "Come on in."

She led Rusty to a small back room and gave him a drink of good whisky. "How many girls could you use?"

"I have orders for five or six."

"I have girls coming here every day looking for work. No way can I use them all. What is in it for me if I find you six of the best whores in all of Mexico?"

"I could pay you ten dollars for each girl."

"Make it twelve and you have a deal."

"I will make it twelve if you will let me have one of your girls and a room for the night."

"I told you before, we don't do business with you colored. But we do have one black girl. Her name is Black Jenny. She is always trying to get us to let black men in. She says they are ten times better in bed than any white man. If I let you take her for the night, you have to stay in the room. My white clients see the likes of you around here, and it would ruin by business."

The madam opened the door and called out for Jenny. She came in, and Rusty could not believe his eyes. She stood six feet tall. Her complexion was a dark shade, like polished steel. All she wore was a g-string and pasties over her nipples. She had long waves of black hair that hung down to her ass. She had a full mouth and eyes that looked at Rusty with a mixture of lust and romance rolled into one.

"Jenny, I want you to take this black man to your room. Show him the best night of his life. Don't let him come to the lobby or the bar. Take a good bottle of whisky with you. Rusty, I want to see you here in the morning."

Jenny took Rusty by the hand and led him to a small room with a bed and a nightstand. She flicked off the pasties and dropped her g-string. "Would you like a drink?"

Not waiting for an answer, she took the bottle and poured it between her bosoms. The clear, brown liquor ran down her belly, around her belly button and she caught it in a glass she held between her legs. Rusty took the drink and tasted the whisky. It was the best he had ever had.

She sat on the bed and invited Rusty to come to her. She peeled off his shirt and let his buckskin pants drop to the floor. She got up, taking a wash basin from the nightstand. He held the washbasin and she washed him. She then poured herself a drink. She used Rusty's manhood, to stir her drink. Jenny and Rusty explored each other until the wee hours. Rusty rose to very wobbly knees the next morning. His only thoughts were that this sure as hell beats shoeing horses for the Army.

Rusty knocked on the Madam's door, and she let him in. Sitting in a circle on the floor of the small room were six beautiful Mexican girls. To Rusty, they almost looked alike with long, black hair, brown skin and black eyes. They all seemed to be in their late teens. Rusty explained what was expected of them, and where they were going. He could see that no buck-board was going to be big enough to haul all these girls back to Loupe Rose's. He was going to have to have a larger wagon.

He told the girls to meet at the Town Square on Friday morning. He would be there with a wagon and they would start the journey to their new life. He set out to find a wagon and a good team.

CHAPTER 47

"One of the girls had the cramps and was not feeling well."

Rusty started looking for a team and wagon to haul his passel of ladies home to Loupe Rose. He soon found that such a thing as a large wagon did not exist in Mexico. He found burro carts, and even one small carriage.

With six women and all the things that women have, he needed a big wagon and a good team. If he just had a way to get them across the Rio Grande he felt sure he could find a wagon in Texas.

As arranged, on Friday morning, he met them at the Town Square. "Ladies, I have been unable to find a suitable wagon to transport you to your new home and new jobs. I am sure that one is available on the Texas side of the river. It is only two miles to the crossing. The river is low this time of year. We will all walk to the river and wade over to Texas. I will get a hotel room for you, find a large wagon, and we will be off in the morning."

The girls looked at each other and giggled, they all seemed game for the adventure. By the time they had made the walk to the river, the giggles were gone. The July sun was very hot, and the road was very dusty. After a short rest on the bank, they all waded out into the brown water. Rusty took little Fellipe on the horse with him.

One of the girls had the cramps and was not feeling well. She had only gone a few feet into the river when she was sucked down by quick sand. Rusty managed to get a rope on her and drag her back to the bank. He put her on his horse with Fellipe and, leading the horse, they started back across. The channel of the river was deeper and swifter than expected. The girls were all swept off their feet. Some could not swim, and all the parcels they carried went floating down the river. Rusty hurried to the other side and deposited Fellipe and the girl with the cramps on the Texas bank. He rode back into the river and managed, with the help of his horse and rope, to save all the girls.

They were wet, muddy, and had lost all of their belongings. Silva took over. She got them all behind some brush and made them strip, one at a time going to the river and rinsing out their clothes. Even in the hot sun, she built a small fire and hung the clothes on the bushes. In a half hour, things were looking a little brighter.

Rusty looked at the girls. Some were weeping, the others were just plain mad. He thought his best bet might be to head his horse north and not look back. He entertained this thought for only a few seconds. He had to stick to his bargain with them and get them to Loupe Rose. He could see that Silva was a natural leader. He addressed her the way he had heard his dad address overseers, with a tone of friendly authority.

"Silva, please make the ladies comfortable. I will ride into town and find a place to stay and bring back some food."

He knew that it was impossible to comfort the girls. Silva, with her new authority, moved among the girls and, in a short time had them in much better moods.

Rusty had not ridden far when he found a woman making tortillas. She also had a pail of honey. He managed to buy some of the tortillas and the honey. He took the treats back to Silva and instructed her to feed the girls. With the warm tortillas and the sweet honey, she had them laughing and in good moods when Rusty returned.

He had been unable to find a hotel in the small town, but luck was with him, and he did find a good covered wagon and a team of oxen. The oxen would be slow, but they could travel in modest comfort in the covered wagon.

It was late afternoon when the party started north. It was working out rather well, and in the cool evening, the oxen traveled much faster than in the heat. The moon was well in the sky when they entered a town that was larger than the river town. The local sheriff stepped out of his office, which was in the jail, and stopped the wagon. Rusty explained what he was doing with a wagonload of girls. Several of them were sound asleep.

The sheriff smiled and said, "The price for going through my town is that I have to sample one of these beauties."

Rusty eyed the jail. "Sheriff, I will make you a deal. I will see if I can get a girl to oblige you, if you will let us stay in your jail until late tomorrow afternoon." Rusty turned to the girls and asked for a volunteer. All of their hands went up.

"Sheriff, it looks like you can take your pick."

He escorted them into the jail to fairly clean cots and fresh wash water. The girls were in seventh heaven. "When things are bad it makes just a little good look very good," Rusty thought to himself. Silva chose to sleep in the wagon with Fellipe. Rusty took the oxen to a small pasture behind the jail and slept in a small stable that was close by.

The sheriff went into the jail with the girls. It was a three-cell jail and there were no prisoners in it. The girls decided to give the sheriff a good work out for letting them sleep in the jail. He put two girls in each cell. The sheriff was in his late twenties and not a bad looking man.

First, he would visit two of the girls in one cell and then go to the next cell. He never had it so good in his life. When Rusty found him the next morning, he was laying outside of the third cell. He had no clothes on, and he was breathing hard. He had claw marks on his back, and his penis look like a piece of raw meat. Rusty helped him up in a chair.

"Looks to me like you had quite a night, Sheriff."

"I've never had so much fun in my life. This is a great bunch of girls you have here. There is a bottle of tequila in the top drawer of the desk. I need a drink."

Rusty got him the bottle and a glass. He started to pour the tequila, and the glass slipped out of his shaking hand, and he poured tequila all over his raw penis. He let out a yell, never having anything burn so bad in his life. He ran out of the jail and jumped in the horse trough outside the door. There he sat in the horse trough, as the six girls gathered on the jail steps laughing their heads off at him.

The townspeople gathered around wondering what in the hell was going on. Rusty managed to get the sheriff's shirt out of the jail. Rusty got him out of the trough and wrapped the shirt around his lower half. The sheriff ran down the street in the direction of his house. The townspeople were laughing along with the six prostitutes on the jail steps. Rusty often wondered, in later years, if the sheriff had been elected again.

When it started to cool off, about four that afternoon, Rusty hitched the oxen to the covered wagon and started back on the trail. He was trying to scheme how he was going to get Bull Short to take Silva. He knew that she would be a perfect woman for him. She was smart and a worker. She had a very pretty, round face. She wore pretty much traditional Indian clothes. The first thing he would have to do was to get her into some better clothes.

It was about four in the morning when the tired oxen stopped by a small creek. It was a good place to camp for the day, in the shade of large oaks, with ample, cool water. The grass was green and good for the oxen. The camp was on the south edge of a small town. Silva cooked them a good meal. Rusty rode into town and bought two dresses that he thought would make Silva look better. They were only a half day from Bull Short's camp.

Rusty called Silva and a tall Spanish girl, named Carmen, off to the side. Carmen was just what Bull had ordered. She stood about 5'8" with long, black hair and the face of a Spanish princess. She was blessed with olive skin, breasts like two browned Parker house rolls, her legs started right where they were supposed to, and she was wide in the crotch.

"Carmen, I have a plan that I want you to help me with. We are soon going to be in a cow camp run by a man named Bull Short. He told me to get him a girl when I went to Mexico, and what he described was a girl just such as you, Carmen. What he needs and really wants, but doesn't know it, is a girl like Silva.

"When we get into camp, I will pair off all the girls with the cowboys. They will be so happy to see all these pretty girls, they will pay good. I will collect the money and keep some, but give most of it to the girls. Carmen, I will pair you with Bull. You be nice to him, but make him miserable. Don't let him have any sexual favors, and keep begging him for more money. Do not do any work for him, and ask him to do things for you."

Then Rusty turned and addressed Silva. "Silva, I will not pair you with any cowboys. Wear this new dress and help the cook with the meals. See to it that Bull's bed is all made up for him. By morning, he will be pretty mad at Carmen. I want you to bring him some coffee with a shot of brandy in it and some bread dipped in bacon grease. That is what he likes for breakfast. When we get ready to leave, I am going to take Carmen with us to Loupe Rose's, and you, Silva, I want to stay in cow camp. Do your best to please Bull, and if I don't miss my guess, he will want to take you to bed the very first night. You have been married, so I know you know how to treat a man in bed. Silva, Bull is a good man and very rich. He will make a good father for Fellipe and a good husband for you. If this plan does not work, I will take you out of Bull's camp when I get back from taking the girls to Loupe Rose's."

The cowboys hated to see the girls leave as Rusty loaded them in the covered wagon. The only exception was Bull. He was very happy to be rid of Carmen. The girls were very happy. They now at least had some money to replace their belongings that had disappeared in the river.

The wagon was barely out of sight when Silva had Bull's clothes washed and hung on the chuckwagon wheels to dry. The camp cook had allowed her to make a small bed in the chuckwagon for Fellipe. When the work was done, Silva served Bull a drink and his meal, but kept well out of his way. She had his bed all rolled out for him, and placed hers not too far away, but behind a patch of mesquite brush.

Bull watched Silva work. He was all horny from being with Carmen and not getting any sexual gratification at all. The small Indian woman looked better all the time.

Silva lay in her blankets smelling the smoke of the campfire and looking up at the bright Texas sky. It had been a long time since she had been with a man. She could feel a stinging fire in her loins. Silva crept through the night and quietly slipped into Bull's blankets.

Bull felt her soft, warm body and let his hands find her small and somewhat droopy bosoms. Silva found his hard member, it was about the size of a small stick of peppermint candy, but it felt good to her to have the warm body of a man close to her.

As if by magic, they were soon locked in each other's embrace. The sweat rolled off them, as the night was warm. Their two rather large bellies merged in a slick rhythm. The he-sweat and she-sweat added to the aroma. The alarm clock went off the same time they did. Bull was an early riser. He liked to work as many cattle as they could before the hot Texas sun got unbearable. Silva gave Bull a tender kiss on the cheek and made her way to help the cook with breakfast.

That afternoon, when they finished branding cattle, a surprised Bull found himself taking Silva and Fellipe down to the creek where Fellipe could go for a swim. Bull had never liked kids, but there was something about this little brown boy that he liked.

Silva and Bull sat on the bank and talked. She told him of her first husband, how he was a cowboy and how the bull had run a horn in his back. He only lived a few minutes. Bull talked of his boyhood on the Gulf of Mexico as a fisherman's son, and how he had gotten in the cattle business. It seemed that a rancher brought a herd of cattle to the gulf to be put on a boat to be shipped east and hired Bull to go back to west Texas to become a cowboy. It was only a short time before Bull had his own crew and was gathering the wild cattle on his own. Bull took Silva by the hand and looked into her dark eyes.

"Silva, I think I am falling in love with you."

"Oh, Bull, I know I love you. I will work hard and keep Fellipe out of the way. Maybe you can teach him to be a cowman like yourself. We must thank Rusty for getting us together. He seems to want to start gathering cattle just like you. My husband had branded a lot of cattle before he died, and he gave me this paper. He said if anything happened to him, the cattle would be mine and Fellipe's, but I had no one to gather them."

She gave Bull a wrinkled and worn paper.

"If I should die all my cattle, branded Double Bar, go to my wife Silva and my son Fellipe," the paper read.

"I would like to give the paper to Rusty and tell him, if he would go south and gather all my cattle, I would give him half."

Bull looked the paper over. "Silva, that sounds like a good idea to me. I have been branding some cattle for Rusty, but this would start his herd much faster and I would not have to brand any more for him. Rusty is a good man, but he has a lot to learn before he is a good cowboy. I could send Blackie with him. He is a good cowboy and could teach Rusty a great deal. Not only that, but he would be riding for my brand, and he would watch your interest. Blackie is the only black cowboy I have and he and Rusty seemed to get on well when Rusty was in our camp."

Silva's only comment as she kissed Bull was, "Bull, you are such a good man, and smart too."

Little Fellipe took Bull's chubby finger in his little hand and looked up at Bull with his big brown eyes. "Can I call you Daddy?"

Bull turned red, and rubbed his boot in the dust. "Well I...well I...don't..."

He picked up the little boy. "Sure-thing. Fellipe, Silva, and Bull. We are all going to be partners and family."

They walked back to camp, Bull let Fellipe ride his horse around camp while Silva helped the cook with the evening meal.

CHAPTER 48

"Lucy, that will start us out on even ground. I have never seen a girl cowboy."

Loupe Rose kissed her brother's cheek and gave him a hug. "Thank you so much for bringing me these fine girls. I got them all cleaned up and they all worked last night. The gentleman they entertained raved about them. I am glad you have use for that wagon. You are welcome to it, and here is some more money for your trouble getting the girls to me."

"Thank you very much Loupe Rose. I'm going to use the wagon as a chuckwagon, hire a few cowboys and gather cattle for a while. I have a lot to learn, but I know I can build a good herd. I'm going back to Bull Short's camp. I think I can work for him a while, and then I will head south. I hear there are a lot of wild cattle along the border. I will be back in the fall. Have a good bed, a good girl, and good steak ready for me."

Rusty got up in the wagon. He had two horses tied behind, and he was off to Bull Short's. He arrived at camp in time for a fine supper prepared by Silva and the camp cook. Bull wasted no time in telling him how happy he was with Silva and the little boy. Bull presented Rusty with a tally book with a brief description and the number of cattle he had branded for him.

Bull had branded fifty seven head for him. Thirty seven were cows, three bulls and he made steers out of another eight bulls.

Rusty worked at roping, branding, castrating, and earmarking cattle for the next week. He was amazed at how well Silva and Bull got on. He did some work remodeling the wagon to make a chuckwagon out of it. He also bought three new horses from a horse trader that came to camp. One of the horses was a big roan. Rusty saddled him, climbed aboard, and immediately found himself spread out on the hard Texas soil. Blackie had a good laugh, but Rusty did not think it was so funny.

He pointed to the big roan and said, "Blackie, you ride the big son of a bitch."

One of the cowboys got hold of the big roan's ears and eared him down so Blackie could get on. Blackie, on board the horse, made the first jump, and you could see the treetops under his belly. He came down hard, spun so fast his head almost replaced his tail, then with his head between his front legs he made several more bad jumps. Blackie sat the saddle as if he was part of the animal. The horse finally came to a stop.

Blackie dismounted, handed the reins to Rusty, and said, "He's going to make a hell of a horse."

Rusty Montana looked at that wild-eyed roan and said, "He looks more like a horse from hell."

Bull had made all the arrangements with Rusty about taking Blackie as a cowhand to help roundup Silva's Double Bar cattle. The morning they were to pull out and head south, Rusty gave instructions to Blackie. "Blackie, you are going to be the foreman. I am going to cook and keep shoes on the horses."

Blackie looked at Rusty with amazement and almost a look of disgust.

"Man, have you gone crazy? The boss can't be the cook anymore than the cook could be the boss. We won't be able to hire cowboys if they know the head boss is wearing an apron and has a fry pan in his hand. Don't you have any ego at all?"

In the world of cowboys, there was a pecking order that was like a religion. The owner, the cow foreman, cowboys, and at the bottom was the camp cook.

"I have learned to be a cowboy and I don't like it. I have eaten dust, been kicked, walked on, bucked off and I don't like it. When I was a little boy, my mother and Bolo kept me around the kitchen a lot. It was a much easier life than being a cowboy. I'll hire the cowboys so they know that I'm the owner, but then they are your responsibility."

Blackie just shook his head. "And your name is Rusty Montana." They headed for town to buy their supplies and see if they could hire some hands.

When they pulled into town, there was a tall young man dressed like a cowboy leaning against a building. The sign read 'Saloon and Girls'. Rusty stopped the wagon and asked if he was looking for work.

"I sure am."

He looked at Rusty and Blackie. "Don't know as I ever worked for a colored boss. I've ridden with many a black cowboy and they were fine hands. What's your deal?"

Rusty explained that they were going south to gather cattle for his own brand and for the Double Bar brand.

"That's the territory of Lord Chitin. He is a real Lord from England, came over to get into the cattle business. He's not goin' to cotton to anybody gatherin' in what he calls his territory. Everybody just calls him the "The Lord", he has some mighty tough hands, in fact he's pretty tough himself. You can expect trouble if you start working cattle along the border."

"We aren't really lookin' for trouble," Rusty responded. "But if it comes, we are ready to fight. You with us or not?"

"Hell yes. I'm with you. I've had a hankerin' to get at the Lord, but couldn't do it alone. I just can't make a deal with a dry mouth. Let's go have a drink and talk this over. We'll have to go across the street. They won't let black boys drink in this saloon. In case of trouble, I'm not a bad shot."

He took out his six shooter, and shot the hat off a little boy walking down the street. The little boy picked up his hat and frowned at the tall cowboy. "I wish you'd quit doing that. You've almost ruined this good hat."

Inside the saloon, Rusty stuck out his hand. "My name is Rusty Montana Chandler."

"Glad to make your acquaintance. My name is Patrick Quick, but everybody calls me Patsy. My ma always wanted a girl, so she called me Patsy, and the name just stuck."

Rusty thought to himself, "With the boss doing the cooking and a cowboy named Patsy, this is going to be one hell of a cow camp. Blackie will probably have a shit hemorrhage." They sat down and ordered a drink. Blackie had taken the horses and the wagon to the livery and went to find them a room.

"What about this Lord Chitin? Does he think he owns South Texas?" Rusty asked.

"He's a bad actor, and if you have the Double Bar brand signed over to you, he'll really be after you. He killed the last man that had the Double Bar brand."

"I got the brand from Silva. She said she was the widow of the man who had the brand. She said he was gored by a bull and died."

"That is pure bull shit. The Lord caught him and tied him to a tree. Tortured him something awful. Drove cactus under his fingernails, and even inserted hot needles in his penis. He was trying to get him to sign the Double Bar brand over to him. He wouldn't sign the brand over. He died a horrible death. The cowboys went back and told Silva he was killed by a bull. They didn't want her to know how he suffered."

Then Patsy said, "I guess I better come clean with you. At that time, I was working for The Lord. Now the Lord is doctorin' all the Double Bar brands. He started brandin' some cattle with a Lazy H. It's real easy to make a Double Bar into a Lazy H. You go hit the range and start branding cattle and there'll be a war."

Rusty had learned more in the last few minutes than he really wanted to know.

"You still want to go to work for me after you worked for the Lord?"

"You bet I do. I got sick of the Lord's double-dealing, and not only that, he fired me."

"Do you know where we could get one more good cowboy?"

"My partner is a real good hand. We rode together for years. The jail's holding the clam, but if you go the bail, you won't go wrong."

They finished the drink, and had one more.

"Let's go over to the hoos-cow and talk to your friend. What's his name? What's he in jail for?"

"Well now, Mr. Rusty Montana, the name is Lucy Quick. She's my wife. She's the best cowhand along the border. She can cut the nuts out of a critter and have him branded while most cowboys are still thinkin' about it. As to why she's in jail, well I guess you'd better talk to her about that. She takes it kind of personal."

They walked into the jail and the jailer took them to a back cell. Lucy was in her mid twenties and had dishwater blond hair and deep set blue eyes. She had buckteeth that could bite a pumpkin to the gut through a picket fence. She had on jeans that had seen better days, and you could not see a sign of a bosom under her plaid flannel shirt. She saw her husband coming and jumped to her feet.

"Patsy, what the hell are you doing runnin' with a nigger?"

"Now Lucy, settle down. This here is Mr. Rusty Montana Chandler. He wants to talk to you."

"Lucy, like Patsy said, my name is Rusty. He says you are a hell of a cowhand. We're going to be gathering cattle. I'd be happy to get you out of here, if you will go to work for me."

"I've seen a lot of cowboys who were niggers, but I never seen a nigger boss."

"Lucy, that will start us out on even ground. I have never seen a girl cowboy."

Lucy's blue eyes took on a sparkle. She broke out in a smile that exposed her large and long teeth.

"Mr. Rusty, I like you. And you bet I'll go to work."

"Guess we should settle a few things before we get too far in this deal. First, why are you in this jail?"

Lucy's big toothy smile came again. "Well, Mr. Rusty, I guess because it's the only jail in town."

She slapped her knee and let out with a big laugh.

Rusty thought about dropping the question, but when Lucy stopped laughing at her own joke she spoke up.

"It's like this. There are a couple of kids here in town, and they're always on the street. Patsy always shot the hat off the little boy, and I would shoot the hat off the little girl. One day I shot a little low and creased the kid's skull. It didn't hurt her much, but the sheriff took a dim view of our playin' with the kids. I rushed right to the kid when I seen I had nicked her. I asked if I could take her to her mother and dad. She said she was fine, that she only had a mother who was a hooker. She said her mother always told her that she probably had a dozen dads. Even after being nice to the kid, the sheriff put me in jail."

Rusty paid the bail, and the three of them went for a drink. Blackie showed up and was introduced. Rusty explained that he really didn't like to cowboy and he was the camp cook.

"If this ain't one hell of a crew," Lucy reflected. "The boss is a nigger, the cook is the boss, a girl is a cowboy, and a cowboy named Patsy."

Rusty gave Patsy and Lucy an advance so they could get a meal and a room.

"Mr. Rusty, I sure do thank you," Lucy said. "I just haven't had this Patsy in bed for most of two weeks. You wouldn't know it by looking at him, but he's a hell of a hand with a woman. Knows what makes us feel good."

Rusty gave orders for all to meet at the livery stable in the morning, and they would go to work or war, which ever came first. Blackie gave Patsy the big roan to ride. The horse did his level best to unseat Patsy, but was unsuccessful. When the horse stopped bucking, Blackie announced, "You're a cowboy, alright."

CHAPTER 49

"Lucy, I have sure had a hankerin' to get in your pants"

Rusty and his cowhands rode out of town just as the bantam rooster, mascot of the livery stable, made his morning wake up call. They rode until noon and set up camp in a box canyon that was nearly hidden in the mesquite brush. Patsy and Lucy knew of the place and thought it a good place to start the gather.

Rusty gave the orders for gathering. "Blackie, I made you foreman. Now I'm going to make you and Patsy co-foreman, as Patsy knows the country. First thing we'll gather all the Double Bar cattle we can find. We'll move them a day or two north before we start branding mavericks. Bring along those Double Bar cattle that have had their brands tampered, and we'll take them with us. I don't want any more trouble with this Lord guy than is necessary."

That evening about five o'clock, Rusty was skinning a javelina which came wandering too close to camp. He would make a fine supper. The three hands drove in a herd of Double Bar cattle. The count was forty-seven, and all were in good shape. Some of the brands had been tampered with and made into Lazy H's. Patsy and Blackie reported that with one more day, they would have most of the Double Bar cattle in that area pretty well rounded up.

They enjoyed a good supper of the wild hog. During the night they took turns at watch, but had no trouble. Before sun up, Rusty had a breakfast of the wild hog and biscuits ready for his crew.

That evening, the cowboys came in with over one hundred Double Bar cattle. The next morning they started north with the herd. The cattle trailed well, and they managed to pick up a few no-brands or mavericks on the way.

Rusty would watch as Patsy would rope the head of the mavericks, and with a graceful swing of his rope, Blackie would lay a loop around the hind legs of the critter. The critter would be stretched out on the hard Texas soil. Lucy, with a stroke of her sharp knife, would cut off the animal's scrotum and remove his testicles. Then she would brand the animal with Rusty's brand.

Patsy would ride in enough to slacken the rope so Lucy could get it off the steer's head. The steer would get up and kick off Blackie's rope. As Rusty

Montana watched this process, he came to the conclusion that he would never make a good cowboy. These hands worked with the grace and precision of ballet dancers. He would just be happy doing the cooking and keeping a tally on his cattle.

That night they had all just gotten in their bedrolls when Lucy had to relieve herself. She was in the buff and squatted by a large prickly pear, where a large diamond back rattlesnake happened to be hunting mice. Bang! The big snake struck right on the left cheek of her ass. She jumped up, and the snake's fangs hung in her butt as she ran back to camp. The men, who had not gotten to sleep yet, watched as this nude woman ran into camp with a six-foot rattlesnake hanging on her like a tail. It was a serious matter, but they just could not help but laugh. This vexed Lucy.

"You rotten bastards—get this snake out of my ass."

Patsy grabbed her and removed the snake and tossed it aside. It was a moonlit night, and Blackie shot the head off the snake. They laid Lucy on a blanket and took her sharp knife and cut a cross where the two small fang holes appeared. Patsy sucked out all of the poison blood, then chewed up a big wad of tobacco and stuffed it in the wound. By this time Lucy was pretty sick, but also mad, as the others teased her about the snake biting her in such a private spot.

The next morning found Lucy pretty sick, but not sick enough to die. They fixed a place in the chuckwagon for Lucy, and trailed the cattle north. Not far into the morning, they saw a group of three cowboys coming. Patsy recognized one riding a big white stallion as The Lord.

Patsy commented as they rode toward the trail herd. "This could be big trouble. It is The Lord himself and he has Pick and Nose with him. They're his bodyguards, and they're cold blooded killers."

Rusty outlined a quick plan to Blackie and Patsy. The two men's mouths dropped open at Rusty's plan, but it was too late to argue. The Lord was in camp.

Rusty stepped down off the chuckwagon he was driving to greet his guest. Just as he hit the ground, he drew his six shooter, and shot the big white stallion right between the eyes. At the same time, Patsy shot one of the bodyguards in the head, and Blackie shot the other in the heart.

The Lord struggled to get out from under his dead horse, and Blackie and Patsy disarmed him. Rusty poked a gun in his belly.

"You've been tampering with brands and we don't take kindly to that. To top that off, I've always wanted a nice white horse robe. The hide off that stallion will make a good one. Come to think of it, you're dressed up pretty fancy. Take off those duds."

They stripped The Lord. Rusty instructed Blackie to go catch a stray mule that had followed the herd for the last two days.

"Get on that mule and get out of here," Rusty ordered The Lord. "The people of south Texas don't like your kind. Here's some money to buy a ticket back to England."

The Lord mounted the mule. Rusty slapped the mule's ass, and the last view they saw was a nude man heading south on a black mule. The Lord never had a chance to utter a word as the whole process took very little time.

The next few days went slow for the herd, as they were short handed. Poor Lucy was getting better but could not yet sit a horse. They managed to add some mavericks to the herd, but there were no more Double Bar cattle this far north. Lucy was well enough to cook, so Rusty took her place castrating and branding. He was much slower than Lucy was. One morning he got bucked off the big roan and pretty badly skinned up. He just didn't like being a cowboy.

Rusty had noticed Lucy taking a shine to Blackie. If there was anything he did not need, it was a jealous husband on his crew. He had not seen them do anything out of line, but it was just the way they looked at one another. Patsy had noticed their behavior and wondered if anything was going on.

Lucy was all healed up and back in the saddle. There were some strays in a deep canyon. It was decided that Lucy and Blackie would go to the east side and Patsy would go on the west side to push them back to the herd. Patsy waited for the pair to get out of sight and then he followed them at a distance.

When Lucy and Blackie were deep in the rimrocks, Blackie made his move. "Lucy, I sure have had a hankerin' to get into your pants."

"Blackie, I've had the same feeling. I'd like you to get into my pants." Lucy slipped off her horse and dropped her pants.

"There are too many rocks here to lay on. Maybe we could do it dog fashion."

Lucy kicked free of her pants and got on all four. Blackie was so excited he could hardly contain himself as he mounted up. He was pumping away when a loop of a lasso fell over his head. He felt the yank as he went over backwards and was dragged for about twenty yards in the gravel and prickly pears. Blackie sat up, seeing stars and half-choked. He removed the rope from around his neck. His body was full of prickly pear stickers and covered with large scrapes and small cuts. He looked over his shoulder and saw Patsy sitting on his horse at the end of the rope. Patsy coiled his rope and rode off to keep the cattle moving.

When Lucy, Patsy and Blackie rode into camp that night, Rusty took one look and asked, "Blackie, what in the hell happened to you?"

It was Patsy who answered the question. "Blackie roped a big bull this afternoon. It pulled his horse down, and he drug Blackie for about fifty yards. We better get his clothes off and the cactus out of him and doctor his cuts."

It took most of the evening to get all the cactus pulled out of Blackie and his cuts and scrapes washed and doctored. Rusty took note that Blackie's horse did not look like he had been pulled down, and Lucy walked a little stiff, like maybe an object had been removed from her a little too fast.

The closest Blackie ever got to Lucy again was to say good morning.

The next day they rode into Bull Short's camp. It was just in time as they had gathered so many cattle they could hardly handle them without additional cowboys.

That night Bull Short and Rusty talked well into the night. They got out their tally books. Counting Silva's Double Bar cattle, they had well over 1000 cattle branded. They decided that they would go into partnership and only use one brand. The brand they would use would be the BVR on the right rib.

CHAPTER 50

"Rusty Montana had heard of a place called Montana."

In the next two years, the BVR Outfit had built a herd of thousands of cattle ranging across west and west central Texas. Rusty was general manager of the BVR Outfit and had an office in Forth Worth. He was very busy keeping tallies, hiring cowboys, and sending them out to the right camps.

Bull Short was his full partner, but Bull just could not stand being closed up in the office. He had his own camp, and Blackie and Patsy each had a camp. There was one problem, they had all these cattle and no place to sell them. If they could have gotten them back east, either the South or North would have loved to have this beef. If they tried driving them east, one of the two sides would confiscate them.

Rusty had heard of a place called Montana. He guessed in a way he was named after it. It had Army camps and miners, both of which would buy beef. Rusty sent word to Bull to come into the office.

"Bull, there's this place up north they call Montana. They've struck gold in the Virginia City and Bannock communities. There are several forts up there trying to keep the Indians under control. We could sell thousands of steers if we could get them up to Montana. I want you to take Blackie and some other good hands and drive at least a thousand head to Montana."

"No way am I going to leave Silva and little Fellipe to go to Montana," Bull answered. "Silva is going to have a baby in about five months. I'm not going to Montana. If you want to sell beef in Montana, you'll have to take a crew and go yourself."

They argued for a while and decided to go have a drink. They both got drunk and argued some more without any conclusions. It was about three the next morning when they decided to go to the local whorehouse. The Madam was a tall, buxom lass who had migrated from Scotland. She welcomed the pair. Rusty Montana was the only man of color she would let in her establishment. Rusty and Bull sat at the bar and ordered a drink.

"Boys, you're in luck tonight. I just got in two new girls, and I know you will like them," the Madam said.

A little blonde came out of a back room and made a beeline for Bull. Bull was pretty true to Silva, but every now and then a little piece of ass in a whorehouse was just what the doctor ordered. In a matter of minutes, Bull had his arm around the little blonde, and they headed off to the room.

A very young and very red-haired girl sidled up next to Rusty. Rusty was pretty drunk, and he never really liked white girls. He gave the girl twenty bucks and told her to go on her way. She acted insulted, but Rusty just smiled at her. He knew very well that she was better off with the twenty bucks than wallowing around with a drunken black man.

The next morning, Rusty found himself in his office, not really knowing how he got there. He did not feel a bit well. One thing had come to him while drinking the night before. He had made up his mind what he wanted to do. Bull came to the office feeling just as bad as Rusty did.

"Bull, how does this sound to you? I want to sell out to you, and as part of the payment, I want 1000 steers rounded up to drive to Montana."

"Just where in the hell am I supposed to get enough money to buy you out?"

"I'm going to price them to you cheap. You go to the bank, and they'll loan you the money. I want to take Patsy and Lucy with me. I'll make Patsy foreman, and I hope I won't have to do much cowboying."

They went to the bank and made the arrangements. Rusty deposited his share in the Fort Worth bank. It was quite a large sum, because in the past two years, he had branded a lot of cattle.

Rusty called Patsy into the office, and they discussed the preparations for the trail to Montana. Rusty informed Patsy that all he wanted to do was cook and keep shoes on the horses. He would fix his bed in the chuckwagon rather than sleep under the stars. Patsy joked that he was missing all the fun.

Rusty and Patsy decided to go to supper that night at a bar and club on the outskirts of Fort Worth. They ordered a drink and steaks. Patsy had to use the outhouse, which was behind the club. He noticed a small corral holding three steers. Cattle being his life, he went to take a closer look, and lo and behold, they all had the BVR brand on them. He thought nothing of it, as he knew that BVR beef was sold to most of the café's in Fort Worth.

Getting back to the table, he mentioned seeing the cattle out back to Rusty. Rusty commented that that was strange, as BVR cattle had never been sold to this club.

"I guess I will have to talk to the manager and find out where he is buying them."

The manager was called to the table. Rusty introduced himself as the general manager of the BVR Cattle Company and asked where he had gotten the cattle.

"I buy them every week from a black cowboy and a young lady that helps bring them in. We butcher every Monday. It is excellent beef. Come on out back, and I'll show you where we kill the beef and get it ready for the dinner trade."

Rusty and Patsy went out back with the restaurant manager and were shown the facility. Rusty noticed a collection of small metal objects on a shelf in the slaughterhouse and asked about them. The manager explained the strange objects.

"From time to time, we find metal objects in the second stomach of the cattle. It seems that these objects are sometimes swallowed by the cattle and fall into the second stomach. It doesn't harm them unless they are sharp objects. If it's a metal object like a nail, it'll puncture the stomach and make the animal sick."

The manager took a bullet off the shelf and held it for Rusty's inspection. "This is a 45 slug that the critter picked up. It was in his stomach, but the animal was very healthy. I don't know why I keep this stuff around, it's just kind of interesting to me."

Rusty thought it was interesting too and made a mental note of it, for no particular reason.

After the meal, Rusty inquired of Patsy as to what he knew about the matter of the cattle being delivered to the restaurant manager.

"I know one thing for sure, that description the manager gave was of Blackie and Lucy. Lucy has been leaving camp every Sunday, says she is going into town to visit her sick mother. I know for sure that her mother is sick, as I went with her once, and the old lady was not well. There was a sexual incident when we were working cattle down south. I thought it was all over between them. However, the past few weeks I have had some suspicions about what they were doing."

They decided that the following Sunday night, Patsy would follow Lucy. Rusty would go to the slaughterhouse of the restaurant and wait to see who showed up.

Patsy followed Lucy directly to her mother's home. She stayed about an hour and went directly home. Patsy confronted Lucy about the cattle stealing. She laughed and gave Patsy a big hug.

"You know I am true to you. I would never steal cattle."

Rusty lay in the brush beside the slaughterhouse, and sure enough, here came Blackie driving three of the BVR steers. The restaurant manager paid him and locked the stolen cattle in the corral. There was no girl with him. Rusty decided it was no use to cause trouble right then. He would get the Texas Rangers and catch Blackie with the money in the morning. He was sure the restaurant manger would identify him. Facing prison, Blackie would surely disclose his female accomplice.

It was four the next morning when Lucy was up saying she could not sleep and had to relieve herself. She went to where Blackie had his bed rolled out.

"Blackie, Blackie it's me Lucy. They are on to us. Rusty Montana and Patsy know about the cattle deal. You better make a run for it. I have Patsy convinced I had nothing to do with the cattle rustling."

Blackie took Lucy in his strong black arms. "Lucy I love you. Come with me."

"Blackie, it's been fun sneaking around, making love with you and rustling cattle, but my heart has always been with Patsy. You run along before the crew gets up. They'll hang you if you stay here."

Blackie's blood boiled. "You white bitch, you mean you never loved me even a little?"

"Now Blackie. Settle down. I didn't say that. I just said that my heart was with Patsy."

They had talked too long. Patsy walked up to them. "Freeze where you are Blackie, or I'll blow your fucking head off."

Blackie went for his gun. Patsy shot his black friend in the shoulder. Blackie spun around and went to his knees, dropping his gun.

"Get up and keep your hands where I can see them."

Lucy started to cry and pleaded with Patsy. "Don't shoot Blackie. Please don't shoot him."

Patsy kicked Blackie's gun out of the way and took his gun off cock, but kept it pointed at Blackie. "We've been through a lot and had a lot of fun, the three of us. Now you're fuckin' my wife and stealin' the Boss's cattle. I should shoot you both. I overheard Lucy say she wanted to stay with me. Those days are over. I can't believe what scum and rats you two are."

Several of the other cowboys had gathered around.

"Bill, go to the corral and get a horse for each of these two no goods. Rusty will be here soon with the Texas Rangers to take you both to jail. I'm going to do you a favor. Now get on those horses and get the hell out of here. I'll try and stall the Rangers long enough to give you a head start. I never want to see either of your faces again."

Just as Blackie and Lucy dropped over the horizon, Rusty and the Ranger showed up.

"Rusty, I will tell you the way it is. Lucy and Blackie had been stealing the cattle. They also had been sharing bedrolls. I have been their friend for a long time. I just couldn't turn them over to the Rangers without giving them a chance." Patsy pointed south. "That's the way they went. If you want them, go after them. They have no guns, and Blackie has a slight shoulder wound. I am sick of Texas. Let's get these critters started for Montana."

Rusty looked at the Ranger and said, "Let them go. I think, in their lifetime, they'll make their own punishment much better than any prison could."

Rusty's true thoughts were, "When push comes to shove, I want Patsy on my side."

CHAPTER 51

"Her name was Min Ling, and her job was to clean Rusty's room once a week."

It was early May when Rusty and Patsy left Texas with a thousand steers and a crew of six cowboys.

Just at dusk on the second night out, two shots broke the silence of the Texas plains. Rusty and Patsy were standing by the cook fire. They looked at each other wondering where the shots came from and why. Then one more shot sounded, and a horse on a far picket fell. The shots seemed to be coming from a small knoll off to the south.

"Patsy, get your horse and go around the cattle to the north. Those shots have them uneasy. I will ride around to the south."

It took all hands to hold the cattle from stampeding. By the time things were settled down, the only damage was the loss of one horse. Darkness had set in and there was no use to search for the perpetrator.

Patsy remarked over a cup of coffee, "I bet that was Blackie telling us good-by."

The trail drive was pretty routine from that point on. They lost some cattle to river fords and had to part with some cattle to wandering Indians who demanded bounty for crossing their territory.

Rusty had managed not to do much of the cowboy work, but kept the horses shod and did the cooking. Patsy handled the crew and the cattle. They sold 500 head in Colorado to miners for a very good price. Rusty gave a large bonus to Patsy and the other cowboys. He put the rest of the money in a Denver bank.

Near Bozeman, Montana, Rusty sold another 250 head to the Army. With what they had sold and what they had lost, they arrived in Virginia City with about 175 head.

Rusty stood, overlooking Virginia City. The September Montana sun was setting behind snowcapped mountains. The yellow of the quaking aspen and the cottonwoods blended into the green of the pines and the white of the new skiff of snow. This was God's country, the most beautiful place that Rusty had ever been. He and his cowboys had finished selling the cattle to the miners. Despite the chance of getting rich with a good gold strike, all the cowboys chose to go back to Texas.

202

As Patsy departed, he said to Rusty, " I just couldn't take digging in the cold ground. I want to see blue bells, mesquite brush and look at all those Texas stars."

Rusty shook hands with all his loyal crew, paid them off, and they were on their way back to Texas.

Rusty decided to keep his chuckwagon, as he could find no ready market. He took a small room over the Chinese laundry. The Chinese family lived below. They were a very hard working family, saving every dime they made so they could return to their homeland. They had two children, a boy about eleven and a girl about seventeen. Her name was Min Ling. Part of her job was to clean Rusty's room once a week.

Rusty took a job working a claim. The claim belonged to a man named Mr. Burger from Missouri. He was a good boss. Rusty did not really like the work, but knew this was the best way to learn the mining business. Rusty kept very much to himself. He did not go to the whorehouse or the saloons in the evenings, but returned to his small room and read all he could find about mining.

As the Montana winter set in, Rusty and his boss were unable to do much work in the frozen ground. Rusty sat in his room remembering his childhood in the old south. He reminisced about the magnolia trees and the warm, humid nights with the fireflies playing in the reeds along the creek. He wondered about his father and his mother, Mary Annabelle. Even though he had been a slave, those were good days. He wondered how the war was going. There were reports that the North was winning. He knew this would be very hard on his father.

A rap on his door interrupted his thoughts. Rusty opened the door and greeted Mr. Burger.

"Good day Rusty. Can I come in and talk with you?"

Rusty liked the man very much and was glad for the company.

"Rusty, it is time for me to go home. I am lonesome for my family. I have a small stake in gold, and as you know, it is very hard to get gold out of Virginia City. The outlaws will kill you for a dry pair of socks, let alone gold. I have a plan that I think will work. First, I would like to trade you my claim for those two horses that you have in the livery. The claim is not real rich, but you are a good worker, and you'll be able to make some pretty good money over the next summer.

"There is a little more to the trade than just the claim for the horse," Mr. Burger continued. "I will throw in my house and all the tools you need to work the claim. You must accompany me for two days. By then we'll be out of outlaw territory, and I will go on to Fort Benton. I will stay in Fort Benton until spring and catch a riverboat back home. We'll only take our guns and pretend we are going hunting. This will throw the outlaws off. They won't realize that I am carrying the gold."

Rusty did not answer right away.

"Hell, I'll do that. Not only does it sound like fun, you're offering me a very good deal."

They went to the livery and got the two horses that Rusty had saved from his Texas trail drive. Rusty noticed that Mr. Burger's saddlebags were very heavy. He most likely had more gold than he let on, even to Rusty. They had not ridden far when they noticed three men known to be part of the Virginia City outlaws following them. They deliberately turned off the trail and headed for the foothills. The three men kept them in sight and just out of reach of rifle shot. There was a bunch of elk lying in a patch of quaking aspen.

"Mr. Burger, I think we should shoot one of those elk. That would convince the three of them that we were really hunting."

While they were dressing the elk, the three outlaws rode up. One of them was named George and had a bad foot.

"What you boys got in those saddle bags?"

Mr. Burger went to his horse and took off the saddlebags and handed them to George. Rusty was very surprised, but showed no sign of it. He kept on dressing the fresh killed elk. George, who had drawn his gun, holstered it. He gave a strange look, and after thanking Mr. Burger, the three rode off.

As soon as the outlaws were out of sight, Mr. Burger mounted his horse and said, "Let's get out of here before they find out that those saddlebags are full of rocks. I have all my gold sewed into my clothes."

They rode hard and fast until they arrived at a stage stop. As planned, Mr. Burger would take the horses and go on to Fort Benton, and Rusty would take the stage back to Virginia City. Mr. Burger did not stop for long. He wanted to put all the distance he could between him and Virginia City.

Rusty arrived back in town the next day. It had turned very cold. Rusty knew that the elk they had killed would be frozen, and if the wolves and other varmints had not eaten too much, it would be excellent food. He rented a horse and went back to the kill. He was in luck. Only a few magpies had found the kill and had pecked on it very little.

Arriving back in town with the elk, he gave half of it to the Chinese family that had been his landlords and took the other half to his new cabin. He made arrangements with Min Ling's father so that she would come and clean his new quarters once a week.

Rusty's new cabin was much larger than his room over the laundry and had good homemade furnishings. The cabin was three-quarter log, with the backside built into the face of a rock ledge.

The next morning, Min Ling came to do her cleaning. Rusty had not been home when she had cleaned his room. Here in the cabin, as she moved with feminine grace about the room dusting and cleaning, he felt a stirring in his loins. It had been a long time since he had been with a woman. Her soft, brownish skin with its amber tone added to his interest, and those soft, brown eyes would meet his from time to time. She spoke very little English. He offered her a bowl of elk stew, which she accepted, and they both ate in silence. After the meal, he took her soft hand and pulled her into his arms. She gently pushed him away and smiled, saying, "Tomorrow. Tomorrow."

The next morning she and her father showed up at Rusty's cabin. She had a small bag with all her belongings. Rusty invited the pair in and the father bowed and presented Min Ling to Rusty.

Mr. Ling spoke no English, but Rusty got the message. Min Ling spoke in her best English, "I told father of our deep love. He said you are a good man, and he brought me to you."

Mr. Ling made a deep bow and left the two standing in the cabin. This was the first time in his life that Rusty was at a complete loss. Min Ling went to the stove and dished two more bowls of the elk stew. They ate, then she removed the dishes from the table and washed them. There was a good, warm fire in the stove, the wind howled outside and the temperature had dropped to ten below.

She came to Rusty and let her dress fall to the floor. This revealed a young, soft, amber body with almost no breasts—just two large nipples. The triangle of hair at the base of her flat stomach was soft as kitten fur. He took her in his arms and they fell back on the bed. He was hot enough to boil, but knew better than to hurry or hurt her.

He took her hand and closed it around him. Her soft hand made two strokes and he ejaculated all over his own belly. Min Ling let out a soft laugh and got a cloth and cleaned him.

She lay back down and took his hand and placed it on her soft patch of kitten fur. It was not long before Rusty was once more ready. He rolled over on his soft brown partner. She let out with soft moans as she locked her legs over his back in a gentle, but vice like, grip. They made love all day long with the wind howling outside and the thermometer stuck at twenty below.

That night, she fried him elk steak and made tea, which she had brought from her old home. Rusty remembered his mother telling him that if he were a good boy, he would go to heaven. He told himself, "I must have been a very good boy."

Chapter 52

"The war is over! The North has won! Lee surrendered to Grant."

Rusty and Min Ling enjoyed a great winter. Three or four days a week, Min Ling would go help her parents with the laundry.

Rusty did some hunting and prepared his tools for spring. Rusty spent a good deal of time teaching Min Ling English and found that she was extremely bright in numbers and arithmetic.

They would go downtown and eat at the café and saloon about once a week, keeping a low profile. Rusty would see some of the men he knew to be outlaws hanging around town. The winter was not too bad, with a cold snap, and then a Chinook wind would come over the Rockies and warm things up and melt most of the snow.

The townspeople would not let Lee Wee Ling, Min's little brother, attend the local school. The only reason Rusty could think of was that he was Chinese. Rusty would spend some of the winter days schooling Lee Wee. He, too, was very bright with numbers.

With the coming of spring, Rusty worked his claim all day. It was producing a little gold, not much more than it took him and Min to live. He could see that it was about to run out altogether. He sometimes wondered if Mr. Burger had known this when he sold Rusty the claim.

Rusty would never forget the day. It was May 15 and Virginia City got one of its biggest-ever spring snow storms. A heavy, wet snow fell all night and all day. He and Min were snowed in. Outside, the snow was four and a half feet deep. They made love and read and made love again.

He looked at the back wall of the cabin, under the stone cliff. He reasoned that if he chipped out a foot or two of the cliffs, they would have more room. He could put the chipped rock in front of the cabin, because when the snow melted, it would be very muddy. He had not made over ten swings at the wall with his pick when a rock fell to the floor, leaving a vein of gold exposed. The vein was six inches high and almost a foot long. Both he and Min dug at the gold all day and into the night. By midnight, they had the wash basin and the dish pan full of almost pure gold.

He and Min hung the curtain, which they had always kept over the wall, and hid the gold under the bed. It was time for decisions. If the town ever found out they had a big strike, the outlaws would stop at nothing to get the gold. They wanted to share some of it with the Min family, but if they did, word would surely get out.

Rusty knew that the Vigilante Committee was meeting every week, and they had already hanged some of the outlaws. Up until this time, Rusty had played a very low-key role in Virginia City. After much discussion, he and Min decided that he should take an active role in the Vigilante meetings. He could at least identify the three men who tried to hold up Mr. Burger.

He sat in the back of the hall as the meeting came to order. He could tell by the looks and the whispers that the group was talking about him. Most likely, they were saying, "What's that nigger who lives with the Chinese girl doing here?"

The chairman rapped the gavel, and the meeting came to order. "Our first order of business is to take into custody the new comer in the back of the room."

Three men seated next to Rusty held him and tied him up. The chairman continued. "Young man, we have been watching you for some time and are very happy that you presented yourself tonight so we did not have to come and get you. It is our understanding that you have been hiding out with that Chinese girl, and working with the outlaws. We know for a fact that your claim is not any good, yet you have money for everything you need."

Rusty took a few steps to the front of the hall. With his hands tied behind him, he pulled himself to full stature and addressed his captors.

"Gentlemen of the Committee. You are right that Miss Ling and I have been keeping to ourselves. This certainly has nothing to do with our working with the outlaws. What it has to do with is the color of our skin. You all know that a black man and a Chinese girl are not welcome in the social realm of Virginia City society. The reason I came here tonight was to see if I could help the community rid Virginia City, and all of Montana, of the outlaw gangs. I can identify three of the outlaws that tried to rob Mr. Burger. There is no need for this identification at this time, as the three did nothing wrong. They confronted Mr. Burger and myself. Mr. Burger gave them two saddlebags full of rocks and they rode off."

There was a murmur of laughter in the hall. Rusty then continued. "As to having money, you seem to have forgotten that I rode into town with a herd of longhorns, which most of you bought at least one. Now, if someone would be so kind as to untie me, we could get on with this meeting."

Suddenly, the door of the meeting room flew open and a young man rushed in. "The war is over! The North has won. Lee surrendered to Grant."

There were some cheers and some boos, but in general, a great feeling of relief. A Mr. Stewart came to Rusty and introduced himself and untied

Rusty. "Sometime I would like to talk to you about the cattle business. But for now, lets all adjourn to the saloon and have a drink."

Rusty joined in with the good citizens of Virginia City for a night of drinking and good fun. The most prominent citizens of the town accepted him. He and Min Ling were invited to the theater as guests of the newspaper publisher for a performance the next night. The men were very respectful. The women still looked down their noses at Min Ling.

When Min Ling and Rusty got home that night, they lay in bed and made plans. Rusty told Min that he planned on marrying her and giving her parents enough gold so they could get home to China. Then he and Min Ling would get their gold out of Virginia City and return to the South. Min Ling lay beside him, gently rubbing his belly with her small hands. She loved the feel of his skin, and it seemed to Min that he was always ready. They made love, and it was after that, Rusty noticed that Min Ling was crying. He raised up on one elbow and wiped her tears away.

"What is the trouble, my little China doll?"

"It will be sad for me to leave my parents and never see China again."

"Min Ling, we are very rich with all of our gold, and I have quite large sums of money in several banks from my cattle business. After we go south and see my family, we will go to China for a visit." This plan seemed to please her. She stopped crying and they fell asleep.

The next morning, Rusty worked the mine in the back of the cabin, and announced to Min Ling that the vein had run out. They had taken all the gold that was in the vein, and it was plentiful.

That night Rusty went to the bar for his meeting with Mr. Stewart. "Rusty, I know you know cattle. My brother, Jim, and I are building large herds here in Montana. We have sold a herd to the Army at Fort Benton. I would like you to trail the cattle to Fort Benton for me."

Rusty's first thought was to politely tell Mr. Stewart to go to hell, that he had all the cattle business that he wanted. Then the thought struck him that it may be a good way to get his gold to Fort Benton, where he wanted to go anyway.

"Mr. Stewart, I would be happy to help you with your cattle drive. I have a good wagon, as I want to take Min Ling with me. We are going to be married. Then we will take a riverboat down the Missouri. I want to return to the south, now that the war is over."

They began gathering cattle the next day. Most of them were ranging on the grass hills and along the meadows of the Ruby River. They would keep them held on the meadows until it was time to start for Fort Benton. When Rusty arrived home after two days of gathering cattle, Min Ling was not home. He paid no attention, as she often went to help in her parent's laundry. It got late and he decided to go to the laundry and see if everything was alright. When he got there, there was nobody around. Upon closer observation, he found that most of their personal belongings were gone.

"She could not have left me. I love her very much. She would never leave me. The townspeople must have run them out of town, or worse." These thoughts gushed through Rusty's mind as he ran to the stage station. He woke the stage master, who was asleep at his desk. "Have you seen anything of the Ling family?"

"Oh yes. They left yesterday on the stage for Salt Lake City. Seems they got homesick for China. We will miss the laundry, but it is good riddance for the town to be rid of those Chinamen."

Rusty slowly turned away and walked back to the cabin, which was now half cave and half cabin after the mine he and Min Ling had carved into the cliff. He checked the hiding place for gold and the wash basin of gold was missing. He sat down at the homemade table where he and Min Ling had shared so many pleasant meals. A tear dropped from his eye to the rough surface of the table. He had loved and lost.

A rap-rap came to his door. Rusty opened it and there was a small boy. He introduced himself as a friend of Lee Wee. Rusty asked him in, and the boy told his story.

"I overheard some men talking, and they told of killing some Chinese people when they were robbing the stage yesterday. I know the Chinese girl was a friend of yours, like Lee Wee was a friend of mine. Could you please go after them and see if you can help?"

"Why didn't you go to the sheriff?"

"The sheriff was the one talking about robbing the coach."

Rusty gave the boy a small nugget and made a request.

"You go tell Mr. Stewart that I am riding south to try and help our friends. Tell him I will be back in a few days, and we will start the cattle drive north."

The boy gave Rusty a big smile and was off on his errand. Rusty saddled his horse and headed south as fast as he could go.

CHAPTER 53

"We had reliable reports that these people had a suitcase full of gold."

When the Ling family was getting on the stagecoach, the station manager noticed that one of the suitcases the Ling's were carrying seemed extremely heavy. He notified his outlaw friends of this fact.

The man driving the coach that day was a small man with a quiet and unassuming disposition. He was known around town to be kind and helpful to people in need. The outlaws had tried several times to solicit him to become one of them because of his job as a stage driver. He would decline the offer. His only fault seemed to be that he was madly in love with a woman who managed the first stage stop south of Virginia City. She was not a member of the organized outlaw gang but was, in herself, a robber and a murderer.

She, at one time, had been a very heavy woman who had lost a lot of weight. Her large bosoms now hung almost to her belly button, she never tried to control these ample bosoms. They would flop from side to side as she walked. Thus she became known as Floppy. She had the reputation of being very cruel to animals. Despite all of this, the driver could not wait to get to that first stage stop to share her bed.

Somewhere south of Virginia City, Min Ling noticed four riders following them. She had heard Rusty talk of the outlaw gangs, and took this to be a warning. She asked the driver to stop the coach. She quickly got the gold out of the coach and hid it behind some rocks. Then, getting back aboard, she ordered the driver to go on.

It was only about a half-hour before the outlaws surrounded and stopped the stage. The Chinese family were the only ones in the coach, and the outlaws ordered them out as they held their guns on the driver. The outlaws ordered the driver to throw the luggage off the top of the stage to the ground. They opened it and spread the contents over the ground, not finding the gold. Their tempers flared. The driver had always had the Lings' do his laundry, and he really liked the Chinese family. What appeared to be the leader of the gang, cocked his gun and asked where the gold was. The driver, thinking that none of the family could speak English, answered for them.

"These people have no gold. They are just trying to get back to their homeland. Where on earth would they have ever gotten any gold? They are just a hard working family."

"We had a reliable report that these people had a suitcase full of gold, and they put it on this stage."

With that, he shot Mr. Ling, hitting him in the neck. Mr. Ling made a grab for his neck and hit the ground hard.

"Now, I am just going to keep killing these people until they tell me where the gold is."

He shot Mrs. Ling in the chest, and she dropped. Her heart pumped her lifeblood out on to the Montana soil.

Min Ling could stand no more. She let forth with a scream and rushed the robber's horse, waving her hands and screaming. Neither the horse nor the man were expecting this move. The horse reared, dumping the rider. In the confusion, the driver was able to get his shotgun and got two shots off at the robbers. They were good shots and found their mark. The remaining robber had had enough and turned and ran.

The outlaw leader picked himself up out of the dirt and stared down the barrel of the driver's shotgun. He raised his hands in surrender. Two wounded robbers tried to get up, but it was too late, the gaping holes in their chests drained out the life giving air and blood. Lee Wee Ling stood, with tears streaming down his face, as he looked down at his dead parents.

The driver gave the orders, as he tossed Min Ling a short rope. "Tie the hands of that no good behind his back."

Min got behind the outlaw and pulled his hands back with authority, tying them very tight.

"Now pull off his boots and tie his feet."

Min did as she was ordered.

"Now get in the coach. We will go back and get your gold and be on our way."

Min dropped to her knees beside her dead parents. "We cannot leave them. We must bury them."

"We haven't time. That outlaw who got away will be back with well armed help."

"Please, let us take their bodies. We can bury them later."

The driver and the two Chinese loaded the poor dead parents in the coach. The driver got the team turned and headed back. When they got to the place where they had stashed the gold, Min and Lee Wee jumped out, and with great effort, got the heavy gold loaded in the coach. The driver again turned the team and headed south.

They had not gone far when the driver shouted down to Min and Lee Wee that there were three outlaws chasing them. "Toss out the gold, and they will stop. It will save our lives. I will toss down the strong box from up here. We have a chance."

Min dumped the gold out on the floor of the coach and tossed out the suitcase. The driver looked over his shoulder and saw that the ploy had worked, at least for the time being. The robbers had stopped and were inspecting what had been dumped. He whipped his tired team to get some more distance between the coach and the robbers.

The driver pulled into the first stage station south of Virginia City with a very tired and lathered team. His two dead passengers and the two very sad and scared Chinese children made a grim load. Floppy, the mistress of the station, greeted the troubled coach. She cooked them a good supper and made arrangements for graves to be dug behind the stations. She then made Min and Lee Wee as comfortable as possible in a clean room with two pallets. It was getting late, and she promised that they would give the parents a decent burial in the morning.

The driver had to take a piss and went out behind the station. He noticed that three graves had been dug. He went back to the kitchen to find Floppy loading her gun, not getting ready for bed as he had expected. He was very horny, and oh, how good she looked.

"What are you loading the gun for? I want to get to bed. It has been a long time since we had a good round of love making."

"We have work to do. We just can't let those young Chinamen take all that gold out of the country. We take the stagecoach and the gold and go on to Salt Lake City and disappear among the Mormons. With all that gold, we could live, as the saying goes, 'happily ever after.'"

"You have to be crazy. You just can't kill those children in cold blood."

"I'm not going to. Here, you take this gun and go in there and shoot them both in the head. They are surely asleep by this time. You must love me enough to do this for me."

Floppy untied her shirt and, taking out one of her long tits, rubbed it gently over the driver's lips.

"Oh, Floppy, I do love you. Lets go to bed and think this over. Maybe in the morning I will feel more like doing such a terrible thing."

"You are such a chicken shit."

Floppy got up and went to the room housing the Chinese children. She found only Lee Wee, sound asleep. Min was gone. Looking out the window, she saw the girl standing by one of the open graves weeping. She gently opened the window and shot the girl in the back, blowing off the lower lobe of her right lung. Min toppled over into the open grave. Floppy turned and saw Lee Wee sitting up on his pallet. She shot him in the face at close range. He fell back on the pallet with his brains splattered on the wall.

Floppy and the driver dragged Lee Wee's body out and dumped it in the grave with Min. Min was gasping for breath and bleeding badly, but she knew that the body was that of her beloved brother. She struggled to get out from under the body, as Floppy dumped in the first shovel full of dirt. She fought hard to keep the dirt out of her face. Despite her wound, she still had the strength to struggle and keep on top of the dirt that was being shoveled in on her.

The driver had stood for all the cruelty that he could stand. He grabbed Floppy and tossed her back from the grave. She fell into the open grave behind him. The driver helped Min to the surface and laid her out on the ground, then ran to the stage station and got a blanket and covered her. She was still alive.

CHAPTER 54

"Were you really planning on burying that poor girl alive?"

Rusty rode his very tired horse up to the front of the stage stop. There were no lights, and there seemed to be no one around. Then he heard a noise coming from behind the main building. There, he found the driver weeping and pushing a woman back in the grave every time she tried to free herself.

The driver did not see Rusty behind him. Rusty dismounted and gave the driver a shove and he landed in the grave with Floppy. Looking down in the grave, Rusty asked, "Just what in the hell is going on around here?"

Both Floppy and the driver tried to talk at the same time, each telling entirely different stories. Rusty pointed his gun at the head of Floppy and ordered her to shut up. The driver looked up at Rusty.

"Before I talk, there is a Chinese girl over there under a blanket. She is about to die and needs help."

Rusty looked in the direction the driver was pointing and indeed, did see a mound of blankets. Rusty began to shovel dirt in the grave, holding the pair as fast as he could. Floppy protested.

"You can't bury us alive."

"I am not going to. I am only going to bury the pair of you to the necks, while I care for the girl. You two be thinking, as I will be wanting some answers."

When Rusty had the pair in dirt up to their necks, he turned his attention to Min. He carried her gently into the stage station and laid her on a pallet. He washed the wound and dug the dirt from her nose so she could get more air. Her beautiful yellow-brown skin was an ash gray. Her breathing was labored, and there was some air escaping from the bullet hole in her lower chest. She was babbling in a low, husky voice, but it was Chinese, and Rusty could make no sense of it.

He tutored her to be quiet, to save her breath for the energy she badly needed. He got a wet cloth and wet her lips. This was all he could do for now, except pray. He turned his attention to the two outside.

Rusty dug down in the grave until he could get Floppy's arms tied, and then did the same to the driver. Removing them from the grave, he took them into the stage station where he could keep an eye on Min.

"Now, I want to know what is going on around here," Rusty demanded.

Floppy was the first to speak. "This here no good driver pulled into my
station with two dead Chinamen and two kids. He told me they were loaded
with gold, and all we had to do was kill them and the riches would be ours.

He shot the boy at point blank and then tried to kill the girl. He is a
very bad man."

The driver then told his story, from the time the stage had left Virginia
City, until the present moment, and he told it very much the way it was,
even adding the details that he had been in love with Floppy.

Rusty looked at Floppy and asked, "Were you really planning on burying that poor girl alive?"

"No. No. I was just trying to scare her."

Rusty got to his feet and went to Min. She was not breathing and was
a ghostly gray with open eyes staring at the ceiling. Min was dead. Rusty had
lost her for good.

He walked back to Floppy, opened her shirt exposing the long breasts,
then took the bone-handled knife, which was made from the bone of his
grandmother's leg, and sliced off Floppy's right breast close to her chest. He
took the bloody trophy outside and put it in his saddlebag. He went back to
Floppy and, with the knife, he split her left breast right down the middle,
doing such and excellent cut that it even left half the nipple on each half.

After the grizzly operation, Rusty said, "Take that you bitch. That will
teach you to bury people alive. Now I am going to sit here and watch you
bleed to death."

The driver, who was still tied, spoke to Rusty in a tone that could have
been used by a Baptist preacher.

"Mr. Chandler, if you sit there and watch Floppy bleed to death, it
makes you no better than she is. The loss of her breasts is a great punishment, which she surely deserved. Now untie me so I can help her, and help
you bury your beloved Min Ling. God bless you Mr. Chandler."

Rusty, with bowed head and feeling as low as a snake's belly, untied the
driver.

Their first order of business was to get Floppy laid out on the bed and
the bleeding stopped. In only a short time, Floppy was no longer bleeding
and even made the comment, "What the hell, my real name was Ruby. I
guess I will just have to go by my real name."

Rusty and the driver spent the rest of the morning laying the Chinese
family to rest. Rusty mounted his horse and slowly rode back to Virginia
City. He rode slowly with his head bowed. He felt the terrible loss of Min
Ling and her family. He felt half-happy and half-ashamed for the condition
he had left Ruby in. He wondered what would become of the driver and

Ruby. He felt that the driver was still in love with her. Rusty left enough gold with the driver and Ruby to tide them over for a while.

As Rusty rode past the butcher shop in Virginia City, he saw two dogs lying on the boardwalk in front of the butcher shop. He thought of his prize in his saddlebag and tossed Floppy's (Ruby's) breast to the dogs. With a dog on each end of the breast, they had a tug of war, and as usually happens, the big dog won the prize and enjoyed a fine meal.

Rusty got to his home and fell into bed. He had never been so tired in his life. He was aroused the next morning by a loud rap on the door. His early morning guest was Mr. Stewart. Rusty invited him in and put on a pot of coffee.

"Rusty, I have some bad news. The Army canceled the beef contract, so we won't be taking any cattle to Fort Benton."

Rusty poured the coffee and the expression on his face showed the disappointment. "Mr. Stewart, I am very sorry to hear that. I was looking forward to the trip. I have a terrible story to tell you."

Rusty told the story of the killing of his beloved Min Ling, and the rest of the gruesome tale of the past few days.

"Would you sell me some cattle? I will trail them to Fort Benton and take the risk of getting them sold."

"Yes, I would love to sell you some cattle."

Rusty agreed to buy 100 head and paid Mr. Stewart for them in gold.

"Do you know where I could hire one good cowboy? I had planned on taking Lee Wee Ling to drive the chuckwagon and Min to do some of the cooking. That is all for not, and I will need at least one good hand."

Mr. Stewart gave this problem some thought. "There is an orphan boy who lives on the streets of Virginia City. The whores let him stay with them when it is really cold. His mother was a whore, but she died about a year ago. I guess he never had a father. He is only about thirteen or fourteen, but he is a hard worker, and I think that he is trustworthy."

"I will talk with him. I know who you mean. He was a friend of Lee Wee Ling's.

After the departure of Mr. Stewart, Rusty got out his gold and started pounding the nuggets into smooth forms. He made them into cylinders about two inches long and an inch in diameter. He was careful to keep the edges very smooth. He remembered the day when he was managing the BVR Outfit in Texas and had visited a small slaughterhouse that killed beef. The manager had a collection of different hardware items that had been found in the second stomach of the cattle. Rusty reasoned that if he could get his cylinders of gold down the cattle, they could carry the gold all the way to Fort Benton for him.

He would have to figure a way to supervise the slaughter of the cattle so he could retrieve the gold. He would cross that bridge when he got to Fort Benton.

He went to bed and could not sleep. He knew a way to get the gold into the cattle, but it would take more help than the orphan boy. He needed a good man he could trust.

Rusty was awakened by a dream, he had dreamed of his ordeal with the driver and Floppy. That was it, the driver. He was a good worker and a man that seemed to have a heart, and one you could trust. He did not even know his name. He was just the driver. This was probably a bad idea. He sure did not want anything to do with old Floppy. Just for the hell of it, he would go to the stage office in the morning and inquire about the driver.

On the way to the stage station, he met the orphan boy and asked him to meet him at his cabin in about two hours.

CHAPTER 55

"Rusty laid out the plans for getting the gold out of Virginia City."

When Rusty inquired about the driver at the stagecoach company, he learned that the driver's name was Johnson J. Johnson. He had left Virginia City and was on a run to Salt Lake City and would be home in about a week. The stagecoach company apparently had not learned of the trouble at the station south of Virginia City and Rusty thought it best not to tell them of the problems. He would just wait a few days and see how things played out.

Rusty arrived back at his cabin to find the orphan boy waiting for him. Rusty invited him in and fixed them a pot of coffee. Rusty introduced himself and the boy said his name was Wally Holt. Rusty began the interview by laying his needs on the line.

"Young man, I am looking for a man to work for me. He must be honest, willing to work long hours, and above all, loyal to me. In return, I will pay above average and treat him with respect. If you are interested, I want to know everything about you, from the day you were born until today. Remember before you answer, loyal, hard working, and honest. If you have any questions before you start, now is the time to ask them."

Wally looked Rusty in the eye and then dropped his eyes to the cup of coffee on the table before him. "Mr. Chandler, before we go on, I must ask you this. My mother never liked darkies. She said they were lazy and could not be trusted. You are a darkie, and that worries me."

Rusty took the boy gently by the chin and lifted his head to where he could look him in the eye. "Wally, niggers, darkies, black people, are just like whites. Some are lazy. Some are criminals. Some lie. I can assure you that I am none of these. However, if you do not feel good about my race, it is best we go no farther with this conversation. Here is a nugget for your trouble in coming over."

Rusty shoved a rather large nugget across the table to the boy. Wally looked Rusty straight in the eye and passed the nugget back to him.

"No, Mr. Chandler. I am very interested in going to work for you. I just thought it was better for me to clear the air about race, so you knew what was in my head."

They both sat at the table and looked at one another for what seemed like an hour, but it was only seconds. A smile turned the lips of both Wally and Rusty. Wally began his life history.

"I think I was born in Dodge City, Kansas. My mother was a whore and the first I really remember, we lived in Wyoming Territory. She would work at night, and during the day, she would stay with me in a small cabin in the alley behind the hotel where she worked. When it was time for me to go to school, she sent me to the local school. The other kids made fun of me for where I lived and the fact that my mother was a whore. I did not go to school much, but somehow I managed to learn to read.

"When I was about seven, we moved here to Virginia City. Mother went to work here as a whore for Madam Maude. Life was about the same, only I had a small room in the basement of the whorehouse. I went to school some with the same trouble I had before. I have managed to get some more learning. When I was about ten, my mother became sick and could not work for a while. She stayed with me in the small room, and I cared for her the best I could. Mr. Johnson, who was one of mother's customers, brought us some food and gave us some money. He is a very nice man.

"One day, Maude asked me to come to the living room of the whorehouse. There was a large, fat man sitting on the couch. Maude introduced us and asked me to go to the room with him. I had no idea what was going on, so I went. It was terrible, the things he wanted to do to me and the things he wanted me to do to him. It was an upstairs room, but I was so scared that I grabbed the wash basin and threw it through the window, then I jumped into the alley. I was very lucky and hit the ground running. This really pissed off Madam Maude, and she made my sick mother leave. Mr. Johnson gave us a small room in his house to live in. I did what work I could, and my mother just got sicker and sicker. In about six months, she was dead. Since that time I've been staying with Mr. Johnson some of the time and mostly on the street when the weather is good."

Rusty held up his hand to cut short the interview. "This Mr. Johnson you talk about is the same Mr. Johnson that drives the stage?"

"Yes. He is a really nice man."

"Do you know where he is now?"

"Oh yes. He is on his run to Salt Lake City. He should be back any day."

"Did you know that was the stage that our friends, the Lings, were on?"

"I know. I bet he did all he could to save the Lings. He would never harm anyone. He hated the outlaws. He was always telling me to stay away from them."

"If you see Mr. Johnson when he gets back, tell him I want to talk to him. What is your last name Wally?"

"It is Holt. My mother said she did not know who my father was, so I could pick any name I wanted. I knew a man named Holt, and I kind of liked him, so I just took the name Holt."

"Wally, for a boy only thirteen, you have had a full life. If you still want to be honest, loyal and hard working, you can have the job."

"Oh, Mr. Chandler! I want the job very much."

They shook hands. "The first thing we have to do is to pound all this gold into oblong cylinders like this one."

Rusty showed Wally one of the shaped nuggets that he planned on putting into the cattle. "We have all this gold to do." He pulled off the cloth that covered the tubs of gold. Wally's eyes popped out so far you could have knocked the pupils off with a stick.

"Now Wally, you can see why you must be honest and loyal. I want no one to know of this gold. I think there is about two cubic feet of gold. It weighs twelve hundred pounds per cubic foot, and is worth about $300,000 per cubic foot."

"Mr. Chandler, I will tell no one. How do you plan to get all this gold out of Virginia City?"

"I have a plan in mind that I think will work, I will tell you about it later. Now, let's get to work and make it into nuggets."

The next day, Rusty bought Wally a horse and saddle. They spent the next few days rounding up the cattle that Rusty had purchased from Mr. Stewart. They held them in a box canyon just outside Virginia City. This activity drew no attention from the outlaws, as they knew Rusty had been in the cattle business and did not think it strange that he would go back into that profession.

After boarding their horses at the livery stable, Rusty and Wally went home to the cabin to find Mr. Johnson waiting for them. Mr. Johnson initiated the conversation.

"Mr. Chandler, I just dropped by to apologize to you for what happened to the Ling family. If I had not had such a hard-on for that Ruby, I could have done much more. I will never forgive myself."

"What did you do with Ruby?"

"In Salt Lake City, I saw the light, and what a real bitch she was. I found a good woman to help dress her wounds. She was still pretty sour at you for cutting her breast, and really was in pain. Well anyway, when I got her settled, I went to the butcher shop for some meat and never went back. I brought the stagecoach back here to Virginia City just like nothing had happened. I hope I never see her again. I have always had troubles with women. I guess I'm just too horny. I imagine that Wally has told you I used to date his mother. She was a wild one."

Rusty looked at Mr. Johnson and Wally. This would be the hands he needed to get the gold out of Virginia City. He wished that he had Sigrid here to help. He was a good, steady man, and if Patsy was here to help with the cattle, it would be perfect. He chased those thoughts from his head and came back to reality.

"Mr. Johnson, I want you to go to work for me. I will pay you more than you are making with the stage line. I want you and Wally to help me get a herd of cattle to Fort Benton."

"Rusty, I'd be happy to go to work for you. When the stage company finds out the details and the real truth as to what happened to the Ling family, I could be looking for work."

Rusty invited Mr. Johnson and Wally into the cabin and made them a big supper of beef stew. When dinner was over and the dishes washed up, Rusty laid out the plans for getting the gold out of Virginia City.

CHAPTER 56

"I have a plan. It is a little crazy, but I think it will work."

Rusty looked across the table at his two employees. He outlined his program to get the gold out of Virginia City.

"As you both know, it is almost impossible to get gold out of Virginia City because of the well organized outlaw gangs. I have a plan. It is a little crazy, but it will work. When I was in the cattle business in Texas, I visited a small slaughterhouse. The manager there told me that he often found heavy metal objects in the second stomach of cattle. In fact, I saw some of the objects that he had removed. Wally and I have spent the past day molding the gold into cylinders. We are going to put these cylinders down the cattle and simply drive the cattle carrying the gold out of the country and to Fort Benton. Do you have any questions?"

Johnson was the first to speak. "How do you plan on getting the gold into the cattle?"

"Wally and I have rounded up the cattle we bought from Mr. Stewart. We are holding them in a small box canyon pasture down the creek. At one end of the pasture, there is a narrow rock formation. We will drive cattle into this area about ten at a time. We will place a gate over the end of the holding area, and the cattle will be packed in so tight all we have to do is hold up their heads and drop the gold right down their throat. Johnson and I can get the animal's head up, and Wally can drop in the gold. We ear mark the ones that have gold, and turn them out, then get in another ten head."

Wally had the next question. "Mr. Chandler, just how do you get the gold out of the cattle?"

"Wally, that is a good question. I have not figured that out just yet. We will try and sell the cattle and just deliver the dressed animal. This will be a lot of work. I hope you both know a little about butchering cattle. It looks like we may be doing a lot of it."

The trio worked very hard getting the gold down the cattle. They could only work at night for fear of being discovered, but by in large, things went well and at the end of the third night, all of the gold was in the cattle.

They spent one day getting their personal belongings loaded in the chuckwagon. Rusty had decided to just abandon his cabin and the spent

222

gold mine dug out behind the cabin. If he sold it, the outlaws would know that he was leaving town.

It was daybreak on a bright May morning when the trio headed the cattle northeast to the river port of Fort Benton. Rusty looked at the sun hitting the still snow-covered mountains. He noticed the new growth of bright green grass. He noticed the new spring Montana wild flowers, the Shooting Stars, the Forget-Me-Nots, and the tall purple Lupine. Montana was a beautiful place. In a way, he hated to leave. On the other hand, he wanted to go back to his roots in the deep south and see his family. He very much wondered what he would find.

Rusty drove the wagon, and Wally and Johnson pushed the cattle along. The first two days, they moved at a good pace. About mid-day of the third day, one of the big steers became sick and fell behind. Rusty ordered Johnson to shoot the big animal. He thought that they were far enough out of Virginia City to check and see if the cattle were still carrying the gold.

They opened up the animal. It took them some time to find the second stomach, as none of them had any knowledge of the insides of a bovine. The stomach was located, and sure enough, there was the gold. Rusty let out a war whoop and did a little dance of joy. Wally and Johnson thought he had lost his mind.

That night, they camped along a clear, cool Montana creek. They killed another animal, harvested the gold, and had a good supper of beef steak. Morning found them just crawling out of their bedrolls, when a small band of Blackfeet Indians rode into camp. Johnson had spent many years in Montana and had done some trapping before the gold strikes. He was able to talk with the Indians using a combination of their language and some sign language. The band of Indians was very poor and hungry. The Blackfeet had been devastated with small pox, and they were not the proud nation they once had been.

"They say they want a beef, that they are hungry. They don't have much fight left in them. I will just tell them to take a flying fuck at the moon."

"No, no, Johnson. Tell them that if they will go up on that hill and wait, we will give them five head all dressed and ready for them."

Johnson was quick to get the picture. "What you are saying Rusty, is that this is a good way to harvest some of the gold out of the cattle and keep the Indians happy."

Johnson passed Rusty's message on to the Indians, and they retreated off about a hundred yards to the top of a small hill. Rusty shot five of the cattle, and they were soon rough-dressed and ready for the Blackfeet. The Indians were motioned to ride in and get the prize. The leader of the Indian band spoke to one of the young braves, and he rode off to the north at a fast gait. Johnson told Rusty and Wally that the chief had told the young man to ride and get the women from camp to finish butchering the cattle. The chief was so happy he gave Rusty a very fancy, beaded medicine bag.

They made camp just outside Fort Benton on a bend of the Missouri River. The next morning, Rusty sent Johnson and Wally into town to scout a market for the dressed beef he planned on selling. They reported back that there was a ready market, and they had received orders for five dressed beef. By nightfall, they had the five beeves dressed and loaded in the wagon for delivery the next morning.

Someone had to stay with the cattle, so Rusty left Johnson, and he and Wally went to town. Rusty took a large amount of the gold, made a deposit in the Fort Benton Bank and turned the rest of it into bank notes. Rusty and Wally collected a good price for the meat, but when arriving back at camp, Johnson was nowhere to be found. The cattle had not scattered too far and Rusty and Wally soon had them rounded up. They were very concerned about the welfare of Johnson.

Johnson rode into the Blackfeet camp, giving the sign of friendship and holding up a bottle of whisky. The chief was very happy to see the whisky, and he also held good feelings toward Johnson because of all the meat that he had received from the white men.

He and the chief drank some whisky, and before long, the chief had offered Johnson a squaw and a teepee for the night. This was just what Johnson had come for. She was middle age and somewhat rounded, but she knew how to please a man. Morning found Johnson so worn out he could hardly get on his horse. He rode into camp just as Rusty and Wally were getting ready to go to town and organize a search party for him. He was not greeted with the same enthusiasm he found in the Blackfoot camp.

"Where in the hell have you been?" Rusty demanded.

"Rusty, I'm sorry. I just knew that there had to be a good squaw in that Blackfoot camp, and I had a terrible hankerin' for a good woman. It's been a long trail, and I do love to get next to a good woman now and then. I know you are going to fire me for leaving camp. I'll just get my things together and get on out of here. I do hope you found everything in good order."

Rusty was so mad he saw black, but Johnson was a good man, and he knew when he hired him that he had a weakness for women.

"Get down off that horse, and let's get to butchering cattle. We only have a few more days of this and we catch the boat down river. Please promise me that the next time you get to hankerin' for a woman that you let me know."

By the end of the week, they had all the cattle butchered, and Rusty rented a house in Fort Benton for them to live in while they waited for a boat to come up the river.

CHAPTER 57

"Johnson spent most of his time in a local brothel."

Rusty spent most of the day posting letters to get his money transferred from the different banks in the west to a bank in Atlanta. Wally got a job helping a local fur and hide buyer. Johnson spent most of his time in the local brothel.

After about two weeks working for the hide buyer, Wally came home and said that he had been laid off, because the buyer was out of money. Wally's boss had told him that he could go back to work when the boat came in to help load the hides. His boss had a large inventory of buffalo hides that he had bought from the buffalo hunters. He also had a good many furs that the Indians had brought in and sold to him. Wally also told Rusty that a boat had been spotted coming up the river. The rumors were that the boat would dock in the morning and would lay over two weeks, as it needed some repairs before it went back down the river.

The next morning, Rusty and Wally were at the dock and watched the riverboat dock. Rusty could not help but overhear the fur buyer and the captain of the boat talking over the deal to ship the furs and hides down river. The riverboat captain made it very clear that the fur buyer could not load his inventory until the captain was paid. The fur buyer offered to give the captain part of the hides for the pay down the river. The captain seemed to be a man with a hard head and refused to let him load his hides until he had the cash.

"Do you know how much he paid for the hides and furs?" Rusty asked Wally.

"I know what he paid for the buffalo hides, because I was with him when he bought a lot of them. The furs, I am not too sure of."

Rusty made a count of the hides on the dock and added ten percent to the price. Calling Wally off to the side where they could not be overheard, he instructed Wally, "You offer him $2,000 for all his hides and furs. Then we will load them and make a deal with the captain to take the hides, furs, and us down the river. If he says that is not enough, you can go up to $2,500, since we really don't know the price of the furs."

Wally went up to his ex-boss and made the offer. The man was very surprised at the boy's offer and asked where he planned on getting that kind of money.

"I am representing a very rich man."

"You mean to tell me that nigger you were just talking to is rich?" Then, not waiting for Wally to answer, he continued, "I can't sell for that kind of money. They cost me more than that."

Wally countered with, "That is the best we can do, and if you don't take it they will just rot on the dock."

"I see that nigger has some horses. If he'll give me the money in gold and two of his horses, you have a deal."

Wally reached out, and they shook hands on the deal. Wally went to bed that night feeling pretty important.

When the passengers were disembarking the boat that morning, Rusty noticed a young girl get off. She was dressed in a long, pink dress, and she was carrying a light blue parasol. Her shoulder length blonde hair glistened in the morning Montana sun. A well-dressed older man escorted her. They were picked up in a buggy owned by the local hotel.

On the way to his rented home, Rusty noticed a broadside in a store window. It read: **MASQUERADE BALL TO BE HELD ON THE DOCK OF THE GOOD SHIP MISSOURI ANN. <u>EVERYONE WELCOME.</u>**

Rusty thought that might be a good time. When he had been camped outside Fort Benton, he found a part of an old Spanish armor that was worn by the Spanish when their expedition had made a brief visit to Montana many years earlier. The helmet was in good shape.

The night of the ball, he put on the helmet and some tight fitting clothes, bought a Civil War sword at the pawn shop, and went to the ball. He saw the blonde girl that had gotten off the boat. She was dressed as a fairy princess, and she really looked like one. Rusty asked for a dance, and as they danced, they seemed just right for each other.

He learned that she was in Fort Benton with her father. They were from England, and her father came west to do some hunting. Later on in the evening, Rusty had another dance with her. It was a slow dance, and he held her close. His manhood became very rigid, and she could feel it against her leg. Rusty suggested that they get some air out on the deck of the Missouri Ann. He held her close. She suggested that he take the helmet off.

"I just can't. It's against the rules. You can only identify yourself after midnight."

She let out a long breath and said, "I would love to get closer to you, but we just can't out here on the deck."

She then let her slim, soft hand drop down and begin to stroke Rusty. The next thing he knew, she had his pants open and his manhood in her soft white hand. When she looked down and saw that large, black organ throbbing in her warm white hand with the Montana moon shining on it, she came very close to fainting. She gasped for air and dropped his manhood like it was red hot. She slowly collected herself and took the organ back in her hand.

"You are a black man. I just don't care. I want you. Meet me up along the river tomorrow."

She gently rubbed Rusty until he shot a large load out into the Missouri River. A large cutthroat trout resting under the boat saw something hit the water. He came up to take a closer look, thinking it might be a meal. On seeing what hit the water, he went back down under the boat.

They went back to the deck and finished the dance. Rusty slipped out before midnight, when he would have to identify himself.

The next day, Rusty rode up the river to meet the blonde girl. He thought, "I really do not want to roll around on the grass and have sex with that white girl. She is a nice girl and would most likely be a good friend. I wish I could think of a way to get out of this deal."

He found her sitting under a cottonwood tree, and her horse was picketed near by. She was in tight black riding pants and a purple shirt that showed ample cleavage. Her long, blonde hair made a fan effect over her shoulders.

"We don't even know each other's names," she said, as she rose to her feet. "My name is Fay Bright."

She extended her hand. Rusty took it and introduced himself. "I am Rusty Chandler. I am very happy to know you."

She turned red and cast her eyes down, looking at her boots. "I wish to apologize for last night. I had too much to drink. I am really not that kind of a girl."

She raised her head and looked Rusty in the eye. Rusty made a deep bow and announced, "I accept the apology, the pleasure was all mine."

They both broke out laughing.

They spent the afternoon sitting on the cool green grass, under a cottonwood tree and listening to the mellow sound of the Missouri making its way to the Gulf of Mexico. Never was the subject of sex mentioned. Rusty told of his days on the plantation as a pampered slave. Fay told of her childhood in England as a spoiled rich girl. They rode back to Fort Benton as the sun was finding its way to bed in the western sky.

They were careful to ride into town at different times, as neither of them wanted to start any rumors. Fay invited Rusty to have lunch with her and her father the next day at the hotel dining room.

Mr. Bright was more than a little shocked when he was introduced to Rusty, and he was a black man. This was a point that Fay had failed to mention to her father. Mr. Bright was polite to Rusty, in sort of an at-arms-length fashion. Rusty noticed considerable perspiration on Mr. Bright's forehead and stains on his shirt under the arms. Rusty learned that, for the next two weeks, Mr. Bright had hired a guide to take him on a hunting trip. He would be leaving Fay alone at the hotel. Rusty promised to look out for her, a situation that did not put Mr. Bright's mind at ease.

CHAPTER 58

"He had a long French name, but everybody called him "Captain Frenchie."

The captain of the Missouri Ann was a young man on his first trip as a captain up the river. He was of French blood, and his family had been associated with river transportation on the Mississippi and the Missouri for three generations. He had a long French name, but everybody called him "Captain Frenchie."

He was a man that seldom laughed and was all business, very protective of his boat, its cargo and his passengers. To describe the captain in a few words, there was no bull shit about him. If the captain had a weakness, it was that he had fallen head over heels in love with Fay Bright.

Other than being very protective of her on their trip up the river, he had not shown a hint to Fay that he was mad about her. As for Fay's part, she thought he was a nice man and a good captain. She never once had thought of him as a lover. This was strange in itself for Fay, because she hardly looked at a man that she did not wonder what kind of a lover he would make.

Rusty, Johnson, and Wally were busy loading the hides and furs on to the Missouri Ann for their trip down the river to market. The loading was under the directions of Captain Frenchie.

Fay came running to the dock, with skirts and long blonde hair flying in the wind. "They have killed my father! My father is dead!"

Rusty and the captain ran back up town with her and they found the wagon and the party that Mr. Bright had hired to take him hunting. The half-breed who was in charge of the expedition stood by the wagon, and in the wagon lay Mr. Bright. Fay ran up to the big half-breed and started pounding on his chest with her small fist and yelling at him.

"You killed my father! You killed my father!"

Rusty gently pulled her off the big half-breed and inquired as to what was going on. The half-breed responded.

"We spotted a large herd of buffalo. Mr. Bright got off his horse, brought his rifle to his shoulder to shoot, and just dropped over. I ran to him and tried to help him up, but it was too late. He was dead."

The doctor, who also served as coroner, was also standing by the wagon. "I just examined Mr. Bright and I see no sign of foul play. I would say the man had a massive heart attack."

Fay put her arms around Rusty and wept on his shoulder. Rusty held her for a short moment and then stepped back. Looking at the half-breed guide he said, "Please forgive Miss Bright. She was just upset."

"I do forgive her. I understand."

Fay looked to her left and saw the captain. She went to him and put her arms around him and started crying on his shoulder. The captain was dumbfounded and put his arms around her and let her cry. She felt so good to him, her warm body against his, he could feel her ribs and spine through the silk blouse she had on. It was one of the best moments of his life.

Rusty asked Captain Frenchie to take Fay into the bar and buy her a drink, while he and the doctor took care of the body. He said he would join them later. The doctor, with the help of Rusty and the half-breed guide, got Mr. Bright into the combination morgue and doctor's office.

Rusty said, when Fay had settled down, he would help her make the arrangements for the burial of her father. Rusty noticed that Mr. Bright had a large wallet in his pocket. He took it and announced that he would take it to Fay. On his way back to the saloon to see Fay and the captain, curiosity got the best of him and he took a look at the contents of the wallet. There was a large sum of money, but what caught Rusty's eye was a paper that read:

> This paper authorizes, for permission of one Nan Cockney, to leave England for a period of 1 year.
> Description: Age: 21—Eyes: Blue—Hair: Blonde—Occupation: chambermaid.

There was another paper authorizing Mr. Bright to leave England. Rusty scratched his head and wondered. Could these be papers for Fay Bright, and if so, just what did they mean, and what was behind them? If she was not his daughter, they must have been traveling as lovers. Rusty placed the paper back in the wallet and went to the saloon. Much to his surprise, he found Captain Frenchie and Fay holding hands over the table. As Rusty approached, Fay dropped the captain's hand and said to Rusty, "It seems that the captain and I have been somewhat fond of each other and were unaware of the fact."

She smiled and took back the captain's hand. Rusty gave her the wallet. She opened it, counted the money, and read the paper. Closing the wallet she said, "I knew that Mr. Bright was a wealthy man, but there is a lot of money here."

Rusty wondered. She had always called Mr. Bright Father, now it was Mr. Bright. He decided to leave it alone for now, but vowed to find out what had been going on.

The next ten days were busy with the loading of the boat. It was late June, and the river was starting to go down. Captain Frenchie was in a rush to get started. He spent every hour he could with Fay, some in bed, and some not. He furnished Fay's small cabin on the Missouri Ann as lavishly as he could with the furnishings available in Fort Benton.

Fay told him of growing up rich in England and how she would now inherit all of the family money, as her mother was dead, and she had no brothers or sisters. She said she had to return to England to take care of the business, but she would return and marry the captain. She would have enough money to buy at least three boats, and Frenchie could hire captains, and he could stay at home with her in the big home she planned to buy for them in St. Louis.

She asked Frenchie to give her some money, because what cash Mr. Bright had left her would not see her through the year, until she got the estate settled in England. Frenchie told Rusty of his plans to give Fay all his savings and also the money his mother had in savings in St. Louis. Rusty hoped it would work out for the captain.

Johnson J. Johnson had planned to go down the river with Rusty and Wally, but at the last minute he decided he just could not leave the Fort Benton whores.

The boat was loaded. All the passengers were to spend the night on board so they could get a good start in the morning. Rusty lay in bed. He found sleep hard to come by. He was almost sure that Fay Bright was, in fact, a chambermaid named Nan Cockney. She had come to America with Mr. Bright as his mistress, not his daughter. He was almost sure that she never planned on coming back to America to marry Frenchie.

Should he tell Captain Frenchie his thoughts? What if he was wrong? He considered both the captain and Fay as his friends. Not friends like the cowboy Patsy or his childhood friend Sigrid, but still friends. He thought of comforting Fay and asking her about her identity, yet it was really none of his business. The fact that he was a man of color would not make his finding in the case as believable as if he were white.

The slow rocking of the boat tied to the dock finally let Rusty find sleep. He was awakened by the sound of the captain giving the crew orders to get under way.

The first day down the river was quite routine, with the crew getting used to their duties and the passengers getting settled for the long trip. Rusty and Wally, though they were paying passengers, worked along with the crew when there was extra duty.

One afternoon Rusty found himself on watch with the captain, as they made their way down the river. The captain spent the afternoon telling Rusty how wonderful Fay was, and how happy he was that he could help her out financially until she got her inheritance, how much he loved every hair on her body and what a good wife she would be. He could hardly wait to introduce her to his mother in St. Louis.

Rusty tried to give subtle warnings to Captain Frenchie, that all things may not be as they seemed. His warnings fell on deaf ears.

CHAPTER 59

"I do not feel the least bit bad about taking his money."

A hard jolt from the boat awakened Rusty. His first thought was that they had run aground. He jumped out of bed and ran to the rail and saw that Captain Frenchie had just hit the dock at St. Louis. The captain looked down from the bridge to see Rusty at the rail.

"Sorry for the rough landing," he shouted down. "There is current along this dock that I haven't seen before."

Rusty went back to his cabin and made ready to get off the boat. He was most happy to be in St. Louis. He was getting closer to home. Looking over his wardrobe, he had very little to wear that would be very good for downtown St. Louis. He put on the best he had and went to find Wally. Wally was standing along the rail looking at all the activity on the dock. Rusty lay his hand on Wally's shoulde,r and Wally turned to greet his employer and friend.

"Wally, let's go ashore, buy some new clothes, have a good breakfast and get the best room in St. Louis."

Wally smiled. "What did I do to deserve such a good boss?"

"That's an easy question to answer. You worked."

Rusty bought a business suit and some more casual clothes and did the same for Wally. They went back to the boat and changed. Then it was a big breakfast of steak and eggs.

They went to a very nice hotel and asked for a room. The desk clerk stood on one foot and then the other. "I am very sorry but we do not furnish rooms to the colored," he announced.

This riled Wally, and he nearly shouted at the clerk, "This is the best man I ever knew. Do you mean to tell me he is not welcome in this hotel?"

"That is correct young man. We take no colored people in this fine hotel."

Rusty could see that Wally was about to hit the desk clerk. "It is okay Wally. You will find a lot more of this in the south than in the west."

Rusty took a large bundle of bills out of his pocket. "Now, Mr. Desk Clerk, would you please give my young friend here the largest and very best suite you have?"

The clerk handed the registration book to Wally. As Wally signed his name, the clerk took the money out of the pile on the desk. Wally turned back to Rusty.

"Mr. Chandler, it would be my pleasure to have you as my guest during the duration of our stay in St. Louis."

After getting settled in the fine hotel and in a fine set of rooms, Rusty told Wally, "Wally, we have to get busy and get our hides and furs sold. Knowing the captain, he will want them off the boat so he can load to go back up the river."

On the way back to the boat, they saw a poster that read:

FUR AND HIDE AUCTION
ON THE ST. LOUIS DOCKS
JUNE 30 AT 10:00 AM
SEE MR. TANNER SKINNERBERG FOR DETAILS

"That's the day after tomorrow," Wally commented. "Let's go see Mr. Skinnerberg. It sounds like a good place to sell our inventory."

They found Mr. Skinnerberg in a small office in a very stinky warehouse not far from where the Missouri Ann laid at rest along the dock. Mr. Skinnerberg was a huge man with black eyes. He was chewing on a stub cigar.

Rusty introduced himself and Wally. "We have a boat load of furs and buffalo hides. We would like to know more about your auction. We want to sell our merchandise."

Mr. Skinnerberg looked very skeptically at the two men before him. "We are very careful what kinds of furs and hides we let into the auction. Skinnerberg only wants the very best. Our buyers expect it."

"Come to the Missouri Ann and take a look for yourself," Wally answered. "We have, along with several hundred buffalo, mink, wolf, fox, martin, ermine, beaver, bobcat, bear and even a few otter."

"Well, young man if you have that kind of fur, I better go take a look."

Mr. Skinnerberg looked at the furs and hides. Wally could tell by the look on his face that he was impressed with the furs and the hides.

"This merchandise would be very welcome at the auction. Can you get it to my warehouse in time? It is only two days' away."

"Never fear, Mr. Skinnerberg, we will have them there on time."

True to his word, Wally had the furs in the warehouse and displayed very well for the auction. Rusty and Wally were very pleased with the prices the furs and hides brought. In the hotel suite that evening, Rusty gave Wally a generous bonus for his good work in handling the fur deal. Wally and Rusty ordered champagne by room service to celebrate their good fortune.

Then Wally turned to Rusty, his eyes lightly moist with tears. "You've been so good to me, I really hate to announce this. I have decided to go back up the river with the Missouri Ann. I really like the hide business and the buffalo hunters will be killing a lot of buffalo for the next few years. With all of this money you gave me, I'll have enough to become a hide dealer. With Mr. Skinnerberg on this end to help me sell, I think I can make a lot of money in the next few years."

"Wally, I hate to see you go, but no way do I want to stand in the way of your success," Rusty assured him. "I am sure you will be very successful. As you know, I get on the boat in the morning to go to Memphis where I will board the train for Atlanta."

They shook hands and drank some more champagne.

The next morning, Rusty was on the Star Queen watching the last of the passengers board. He was surprised to see Fay Bright kiss Captain Frenchie good-bye as she boarded. The first person she saw when on board was Rusty.

"Rusty, I am so glad to see you. I am on my way to New Orleans to catch a steamer to England. This will be such fun traveling with you."

"Fay, it will be good to have some company. I leave the Star Queen at Memphis, but we will have a few days. Will you be my guest for dinner tonight?"

"Thank you. That would be very nice."

They parted to their individual cabins. The Star Queen was an almost new ship and one of the finest on the river. Her decks were polished, and she sparkled white in the morning sun as she left the dock for her trip down the river.

Later that morning, Rusty was lounging on the deck and struck up a conversation with a young girl. It turned out that she was with an acting troop, bound for New Orleans, to star in a play that was being produced in that gulf city. She had been born in England but had migrated to the United States and was enjoying a fine career as an actress. Rusty thought of a plan.

He hired the girl to do some acting for him. He explained what he wanted and wrote her a short script.

Rusty was seated in the back of the ship's dining room when Fay made her entrance. She was dressed in a long, pink dress with light blue gloves, and her hair was tied in a high bun on top of her head. She was beautiful. It was easy to see how a man could fall for her. Rusty seated Fay. They had a fine dinner. Fay spoke of how much she loved Captain Frenchie, how she had met his mother, and how the old lady just loved her, and she had given Fay all of her savings to help her out.

Rusty had just ordered an after-dinner drink when a young girl approached the table. She stopped about three feet from Fay, reached out with both hands, and addressed her with a very English accent. "Nan, I cannot believe it is you. When did you come to America?"

Fay looked dumbfounded at the strange girl. The actress continued, "I have not seen you since we worked at the Bright Estates. You were a chambermaid, and I worked in the kitchen."

Fay's mouth dropped open, and the actress continued. "I remember what a time you had carrying those chamber pots down those long stairs. Do you remember the day you dropped one? What a mess."

"Oh, that was not me. That was the other maid, Billy. I had to help her clean it up."

Fay was hooked.

The actress made a few other mundane comments about the kitchen maid and the chambermaids and excused herself.

Fay turned and looked at Rusty with a look that said, "I forgot you were here, I forgot where I was."

Then she said, as if nothing had happened, "Now you know."

"Fay, I have been very suspicious of you for a long time. I really don't care what your relationship was with Mr. Bright. But what you are doing to Captain Frenchie makes me just plain sick."

"Mr. Rusty, I want you to know my side of the story. I was raised on the wrong side of London. I had no father. My mother was a fish vendor on the waterfront. I have had very little schooling. In fact, I cannot read or write. At sixteen, I went to work as a chambermaid in the home of Mr. Bright. He was very rich and had a beautiful wife. His son, who was about my age, would rape me every chance he got. I was afraid to resist because they would fire me. His parents knew this and did nothing.

"One morning I was getting ready to go to work, I was standing in front of my mirror with nothing on. I decided, right then and there, that I was young and pretty. I did not want to grow old vending fish on the waterfront. The only thing that I had was a small triangle of blond hair between my legs. From this day forward, I was going to use that small triangle of blond hair to get what I wanted in the world. I called it my Golden Triangle.

"I went to work that day, and I was making a bed in Mr. and Mrs. Bright's room. Mr. Bright came to get some shoes out of the closet. He asked me to get them for him. I bent way over in my short skirt and let him take a good look. When I turned, with the shoes in my hand, I could see that Mr. Bright was interested in what he had seen. When I started to hand him the shoes, I dropped them, then I bent low to get them and let Mr. Bright look down my blouse. I set the shoes on the bed and took Mr. Brights' hand and said to him, 'Mr. Bright I have something I would like to give you.' I still had a hold of his hand. I pulled up my skirt and placed his hand on my Golden Triangle.

"We made love all afternoon on his big bed. The rest of the family must have been gone, as Mr. Bright seemed to have no fear of anyone catching us. It was a lot better with Mr. Bright than his son. Even though he was twice my age, he was a good lover. I must say that I really enjoyed the afternoon. Just before he left the room, I asked him for a better job," Fay continued.

"He said, 'I will see what I can do.' He was gone. The very next day he asked me if I would like to accompany him to America. He said he would double my pay and pay all the expenses. He said I would have to pose as his daughter. You know the rest of the story and how I put the Golden Triangle to work on Captain Frenchie. I do not feel the least bit bad about taking his money. A girl has to get along and do what she has to do, if she don't want to spend her life selling fish. Thank you for the dinner. Now if you will excuse me, I have to go see if I can find a job for the Golden Triangle."

Rusty went to his cabin and hoped that there were not too many women in the world like Nan, Fay?

CHAPTER 60

"Man overboard! Man overboard! Rusty yelled."

The Star Queen was only twenty-four hours out of Memphis. Rusty woke to the gentle sounds of the big wheel on each side of the boat gently pushing the Star Queen down the big river. He had to take a pee, so he got up and went out on the deck. It was a full moon and a most beautiful night. Nobody was about, so he decided to just pee over the side. He opened the rail and stood, watching his addition of water to the Mississippi and thinking it was not going to make much difference. The pilot made a quick turn to miss a snag, and splash, Rusty fell over the side.

"Man overboard. Man overboard," Rusty yelled.

He watched as the Star Queen made the slow turn around the bend and disappeared down the river. He swam to the east bank, which was not a great distance. Standing in mud up to his ankles, in his nightshirt with the mosquitoes swarming over him, he thought, "this is not a fun place to be." He managed to climb up the steep, muddy bank and found a deep forest with thick underbrush that a man could hardly get through. It was darker than the inside of a tomcat, as the moonlight could not reach the forest floor. Rusty decided to try and rest until daylight

When the first rays of sun hit the forest floor, Rusty gathered his bearings and decided to stay close to the riverbank and try to make his way to a cabin or a settlement. It did not take long for the July sun to get very hot. The mosquitoes seemed not to notice the heat, as they chewed on every part of Rusty's body. It seemed that the thorny branches actually reached out to scratch his body.

Just before noon, Rusty heard the sound of children playing. He peered through the under brush and saw a cabin and two young black children playing with a bitch and her litter of pups. Rusty positioned himself, staying behind the underbrush, and called out to the children.

"Could you please get your Mother or Dad? I need clothes and I am lost."

The children ran into the cabin. A young black woman appeared at the door. She was dressed in a red and white cotton dress with a turban around her head. She appeared to be in her mid twenties. Rusty stayed behind the brush and addressed the young woman.

"Ma'am, my name is Rusty Chandler. I fell off of the riverboat last night. I have no clothes, and I am lost. Could you please help me?"

The woman disappeared into the cabin, returning with a pair of gray pants from an old confederate uniform. She tossed them over the brush to Rusty.

"We found these on a dead soldier a few years back. They are too small for my husband."

Rusty put on the pants, thinking all the time that her husband must be one hell of a man, as Rusty was not small and the pants were too large for him. Rusty stepped out from behind the bush.

"God must have sent you," the woman said. "My husband is in the city getting supplies, and the milk cows have run off. I can't leave the children to look for them. Could you please help me? They weren't milked last night, and if they go much longer it will ruin them and my husband will be very mad. First, you must clean up, and I will fix you some food."

Rusty washed up and found that, though his wounds had bled profusely, they were not deep and would soon heel. She served him hot corn bread and salt pork. Rusty had not had such good food since he had left the plantation years before. While he hated to waste time looking for the family's cows, he had no choice. The cows were very important, as the family made cheese as a supplement to their income. It was after dark when he finally got back to the cabin with the cows. He helped the young wife milk them, and she fed him a supper of more hot corn bread, with fried chicken and watermelon.

She put the kids to bed and asked Rusty to spend the night, as he could not find his way in the dark. Rusty was very tired. He had slept very little in the last twenty-four hours. He accepted the invitation. She made him a pallet on the floor, and she went into the other room where she had put the children to bed. Rusty could not help but notice her nice wide hips and ample bosoms. While he had been hunting the cows, she had bathed and she now carried a sexy, clean musky odor.

Rusty slept what seemed only a few minutes and woke. He heard a small voice say, "Rusty are you awake?"

"Yes."

She settled in beside him and took hold of him. She let out with a small gasp and wasted no time in formalities. She raised up and settled on top, her warm and waiting body was ready. The only sound in the cabin was her low moaning as she, gently at first and then with vigor, made love. "Oh, Rusty. It feels so good.

The door of the cabin opened and quickly filled with the shape of a huge man holding a lantern. Rusty could make out the form of a gun tucked in his waste band. The young mother screamed and jumped to her feet.

"Abraham, what are you doing home?"

Rusty jumped up and, before the man could absorb what he was seeing, Rusty ducked under his arm and ran out of the cabin into the night. He
felt the wind of the bullet pass by his head as he disappeared into the dark
forest.

Rusty sat down on a log. His mind was reeling with thoughts. "Here I
sit, a wealthy man," he thought. "Not a stitch of clothing. Not one penny to
buy any, even if there was a place to buy them. If I don't get to Memphis
soon, the Star Queen will be gone. I have to hope that they take off my luggage and store it. I wonder if I have been missed? I can't do this alone. I have
to have help."

Rusty managed to get a little sleep before sun up. He was on a trail that
led south and knew that it would eventually end up in, or very close to,
Memphis. Despite his brown skin, he was starting to sunburn very badly. He
found some swamp plants with large leaves and made a make shift cloak.

The sun was about center sky when he heard voices behind him. He
hid in the brush along the road. It was two young white men who were talking and passing a jug back and forth. They were drunk as skunks. Rusty
stepped out and tried to tell his story. They just laughed at him.

"You are the guy that was with Abraham's wife, and he caught you. He
told us all about it. He said, 'don't help the goddam nigger. Just leave 'im to
the sceeters and the sun. It'll take care of 'im.' Look at you. Dressed like
Adam. Are you trying to play first man?"

They both had another good laugh, and rode on.

Rusty went into the forest and lay down, trying to get some rest in the
afternoon, so he could travel again after dark. The sun had set when he
woke. He moved on down the road a good pace. He heard a horse snort and
stopped. Going on, he found the two young men, both asleep or passed out.
They had not taken care of their horses and left them saddled and tied to the
tree. He found a set of clothes in one of the saddlebags and quickly dressed.

Taking a piece of charcoal from the dead fire, and finding some
foolscap, he left a note.

"Sorry I had to borrow your horses. Pick them up at the sheriff's in the
next town. I will be happy to pay you for their use and for the clothes.
Rusty Chandler

He took both horses so they had no way of giving chase. Now he at
least had some clothes and a pair of horses, even if he had almost stolen
them.

Rusty rode hard, and to his surprise, in two hours he was in the outskirts of Memphis. In another half-hour, he was at the sheriff's office in
Memphis. He dismounted and started to enter the office just as the sheriff

came out. The sheriff stopped on the top step of the office and looked down at Rusty.

"Where did you get those horses?" he demanded.

Rusty gave him a thumbnail sketch of how he had fallen off the boat, got caught with Abraham's wife, and borrowed the horses from the young men on the trail.

The sheriff went back in the office and came out with a wanted poster. He looked at Rusty, then at the horses. Then he took another look at both of them.

"Young man, that story is so far fetched, I think it must be true. These horses where stolen from a plantation north of here by two young white men. They also took a stock of homemade moonshine. There is a reward for the return of the horses and the capture of the young men. Now, where did you say you so-called borrowed the horses?"

Rusty described, as best he could, where he had taken the horses. The sheriff invited Rusty into the office. He gave orders to a pair of deputies to take the trail north and see if they could find the robbers.

"With all due respect, sir," Rusty addressed the sheriff. "I am really in a hurry to get to the river docks and see if I can catch the Star Queen before she gets underway down river. I think I still have a chance of getting my luggage."

"What's your name?"

" I'm sorry. I am Rusty Chandler. I forgot to introduce myself."

"You know you may have a reward coming. I can't let you go until we find the robbers, and make sure that your story is on the up and up. The docks are not far. I will escort you, and if your luggage is really on the Star Queen, it will help in clearing you of the robbery."

When the sheriff and Rusty rounded the corner and saw the Star Queen still tied up to the dock, it was one of the prettiest sights that Rusty had ever seen. They were greeted at the gangplank by the captain.

"This is a surprise. You two are just the men I was getting ready to look for. Miss Fay Bright came to me just before we docked and asked if I had seen Mr. Chandler. I said I had not, and she said he was missing. She wondered if she might have the key to his cabin. She said he might be inside very sick. I accompanied her to the cabin, and we found it empty."

"Then, just as we docked, Mr. Gill Lucky, a professional gambler we had on board, came and accused Miss Bright of stealing his money. He said he had taken her to bed and when he woke in the morning she and his money both were gone. We found his money on her person, and we have her locked in her cabin. She said something about the stolen money being for the use of her Golden Triangle."

CHAPTER 61

"Do you wish to make a statement before I sentence you?"

The gavel came down hard on the bench.

"The State of Tennessee versus Miss Nan Cockney, alias Miss Fay Bright. The accused is charged with stealing $1,000, give or take a few dollars, from one Mr. Lucky. How does the defendant plea?"

"Guilty, Your Honor."

"Do you wish to make a statement before I sentence you?"

"Your Honor, my name is Rusty Montana Chandler. I am a friend of the defendant. If you release the defendant to me, I will pay Mr. Lucky back his money, and court costs."

"Mr. Chandler, if you will promise that she is out of town by sunset, it will be ordered."

"I promise to have her out of town by morning."

"Defendant is released into the custody of Mr. Rusty Chandler. Next case."

Rusty took Fay by the arm and walked her out of the courtroom.

"Thank you very much for doing that for me," she said.

"I did not do it for you. I did it for Captain Frenchie."

"What has Captain Frenchie got to do with this?"

"Fay, in your heart I can't help but think you are a good person. What you are doing to the captain and his mother is terrible. You are taking his love and his money, plus his mother's money. Will you please consider this? It is quite simple. Get on the next riverboat up to St. Louis and give your Golden Triangle to Frenchie, God knows he has paid for it. It would be just like a fairytale for you. You can 'live happily ever after.' He is a good, hard working person and he would be very good to you. You take his money and his love back to England with you, and what do you have? You will never forgive yourself."

She locked her arm in his as they walked toward the docks. Rusty was not too sure he felt comfortable with this, but he went along.

"Rusty, how many chamber pots have you emptied and cleaned?"

"I have done that, and don't you forget I was raised a slave. I will admit a pampered one, but still a slave. So don't get tears in those eyes and tell me the tale of the poor little chambermaid. One more thing. Don't tell me that

241

your Golden Triangle is the only thing you have to make a living with. You are young, pretty, very smart and a hard worker. If you have your head set on being disappointed and embellished in sadness, get on the boat and go to England. If you want to be loved and pampered, get on the other boat and go to St. Louis to your Captain Frenchie."

Fay had a lump in her throat, she felt like she had swallowed a large stone.

"Rusty, what are you going to do?"

"What am I going to do? For Christ's sake, I am going home. I have told you that a dozen times. I would have been there now if I had not spent a week trying to keep you and that Golden Triangle out of jail."

They had arrived at the docks, and there were the two boats, one headed up the river and one down. Rusty grabbed her by the shoulders and shook her gently.

"You have plenty of money. Get a ticket on whichever boat you wish. I am going back uptown to pay off your bills, and then I am headed for Atlanta."

Rusty turned and walked away and never looked back.

CHAPTER 62

"Rusty, Rusty, my boy Rusty Montana"

Before leaving Atlanta, Rusty had bought a fine carriage and a fine team. Rusty had also purchased some fine clothes and even a diamond stick-pin for his tie. He wanted to arrive at his home looking as though he had done well.

Rusty stood in the lane leading to Cottontail Plantation. Home at last. The mansion looked in disrepair. The porch was sagging, and two of the pillars were missing. It needed a new roof and a coat of paint. The glade sloping down to the creek showed signs of a flood that had washed all the nice green lawn away.

As Rusty got closer, he could see that the lean-to that had been home to him and his mother had burnt, and the backside of the mansion had suffered fire damage. The fields had not been cultivated and had grown to tall weeds. The stable where he had spent so much time was still in fair repair, with just a few doors sagging. For a place that he remembered as so busy, with people laughing and working, he saw no activity. He vowed to do something about it.

Rusty knocked on the door, and after a long wait, a heavy black woman answered. She looked Rusty up and down. In a voice that would have cut a steal rod, she demanded, "You're one fancy nigger. What business you have here?"

Rusty removed his hat and spoke in an even voice. "My name is Rusty Montana Chandler. I was raised on this plantation. I wondered if you might know where I can find Mary Annabelle? She was once a slave here."

"She lives down in that little house on the back side of what used to be Hanging Magnolia Plantation. She lives with a white man. They come up here pokin' around now and then, tellin' me how things use to be around here. It gets pretty old, I just have to run 'em off."

"Who owns this plantation now?"

"You're just full of questions, and I ain't doin' any more talkin'."

She slammed the door in his face.

Rusty got back in his rig and drove to the old Hanging Magnolia Plantation. All that was left was the chimney, standing in the ashes. He drove to the back side of the plantation. The fields, which were once rich with cotton, stood covered with knee-deep weeds. There was what looked to be about forty acres producing a poor crop of cotton.

The house that used to be the house of the overseer of Hanging Magnolia was much as he remembered it. It was well kept, and there was a good garden growing in the back. There was a tall woman in a bright red dress weeding the garden. She stood up and looked at her visitor coming into the yard. She had a strip of white hair about one inch wide running through the front of her hair. Otherwise, Mary Annabelle had not changed.

Rusty stopped and looked at her. "I really never knew how much absolute beauty she had," he thought. She did not recognize Rusty at first. He took off his hat and smiled. She stopped.

"Rusty! Rusty, my boy Rusty Montana!"

She dropped her hoe and ran to him. She was all over him like a wet blanket, hugging him and kissing him on both sides of his cheeks. While weeping and laughing, she held him at arm's length and said, "You are a sight for sore eyes. Oh, Rusty, I prayed for you everyday. I knew you would come back to me. Come, I will fix you some tea."

They went inside and Mary Annabelle went to what looked like a bedroom door and peeked in, then closed the door quietly.

"Mas Malcolm has been very sick for almost a month. We will talk a while before we wake him. The girls will be over later to see him. They come by everyday."

"By girls, you mean Evelyn Lucille and Mandy Ann?"

"Yes."

"Tell be about them first."

"Well, Mandy Ann still teaches at the school," Mary Annabelle explained. "I help her from time to time. She married a Yankee solider. She has no children. There is a group of them still here to keep us southerners in line. The fact that Mandy Ann married one of them does not set well with Master Malcolm. Evelyn Lucille, as you know, is married. She and her husband managed to hang on to some land down the road apiece. They farm and do quite well. Evelyn Lucille has a boy, seven and a girl, five. The girls will be so happy to see you. We talk of you often."

"You say Malcolm has been sick. How bad is he?"

"He has not been good since the northerners took the plantation. They used the house as a headquarters for the officers. They used the stable for their cavalry mounts. They kicked him out, so he came down to this house and brought me with him. Everything was gone. He was a very sad man. He has not been well since the war, but he is getting much worse. I am very worried about him."

"Who owns the plantation now?"

"It belongs to some carpetbagger who lives in New York. He doesn't farm it much and keeps that old black woman to care for the house. I call her Old Black Bitty Hen. She's so fussy and mean."

"How did the New Yorker get the plantation?"

"I don't know. Those carpetbaggers seem to just take what they want and take, take, take. We must go in and wake Master Malcolm before the girls get here. I have to comb his hair and get him looking sharp for his daughters. You wait right here and drink your tea."

Mary Annabelle went into the next room and in a few minutes called for Rusty to come in.

Malcolm was sitting up in bed. His hair was snow white and his face was very gaunt. He was not that old of a man.

Rusty heard Mary Annabelle say, just as he walked in, "You have some company."

Malcolm had no reaction when he looked at Rusty.

"Do you remember me? I am Rusty."

Malcolm's mouth dropped open. He said not a word, and a tear ran down his right cheek. The room was silent. Rusty was the first to speak.

"I am Rusty. I used to work in the stable with Mr. Rideout."

In a voice that seemed very strong for Malcolm's condition, he said, "Rusty, of course I remember you. Sit down. Mary Annabelle, bring us some tea. Tell me all about yourself. You look very prosperous. Wait, Mary Annabelle, bring us some good whisky."

Mary Annabelle came back with two glasses of moonshine. They had no whisky. Rusty tasted his and started to make a face and caught himself.

"This is a fine drink, Master Malcolm."

"I wish I had some good Kentucky whisky for you, but the damn Yankee's took everything we had. I guess your eyes tell you what has happened to us. You look like a million dollars. Tell me what you have been doing since the war."

"I will tell my story, but first, you remember the gold you gave me when I left during the war?"

"Yes."

"I would like to pay you back, with interest."

Rusty handed Malcolm a bag of gold about the size of a quart jar. It was so heavy Malcolm could not hold it, and it dropped onto the bed. He managed to pick it up.

"Thank you. Thank you very much," Malcolm said.

He handed the bag back to Rusty. "Please take this and deposit it in our local bank in the morning. I do not want that much wealth around the house."

Rusty took back the heavy riches.

"I will be very happy to do that."

Rusty outlined the past years, from the time he and Sigrid left the plantation. He even told Malcolm about sending Sigrid snipe hunting while he made love to Hazel Nut in the barn. Malcolm smiled at the story. He told of getting to Texas and finding Loupe Rose working in a hotel in Texas, but he did not go into detail. Malcolm was very happy to know where Loupe Rose was. He had not heard from her. He told of going into the cattle business with Bull Short, and how he had trailed the cattle to Montana. He told about Virginia City and of hitting it rich and getting into the fur and hide business in Fort Benton.

When Rusty had finished, Malcolm commented, "Rusty, you are quite a man." He then nodded his head and fell asleep.

Mary Annabelle took Rusty by the hand and led him out of the room. They had just sat down when a rig pulled up in front. Rusty looked out and saw immediately that the driver was Evelyn Lucille, still trim and very attractive. Beside her was a very fat blonde. On closer observation, Rusty saw that it was Mandy Ann. He could not believe the weight she had put on. In the back seat of the rig was a colored boy, quite black, but with reddish hair. He appeared to be about nine years old. Mandy Ann was the first into the room as the boy and Evelyn Lucille tied up the team outside. Mandy Ann knew Rusty immediately and rushed to him, throwing her arms around him.

"Rusty, you are home. Evelyn Lucille and I were wondering who had the fancy rig and team outside. I am so happy to see you. You look wonderful."

Evelyn Lucille came in, with the boy a pace behind her. She, too, ran to Rusty and hugged him.

"Rusty, you are so handsome, and those fancy clothes. That good rig outside must be yours. Don't tell me you struck gold."

The boy stood back and looked at Rusty. Rusty returned the stare. It was Mary Annabelle who went to the boy and put her arm around him. "Thursday, this is your big brother, Rusty Montana."

CHAPTER 63

"Well if it's not that fancy Nigger again."

"Somebody shit in the water pail."

"No, those are sweet taters I'm fixin' for supper. If you don't quit talkin' like that, I'm goin' to wash your mouth out with soap."

It would not have been the first time that Thursday had his mouth washed out with soap for the language he used. He was a good boy and did well in school, but he was handful and often in trouble. When he was good, he spent a lot of time playing with his pet red rooster. Mary Annabelle did her best to try and bring him up to be a good citizen.

Rusty had been home about three weeks. Malcolm's condition was no better. Rusty had talked to the doctor and he had said that there really was not much wrong with Malcolm except acute alcoholism, and he was psychically ill from losing everything to the Yankees. The doctor said he had talked to the daughters about his condition, but they were so busy with their own affairs that they just let Mary Annabelle take care of him and she kept giving him the moonshine. Rusty had instructed his mother to quit giving him the moonshine.

"There are only two things that make Master Malcolm better," Mary Annabelle would say. "One is to keep that Yankee husband of Mandy Ann's away for him. The other is to give him moonshine."

When Rusty had taken the gold he had given Malcolm to the bank, he had a long talk with the banker. The banker knew who owned Cottontail Plantation and what his address was in New York. Rusty found out from the banker what a fair price for the plantation would be and told the banker to have a deed drawn selling the plantation to Rusty. Rusty then posted a letter to the New Yorker and told him that the money for the plantation was in the bank, and if he signed the deed and sent it back, the banker would deposit the money to the New Yorker's account. It had been two weeks, and Rusty had not heard a word. He dropped by the bank that afternoon and the banker called Rusty into his office.

"Rusty, I'm glad you dropped by. I heard from New York yesterday. He signed the deed. Cottontail is all yours. I was going to dispatch a messenger to tell you, but things are looking up here in the South, and I just did not have time."

Rusty had never been happier in his entire live. The first thing he did was to go see Evelyn Lucille's husband. His name was Leo Burnheart. His ancestors had farmed in southern Russia and had passed their skills down the line. Leo had the best crops in the county and was a hard worker.

"Leo, I don't want you to utter a word of what I am going to tell you. I want it to be a surprise for the entire family," Rusty said.

He showed Leo the deed. Leo smiled and asked, "How on earth did you get this done?"

Rusty explained everything to him, and Leo congratulated him on a good piece of work. "What are you going to do with it, now that you own it?" Leo asked.

"That's where you come in. You're a good farmer. I want to rent it to you. All I want is for mother and Master Malcolm to be able to live in the big house. I'm going to fix it up. Your rent will be that you see to it that Mary Annabelle and Malcolm have no wants the rest of their lives. Can you agree to this?"

"Oh yes. We've wanted more land to farm. If it's all right with you, I'd like to move Evelyn Lucille and the family right away. There's plenty of room, and Evelyn Lucille loves her father very much. She'd like to help Mary Annabelle with his care. I guess Thursday would live there also?"

"No. Nobody knows this yet, but I'm going to take Thursday with me," Rusty replied. "I want to go back out west. I feel there is a lot of opportunity in California. Thursday is just too much for Mary Annabelle to handle. He will be better off with me. Now remember, not a word about this. I'm on my way right now to kick that old bitty out of the mansion and hire workers to fix it up."

They shook hands and Rusty was gone.

Rusty knocked on the door of the Cottontail Mansion and the lady came to the door.

"Well if it's not that fancy nigger again. I was sorry the other day when I kicked you out. Not many as good lookin' as you in these parts. You come on in and get in bed with this old mamma, she'll show you a thing or two." "That's not why I came back. In fact it's about as far from the reason as you could get. I have a deed to this property, made out to me, and signed by your boss. I'm coming in the morning with workers to remodel the mansion, and I want you out of here."

She stepped out on the porch. Looking Rusty in the eye, she lit into him. "I ain't never been no slave. I'm a northern nigger. You just can't kick me out. A black woman here in the south can't even find a place to live, let alone a job."

She sat down a little too hard on the old porch swing, the chain broke and dumped her, unceremoniously, onto the porch floor. Rusty helped her to her feet.

"You've been staying here, being paid, you must have enough money for a train ticket back up north. The fact is, I don't much care where you go or how you get there. I have men coming to work, and I want you out."

"You're not very kind to a poor old black woman."

"It was only a few minutes ago, you wanted to climb my frame, and now you're begging for mercy," Rusty said.

What neither of them had noticed while they were arguing was that Thursday was standing around the corner, taking it all in. Thursday had been out in the forest hunting squirrels with his slingshot. He thought, "if my brother wants her gone, I guess the least I could do is help."

He fired a shot at the right cheek of her ass. She jumped down off the porch. Thursday ducked back, and when Rusty looked around, he saw nothing. Thursday saw another chance to hit his target. Wham! A good sharp stone, right in the left side of her ass. She started down the road at a good pace. Thursday saw yet another shot and took it - right between her shoulder blades. She picked up speed as she got out of range. Thursday ran behind the house, out of sight, and back to his house. Rusty still had no idea of what went on.

That night at the dinner table, Thursday proudly announced to Mary Annabelle that he had helped his brother get rid of the old bitty from the mansion. Rusty looked at Thursday with unknowing eyes. Thursday reached in his hip pocket and held up the slingshot. Rusty would have liked to laugh, but held back.

"Thursday, that was not a very nice thing to do," Rusty scolded.

"You asked her to go, and she just stood there. I wanted to help," Thursday explained.

Mary Annabelle could stand the curiosity no longer. "Will someone tell me what is going on?"

"This was supposed to be a surprise, but little loud mouth here has let the cat out of the bag," Rusty said. "I bought the Cottontail Plantation. I'm going to have it fixed up, and we will all move down there. Leo is going to do the farming. I've already talked to him, and he is very excited. We will fix up the old study for Malcolm. I bet, when we get him moved and try to get him off the moonshine, he will get well. The only problem I see is if Mandy Ann and her soldier move in. Malcolm will not be very happy. I will have to talk to Mandy Ann tomorrow."

Mary Annabelle had tears running down her face. "Oh Rusty. My good Rusty. Thank you. Malcolm will be so happy, and I will do everything I can to make him well. Rusty, I have never been happier in my entire life."

Thursday got up from the table, stood straight as an arrow, turned and walked out into the yard. Rusty and Mary Annabelle looked out and saw him holding and petting his pet red rooster.

"What do you suppose is bothering him?" Rusty asked Mary Annabelle. "It must be something about moving that he doesn't like."

Mary Annabelle knew, but she would not tell Rusty. Thursday did not want Malcolm to get well. The boy hated him. One time, when Malcolm was drunk, he heard him tell Mary Annabelle that she should sell Thursday, as they really did not need him. Mary Annabelle did her best to make it up to Thursday by explaining to him that Malcolm was just drunk and that he could not sell him, as all Negroes were free. It was not like the old days.

Nothing more was said about Thursday. Rusty and Mary Annabelle went on talking about the plans to move and everything that had to be done. "Rusty, I think we should go tell Malcolm. He'll be so happy that he might decide to quit drinking."

"Okay Mary Annabelle, whatever you think."

They went into Malcolm's room and sat by his bed. Rusty smiled at his aging father. "Malcolm, I purchased the Cottontail Plantation and, in a few weeks, we will all be moving back."

Malcolm sat up in bed. You could see he was about to cry. "Thank you my son," he uttered.

This was the first time that he had ever identified Rusty as his son.

"You were a good boy and grew into a good man. I wish Thursday were more like you. Now Mary Annabelle, if you would get me my medicine, I promise that it will be my last. I am going to get well. Having the old plantation back means everything to me."

Mary Annabelle got him a glass of moonshine. While he was drinking it, Rusty tried to make him feel better about Thursday.

"Thursday is a good boy. Leo is going to farm the old plantation, and I will see to it that he puts Thursday to work. He needs work along with his schooling. Mandy Ann says that he is a good student."

Malcolm had finished the moonshine and was fast asleep.

CHAPTER 64

"She wondered how a red feather got in her hand bag."

Malcolm had given Mary Annabelle a small derringer to protect herself when the northern troops were coming. Thank goodness she never needed it, but she always kept it hidden. One day Thursday was exploring and found the gun. He did not bother the gun, but he did remember where it was.

One morning at the breakfast table, Rusty and Mary Annabelle decided to go to the Cottontail Mansion and look it over.

"You empty Malcolm's chamber pot, and then wait for Mandy Ann to come to take you to school," Mary Annabelle instructed Thursday.

Thursday hated the chamber pot job. He got it done and noticed that Malcolm was still asleep. It was about fifteen minutes before Mandy Ann came for him, as she did every school morning. Thursday went to the dresser and got the gun. He went to Malcolm's room and found him still asleep. He carefully laid a pillow along side Malcolm's head. Thursday placed the gun on the pillow and put another pillow over the gun and fired. Thursday waited a few seconds and took Malcolm's lifeless hand and placed it around the gun, putting the pillow back on top of the gun and Malcolm's lifeless hand. For some reason Thursday could not explain, he placed a red feather from his rooster between the pillows. Thursday had just finished his breakfast when he heard Mandy Ann's rig pull up outside. He grabbed his books and jumped in the rig and headed off to school.

Rusty and Mary Annabelle returned to the kitchen, and Mary Annabelle was fixing some tea. Rusty was at the kitchen table drawing up plans for the Cottontail Mansion remodeling job. Mary Annabelle served the tea.

"I had better check on Malcolm," Mary Annabelle said.

Mary Annabelle entered Malcolm's room and found he was still asleep. She spoke to him and got no answer. On closer inspection, she saw the bloody pillow. She picked up the pillow and saw the gun in Malcolm's hand and the red feather. She picked up the feather and held it tightly in her fist. She walked back into the kitchen.

"Malcolm has shot himself."

Mary Annabelle kept on walking, in a complete state of shock. Mary Annabelle stopped under a large southern pine in the yard. She leaned against the large tree. Tears streamed down her face, yet she was not crying. How could he have killed himself? He seemed so happy last night about moving back to Cottontail Plantation. What about the red feather? She had never mentioned any Voodoo to Malcolm, and never a word about the red feather. In fact, she had hardly thought of Voodoo since the war and the breaking up of slavery. Her only religion was Christianity and going to the local Baptist Church. Malcolm seldom got out of bed, but he did know where she kept her gun. She loved him so much. Life would never be the same without him.

She opened her hand and blew the feather out into the light southern breeze.

Rusty went to the bedroom and gently covered Malcolm's face with a sheet. Then he went to Mary Annabelle and put his arm around her.

"Come back in and finish your tea. I know how much you loved him. I must go tell Evelyn Lucille. I think it best we wait until school is out to tell Mandy Ann and Thursday."

When Evelyn Lucille learned of her father's death, her eyes filled with tears. "It's sad that he never got to go back to Cottontail Plantation," she said. "On the other hand, he knew it would not be the same. I hate to say it, but it may be for the best. Please don't take it personally, but the thought of an ex-slave owning the Cottontail bothered him. He loved you, but in his mind, you and Thursday were still slaves."

Rusty and Evelyn Lucille made plans to meet that evening with Mandy Ann and Mary Annabelle to plan Malcolm's funeral.

Mary Annabelle sat at her kitchen table and cried and thought, then cried some more. Her love for Malcolm had been long, sometimes hard, but very real. Like a strike of lightning, a thought hit Mary Annabelle. There is no way Malcolm could have known where the gun was kept. She had moved it after Malcolm had become sick. The timing was not right either. It would have been very hard for Malcolm to get the gun, get back into bed and arrange the covers and pillows. She and Rusty were not gone that long. Yet if someone just got the gun and shot the sleeping man, there would have been plenty of time. The red feather - someone else put it on the pillow, not Malcolm. There were so many things about Voodoo that could not be explained. Thursday was the only person around. Oh no. Not Thursday, she and Malcolm's youngest child. She must get these thoughts out of her mind.

Mary Annabelle cooked a modest supper for all of Malcolm's children that evening. She had spent the afternoon getting Malcolm's body ready for burial. The undertaker in the village had died recently, and there was not another one for miles. Rusty had the carpenter shop in the village make a pine coffin, and he had helped Mary Annabelle get Malcolm arranged so that he looked pretty good when the girls arrive. Evelyn Lucille and Leo came, but Mandy Ann's husband was on patrol and could not be in attendance.

It was decided that Leo and Rusty could dig the grave in the Chandler family plot at the Cottontail Plantation. Mandy Ann was to make arrangements with the preacher in town, and the funeral would be the next afternoon. The weather was very hot and it was decided that they should bury Malcolm as soon as possible.

While the family was making these plans, Mary Annabelle and Thursday sat in the back of the room and did not participate in the arrangements. Mary Annabelle watched Thursday and when the evening was over, she was sure he was the one who had pulled the trigger, not Malcolm. Oh, but what to do about it? She could not live with it, yet she could not tell anybody what she knew had happened.

The next afternoon, it rained in a brutal down pour. The grave filled half up with water and everyone was huddling beneath their umbrellas. Rusty, Mary Annabelle and Thursday took their places several paces behind Evelyn Lucille's family and Mandy Ann. It was the old custom, and Rusty knew that Malcolm would not want the colored part of his family with the rest of his family.

Mandy Ann's husband was still out on patrol. The preacher gave a short sermon, and they all recited the Lord's Prayer. Rusty had Thursday take his sisters back to the house. He did not want them to watch while he and Leo lowered Malcolm's coffin into the grave that was half filled with water. It was a real mess. They had to hold the coffin down with long poles until it filled with water to keep it from floating to the top. Then the lid of the coffin floated to the top. Then up came Malcolm. They pushed him back down with the poles. They finally had to just lay the lid aside, hold Malcolm down with a pole, and fill the grave, coffin and all, with the mud.

Everybody was thinking how Malcolm's funeral would have been in the days before the war, but nobody said anything. There would have been at least a hundred friends and slaves to bid him his last farewell. The way it was, he was laid to rest as so many were, just a victim of the war.

Rusty and Leo finished the dirty and depressing work, and turned to find a woman standing, watching them. She was tall, dressed in a dark red, long velvet dress with a black hat and gloves. Rusty Montana introduced himself and Leo Burnhart.

" I am happy to see you again. I remember when you were a child. My name is Golden Finch, and I was wondering where I might find Malcolm Chandler."

Rusty then remembered her. He never had liked her. She treated slaves in an underhanded way. Rusty turned and pointed to the fresh grave.

"Father is in the grave we just filled."

Rusty seldom used the word "father", but in this case, he gave it some emphasis. He could see that Golden Finch had gotten the message as she looked at the black man. She stepped around the two men and stood by the grave in the pouring rain with mud up to her ankles. Rusty and Leo walked to the road where her fine coach was parked with a waiting driver. Golden stood by the grave for a few minutes and then returned to the coach.

"I am so sorry Malcolm is gone. I was in France attending to my wine business when the war broke out, and I just stayed over there until now. I lost all contact with my southern friends. Where are Malcolm's daughters?"

"They are over at the small house on the old Hanging Magnolia Plantation. I think you remember where it was. They will be happy to see you. Leo and I are so wet and dirty that we are going over to the creek and wash up a little before we go home."

Golden looked the two men up and down. She gave a shy smile and said, "I hope all that dirt going into the creek doesn't kill every fish between here and New Orleans."

Golden pulled up in front of the house and left her driver with the rig. Evelyn Lucille and Mandy Ann were very happy to see Golden. Mary Annabelle was not that happy because of the relationship that Malcolm had with Golden. Mary Annabelle fixed some tea and sent Thursday out to the rig with some hot chocolate for the driver.

The driver asked Thursday if he would watch the team and rig for a bit while he went to the outhouse. Thursday was very happy with his new responsibility. He happened to notice Golden's hand bag in the seat of the coach. Thursday opened it and found it contained, among other things, a diamond broach and considerable cash. Thursday took the broach and the money and hoped that Golden did not open the purse until she was way down the road. Thursday also left a red feather in the purse. Thursday considered himself a rich man. The driver came back and gave Thursday a coin for watching the team and coach.

Golden had enjoyed her visit with the girls, and everybody was brought up to date on the goings on over the past years. Evelyn Lucille asked Golden to stay the night, as it was getting late. Thursday was thinking he had to find some way to get his loot back in the handbag, then luck saved him.

Golden thanked Evelyn Lucille for the kind offer but said she must be on the road. Golden was not too far down the road when she opened the handbag to get a handkerchief and noticed the red feather. She picked it up and tossed it out the window of the coach. She did not notice the missing items. She did wonder how the red feather got into the handbag.

CHAPTER 65

"It was possible that the law could send Thursday to the gallows."

Rusty hired ex-slaves to work on the remodeling job. He paid them well, but oh the troubles he had. They were used to being stood over with a whip to do their work. When there was no overseer whip, there was no reason to work.

He started paying them every evening each day. If they had any money they would not come to work. He started paying them on Saturday night and this worked some better. Rusty thought they were good enough people, they just did not understand work for pay.

One older man had been a slave on Cottontail Plantation and had done some carpenter work for Mr. Readwright when he had his wooden leg factory. He was a good worker and understood what Rusty was going through. One day Rusty was complaining to him about the poor quality workers.

"Mr. Rusty, you get yourself a whip."

The next morning, seven of the ten employees showed up. Rusty lined them up and gave a short speech.

"Starting today we are going to work hard and get this job done. You are paid well, and you don't get the work done. I am going to the village and get the three that are not here. When I get back I want all those bricks laid, and make them good and straight."

He turned and started for town to get the no-shows. He looked back, and his crew was laughing and goofing around with no thoughts of work. He walked back to the job sight. Taking the whip he raised a welt the size of a hen's egg on the ass of one of the ringleaders.

"Now get to work."

One of the men started to laugh. Rusty gave him a good pop with the whip. His crew went to work. In town, he found the three other workers drunk or too sick with hangovers. He rounded them up and forced them back to the job. The whip came in handy for this mission.

The following day, Rusty only had one of the crew missing. Rusty served them coffee and gave them a talk about doing quality work. It was a difficult transition for the slaves to go from slavery to a free labor market. It was going to take good leadership on the part of the southern leaders.

It took three weeks before the mansion was ready to receive its occupants. Evelyn Lucille and her family were the first to move in. It was much a different life than before the war, but the family was very happy. Leo had crews of men working the fields to get in the crops. Evelyn Lucille did not know how it would feel when Rusty moved into the mansion. This would be something new, the slave being the master.

Mandy Ann and her husband decided not to move to the mansion, as he had orders to report to Fort Abraham Lincoln in Bismarck, North Dakota. He would be joining the Seventh Cavalry under the command of a General Custer. Mandy Ann was going to join him later. They were both excited about their move to the west, and it meant a promotion for Mandy Ann's husband. Mandy Ann hoped she could get a job teaching at the fort.

Just before Mary Annabelle and Thursday were to move into the mansion, she informed Rusty that she would rather stay in the little house. Rusty was shocked and hurt.

"Mother, the real reason for my buying the plantation and fixing up the mansion was so you could live in comfort. I had a room especially decorated for you. Thursday would be closer to school, and Mandy Ann would not have to pick him up every day. You could help Evelyn Lucille with her family, which I know you enjoy, but you would only have to do just what you wished."

"Rusty, I would just not feel right back at Cottontail Plantation without our Malcolm."

She went to Rusty and put her arms around him. "I hope you understand."

Rusty was disappointed, but he did understand. He decided it would be a good time to tell Mary Annabelle that he planned on going back to the west.

"What I want for you, mother, is what you want. If you are happy here in this smaller home, you just stay here. I think, for me, there is more opportunity in the west. I am going to San Francisco and get in the shipping business. I plan on heading back out west in a few weeks. I will, of course, keep in touch with you, and I will return from time to time. I think it would be a good idea if I took Thursday with me. I could finish teaching him with the schooling he needs, and he would be great company for me."

A look and feeling of pure panic came over Mary Annabelle. To keep her knees from shaking, she sat down. "Rusty, things are happening too fast. I must have a talk with Thursday. I hate to have you take Thursday, but it could be that it would be best. I just need time to think. Please let's not discuss any more plans for at least a week and give me time to straighten out my thoughts."

Rusty readily agreed, knowing that his mother had been through a lot in the past month.

While Rusty was having the conversation with Mary Annabelle, Mandy Ann was reading a letter that she had received at the school.

> Dear Mandy Ann,
>   I want to thank you and all your family for the good visit we had when I was recently at Cottontail. I can not express my feelings of loss on the passing of Malcolm. I know how hard it must be on your entire family.
>   The next subject I wish to address is not pleasant. Please understand that I am, in no way, accusing Thursday. But let me tell you what happened.
>   When I was visiting with you and Evelyn Lucille, my driver left my team and coach in the care of Thursday. That evening when I got to my hotel room, I found I was missing from one of my handbags, a large sum of cash and a very expensive diamond broach that my mother had left me. There had been several other people that afternoon that had access to the handbag, and I am checking them all out. I was very suspicious of my driver, but on very close questioning, I am sure that he had nothing to do with the missing articles. I feel the same about Thursday, but could you please question him for me to help clear up the matter. There was a strange object in my handbag when I opened it. It was a red feather.
> With love,
> Golden Finch

Mandy Ann knew Thursday too well to think he had anything to do with the theft. Thursday and Mandy Ann had always been close. He had been her student since the first grade. He was a fair to good student. He had been in no serious trouble. She would talk it over with Mary Annabelle. She asked Mary Annabelle over to her house that evening.

"Mary Annabelle, I received this letter from Golden Finch today. Please read it and see what you think."

Mary Annabelle read the letter and hoped she did not show the great anxiety that she was feeling. With a shaking hand, she handed the letter back to Mandy Ann.

"I am sure Thursday had nothing to do with this, but I will talk to him and let you know tomorrow what he has to say."

Mary Annabelle found sleep impossible. Her son had committed murder and now a major felony. If the rest of the family knew, they would insist that the law be called. It was very possible that the law would send Thursday to the gallows. The fact he was a child, and did not understand, would help. He was a colored child, and that was against him. She felt she must get Thursday out of the country. He could not go west with Rusty, because it would look like Rusty was involved. Not only that, but there was not time. Something must be done. She went to Thursday's room and woke him.

"Thursday, this is very important. I know what you have done. I know you killed Malcolm, and I know you stole the money and the broach from Miss Finch. You could be hanged."

"So what? I hated Malcolm, and I really needed some money. That old hag of a Finch has plenty."

"If you get the money and the broach right now, I will keep your secret about Malcolm. You must return it to Mandy Ann so she can get it back to Miss Finch. I am sure Miss Finch will not punish you for what you have done."

"I don't have all the money. I bought a horse."

"You bought a horse! Where do you keep him?"

"I have him hid down in the woods."

"You must give back what money you have left and the broach. I will beg Mandy Ann to explain it to Miss Finch. We can only hope and pray that we can keep the secret about Malcolm's death. You have done very wrong, but you are my son and I will try and help you this time."

By the time Mandy Ann arrived to pick up Thursday for school, Rusty had left the house to go work at the Cottontail Mansion. Mary Annabelle took Thursday out to Mandy Ann's rig.

Thursday had decided during the night that he did not want to die at the gallows. He was going to do as his mother had said. He did have the horse for his trouble. Still, he did not feel right about the horse. He was going to sell it and send the money to Miss Finch. Thursday had made up his mind he wanted to be a good man like Rusty, and yes, like his mother. She was a good lady.

"Thursday has something to tell you," Mary Annabelle said.

"Miss Mandy Ann, I did take that lady's money and her broach, here it is in this bag. You can send it back to her. All the money is not there. I bought a horse with some of it. I will write her myself about getting that money back to her. Please tell her I am very sorry."

"Thursday, you are doing the right thing. What you did was very wrong. You can be very thankful that Miss Finch is a forgiving person."

Thursday got in the rig with Mandy Ann, and they were off to school. Mary Annabelle watched them go with a feeling of surprised relief.

Mary Annabelle started back to her house, and an old newspaper blew across her path. She picked it up and read the headlines.

"LIBERIA-NEW COLONY FOR EX-SLAVES A SUCCESS"

CHAPTER 66

"He took the rope off Thursday's neck."

Rusty came home that afternoon and learned that Thursday had robbed Miss Finch. His reaction was to punish the child, but Mary Annabelle told him, in no uncertain terms, to leave the boy to her and Mandy Ann. Then she took out the newspaper she had found blowing in the yard and asked Rusty to read it. Rusty read about the slave colony of Liberia.

"It sounds good, but what has that got to do with our family?" Rusty asked.

"I want to go to Liberia to live, and I want to take Thursday with me," Mary Annabelle answered. "There is nothing left here for me, now that Malcolm has left me. Evelyn Lucille and Mandy Ann treat me like I was still a slave. I feel they don't think of me as a person. I have always wanted to be a teacher. The people of the south will not let me teach white children, and schools for black children are very few. I could become a teacher in Liberia. It says in the article that they need teachers. I feel in my heart that Thursday is changing, and he is very sorry for stealing, but at the very best, he will always be known in this community as the boy who stole."

"You are going back out west, and I just don't want to live here anymore," Mary Annabelle continued. "I feel there is no place here for Thursday or me. As for you taking Thursday with you, please do not take my boy from me. He needs me, and I need him. The article says that you can catch a boat out of Savannah, and just look, the fare is not a lot of money. Will you please take us to Savannah and help us catch a boat? I want to leave in the morning."

Mary Annabelle put on her best dress and went to Evelyn Lucille's and said good-bye. Evelyn Lucille was taken aback and very shocked. She told Mary Annabelle that if that was what she wanted to do then, by all means, she had her blessing. Next, Mary Annabelle went to Mandy Ann, and Mandy Ann had a fit.

"You can't take Thursday away, and you can't leave us! You have been part of the family for most of my life. I love you and Thursday very much. Please stay with us," Mandy Ann pleaded.

Mary Annabelle sat down and explained the reason she had for leaving. Mandy Ann was a reasonable person, and when Mary Annabelle had finished her story, she hugged Mary Annabelle and took her by the hand.

259

With tears running down her cheeks she said, "Come, Mary Annabelle. I will help you pack. I guess I never really understood what being black means. I never think of you or Rusty or Thursday as black. I can see by what you say that even I treat you as black, but honest Mary Annabelle, I never see you any different."

It was Mary Annabelle's turn to get teary-eyed. "I love you and Evelyn Lucille very much. I just want to spend the rest of my life with free black people and see if I can make a difference."

The next morning found Rusty and Mary Annabelle in Rusty's rig and Thursday on his almost stolen horse. Thursday had decided, on his own, to ride the horse to Savannah and then give it to Miss Finch. He told Mandy Ann that he wanted to apologize to her personally. There were tears and good-byes and more tears. There was an early morning fog, and the buggy, with its party, headed for Savannah and a new world. It disappeared from sight one hundred yards from the house.

They stopped at an Inn and boarding house the first night. It was not the best place, but it was clean, and they took black guests. Rusty went in to register for the room and came back to the rig.

"The inn keeper is a tall man and he has no ears, but he is very nice. Come in and meet him."

Mary Annabelle thought, "the poor man." She remembered how sorry she felt for Tall Boy when Malcolm cut off his ears. She wondered if this man had tried to run away when he was a slave. Mary Annabelle entered the small lobby and could not believe her eyes. It was Tall Boy, now a handsome man.

"Tall Boy! Tall Boy it's me, Mary Annabelle."

Tall Boy came from behind the counter, and they embraced. Rusty, Thursday, and a rather large black woman stood watching Tall Boy and Mary Annabelle as they began to chatter a mile a minute. Mary Annabelle was the first to realize they had people watching. She stopped the chatter and introduced Rusty and Thursday to Tall Boy. She explained that Malcolm had bought them both at the same time and how Tall Boy had run away. Tall Boy introduced Rusty and Thursday to his wife, Columbine. Mary Annabelle went to Columbine and gave her a hug.

"Do you remember the night you and I and Pansy sat in the room at Wanderlust Lodge and talked girl talk?" she reminded Columbine.

Tall Boy, with the help of Snowflake, had made it to Canada where they ran a boarding house for several years. Then, after the war, they had a chance to get this small inn and came back to Georgia.

The three ex-slaves visited most of the night. They could even laugh at some of the most terrible moments they had spent together in the early days. Rusty and Thursday managed to get some sleep.

Arriving in Savannah, they took a small room not far off the water-front, and booked the three horses into a livery. Thursday said the first thing he wanted to do was to go see Miss Finch and give her the horse that was rightly hers. With a little trouble, he found Miss Finch's office. There was a very pretty young black girl behind a desk. She asked if she could help.

"I would like to see Miss Golden Finch," Thursday stated.

"Miss Finch had some errands to run. She should be back soon."

Thursday took a seat on a bench along the wall and looked at the pretty black girl. He had never paid much attention to girls or even liked them too well, but as he watched this girl work on her journals, he noticed how pretty she was. He even liked the ankle he could see under the desk. Thursday was as nervous as a cat in a room full of bulldogs as he waited for Miss Finch.

When Miss Finch arrived, she studied Thursday with a puzzled expression. Thursday stood with his hat in his hand.

"Ho. You are the young man that stole my money and broach," she announced.

"Yes mam. I did do that, and I am very sorry," Thursday said.

"Just one moment young man. I want to send Alice here on an errand. I will be right back to talk to you."

She called the girl in the back room, and soon the girl came out, put on a sweater, and left the office.

"Now young man, what do you have to say for yourself?"

"I am very sorry I took your money and jewelry. My teacher, Miss Mandy Ann, has sent most of the money and the jewelry back to you. I had spent some of the money on a horse. That is him tied outside. I want you to have him for the balance of the money. I will never steal again."

"I should hope not. What kind of punishment do you think you should have?"

Thursday mouth dropped open. "Miss Mandy Ann said you would forgive me if I returned the stuff I stole and apologized to you."

"I will forgive you when I see you looking out through bars in the Savannah jail," she snapped.

Thursday thought he knew what it was to be frightened, but not like this. "They will hang me," he thought. He started for the door, but just as he got to the door, there stood a deputy sheriff and Alice. The deputy was a young, good looking black man.

Thursday started to cry as the deputy grabbed him and sat him back down on the bench. He tried to put handcuffs on Thursday, but his wrists and hands were so small that the cuffs just dropped off on the floor. The deputy took a cord and tied it around his neck and held it like a dog on a leash.

"NOW, what is going on here? Miss Alice tells me you stole from Miss Finch."

Golden did not give Thursday a chance to answer the charges. "Yes, the little demon is a thief, and I want him locked up for a good long time. I see you are a black deputy. Since when do we have black sheriffs in Savannah?"

"Mam, the northern army appointed me and several other black deputies to keep the law and order after the war."

"Well, I do not approve of black officers of the law, after all, what do you know about law and order? Get out of here and take that little black thief you have on that leash. Get him locked up, and I will come to the jail later to press charges and talk to the sheriff."

The deputy led Thursday out into the street and headed for the jail. He asked Thursday to give him the details of why the white lady was so upset. Thursday told the truth of just what had happened, how he had stolen the money and jewelry, how his teacher had said if he would send it back and apologize that things would be alright, and that he had just went to Miss Finch's office to give her the horse. He also told the deputy that he was afraid that he might be hanged.

The deputy looked down at Thursday. He knew that if he took him to the Savannah station and Miss Finch pressed charges, Thursday was, indeed, in a lot of trouble. He took the rope off Thursday's neck.

"I am going in this store and buy a cigar. When I come out, you be gone. Never show your face in Savannah again. You will be a wanted man, and every policeman and sheriff in Savannah will be on the lookout for you. I will report that you got away from me. If anyone finds out that I let you go, it will be my neck. So just get out of town."

Thursday found his way back to the room and told Rusty and Mary Annabelle his story.

CHAPTER 67

"I just talked with the captain, and he was very rude."

It was decided that Thursday should stay in the room until passage to Liberia could be found. Mary Annabelle would stay with him, and Rusty would go look for a ship to Liberia. After scanning the local paper, Rusty found an ad.

> The freighter, Hawk, leaves port September 20.
> Port of calls: Liberia and South Hampton.
> Room for small number of passengers.
> See Captain A.B. Marsh at Pier 20.

Rusty made his way to Pier 20 and found Captain A.B. Marsh aboard a medium size, but well-kept, freighter. Captain Marsh had snow-white hair, small blue eyes, and smoked a pipe that curved down his chin. Rusty introduced himself and asked the captain if he had room for two passengers to Liberia.

"Depends. Might and might not."

Rusty did not like the looks of the captain.

"I have the money to pay."

"In that case, I guess I have room for two more."

"I wonder if I might see the accommodations?"

"Go below and take a look."

Rusty went down a narrow ladder to a dark hold with narrow bunks in narrow, dark halls. No way that he would send anybody to Liberia or any place else with this kind of quarters. He went back up topside and told the captain that he was not interested.

"You high fallootin' niggers, since you got your freedom, nothin' is good enough for you. Just get off my ship."

As Rusty was leaving the ship, a young man dressed as a sailor stopped him. "The captain kicked you off the ship, did he?"

"Yes he did. He is a very rude man."

"The company that owns the shipping lines always places those ads to get passengers for additional income. The captain, he don't like passengers, so he just figures a way to run them off. Don't take it personally."

263

"Thanks for the warning. Do you know where I might find passage for my mother and young sister to Liberia?"

"Why don't you stop in at Bird of Prey Shipping Lines. They own the Hawk and two other ships: the Eagle and the Falcon. The office is right around the corner, and the owner is a nice old man. Maybe he can help you."

Rusty thanked the young man and went on his way. He thought it a waste of time to stop at the Bird of Prey office. Then he looked up and saw the sign, Bird of Prey Shipping Lines. He thought, "well, what the hell, just as well stop in."

There was an old man behind a desk piled high with paper. He looked over his glasses at Rusty and asked if he could help him.

"I was wondering if you knew where I might get passage for two passengers to Liberia."

"Yes. Just go down to Pier 20 and talk to Captain A.B. Marsh. It is my ship, but he is the captain and we need passengers to help pay the bills."

"I just talked with the captain, and he was very rude."

"That damn Marsh. I should fire him. I'm getting too old to run a line. I would sell out, if I could find a buyer. All the fancy lines up north get the good shipping. We southerners don't get much since the war. That's going to change though. Things are getting better, but I'm too old."

Rusty thought, "Why not? I love the south. It should be just as good as San Francisco for a shipping business."

"How much do you want for your line?" Rusty inquired.

"Why do you ask a question like that? You blacks have no money."

"Just tell me what you want for the line."

The old man never looked but gave Rusty a price.

"What all do I get for that much money?"

"Three ships. The Hawk is tied at Pier 20, the other two are on the high seas. You also get this office and five water front docks. I was going to expand and have two more ships but I never got around to it, and I am too old."

"I will be here in the morning with your money," Rusty promised.

The old man looked up, shook his head in disbelief and went back to work.

Rusty went to the local bank and requested that they transfer funds from his Atlanta bank into his new account at the Savannah Bank. Just as he was leaving the bank, he heard a woman say, "There he is, that is the little thief's brother. Arrest him."

Rusty looked up and saw Golden Finch going by in her carriage. Rusty had only advanced a block or so when a Savannah policeman stopped him.

"Is that true? Are you the brother of the boy that stole from Miss Finch?"

"Yes, the boy is my brother," he responded.

"Where is the boy now?"

"I have no idea. He and his mother left Savannah."

Rusty just kept on walking, and the policeman did not say more. Rusty did not go in the direction of the rooming house where Mary Annabelle and Thursday were. He kept close watch and noticed that he was being followed. He went directly to Miss Finch's wine import office. Like his brother, the first thing he noticed was the pretty black girl behind the desk. The black girl, Alice, seeing the handsome brown man, had an almost burning sensation in her loins. Their eyes locked, and Rusty smiled at the girl. One thing he did inherit from his father was his reaction to seeing a pretty black girl. Instant hard-on. Golden was in and took Rusty to a back office where she offered him a glass of fine wine.

"I understand that you will not tell the police where that little thief is."

"That is very correct. Furthermore, I think you are being very unfair with Thursday. He has returned all your property and has apologized to you. Why can't you find it in your heart to forgive a young boy who made a terrible mistake, but is trying to correct it? Sending the child to jail will prove nothing, and it will do no good."

"Your brother is a felon, and if you don't tell the police where they can find him, I will have you arrested for harboring a criminal. I have hired Pinkerton detectives to look for your brother and to follow your every move. I do not believe for one second that he has left Savannah."

Rusty decided that if this was the kind of hard ball Golden wanted to play, he might just as well be the pitcher. It was about five in the evening when he left Golden's office. He went straight to the City Park where he could see for a block each way. He sat on a bench, and he noticed a man sitting on a bench on the other side of the park. He just sat there, and when it was good and dark, he lay down on the bench, and got some sleep. He woke up and very quietly, in the dark of the night and staying in shadows, went to the room where Mary Annabelle and Thursday were. They were very happy to see him. He quickly outlined a plan, giving them instructions about what to do in the next twenty-four hours.

Next, Rusty changed into his best suit and even put his diamond stickpin in his tie. Then he sneaked back to the park. Just as Rusty thought the detective was asleep on the bench, Rusty sat down on a bench just across from the sleeping man. At daybreak the detective woke, sat up, and rubbed his eyes. Then he saw Rusty just sitting there looking at him, very obviously in a new clean set of clothes. The detective jumped up and walked away. Rusty noticed a brown stain appear on the seat of the man's pants as he walked off. He had just, plain and simple, scared the shit out of him.

Rusty hung out at the park until the bank opened. When he got to the bank, the banker had his money ready for him, all in bills and in a leather brief case. Rusty first stopped at a haberdashery and bought a man's shirt, pants and shoes in small size. Then he bought a dress for about a twelve year old girl. His next stop was a law office. He had a lawyer draw up a deed to three ships, the five docks and the real estate beneath the office of Bird of Prey Shipping Lines. Then he set off to the office of Bird of Prey Shipping. The old man was behind his desk. Rusty placed the brief case on the desk and opened it, then placed the deed in front of the old man.

"Here is the money for your business, every penny you asked for. Just sign the deed, and I will be the new owner."

The old man looked at Rusty with a faint smile. "It looks like all the money to me."

He signed the deed, closed the brief case, picked it up and walked out of the office. He handed Rusty a key on the way out. He never said another word. The only thing Rusty ever heard of him was he read his obituary in the local paper about three years later.

Rusty took the signed deed and went to the Hawk. The young red headed first mate was giving directions to some workers who were loading freight on the ship. Rusty called him off to the side and showed him the deed. The young sailor backed off a couple of steps and gave Rusty a salute. "First Mate Clayton Fraser at your service, Sir."

Rusty smiled. He could tell by the way the sailor talked, he was a Scotsman. "It is no longer First Mate Fraser, you are now Captain Fraser."

"Oh, thank you Sir. I will do a good job. What about Captain Marsh?"

"Let's go aboard and give him his walking papers."

The new Captain Fraser led Rusty on board, and they went to the bridge where they found the old captain.

Rusty drew himself up to full stature and announced, "I have purchased the Bird of Prey Shipping Lines, I want you to get your personal gear and leave this ship. Clayton Fraser here is the new captain. I have some very special passengers coming on board. Yesterday you seemed not to like colored people, and these passengers are colored. I don't want the likes of you around here when they come aboard."

CHAPTER 68

Rusty and Captain Fraser managed to get A.B. Marsh off the boat. Rusty then turned his attention to Captain Fraser.

"I hope I can trust you, Captain. Within the hour, a man and a girl will arrive to board the ship. Please make them welcome. They are really my mother and little brother. I will explain later. Make them comfortable in the captain's cabin for this trip. As soon as you deliver them to Liberia, you can have the cabin. I have some business to take care of and will be back this evening."

Captain Fraser assured Rusty that everything would be taken care of.

Rusty went directly to Golden Finch's office. Alice looked up from her work. Seeing Rusty again, there it came, the burning in her loins. On Rusty's part, instant hard-on.

"Miss Alice, I have purchased a shipping company. I am in need of an office girl to take care of the paper work and the ledgers. I will pay you twice what Miss Finch is paying you if you will come to work for me."

Rusty could see Golden Finch listening through an open door to the back office. She jumped to her feet. "You cannot come in here trying to hire my help. Now get out of here! You have caused me nothing but trouble."

Rusty noticed a manifest lying on the desk showing an order for a shipping line to pick up a shipment of wine in France for Finch Winery. Rusty picked up the manifest, crossed out the name of the other shipping company, and wrote "Bird of Prey Shipping Lines" and placed the manifest in his pocket.

"Thank you for the shipping order. The Hawk will pick the shipment up, and you can pick it up at Pier 20 in about three months."

Golden was so mad her face was purple, and her body gave off an odor of anger. "You can't do this to me!"

Rusty looked her straight in the eye. "I can, and I just did. Come on Alice."

Rusty took Alice's hand, she grabbed her coat off a hook by the door, and they were gone. They arrived at the Bird of Prey Shipping office and looked at the mess of papers on the desk.

"Go through all these papers and see if you can make any sense of them. I have to go to the docks and see if mother and Thursday are aboard the Hawk. I will be back around six this evening. If you are free, we can go to supper, talk business and maybe other matters."

He gave Alice a wink, and she almost peed her pants.

267

Alice picked a paper up from the desk and read it. "Read this. If your mother and brother want to go to Liberia, it looks like they will have to fill out this form."

Rusty read the paper. It was a form that was to be filled out by all ex-slaves who wanted to make their home in Liberia.

"Yes, thank you for finding this. I will have mother fill it out."

Rusty headed for Pier 20 and the Hawk. Arriving at the pier, he found his mother and Thursday still in their disguises, and he had to laugh.

"You two are a sight for sore eyes. You can get back in your regular clothes. The Savannah Police would not dare try and board the Hawk. Here is a paper you have to fill out before you can live in Liberia."

Mary Annabelle read the form. "Rusty, it says here to list your first name and your last name. I have no last name."

Rusty took the form and read it. "Put Chandler for your last name."

Mary Annabelle broke into tears. "There is nothing that would make me happier."

She sat down and wrote, "Mrs. Mary Annabelle Chandler." In all these long years, this was the thing she wanted most and now, at long last, she was Mrs. Chandler.

Captain Fraser appeared and gave Rusty his traditional salute.

"Sir, we are ready to get underway. Our mission is to deliver a cargo of two passengers to Liberia, along with a shipment of hand tools. From there we go to England and deliver a shipment of cotton. Then we return to France, pick up a shipment of fine wine, and deliver it to Pier 20 in Savannah."

"Very good Captain Fraser. We will see you in a few months."

Rusty kissed his mother, shook Thursday's hand, and went down the gangplank and off the ship. He watched until the sun set in the west and no longer furnished light to see the departing vessel. He could see Thursday standing on the rail and waving at him. It was pretty dark, but Rusty could have sworn that he saw Thursday fall over board.

Rusty went back to the office and took Alice to supper. They had such a romantic, hot and steaming evening, it was impossible to describe in the printed word.

THE END